Sail Away
With Me

Sail Away With Me

SUSAN FOX

ZEBRA BOOKS
KENSINGTON PUBLISHING CORP.

http://www.kensingtonbooks.com

ZEBRA BOOKS are published by

Kensington Publishing Corp.
119 West 40th Street
New York, NY 10018

All Kensington titles, imprints, and distributed lines are available at special quantity discounts for bulk purchases for sales promotion, premiums, fund-raising, educational, or institutional use.

Special book excerpts or customized printings can also be created to fit specific needs. For details, write or phone the office of the Kensington Sales Manager: Attn.: Sales Department. Kensington Publishing Corp., 119 West 40th Street, New York, NY 10018. Phone: 1-800-221-2647.

Zebra and the Z logo Reg. U.S. Pat. & TM Off.

First Printing: October 2018
ISBN-13: 978-1-4201-4598-4
ISBN-10: 1-4201-4598-3

eISBN-13: 978-1-4201-4599-1
eISBN-10: 1-4201-4599-1

10 9 8 7 6 5 4 3 2 1

Printed in the United States of America

AUTHOR'S NOTE

I'm delighted to continue my Blue Moon Harbor romance series. Bookseller Iris Yakimura was introduced in the first book in the series, *Fly Away With Me*, and I knew she'd deserve her own love story one day. Musician Julian Blake was also briefly mentioned in that book, when heroine Eden saw him onstage and said he looked like a "tarnished angel." Her comment was more perceptive than she realized.

If you're familiar with my books, you know there's always a heartwarming romance with a happy ending. You know that I write about characters who are complex, with weaknesses as well as strengths, with tough challenges to face, and with lessons to learn. And you know that I also address some serious contemporary issues. *Sail Away With Me* was in some ways the toughest novel for me to write, because of one issue it addresses.

Sail Away With Me is a story about strength and growth and moving forward with life. It's about wisdom, the support of family and friends, and the journey toward finding true love. It deals with the heroine's struggle to overcome her painful shyness and the hero's attempt to overcome past trauma. The trauma of child sexual abuse.

Child sexual abuse is a crime, and it is a horrific subject to think about, but I wanted to write about it because it's more prevalent than we'd like to think. It's impossible to collect accurate statistics because the crime is underreported and because definitions of sexual abuse vary. However, I've seen information indicating that in the United States, a child is sexually assaulted every eight minutes, and that one in five girls and one in twenty boys is a victim.

In most cases, the experience is traumatic and has an impact on the child's emotional development and on her or his adult life. It can cause suicidal thoughts.

The crime is underreported for a variety of reasons, including the child's embarrassment and misplaced feelings of guilt and shame, as well as implicit or explicit threats from the abuser. Also, the child often fears that she or he won't be believed, as against the word of an adult—and, sadly, that is often true.

If you know or suspect a child is being abused, your first priority should be the child's safety. In an emergency situation, call 911 or any other local emergency service. There may be a legal obligation, in your jurisdiction, to report abuse. Obtaining counseling support for the child should be considered. There are numerous online resources to provide more information about the crime of child sexual abuse and the needs of victims, and to point you to resources in your community.

If you're an adult who was abused as a child, you can find support resources as well. For example, do an Internet search for "adult survivors of sexual abuse."

Moving on to a more pleasant subject, it's time to say thank you. The first one goes to the readers who enjoy my books, tell their friends, maybe write a review, and occasionally drop me a note. Those notes are so very encouraging on the days when my writing muse is being ornery.

Thank you to all the wonderful folks at Kensington, especially my editor, Martin Biro, who is always a delight to work with, and his assistant James Abbate, who makes all the admin-type things run so smoothly. Thank you, too, to my agent, Emily Sylvan Kim, of Prospect Agency. We've been together ten fabulous years!

I'm so grateful to my critiquers, who provided valuable

feedback on this book: Rosalind Villers, Alaura Ross, and Nazima Ali. Thanks also to the following people who helped with odds and ends of research: Roberta Cottam, Vanessa Grant, Sharon Gunn, Solveig McLaren, Andrew Hull, Luranah and Alasdair Polson, Yvonne Rediger, and Éliane Verret-Fournier. All errors (and deliberate bendings of the truth) are mine, not theirs. Very special thanks to Roberta Cottam, who came up with the title of this book.

I love sharing my stories with my readers and I love hearing from you. You can email me at susan@susanlyons.ca or contact me through my website at www.susanfox.ca, where you'll also find excerpts, behind-the-scenes notes, recipes, a monthly contest, the sign-up for my newsletter, and other goodies. You can find me on Facebook at facebook.com/SusanLyonsFox.

A footnote:

I finished this manuscript in the fall of 2017, having no idea how much our world—at least in Canada and the United States—would change in the coming year in terms of outing and condemning sexual abuse and sexual harassment. The #MeToo movement began in the fall of 2017 and Time's Up followed at the beginning of 2018, and they continue to gain momentum. I'm encouraged to see that victims are feeling empowered to come forward, and also to see sexual predators being exposed and sanctioned for their actions. I wonder if the initial response by the police and community to Julian's allegations would be any different today . . .

Chapter One

Carrying his favorite acoustic guitar in its travel-worn case, Julian Blake climbed into the old black van his dad and his dad's bandmates used for their local gigs. Sitting in the driver's seat, tears burned behind Julian's eyes. Would he ever again feel the joy of sharing a mic with his father, Forbes, the man who'd taught him to play a miniature guitar before he was even forming full sentences? The team of doctors gave his dad a less than 50 percent chance of being able to play again, odds that Forbes was determined to beat.

Letting out a growl of impotent rage at how fucked up fate could be, Julian put the standard-shift van in reverse and backed down the driveway. A few minutes later, he reached the two-lane road that more or less bisected the tiny, largely undeveloped island into east and west halves. Turning north, he resisted the urge to speed. Deer, rabbits, and squirrels often darted onto the road regardless of oncoming vehicles. *He* would be a careful driver. Unlike the drunk off-islander who, two weeks ago, had lost control on a curve and smashed into Forbes, who'd been walking along the shoulder of this very road.

That accident had brought Julian rushing from Vancouver to Destiny Island, the place he'd fled as a teen. He hated even breathing the air here, and normally made only a couple of short visits each year. But now he had no choice, because Forbes and Sonia needed full-time live-in assistance.

Julian fisted his left hand and thumped the wheel. *Enough with the negative thinking.* Thanks to a professional development day at the high school, his stepmom was at home with his dad. Julian could escape to his longtime sanctuary, where the vibes of old guitars, bells, and laughter rang in the boughs of the ancient apple trees. In the late sixties and early seventies a commune had flourished briefly there, but since then the land had been deserted. There, with his guitar, he would find a few hours' solace. With luck, the beginning of a song would come to him. He was behind in working on the next album. It was the end of October, and he'd told his bandmates and label he'd have the songs written by Christmas. The Julian Blake Band had booked tours for next year, promising new music.

Pressure crippled his muse, seductive and elusive creature that she was. He owed his life to her, to his music, and he would always honor them. The tattoo on his right arm, of a few bars of "Ache in My Soul," the song that had saved his life, served as a constant reminder.

Passing Quail Ridge Community Hall, Julian remembered playing there with B-B-Zee, his dad's band, on his last visit to the island back in May. *Please let that not be the last time.*

The scenery on either side of the road hadn't changed since he'd last come this way. That was typical of Destiny, a pro-green island with a lot of agricultural land and parks. One of the farms had a "For Sale" sign in Island Realty's distinctive blue and green, displaying Bart Jelinek's white-toothed, horn-rimmed photo. Julian swallowed bile, forced air into his pinched lungs, and rubbed his fingers against the jeans pocket that held his much-mended guitar pick. His reminder; his talisman.

If all he saw of that asshole Jelinek was an occasional photo, he'd count himself lucky.

Iris Yakimura had worn lightweight Skechers to do her tai chi, but now she tugged them off and wriggled her bare toes in October-crisp yellowed grass. She also pulled off the twist of patterned silk that secured her ponytail, and shook her long black hair loose.

One of the aims of tai chi was to align your chi—vital force—and the seamless flow of exercise, stretching, and deep breathing gave her a sense of control, grace, and strength. Tai chi was the perfect way to exercise and center herself, a discipline where she knew exactly what to do next.

Practicing mindfulness, she closed her eyes and breathed deeply, savoring the morning air tinged with the baked-in heat of dry arbutus leaves, a whiff of ocean freshness, and an indefinable something that confirmed that, despite the Indian summer days they'd been experiencing, it truly was autumn. Soon the rainy hours would outnumber the sunny ones, and Christmas was less than two months away. That knowledge was like an underpainting that lay beneath a finished work of art, mostly invisible and yet adding subtle, moody nuances. Didn't every moment of life contain elements of yin and yang, dark and light, past and future as well as present?

She opened her eyes and gazed at the tumbledown remains of a cabin, smothered by blackberry vines, its weathered gray boards remnants from the commune or perhaps even the old homestead that predated the hippies. A robin trilled its cheerful song from the branch of a gnarled apple tree and she smiled, appreciating the present even more due to her awareness that winter was approaching.

Was it odd that she, whose life was governed by order and control, should be drawn to this gentle wilderness where once hippies had sung, danced, taken drugs, and made love? Here, the flower children had sought freedom from social constraints. Iris, in contrast, had been taught by her family to value conformity, to never stand out, because even such a basic right as freedom from persecution could never be taken for granted. As the old Japanese saying went, *The nail that sticks up gets hammered down.*

Clad in yoga pants and a light cotton sweater, she spread a striped blanket on the stubbly grass, sat on it, and took a water bottle from the woven basket she'd carried in from the road. The dirt track into the old commune was so badly overgrown and rutted that she always left the Chevy Volt in a small pullout a short way back on the narrow one-lane road.

These visits to the commune, a place she'd learned about as a teen from one of the old hippies who shopped at her family's Dreamspinner bookstore, were her secret. Her parents wouldn't approve of her trespassing. But this was abandoned property. Its ownership was tied up in a German trust, and the trustee and beneficiaries never visited. Nor did the islanders, who'd either forgotten it existed, didn't want to trespass, or preferred the beaches, lakes, and parks. Iris was the only person who valued this place, so she felt no guilt over her visits.

She took the shiny new paperback from her basket. A voracious reader and a knowledgeable bookseller, she at least skimmed almost every book that Dreamspinner stocked, but her favorites were romance novels. They reinforced her belief that even a shy woman like her could realize her dream of finding a loving partner and raising children together.

And that made her think of her and her aunt's planned

trip to Japan next spring. It would be Aunt Lily's second time in that country, but the first for Iris. Her Japanese grandparents came to Destiny every few years, and Iris was in regular touch with them and other relatives in Japan through email, social media, and old-fashioned letters and cards. She'd like to visit them, and to tour the country where her mom, Grandmother Rose, and Grandfather Harry's ancestors had been born, even though she anticipated being in a more or less constant state of anxiety. The idea of so many new people, sights, and activities was overwhelming.

Might one of those new people be the man who'd play the role of hero in her real-life romance story? She didn't believe in magical thinking, but still, she would be twenty-five then, and that age was significant in Yakimura family history.

Her dad and his father were both shy like her. When her dad traveled to Japan at the age of twenty-five, he had met her mom and found love. And, though his parents, Harry and Rose, had first met in British Columbia as young people, at an internment camp, they were separated when Rose and her family were deported to Japan. Harry and Rose had not reunited until Harry, aged twenty-five, traveled to Japan. He brought Rose back as his bride.

If Iris didn't share her dad's and grandfather's destiny, it wouldn't be a disaster. She was young and had no need to rush. Her best friends hadn't met their true loves until they were a few years older. But still, there was nothing wrong with dreaming.

She put down her book and lay on her back, gazing at the sky, no longer the vivid blue of summer but a faded, cool shade. In Japan, might she find a man who'd appreciate all aspects of her personality, who'd love her deeply and truly, who would return home with her to build a life together on the island she loved?

In an attempt to shut down his brain, Julian turned on the CD player and immediately recognized Peter, Paul and Mary's poignant anti-war song, "Where Have All the Flowers Gone?" Forbes had created his own mixtapes, many featuring favorites from his youth.

Julian turned onto a side road, then another, its single lane fringed with woods. No homes were visible, only an occasional dirt or gravel lane asserting itself amid the greenery. He passed a small blue car tucked into a clear spot beside one of those rough driveways.

The old cutoff to the commune was obscured by trees and brush, and only long experience guided him to it. Even had there been space to park along the road, he wouldn't have; the logoed van could draw attention to the hidden entry. The van was already battered, so he didn't worry about the brushy fingernails that scraped its sides as he eased it through the foliage. He emerged onto a rutted, barely-there track overgrown by grass and salal. Since he'd first come here, when he was eleven, he'd never seen another soul. Only, in his imagination, the ghosts of long-haired hippies.

He bumped down the road slower than he could have walked, and pulled to a stop. Taking his guitar case, he made his way across the rough, dry grass toward his favorite spot by the old apple trees.

It was his dad who'd brought him here that first time. When Forbes had fallen for Sonia, a Destiny Islander, he and Julian had moved from Victoria to the island. Forbes mentioned that he'd lived here, in a commune, for a few months when he was in his late teens. Julian, who'd grown up on his dad's stories of magical places like Woodstock and Haight-Ashbury, had made Forbes show him, but the visit hadn't lasted long. Forbes said it brought back bad memories of the commune leader, a manipulative jerk with a massive ego. As far as Julian knew, his dad had never come again.

Julian, lacking those bad memories, had imagined a wondrous time of freedom, laughter, and music: folk songs, protest songs, rock. When his life had turned to shit thanks to Jelinek, the abandoned commune became his secret refuge, a safe place he could reach in an hour on his bicycle. A place to cry and scream, to play music with no one listening, to pour his emotions into the notes and words and, when he was lucky, to feel the muse inspire him.

His brain drifting, it took him a moment to realize that he wasn't imagining a hippie girl sprawled on the grass. This was a live woman in contemporary clothing, glossy ribbons of long black hair swirling around her as she reclined on a green striped blanket with her eyes closed. A paperback novel lay beside her, its cover showing a man and woman embracing.

Damn. So much for the solitude and peace he'd sought.

Julian started to turn, but his gaze was drawn to her face. He saw elegant features, smooth skin a shade of olive lighter than his stepmom's Mediterranean complexion, arched black brows, long black lashes, and delicate lips.

Her classic beauty called another image to mind. Was this the woman he'd noticed in the audience at the community hall in May? Julian had been onstage, performing with B-B-Zee in the relatively well-lit old converted church, when he'd seen the two pretty women, one blond and one brunette. The blonde—Miranda Gabriel, who was now engaged to his stepbrother, Luke Chandler—had been more blatantly sexy, but it was the brunette who'd made Julian's gaze linger. And it was she who'd vanished right after the final set. When Julian met Miranda, she'd said her friend was shy and didn't go out much.

He should vanish now, respect the woman's privacy and his own. But he didn't. Some instinct he couldn't define compelled him to stay. He lowered himself to the grass near her, opened his guitar case, and quietly began to tune. As his fingers moved, the stress that had kept him constant company since he'd heard of Forbes's accident eased from his body.

Julian began to play, not composing but warming up his fingers and the guitar strings, letting the music drift free, wherever it wanted to go.

Iris dreamt of butterflies, a dozen or more, colorful flutters of wings stirring the air to create gentle notes of music.

Gradually she woke, seeing poppy red behind her warm eyelids, then forcing her eyes open. Her vision a little unfocused, she saw . . . not butterflies, but a male figure, seated. A golden-haired head haloed by sunshine, bent over a guitar.

Her vision sharpened and her brain jerked to full awareness. She wasn't alone. Not only that—her body froze and her eyes widened as she recognized the man who sat on the dried-out grass only a few feet away. Burnished blond hair, tanned skin, the tattoo of musical notes that wound down his right arm. A faded-to-charcoal black tee and well-worn jeans on a rangy, almost too lean body. But mostly, his rapt expression. He was oblivious to her presence, intent on the poignant notes that slipped like tears from his guitar strings.

Julian Blake.

They'd gone to the same school, briefly. Not that he'd have ever noticed her. Though her outgoing mom urged her to socialize, Iris's peace of mind came from fading into the background. Julian had been three years ahead and she'd certainly noticed him. He was a nail that very much stuck up, strikingly handsome in an edgy way, and a rebel. He skipped class, avoided the other kids, and gave the appearance of not giving a damn about anything. He'd reminded her of the "boys from the wrong side of the tracks" in the romance novels she devoured: fascinating and dangerous. When he dropped out of high school and disappeared, she wasn't one bit surprised. Her imagination envisioned him either self-destructing or doing something amazing.

For a girl who'd never even spoken to the boy, it was ridiculous how pleased she'd been when her latter prediction came true. His music was on the radio and on her iPhone; the Julian Blake Band had won two of the Canadian music industry's prestigious JUNO awards and, she believed, deserved even more. His songs were poignant, a tapestry woven of pain and beauty.

Her gaze dropped from his face to his hands, his fingers plucking and strumming emotion from those six simple strings. So graceful, so deft, and yet so masculine and strong. So respectful and yet commanding. Heat rose in her body as she imagined those hands, those fingers, on her body, creating magic. Her cheeks warmed as she remembered the fantasies that had given her nighttime pleasure ever since last May, when she'd seen him perform live for the first time.

"Hey, you're awake."

The soft, husky voice made her jerk up to a sitting position. Her gaze darted to his, which was on her face rather than the strings he continued to strum, and then dropped again. Shyness was as much a part of her as her black hair. No, more a part, because if she wanted to, she could dye her hair. Her shyness was ingrained, it had its benefits, and in familiar situations she knew how to cope with it. But being alone with a man—with a man she'd had sexy, romantic dreams about—made her heart race. All she wanted was to escape.

She kept her head down, not meeting his eyes. "I'm sorry to disturb your playing," she said in a soft rush of words. She picked up her book and water bottle, placed them in her basket, and began to rise. "I'll get out of your way."

"No, wait." The music cut off. "Hold on a minute."

She froze, averting her head so a wing of long hair hid her face from him.

"I've seen you before," he said.

His comment startled a response from her. "You have? Where?" He couldn't have noticed her all those years ago at school, nor when he'd performed with his dad's band this past spring. But nor could this be a pickup line. A celebrity like Julian Blake would never waste time flirting with a totally ordinary woman like her.

"At the community hall. You were with Miranda."

"I . . . yes, I was." He really had noticed her?

Politeness and honesty made her go on rather than follow her instinct to flee. She took a deep breath, acknowledging her anxiety rather than trying to deny or resist it, because neither of those techniques ever worked for her. Another breath, trying to center herself and calm her nerves. "You were wonderful." Hastily, she amended, "I mean, you and B-B-Zee. It was a wonderful evening." Still concealed behind a curtain of hair, she squeezed her eyes closed. *Shut up before you gush on and say his music is wonderful.* Could she be any less skilled when it came to talking to guys?

"Thanks. I always enjoy—" His first words were easy, but he broke off, and when he resumed again, his voice was gruffer. "I enjoy playing with Forbes and the guys."

Now she remembered. How self-centered she'd been. Remorse and compassion made her meet his gaze. "I'm so sorry about your dad's accident." She'd heard that Forbes's entire left side—shoulder, arm, lower back, pelvis, and leg—had been shattered.

"Yeah, thanks. Me too."

She was sorry to hear the pain in Julian's voice, yet focusing on his situation helped ease her nervousness. "How is he doing?" Though she didn't know Forbes well, on the occasions they'd met she had sensed he had a gentle, creative soul.

Julian sighed and put down the guitar. He ran a hand through already tousled hair, hair that framed his lean, handsome face and brushed his shoulders. Iris noted mauve shadows under eyes the innocent blue of forget-me-nots. Lines of strain around his eyes and mouth made him look older than his real age, which she guessed was twenty-seven.

"The doctors say he's doing as well as can be expected. But he's in a lot of pain, and there's a long road ahead of him." He swallowed. "They say he might not walk again. Or even be able to play music."

"That's terrible. Poor Forbes."

"He won't accept that prognosis, and I'm glad. It keeps him motivated when therapy's so painful."

She winced in sympathy. "Determination is so important. I wish him all the best."

"Triple-B-Zee's supposed to play at Luke and Miranda's wedding. That's my dad's goal, to be able to do that."

Triple-B-Zee was Forbes's band—Blake, Barnes, and Zabec—with the addition of Julian. And the wedding date was Saturday, December twenty-ninth. "I truly hope he can."

"Me too." The words grated and he coughed. "Damn, I didn't bring anything to drink."

"Here, have some of my water." She grabbed her own bottle and extended it toward him. "In fact, keep it. I should go and let you get back to your music."

He wasn't close enough to take it from her hand, but rather than rise he scooted forward on the grass, ending up sitting a couple of feet away. Too close for her comfort.

"Thanks." He took the bottle, his hand not touching hers, uncapped it, and downed a long swallow.

Seeing his lips where hers had recently been sent a warm shudder through her body.

"But I interrupted your quiet time," he said. "Don't let me chase you away."

"No, it's . . . I'm . . ." *I'm off balance, embarrassed, and painfully inept at talking to people I don't know, about anything other than books.* She ducked her head again, yet her skin quivered as she felt his gaze.

"I get it. If the idea of listening to me try to work out a new song makes your ears wince . . ." His hand entered her field of vision. Delicately, he eased strands of hair back from her face. His fingers brushed the lobe of her ear, light as a butterfly's wings, and she trembled. "Makes you want to run away . . ." Now, in front of her eyes, he used two fingers to make quick, running steps.

A giggle burst out of her and she covered her mouth, too late to call it back. "No, of course not." The idea of listening to him create music fascinated her. How incredible to witness that process. *His* process. Julian Blake's, a man whose music spoke so intimately to her.

She could become invisible to him, as she'd been when she had first awakened and seen him so raptly intent. Then she'd be free to study his fingers, his expressions. To listen and react to the notes that flew from his guitar strings into the October air. But politeness and the high value she placed on privacy made her say, "Still, I don't want to intrude."

Now she dared to look at him, and saw a twinkle in those stunning blue eyes. "I'm the one who intruded. A polite woman would stay, not make me feel guilty for doing it."

Had he somehow guessed that she tried, at all times, to be polite? Not simply out of social convention, but out of respect for others' feelings. Those forget-me-not eyes were too compelling, so she gazed down at her knees, clad in clingy gray yoga pants, as she deliberated. After a moment, she succumbed to temptation. "Then I will stay."

"Promise not to be too harsh."

"I could never—" she protested vehemently, breaking off when she raised her head and saw him grinning. She found herself smiling back, and that amazed her.

He was, hands down, the most handsome, sexy, fascinating man she'd ever met. He was a celebrity in the Canadian music scene. Yet she felt . . . not comfortable, but more at ease than was typical with strangers. Perhaps it was because she'd seen him around, back when he was just a rebellious teen. Or maybe it was because he, like she, was sensitive to the nuances of people's behavior. In her case, it came out of shyness. In his, she guessed it was an intrinsic part of his creative soul.

His teasing grin eased into something gentler and warmer. "I don't know your name."

"It's Iris. Iris Yakimura."

"Iris." He studied her face and, though she felt heat in her cheeks, she managed not to duck her head again. "Your parents couldn't have chosen a more perfect name."

Why did he think that? She wasn't bold enough to ask.

"You've seen me play, so I think you know my name," he teased.

Throat suddenly dry, she murmured, "Julian Blake." The name was, like many of his songs, an intriguing mix of contrasts. The three syllables of his given name were supple and melodic; the single one of his surname was crisp and powerful. She loved his name. More than once she'd whispered "Julian" into her pillow, in the throes of a romantic fantasy.

How unbelievable that she was here now with the real man, in this serene and evocative environment, and that he was going to play for her. Well, not exactly *for* her, but she'd be a witness to his creative process. He had asked her to stay.

Or maybe she was dreaming again. If so, she'd prefer never to wake.

Chapter Two

Why had he asked Iris to stay? For Julian, composing was a solitary process. He sought his bandmates' input only for fine-tuning. Maybe it was humility, maybe pride, or perhaps just his solitary nature, but he liked to fumble around on his own until he hit on a particular pattern of notes or words that sank deep inside him with a sense of rightness.

Yet, oddly, he had that same feeling of rightness about Iris being here. From the moment he'd laid eyes on her in May, a slim, elegant, lovely flower amid the enthusiastic audience at the community hall, Julian had sensed she was special. He would have expected a calm confidence that matched her serene beauty. Instead, though her slender body, clad in a purple top over gray leggings, formed graceful lines, those lines often communicated reticence or even retreat. Shyness, as Miranda had said, and maybe something more. Perhaps, like him, an appreciation of solitude and a wariness of trusting others?

If so, Julian hoped her reasons were nothing as dark as his. He didn't think they were. He sensed that her soul, behind her reserve, was one of pure light with no heavy, barred doors caging black, malignant secrets.

"What you were playing before," she said hesitantly, "was lovely. Is that a new song?"

He shook his head. "No. Not yet, anyway. I was just messing around."

"It sounded like butterflies. And maybe tears." A smile flickered on delicate, untinted lips. As far as he could tell, she didn't wear a speck of makeup, and she didn't need it. In a low, musical voice, she said, "It seems to me that in every one of your songs there are tears. If not in the lyrics, then in the music."

That was perceptive. "Name me a true story, even the happiest one, that doesn't involve some tears. Even if they're only due to a fear that the joy may end."

"Yes." Her eyes, a rich, dark brown fringed by long black lashes, didn't drop this time. "Like yin and yang."

He gestured to the basket where she'd tucked her book. "How about in romance novels?"

She nodded. "Yes. The tears make the happy endings more poignant. The message is one of hope. That through a combination of luck in meeting the right person, and strength in confronting challenges and one's personal demons, each person can find a lifelong love."

A pretty dream for a pretty girl on a pretty day. A dream as trite as the word *pretty*. Iris didn't strike him as stupid, but was she that naïve? Didn't she understand that for some people, personal demons made the concept of a lifelong love impossible? Not wanting to insult her, he strove for a neutral tone. "You're a romantic."

Her chin came up. "Do I take it you're a skeptic? A cynic, perhaps?"

"I'd say I'm a realist."

Her lashes fluttered down and she said softly, "Then I do not like your reality."

Sometimes a phrase he heard or read struck a resonating bell, and Iris's last sentence was one of them. If she'd used the less formal *don't* rather than *do not*, her comment wouldn't have had the same impact. His muse repeated it. *I do not like your reality.*

It was what Forbes felt when the doctors said he might never again walk or play the guitar. Behind that simple, dignified phrase could lurk such fear and anger. Such despair. But also, as a grace note, hope. The kind of hope that Iris found in her novels.

Automatically, Julian's hands reached for his guitar. Settling it comfortably against his body, he bent over it and gave himself over to his muse, letting her guide his fingers, his thoughts. And the magic happened, as it had uncountable times in the past. He paired words and music, tried out combinations, went back, moved ahead. Immersed in the music, his conscious mind forgot his surroundings while his subconscious drew energy from the gnarled trees, the ghosts of the hippie kids, and from his quiet, sensitive companion.

Finally, he reached an impasse. The song wasn't quite right, but continuing to fuss with it might undo the good he'd created. Lowering the guitar, he rotated his head and shrugged his shoulders, unwinding the tightness of total concentration.

Iris lay on her side on her striped rug, one arm pillowing her head, watching him.

A little embarrassed at having gone through his creative process in front of her for God knows how long, he said, "Sorry for inflicting that on you, but your words gave me an idea."

She shifted gracefully, ending up sitting cross-legged. "I'm honored that anything I said could inspire a song." As was often the case, her voice was so low he could barely hear her words, which made him focus harder and value those words more highly. She went on. "This is Forbes's song? He's the lark that was shot by an arrow."

Julian nodded.

"You've conveyed his pain and anger. Also his determination and hope, which are intertwined with fear." She pressed her lips together.

"I hear a *but*."

"I'm no songwriter, but I was comparing Forbes's story to that of my grandmother."

"Go on."

"She had ALS and died three years ago. She was eighty-seven."

"God, I'm sorry. That's a hell of a disease."

"Yes, it was very sad. Grandfather Harry died several years earlier, of a massive stroke. It was sudden, a shock, but he didn't suffer. For Grandmother Rose, it was a slow, inevitable process of physical deterioration toward death. We still had times of joy, joy that she was alive and we could share things with her. Share love. Her determination was to live and die with dignity, but she—we—didn't have certain things that Forbes and those of you who love him have."

Intrigued, he asked, "What things?"

"Forbes will survive, no matter what limitations his injuries inflict. You have that joy, and relief. He and your family, and his caregivers, also have power. Power to effect change, to improve his situation. With Grandmother Rose, the progression of her disease was relentless and inevitable. When you are powerless to help someone you love deeply, who is suffering so much, it's a very painful thing."

"I'm so sorry you went through that." It was bad enough watching Forbes struggle. Iris made him imagine her family's situation, and he wanted to write that song, too. He rarely told his own stories, at least not directly. He sang about other people's lives and dilemmas, and he tried to do it with empathy, to honor and convey genuine emotions.

His fans told him his songs resonated with them, making them feel understood and less alone. This was what gave his own life value. He ran a hand over his tattoo, the visible reminder.

"Thank you," he told Iris. "For sharing that story and for your advice. It'll help me when I get back to working on the song."

"You won't do that now?" She sounded disappointed.

"I'm played out for now." He cleared his throat. "And parched." Starving, too. He'd been so eager to get to the commune, he hadn't thought to bring food or drink.

"I have more water." She reached in her basket. "Staying hydrated is important."

His lips curved. His stepmom—unlike the mother who'd run out on him and his dad when Julian was four—always said stuff like that. Iris was different in many ways from the fangirl types he typically hooked up with. But he was attracted to her. Definitely attracted, now that he'd put aside his music and was concentrating solely on her.

He reached for the unopened bottle, this time ensuring that his fingers brushed hers. She gave a soft gasp and pulled her hand away. He guessed she was attracted to him, too, unless those blushes and sideways looks were due simply to shyness. He also guessed, from what she'd said about the hope of finding true love, that she wasn't dating anyone special.

All the same, he doubted the two of them would hook up. Iris was into romance and love, two concepts he shunned. People did horrible things in the name of love; as a victim of that horror, he was too damaged, too wary, to contemplate anything more than casual relationships. He was damned lucky he'd at least come out of the hell of abuse to have a normal sex life.

Not wanting to hog her water, he took only a couple

of sips. Her basket was in the shade, and the water was cool and refreshing. He set the bottle down on the grass between them.

"I brought lunch," she said in that hesitant manner of hers. "I'd be happy to share it."

"That's a kind offer and I'm happy to accept." He was hungry not only for food but for more of her company, even if they would never be lovers.

"It's nothing special." She ducked her head again, hiding behind that glossy long hair. "Only a tuna sandwich." Her voice dropped so low he could barely hear. "I like tuna. Tinned albacore, for sandwiches. It's not exactly gourmet. Oh, and I use alfalfa sprouts and I know not everyone likes—"

"Iris." He cut into the apologetic flow of words. "It sounds great. More often than not, I forget to eat, or food's just fuel grabbed on the run. A homemade tuna sandwich will be a treat. And I happen to like alfalfa sprouts."

"Well, then . . ." She reached into her basket again, coming out with a neatly wrapped sandwich. When she unfolded the waxed paper, he saw nut-studded bread, chunky filling, and a fringe of green-leafed sprouts. As far as sandwiches went, it was an artistic creation.

He'd guessed, particularly from her comments about his music, that she might be creative herself. Or perhaps a perfectionist, or maybe both. Julian was infinitely curious about people, and Iris intrigued him on many levels. If he pushed, likely she'd retreat. So for the moment, he took the triangular half she gave him, and ate.

He took small bites, enjoying how the crunch of chopped celery, the tang of green onion, a lemony mayonnaise, and the nuts and seeds in the bread complemented the tuna and sprouts. "You know how to build a sandwich."

"You can have this, too." She held out the half she'd barely nibbled.

"Thanks, but I feel bad enough taking half your lunch."

After that, they ate quietly, her sitting cross-legged on her blanket with her well-stocked basket, him on the grass close by, with only his guitar and its case. He was reminded of a song his dad used to sing to his mom when Julian was a tiny kid. Something about a princess in a castle, and a peasant suitor who longed to scale the walls and reach her. After his mother ran out on them, Julian never heard that song again. She hadn't been a princess, only a groupie. When Forbes's musical talent and drive didn't lead him toward celebrity, she abandoned him and their four-year-old for another rising musician.

It occurred to Julian to wonder if Iris might be a groupie, albeit a more subtle, perceptive one than the women who threw themselves at him after concerts. As an artist, he knew subtlety could be more effective than blatancy. But no, everything about her rang true, as genuine as the pure resonance of a plucked guitar string.

She reached into her basket once more, producing a bunch of red seedless grapes, which she handed him. He tore off a couple of clusters and gave back the rest. Her lips curved softly and he figured she had guessed he'd do this.

"Tell me something about yourself, Iris."

"Oh, there's not much to tell." She ran graceful fingers through her hair but didn't pull it back from her face. "I heard an interview with you on CBC Radio in the summer. You said you're working on a new album?"

"I am, though it's coming slowly."

"Because of Forbes's accident?"

"Yeah." Because of the time commitment involved in helping his dad, the worry over Forbes's condition, and the stress of being back on Destiny.

"Are you concerned you won't get it finished in time?"

"Why don't you want to talk about yourself?"

"Oh!" Her eyes, deep and wary like those of a startled deer, widened. Then she gazed downward again, speaking to her gray-clad knees. "It's easier to talk about other people."

"Why is that?" he asked gently.

"Because I'm shy," she confessed to her knees. "And an introvert. I always have been."

"By introvert, you mean that you recharge your energy by being alone?"

"Yes. And that I'm introspective. But I do like people and I'm interested in them, honestly. So it's good when they talk about themselves. I'm happy to listen. Or I can talk about books. I like to talk about books."

"Books. Romance novels, you mean?"

"All kinds of books." Now she did glance up, passion in her eyes as she went on. "I love books. They've been a part of my life forever. Like music for you, I think?"

He nodded. "Go on."

"My family owns Dreamspinner, the bookstore. You know it, don't you?"

"Right." He'd been in a few times back when he was in school. "Cool store. Did your family open it or buy it from someone else?"

"Dad and Aunt Lily opened it. At the time, the only books sold on the island were a few dozen in those wire racks in the grocery store and pharmacy. They joke that it was a matter of necessity, so they'd have good books to read. That was before online shopping."

"I've heard that online shopping and piracy have hurt bookstores. I hope Dreamspinner's doing okay."

She nodded. "The islanders are loyal, and they're the core of our business. We tailor our stock to meet their needs. Even the ones who've mainly gone to digital still come in for something special. And of course tourists buy books about the island, as well as Canadiana and vacation reading. People like it that we sell only books and magazines, not everything else under the sun."

"Sounds like a good business model. Kudos to your family."

"Thank you. Of course we do also have the coffee shop, and that's provided an excellent supplementary income."

"There's a coffee shop? There didn't used to be, did there?"

"My mother added it." Her smooth brow wrinkled. "More than ten years ago."

"Seems like I never have time to get into the village." It wasn't a lie, just not the whole truth. He avoided Blue Moon Harbor village, where Jelinek's realty office was located. He didn't want to even think about the man, much less risk running into him. "You work at the bookstore and the coffee shop?"

"The bookstore only. Mom, who's an extrovert, handles the coffee shop."

"So you talk to customers every day. Is that hard?"

"I've learned how to do it."

This woman truly did fascinate him. "Tell me what you learned."

She flushed. "It's too embarrassing, and you can't really want to know."

But he did. He wanted to know more about sensitive Iris. So he told her something that few people knew. "You may not believe this, given my public persona, but I'm an introvert, too, and a private person." He didn't go on to say that, while she'd said she liked people, he had trouble trusting and getting close to anyone. "I like performing and sharing music, but the other stuff, the interviews and so on, that's tough for me. I had to learn how to do it."

"Honestly?" Her gaze went unfocused, like she was

examining that notion. "Yes, I believe you. When you're interviewed, you talk about the music and the band, not about yourself. People see you as a loner, and a little mysterious."

"A loner, yes. As for mysterious, that's not my intent. I'm just not very interesting." He'd far rather appear boring than have anyone pry into his past.

"I doubt that's true. I think you choose to share your deepest self not in interviews but through your songs. Even if they're other people's stories, even if the emotions in them are universal, you feel them on a deeply personal level and you sing very intimately." The delicate pink of her cheeks deepened. "It's like a communication between souls."

"Thank you, Iris." It was one of the most touching, perceptive compliments he'd ever received.

"How do you handle the public part?" She shuddered. "I can't think of anything more terrifying than having cameras aimed at me and microphones stuck in my face."

"Rather than be the real me, the guy who's happiest alone with his guitar, I play the role of a more outgoing person. It's a performance. Actually, more so than when I'm onstage." Jelinek had been his teacher, all those years ago, forcing the young Julian to learn how to don a mask that hid the dirty, broken, terrified part of himself. *Remember, Julian, this is our secret.*

"You're happiest alone with your guitar. I'll go now." Julian was polite, amazingly so for a celebrity, and she'd let herself be lulled into thinking he enjoyed her company. But she'd seen the flicker of anxiety tighten his handsome features. Of course she was intruding.

"No, wait," he said.

She rose to her knees, picked up the waxed paper from the sandwich, and folded it. "I apologize for disturbing your quiet time. I'm sure such time is rare, given all you have to do for your father." She began to gather up the grape stems.

Julian grasped her wrist, gently but surely. "Stop, Iris. Listen to me."

She gazed down at his tanned hand, the deft hand that created musical magic, circling her narrow, paler wrist. Her skin warmed under his touch. To her chagrin, a good part of that heat was arousal. "I'm listening."

"Look at me."

She forced herself to meet his gaze, and saw concern and frustration in his blue eyes. How could she be aroused when this man was so clearly troubled?

"I should have said I'm *usually* happiest alone with my guitar. But I enjoy your company. You give me something pleasant to focus on, at a time when things are stressful. Don't go."

So she was a distraction. A pleasant one. Her lips curved. Most women might not be flattered, but for her it was a fine compliment. And the touch of his bare skin on hers, innocent as it was, was a sensual stimulation she would long remember. "If you mean it, then I'll stay." Her smile widened. "I have cookies. Lemon cookies."

Now he released her, smiling back, and the loss of contact brought regret as well as relief. She took out the plastic bag of cookies, unzipped it, and offered it to him.

"I'm coming to think that's a magic basket." After the first bite, he said, "These are great. Sweet, but tangy." He studied her. "You brought a substantial lunch for one slim woman."

She was holding a cookie in one hand but brought the other hand to her face, fanning her fingers in front of it in hopes of somehow concealing her embarrassment. "I eat like a pig. It's not a very feminine quality." Exercise and good genes meant she never gained weight.

"I've never understood women who subsist on celery sticks and zero-fat yogurt." He tilted his head. "Feminine means womanly. Womanly means healthy and natural."

"Sadly, the advertising industry disagrees. I hate how ads impact girls when they're young and don't have the knowledge and common sense to reject them. Early influences can be so powerful." That was more words than she normally strung together with anyone who wasn't a family member or close friend. What was it about Julian that made her so talkative?

"Yeah, they can." His grim tone confirmed his agreement and suggested he might be remembering something unpleasant from his own youth.

Yakimuras didn't pry, so she wouldn't ask Julian to share his secrets. She nibbled her cookie, enjoying the zesty bite of the threads of lemon peel.

After a moment, Julian said, "One of your techniques is to get people talking about themselves. Another is to deflect, to change the subject."

"What are you talking about?"

"I asked how you deal with customers."

He hadn't forgotten, and it seemed he actually did find her interesting. "I breathe deeply and try to center myself, to remember there's no rational reason to be anxious. I talk to them about books, answer questions, and make recommendations. I'm well informed because I love reading and I at least skim most of our inventory." She considered. "I received excellent advice from my father and aunt. They're shy introverts as well." She gave a tiny grin. "Honestly, Mom despairs of the lot of us."

Julian gave a husky laugh. "Interesting phrasing."

Embarrassed again, she said, "I pick up expressions from books I read. Miranda teases me about it."

"It's cute. Anyhow, sorry to interrupt."

"That's okay. Anyhow, Dad and Aunt Lily pointed out to me that shyness is often about self-consciousness, which is self-centered. We should instead focus on the other person's needs and feelings."

"Hmm. That sounds wise. Tell me more. Do you actually think about customers' feelings?"

"Yes." Warming to her subject, she said, "Is the customer rushed and stressed, worried about something? Then I will serve them as quickly as possible, and not add to their stress. Or, as is the case with many of the locals, are they in no hurry, willing to spend time finding exactly the right book or just wanting someone to talk to? Is the woman browsing the 'end of relationship' advice books feeling sad, or is she angry? Or take the young man who's loitering suspiciously. Does he intend to steal a book, or is he afraid to ask where the erotica or self-help section is located?"

"Hmm."

"I try to remember that it's not about me, it's about them. I want their experience at Dreamspinner to meet their needs and suit their mood as perfectly as I can."

"Are you a perfectionist?"

She gave her head a quick shake. "Perfection is impossible. But to strive for some measure of harmony, even of beauty in what we do . . . Well, I think that isn't a waste of time."

"Hence the tuna sandwich that's a work of art."

"Now you're laughing at me." Normally, that would make her cringe, but from Julian it had a gentle feel, like the way her good friends Miranda and Eden teased her.

"No, not laughing. It was an excellent sandwich and I appreciate it." He was sitting with his knees up, his arms resting on them and his hands loosely clasped. With his faded clothing and longish hair, his outdoorsy tan, the burnished wood guitar beside him, she could imagine him as a hippie back in the commune days.

She'd read about those times. The birth control pill was new; women's sexuality was as uninhibited as men's; free love was the norm. People took mind-altering drugs. If she'd lived back then, would she, perhaps with the aid of magic mushrooms, have overcome her inhibitions and made love in the grass with a sexy, creative, amazing man like Julian?

"I understand how focusing on others helps you with your shyness," he said. "I do that with interviewers. But, Iris, sometimes it *should* be about you, because you're as important as anyone else."

"Not with customers. But yes, with friends, it's often about me. Like when Miranda urged me to stop hiding away and attend the Triple-B-Zee performance last May, and she went with me." Iris had gone in part to support Miranda, who'd broken up with Luke and was agonizing over whether he might be there. But the factor that had tipped the scale was the lure of seeing Julian perform.

Now here he was, right in front of her. He had played, if not exactly *for* her, in front of her. He'd listened to her input—and now she couldn't believe her audacity. He was a double JUNO winner! Suddenly, this was all too much. Her senses and emotions, her flaws and vulnerabilities, were on overload. "I need to go. I have commitments." Her only actual responsibilities were to clean the condo she and her aunt shared, and prepare dinner for the two of them before Aunt Lily returned from working at the store. But family duties mattered a great deal, and so did the need to be alone for a while.

Perhaps Julian heard the resolve in her voice, or he, too, craved time alone, because this time he didn't protest. "I've enjoyed talking to you, Iris. Let's do it again."

"Oh!" Her eyes widened. It was the last thing she'd expected him to say. "I . . ." She could see Julian again. But today was special. She'd managed to communicate semi-articulately and he'd been understanding, sensitive. Another time, she'd be tense, get tongue-tied. If she never saw him face-to-face again, she could hang on to this magical memory.

"Are you involved with someone?" he asked.

She ducked her head to hide the longing in her eyes. The longing for something more than would ever be possible between them. "No," she said softly. "But I don't think it's a good idea, us seeing each other again." She rose and gathered her blanket, not bothering to fold it, picked up her basket, and hurried away.

Chapter Three

In the several days since he'd visited the old commune, Julian hung on to the memory of those few hours of peace, of music, of Iris's company. He spent most of his time helping Forbes and Sonia. A few of his dad's close friends dropped by to offer assistance, but fortunately Bart Jelinek wasn't one of them. Julian didn't know what he'd do if he ever came face-to-face with the man.

You're a special boy, Julian.

Would he, who'd never hit a person in his life, haul off and beat him up?

Remember, this is our secret.

Or would he turn into the cringing kid again, feeling dirty, broken, vulnerable? One thing was certain: he never wanted to find out.

Midmorning on the first Sunday in November, Julian was cleaning up the kitchen after a late breakfast, while Sonia got Forbes settled in the front room. They were expecting Julian's stepbrother and his family.

Luke, despite being busy with his work as the island's only vet, raising twin boys, and being recently engaged, had popped in at least every couple of days. He'd done shopping for them, picked up prescriptions, delivered goodies his fiancée had baked. Until today, Forbes hadn't felt well enough to deal with his grandkids' boisterous enthusiasm, so Miranda and the kids had stayed at Luke's house—the house she and her young daughter had moved into. Julian counted it as a great sign that yesterday Forbes had suggested this family visit.

And here they were, chestnut-haired Luke coming through the kitchen door along with his four-year-olds and Miranda. It seemed they hadn't brought Ariana, Miranda's daughter. Before Julian could ask, Brandon and Caleb sprinted toward him yelling, "Uncle Julian!"

It was the first time he'd seen his nephews since his brief visit back in May. Squatting down and hugging an armful of squirming, reddish-haired boys, Julian said, "Who on earth are you guys? You can't be my favorite nephews. Caleb and Brandon are little kids, and you're so big." It was true; they'd grown inches and pounds. Though they were identical twins, there were superficial differences—like clothing choices and Caleb's longer hair—and they had different personalities, so Julian never had trouble telling them apart.

"It's us, it's us!" Brandon, the outgoing, impulsive twin insisted.

"We're your *only* nephews," Caleb, the quieter, more reflective boy, stated reproachfully.

Julian laughed, his spirits lighter. The kids were a shot of pure sunshine. The same as Iris. Thoughts of her gave him moments of solace. Though she'd turned him down when he phoned Dreamspinner and asked if they could get together, he would try again.

After a mock wrestling match with the twins, he rose. "Take off your jackets and shoes, kids. Then you can go find Grandma Sonia and Granddad Forbes. But be careful, okay? Granddad is hurting and you can't hug him."

The boys shed their outdoor clothing on a chair and

roared off, and Julian faced Miranda. She was slim and pretty in jeans and a long-sleeved blue tee, a late-summer tan accenting her blond hair and grayish-blue eyes. Her face bore a wary expression.

He hadn't seen her since May. The night they'd met— and kissed. She and Luke had been broken up and Julian hadn't even known they'd been dating, because she hadn't told him. But she'd stopped the kiss immediately, confessed the truth, and said he wasn't the man she wanted. Julian had been pissed off because even though he and Luke weren't particularly close, his stepbrother was a good guy and Julian would never betray him. But when Miranda had explained, Julian saw she wasn't a bad person, just hurt and confused.

Luke had, by pure bad timing, witnessed the kiss. The next day, he confronted Julian, who enlightened him. And, he liked to think, played a part in getting the couple back together. So, though this meeting was awkward, his conscience was clear. He grinned at her. "Hey, Miranda. Good to see you again."

"You too," she said guardedly.

"I owe you a thank-you."

"You do?"

"You gave me one of the songs for the new album." One of only three he'd completed, though he felt good about the Forbes-lark one, "Your Reality," that he'd started at the commune.

Miranda's brows rose, the wariness fading. "You actually wrote that song?"

After their kiss, she'd been down on herself. He'd told her he figured she was better than she thought, a comment that triggered his muse. "Yeah. It's called 'You're Better than You Think.' I'll play it for you—" He intercepted Luke's scowl, an impressive one from a guy who was a couple inches taller than him and carried a good twenty pounds more of solid muscle. "For *both* of you," he clarified. "By the way, congratulations on the engagement."

Miranda's smile was relaxed and genuine. "Thanks, Julian."

"I'll dedicate the song to you. If that's okay?" His questioning glance went from her to Luke and back again.

Her smile turned into a wry grin. "You couldn't dedicate a song called 'You're Fabulous and Amazing' to me?"

The three of them chuckled, and she went on. "Yes, I'm flattered. As long as you don't reveal how the inspiration for that song came about."

"No one knows but the three of us," he said, "and I'm not planning on changing that."

"The three of us and a girlfriend of hers," Luke said dryly.

Was it Iris? "Uh, what friend is that? Might I know her?"

"Glory McKenna," Miranda said. "She was in Aaron's class at school."

Relieved, he reflected but didn't come up with a face to match the name. "I don't remember her. But then I didn't hang around school any more than I had to."

"You and me both," she said.

He wondered what her reason had been. For him, it had started with resentment about being forced to move from Victoria to this backwoods island. Even worse, he'd lost his close bond with his single-parent dad when Forbes went crazy over Sonia. And then the kids at school all knew each other, and Julian didn't—and wouldn't—fit in. Then Jelinek had come into his life, and misery had turned to sheer hell.

Destiny Islanders had a bunch of sayings about how the island was some people's destiny. In Julian's case, destiny had sucked.

"Mommy!" a petulant little voice said, and he gazed down to see a small girl emerge from behind Miranda, one hand gripping the leg of her mother's jeans. Her brow furrowed as she stared at Julian. She was a cutie, with her curly black hair, dark skin, and deep brown eyes, so unlike her mom in appearance.

He bent again and smiled. "Hey, who's been playing hide-and-seek? I bet you're Ariana. Luke's told me how pretty and smart you are." His stepbrother had fallen in love with Miranda's three-year-old just as deeply as he loved the child's mother.

"I pitty," the girl agreed. "You Luke brother?"

Luke ruffled her hair. "That's right. This is my brother, Julian."

It felt odd, hearing himself described that way. Julian had been eleven and Luke twelve when their parents married, and the boys had always referred to themselves as stepbrothers. They hadn't disliked each other, but they'd both been less than impressed with the marriage and had kept to themselves. In later years they'd become more friendly, but he'd never thought of Luke as his brother. Still, the concept of stepsiblings was likely too complicated for young Ariana.

"I get brothers," Ariana said. "I get a daddy, too. When Mommy marries Luke."

"Yes," Julian told her, "when your mom and Luke get married, he'll be your daddy. Brandon and Caleb will be your brothers. And me, well I guess I'll be your uncle." That aspect of the situation hadn't dawned on him before. He glanced at Miranda. "If that's okay with you."

The bewilderment in her eyes told him she hadn't thought of that either, but then it cleared and she smiled warmly. "Uncle Julian. How about that?"

"I has unc," Ariana said. "Unc Aaron. He's a pilot!"

"I know him." Miranda's brother owned Destiny-based Blue Moon Air and had often flown Julian when he visited the island.

"Some people," Miranda said, hugging her daughter against her side, "are lucky enough to have two uncles."

The girl processed that and then beamed. "I lucky!"

"I think we're all pretty lucky," Miranda said. Then she frowned. "Except poor Forbes, of course. It sounds as if he has a tough road ahead of him. But Luke says he's a fighter, and that he's determined to be able to play at our wedding."

She and Luke were getting married between Christmas and New Year's, which would make for one crazy holiday season, but who was he to judge? In fact, he suspected they might've chosen the date in part because of Julian himself, knowing that he always visited for a few days at Christmas.

"Forbes's bones may be shattered, but he's one determined guy," Julian agreed. "Nothing can break his spirit."

"Has he always been that way?" she asked.

"Uh-huh. Like when my mother ran off with another guy and it was just Forbes and me. There he was, a musician making money from some gigs and working part-time for a construction company, and suddenly he was a single parent with a four-year-old. But he handled it. He was a good dad."

Forbes had shared music, his love of it and his knowledge and skill. He'd kept his son fed and clothed, kept a roof over their heads. Julian remembered a series of babysitters— from grandmotherly types to girlfriends of Forbes's—and sometimes he'd hung out in a corner of a restaurant where his dad was playing, or at the woodworking shop when his dad got an apprenticeship. Social services mightn't have considered it an ideal childhood, but Julian always knew he was loved and always felt safe. Ironically, it wasn't until his father moved them to this tiny island to form a blended family, that Julian had felt neglected and been in danger.

A tug at the leg of his jeans made him look down, to see Ariana's pouty face gazing up. "Unc Julie, I want to play."

He found a smile. "That can be arranged. Hey, do you like music?"

"She does," Miranda said. Teasingly, she asked, "Do you know 'Itsy Bitsy Spider'?"

He laughed. "I bet I can figure it out. Better yet, maybe she'd like to fool around with a keyboard. How about I take her out to the studio and you two can visit with Forbes?"

Miranda stooped and addressed her daughter. "Would you like to go make music with Uncle Julian, sweetie?"

"Yes!" It was an emphatic approval, and the girl held out her hand to him, clearly expecting him to take it.

Julian accepted that small hand gently, feeling the immensity of the gesture. She was so trusting. So innocent. It broke his heart that a child's trust could be so easily exploited, her or his innocence shattered as drastically as that accident had trashed Forbes's body.

He guided her out to the building that had been the original garage. Soon after Forbes and Sonia bought the house, Forbes, who was a wood craftsman as well as a musician, had renovated the garage to create a music studio and a woodworking workshop.

In the studio, Julian showed Ariana the keyboard and she pounded away enthusiastically. He picked up his guitar, strumming and plucking in accompaniment, the two of them creating a noise that most people would never call music, but Julian found oddly pleasing.

The door opened and Jonathan Barnes, the second "B" in B-B-Zee, stepped in, smiling. "Am I interrupting a jam session?"

Still playing, Julian said, "Want to join? Forbes wouldn't mind if you used his guitar." Jonathan normally played the bass guitar, but he'd do fine with Forbes's instrument.

"Thanks, but I can't stay. There's something I want to ask you."

"Okay." Julian put down his guitar and walked over to him, leaving Ariana in her own world of musical expression. "What's up?"

Bald-headed Jonathan stroked his neat gray beard, and the smile had disappeared from his lips. "The band has a booking on November twenty-fourth. I've been trying to find another group to fill in, but haven't located one that's available and plays the right kind of music."

Julian said, not liking the idea one bit, "You want me to fill in for Forbes." His dad's two bandmates were talented musicians and good guys, and Julian had played with the band a number of times, for the pleasure of making music with his father. But every time he joined B-B-Zee at Quail Ridge Community Hall, Julian was antsy, fearing that Jelinek would be in the audience. So far it hadn't happened, which he suspected meant that the man was avoiding him just as much as Julian steered clear of his abuser.

He realized his hand had automatically gone into his pocket, and he was fingering the old, mended guitar pick he'd carried for more than ten years. It was his reminder that even if Jelinek had broken him, he had survived. Even if he carried shame and guilt like rot at the core of an apple, he still had worth, something to contribute to the world.

"It's Jane and George Nelson's sixtieth wedding anniversary," Jonathan said. "You've seen them. He's in a wheelchair and they're always out on the dance floor when we play."

"Oh, man." Yeah, he'd seen them, her in her husband's lap as he maneuvered his chair around, both of them obviously still in love with each other. It was like the fairy-tale ending of one of Iris's books, except that this fairy tale was a real-life one.

"They're huge fans. They really want B-B-Zee."

"I'm pretty busy helping Forbes and Sonia."

"I'm sure, and I don't want to pressure you." Jonathan's brow was furrowed. "It's just, it's the Nelsons. And, though he'd never tell you this, Christian could use the income."

Julian couldn't quite suppress a groan, but fortunately Ariana's keyboard-hammering drowned it out. Jonathan Barnes and Christian Zabec were both, like Forbes, in their sixties, but none of them had retired. Jonathan and his wife did okay, running the Once in a Blue Moon B and B on the harbor, but Christian was a bit of an eccentric. A former American, he'd drifted around until he settled on Destiny, but the island and B-B-Zee were about the only "settled" things in his life. He'd never had a long-term relationship nor a real career. He was good at fixing things and did odd jobs for islanders, but he didn't have a reliable income. Still, Christian was a decent guy. And Julian's dad would feel like crap for disappointing the Nelsons.

How could Julian say no? He couldn't tell the band members he was afraid Jelinek might be one of the guests. "Where's the party, and how big is it? Do you know who'll be there?"

"It's at the community hall, so you know the setup, the acoustics. Jane and George's relatives from all over the place will be there, and many of their island friends. Same as for their fiftieth." He scratched his bald head. "Oh, I guess you don't remember that. You weren't on the island then."

"No." Ten years ago, seventeen-year-old Julian had been in Vancouver. He'd played music on the streets and anywhere else he could, and found jobs waiting tables in cheap diners. He'd avoided drugs and managed to survive without having to sell his body the way so many runaways did. Music made life worth living, and he was grateful he hadn't actually offed himself as had been his plan when he ran away from home. He'd gotten back in touch with Forbes and Sonia after disappearing for almost a year, but no way had he wanted to visit the island.

"Forget it," Jonathan said. "I shouldn't have asked." Julian saw the disappointment in the older man's greenish eyes, disappointment not only for having to say no to the Nelsons, but disappointment *in* his friend's son.

He suppressed another groan. Then, fingering the familiar shape of the guitar pick, he realized he'd been ignoring its message. He was no longer a shattered, suicidal kid. Despite his emotional scars and the guilt that would always haunt him, he was a man who'd built a successful career in a tough industry. He had a healthy sex life despite the abuse. He'd come one hell of a long way—yet he was still letting fucking Jelinek control his actions. "I'll do it." The words burst out roughly, making Jonathan's silvery-gray brows rise.

Tempering his tone, Julian said, "I want to. I'll need to get up to speed on your playlist. Let's schedule some rehearsal time." He took out his phone and brought up the calendar that showed Forbes's numerous medical and rehab appointments.

As Jonathan called Christian, Julian had a second revelation. Did Iris work at Dreamspinner on Sundays? If he wasn't going to let Jelinek rule his life, he should stop avoiding the village.

Iris was busy with a steady stream of customers. The weather's perfect blend of sunny warm and autumn crisp had resulted in the morning ferry offloading a horde of day-trippers. Most were foot passengers, coming to browse the stores and enjoy a nice lunch. Under the influence of Indian-summer euphoria, they were happy to pull out their debit and credit cards to self-indulge or get an early start on their Christmas shopping with one of Aunt Lily's silk-screened scarves at Island Treasures, a stuffed seal at Blowing Bubbles for a child or grandchild, a new book to savor on a chilly winter evening.

As always, Iris focused on her customers' needs and tried to find them the perfect book, be it a thriller by reclusive island author Kellan Hawke, a history of Destiny Island, a travel guide to some exotic destination, or a slim volume of love poems. But even as she worked diligently, Julian Blake was on her mind. He had phoned a few days ago and suggested they get together. Flustered, she'd turned him down. If he saw her again, she'd screw it up, which would tarnish the memory of that perfect afternoon when Julian Blake had been less the celebrity and more a relatable man.

Iris hadn't told a soul about those hours at the abandoned commune. There were no words to convey how magical that time had felt, and she enjoyed hugging the secret close to her heart. Still, it shouldn't distract her from work.

Destiny residents Thérèse Bellefontaine and her daughter, Marie-Claude, were arguing loudly in the Young Adult section.

Iris walked over. "*Puis-je vous aider?*" The Bellefontaine family was fluent in English but appreciated the opportunity to speak French, as did Iris.

The pair responded in French, talking across each other, conveying their opposing wishes. Up for the challenge, Iris found several books she hoped would satisfy both the older-than-her-years girl and the mom who wanted to keep her daughter a child forever. After some mother-daughter negotiation, Thérèse held up two books. "*D'accord?*" she asked Marie-Claude.

"*D'accord*," the girl agreed.

Thérèse gave Iris a rueful smile. "*Merci pour votre patience.*"

"*De rien.*" She breathed a quiet "Whew" as the pair went to pay for the purchase.

"*Pardon*," a male voice said from behind her, "*peux-tu m'aider?*" Silly her, the husky voice reminded her of Julian.

She turned and—*Oh my gosh*. This was no dream, but the man himself, looking amazing in well-worn jeans and a navy T-shirt. Her heart fluttered crazily, like a trapped bird, the way it always did when she was anxious. Except somehow, this time, the feeling wasn't so scary. She took a deep breath, striving for calm. He was a customer, albeit one with whom she'd shared a few special hours.

"*Bonjour*, Julian. *Quel genre de livre cherches-tu?*" Was he shopping for Forbes, or for himself? As she did with all customers, she studied him more closely, for clues as to his mood. His pose was casual, with his right hand thrust into the pocket of his jeans, yet his body looked taut rather than relaxed. The lean angles of his face were strained, he looked pale under his tan, and dampness glossed his skin even though it wasn't misty outside. Concerned, she switched to English and asked, "Has something happened with Forbes?"

"No, he's fine." Julian frowned. "Why would you say that?"

"You look . . ." Afraid, actually; almost ill with fear. But that made no sense. "Stressed."

He ran his left hand across his brow and her sharp gaze caught a tremble in his fingers, those fingers that never faltered when he played the guitar. "I'm okay."

She didn't believe him, but wasn't about to challenge his words. "That's good. Perhaps I can find a book that will help distract you from your worry about your father."

The lines of his face relaxed a little, a hint of curiosity showing. "What book would you choose for me, Iris?"

About to protest that she knew almost nothing about him, she stopped herself. He had tossed out a challenge, one that was particularly suited to her skills.

He needed distraction, so perhaps a thriller. He wrote beautiful lyrics, so might enjoy poetry. His songs told stories; he might find inspiration in a collection of short stories. All those things were possibilities, yet they were the conventional choices. An idea struck her. Maybe it was a crazy one, but if so then she'd find him something else. "Give me a minute. Perhaps you'd like to go into the coffee shop? We have excellent coffees, teas, and baked goods."

"No," he said quickly. "Thanks, but I'll wait here."

Was it her imagination or had he paled again at the mention of food? Was the man ill? Or perhaps on drugs? She'd seen no sign of drug use in their time at the commune. As she walked through the store, another explanation occurred to her. In the crowded coffee shop, fans might recognize him and pester him at a time when he'd prefer privacy. She hated to even imagine what a life of celebrity was like.

A few minutes later she returned to find Julian staring at, but not seeming to see, a display of Christmas novels—which seemed to come out earlier and earlier each year. He glanced up, looking relieved. "There you are. What do you have for me?"

He took his right hand from his pocket when she held out two hardcover books, both longtime favorites of hers. He took them and looked at the one on top: a volume including both *Winnie-the-Pooh* and *The House at Pooh Corner* by A. A. Milne. Frowning, he examined the second book: *The Tao of Pooh* by Benjamin Hoff. He gazed at her quizzically. "A kid's book? I mean, I've never read it, but *Winnie-the-Pooh* is for children, right?"

"Never read Pooh? Seriously? Didn't your parents read it to you? Or with you?"

He shook his head. "Not that I know of. Mom left when I was four and I don't have many memories. And Forbes sang bedtime songs rather than reading to me."

Iris's parents, her aunt, and her Yakimura grandparents had all been huge readers. She couldn't remember when she'd gone from listening to bedtime stories to being able to read the words herself; it had been such a natural transition.

But Julian had asked a question and she knew how to defend her choices. If a customer said no, she learned from the objections he or she raised. "In these books, you'll find entertainment, humor, and wisdom. They'll give you something to relax with, but also ideas to muse on. Who knows, perhaps even inspiration for a song." She gave a small grin. "As you'll see, Pooh composed songs himself." In Julian and in his music, she sensed a connection with nature, the universe, and the principles of the Tao, yet occasionally she saw signs of a deep unrest. She sensed a soul that needed guidance as well as gentle humor.

He studied her face and she dropped her gaze, accepting his perusal but unable to stare back into his eyes. After a moment, he said, "Okay, I'll try them. But to be honest, I didn't come here for a book."

"No?" She darted a quick look upward.

"You turned me down when I phoned. I thought I might be more persuasive in person."

Her heart fluttered again and she glanced around. Was anyone watching them, and if so, what did they think about this odd pairing of sexy, popular musician and unassuming island bookseller? More important, what was Julian thinking? Men didn't ask her out. The only guy she'd ever dated had been a fix-up by her friend Shelley, back in university.

"I don't understand," she murmured, her gaze on the

tan, soft-soled loafers she wore with sage-green pants, a cream blouse, and one of her aunt's gorgeous silk-screened scarves. "Why are you interested in me?"

"Because you're interesting, Iris. I enjoy your company. You're easy to be with."

She knew she could be interesting, and that some people enjoyed her company. Not just her family, but her new friends Miranda and Eden, her oldest friend Shelley, and the members of the book club she belonged to. But Julian was used to far more exciting female companionship.

Although perhaps now, with his father in such bad shape, he wasn't looking for excitement. Perhaps he sought a more peaceful respite from his caregiver responsibilities, and from the unrest she sensed in his soul. So, not a date perhaps, just friendship. Cautiously, she said, "This is a time in your life when you could use a friend who's easy to be with?"

His blue eyes, still stunning even though they looked strained today, closed briefly. "I guess I could." He opened them again, dazzling her. "Will you be that friend?"

A friend. It was amazing to think he might want her friendship, and ridiculous to wish, for one tiny moment, that they might share something more. Iris believed that one day a man would see and value her many attributes, and fall in love with her. Her girlfriends supported her in that belief. But no way would Julian Blake be the man. His life path and hers took opposite directions, even if for this short time those paths might intersect. If she practiced mindfulness, she could enjoy that intersection without wishing for the impossible. She breathed, centered herself, and raised her chin. "I'd be honored to be your friend."

For the first time, his sensual lips curved into a smile. "The honor is mine, Iris Yakimura. So, when—"

A loud male voice cut him off. "Behave yourself and do as I say!"

Tension gripping her, Iris swung around to see a middle-aged man with a boy of eight or nine, the red-faced man grabbing a book from the boy's hand. She studied them closely, noting that the boy, while pouting, didn't look particularly distressed. Relieved that intervention didn't seem to be required, she turned back to Julian.

He was staring at the man and boy, too, and he looked shocky again, pale and sweating. "Fucking island," he muttered, low enough that only she could hear.

"Julian?" What was wrong?

"Oh, fuck," he said roughly. "You don't need to be with a guy like me. Forget it."

She gaped at him as he turned on his heel and stalked toward the door, almost running. He flung open the door and disappeared outside, taking the books with him.

Chapter Four

For three days, Iris had puzzled over Julian's behavior. He had phoned Dreamspinner later on Sunday, getting her father, and apologized for inadvertently leaving without paying for his books. He'd put them on his credit card. He hadn't asked to speak to her.

Even if he wasn't on drugs, he was moody, erratic, irrational. She should, as he'd said, forget all about him. Yet how could she forget the sensitive guy who'd shared his music and his worries about his father, who hadn't told her she was crazy for being so shy but had instead exchanged coping strategies?

Will the real Julian Blake please stand up?

On Thursday morning, she rose, made her bed, and put on her workout clothes. Before starting tai chi, she gazed appreciatively around her room. This, the smaller of the two bedrooms in the third-floor condominium she and her aunt shared, was Iris's sanctuary. She had chosen minimalist furniture with elegant lines, mellow colors, and a few items of art that spoke to her soul. Her aunt's room was similar, but also set up for creating fabric art.

Iris did her tai chi facing the sliding glass door, enjoying the view of Blue Moon Harbor village and docks. In the garden of the condo building, a breeze stirred the last tenacious leaves clinging to the maple and mountain ash trees; dancers in bright yellow and orange skirts, they swirled to its melody. Were they oblivious to, or defiant of, the fact that soon they'd fall and be trampled underfoot?

On the pale green wall on one side of the balcony door, above a tall mauve orchid plant, hung her Mindful Living calendar. The November photograph was of three small brown bowls with candles burning in them. The quote, attributed to Buddha, was about how one candle could light thousands without itself being diminished, and that the same was true when you shared happiness. Each month, she mused over the saying, parsing the levels of meaning and seeking guidance for her own life. In general, she was a happy person. The same, she sensed, wasn't true of Julian. Should she try to share her happiness with him, or was that a fool's errand?

When she'd finished tai chi, she took down the calendar and turned to the previous page, to refresh her memory. This image was of another little brown bowl and a twig with red berries. The saying, from Søren Kierkegaard, was about patience and how you shouldn't expect to immediately reap the rewards of what you'd sown. Iris had always been a patient person, so she hadn't spent much time reflecting on that quote last month.

But now, again, she thought of Julian. Yes, he had flaws, frailties. But she, the woman whose shyness and introversion in some ways enriched but also in some ways restricted her life, should not leap to a hasty judgment of him, just because he was less than 100 percent mellow and perfect.

She sensed that he wasn't a bad person. More likely, a person in pain. If he'd said he had no desire to be with her, she might have believed him. But he had said *she* didn't *need* to be with a guy like him.

Perhaps she didn't. Perhaps she did. Perhaps *he* in fact needed her. She had queried whether he could use a friend, and he'd said yes. In her mind, those words resonated as truth. "What shall I do?" she murmured.

What should she take from the advice about patience? Should she wait and see if Julian returned? Had she done enough to sow the seeds of potential friendship and trust, to share her happiness with life?

She mused on that as she showered and then dressed for a day at the store. As usual, she chose slim tailored pants and a shirt in gentle tones, and added one of Aunt Lily's scarves. In the kitchen, her aunt, slim and lovely in a simple cotton yukata kimono in a rusty-orange shade patterned with hemp leaves, was gazing into the fridge. They exchanged morning greetings, speaking in French. When the family members were alone together, they spoke either Japanese or French. Japanese, to honor their heritage and to respect their relatives in Japan. French, because as good Canadians they believed in speaking both official languages.

Aunt Lily said, "I can't decide what I want for breakfast."

Sometimes they ate Japanese: miso soup, rice, the fermented soybeans called *nattō*, or perhaps grilled fish. Other times, it was bacon and eggs, pancakes, or French toast. Or yogurt, granola, and fruit, or porridge with maple syrup on cold days. So many choices.

"I feel like having an omelet," Iris said.

"That sounds good to me."

Iris took chives, mushrooms, and cheddar from the fridge and chopped and grated while her aunt whipped eggs, milk, salt, and pepper. They made individual omelets, each in its own small pan, preferring the symmetry of an entire folded-over omelet rather than a larger one cut in half. Their plates were ivory with a dark blue, geometrically patterned border. The golden omelets oozing cheese, with a garnish of sliced red-skinned apples, looked lovely, reminding Iris of Julian's comment that her tuna sandwich was a work of art.

He created art with his music. Her own ways of adding beauty to the world were tiny, yet even small things could be consequential. Perhaps she could ease his worry and pain if he permitted her to. She might suffer pain herself—from harsh words, rejection, or the simple loss of his company when he inevitably left the island—and yet her life would be richer for knowing Julian Blake. When her beloved Grandmother Rose was dying of ALS, Iris had learned that joy could exist, even glow more brightly and poignantly, when there was also pain.

"Something's on your mind," her aunt said as they sat at the small table in the living room, by the sliding glass door. "Would you like to talk about it?"

Iris raised her gaze from her plate and smiled. Sometimes it wasn't enough to wait and wonder. How could you expect a bountiful harvest if you weren't diligent about sowing seeds and tending them? "Thank you, Aunt, but I know what I'm going to do." Their family wasn't big on touchy-feely conversations.

"Then I hope it turns out well."

"Me too." Iris rose and went to the kitchen to rinse her plate and put it in the dishwasher. Her aunt remained at the table, sipping coffee.

"I'll see you this afternoon," Iris said before leaving. She was working the morning and afternoon shifts, and Aunt Lily would be at the store for the afternoon and evening. Dreamspinner was open every day except Monday, but the only evenings were Thursday, Friday, and Saturday, unless there was a special event like a reading by a visiting author.

Iris's aunt would spend the morning either creating more

of her wearable art, going for a long walk, or reading in her chair by the window. Lily was an intelligent, sensitive, beautiful woman. She had never married, rarely dated, and seemed content. If she missed having a life partner or children, she didn't confess to it.

In many ways, she was an excellent role model for singlehood, yet Iris wanted more. The calm, orderly life of an independent single woman was fine, and Iris would always need some personal space and time, but she also craved the noise, mess, and love of a life-mate and kids. Perhaps next spring, in Japan, she would meet that special man, the one who'd love her and want to come to Destiny Island and create a family with her.

Iris and her aunt co-owned the hybrid-electric Chevy Volt, but today, like most days, Iris walked the kilometer and a half to the store. She enjoyed being outside, stretching her legs, and listening to an audiobook. She alternated French and Japanese ones.

The Dreamspinner coffee shop was already humming, and a couple of customers waited outside the bookstore, following her in when she unlocked the door. She assisted them, greeted her parents when they arrived, and then holed up in the office, summoned her courage, and called Sonia and Forbes's house.

"Hello? Russo and Blake residence." The voice was Julian's.

Trying to sound calm, she said, "A friend doesn't tell another friend to get lost."

There was a pause. "Iris. I don't think I was that rude, was I?"

He was talking, not blowing her off. The soil was receptive to the seed she was offering, which strengthened her resolve. "The message was clear. However, you'd also said you wanted to be friends. A friend doesn't accept a blow-off when it's delivered out of pain."

Another pause, then a hesitant, "Pain?"

"I could see you were hurting. I think you really could use a friend. Someone who'll offer support and not be judgmental."

"Not judgmental," he echoed thoughtfully. "Does that include not prying into my issues? Just letting me be?"

She gave a soft laugh. "I'm a Yakimura. We mind our own business." Even within the family, they respected each other's privacy. "Julian, what is it you need?"

"Oh, God. I need what I can't have. I want to, oh, I don't know. To fly away. But not in a plane or helicopter, they're noisy. Something silent. A glider, maybe. Skydiving, except then I'd be plummeting back to earth." He gave a soft groan. "Listen to me. I'm not making sense."

"Maybe you are." Though her life was generally happy and pain-free, Iris, too, sometimes yearned to escape normal life, and to feel free. She couldn't give Julian a glider flight, but maybe she could offer something comparable. "When can you next get a few free hours?"

"Uh, Saturday, I guess. Annie and Randall are coming over for the day."

She knew them, of course. They were longtime friends of Sonia and Forbes as well as being Luke's in-laws, the parents of his deceased wife, Candace. "That will be nice for Forbes." Iris usually worked Saturdays, but her family was flexible about adjusting their schedules to accommodate one another. Besides, she'd looked at the forecast and the weekend was supposed to be nice, and her plan did require decent weather. "Saturday it is."

"You want to meet at the commune?"

She would enjoy that, and perhaps he'd play for her, but that wouldn't give Julian the free-flying escape he craved. "Not this time."

"Look, I, uh, I'd rather not hang out in the village."

"That's not what I have in mind."

"Should I ask?"

"No. Let it be a surprise."

"Iris, I . . ."

"Trust me," she said softly.

Trust her. Julian wasn't big on trust. And how could he trust Iris to plan an activity when she had no idea that merely setting foot in Blue Moon Harbor last Sunday had almost made him puke? Fucking Jelinek did still rule his life.

Iris liked to please people. If whatever she had in mind didn't work for him, she'd likely be amenable to a change of plan.

She had told him to dress casually and warmly, so he hoped they'd be doing something outdoorsy like going to the beach. Jelinek, the successful Realtor, would be hard at work on a sunny November Saturday, not hanging out at the beach.

Julian had refused Iris's offer to pick him up, and hadn't told Forbes and Sonia he was seeing her. His family didn't ask. Sonia characterized her son, Luke, as a dog, open and sharing. Julian, she said, was a cat, independent and reticent.

He'd agreed to meet Iris at the community center parking lot, only a couple of miles from Forbes and Sonia's house. Shortly after breakfast, he set out on foot, toting his guitar out of habit. He found Iris sitting in the blue Volt that had been parked near the commune. He put his guitar case on the back seat and climbed in beside her.

The trite phrase "easy on the eyes" might have been invented for this woman. She wore slim-fitting navy jeans and a cream-colored cable-knit sweater, and her long hair was pulled into a low ponytail secured with a twist of patterned blue fabric. The style highlighted her elegant features and meant she wouldn't be able to hide behind wings of black hair.

"You brought your guitar," she commented.

"It's kind of attached to my hand. I don't need to play it."

"I hope you do." Driving from the parking lot, she said, "When do you need to be back?"

"No particular time. Annie and Randall should be at the house by now. You know them, right?"

"Yes. They're both regular customers. Nice people. You'd never guess they were so wealthy, would you?"

"No. They're unpretentious." Annie had created a spectacularly successful video game in the 1980s, and several other popular ones since then. Randall was an excellent photographer, but it was his wife's work that made them billionaires. "They'll look after Forbes today, so Sonia can do some chores and take her mom out for a long lunch." His stepmom's mother was in her eighties, living in her own home, resisting either moving to a seniors' facility or moving in with her daughter and son-in-law.

"That'll be a nice break for Antonia. She isn't able to get out very much now, is she?"

"You really know what's going on around here, don't you?"

"Most of Destiny's residents come into the store and the coffee shop."

He had guessed that, when he'd seen the busy coffee shop on Sunday, which was partly why he'd almost had a panic attack. Then he'd heard that man ordering the boy to obey, and for a moment he'd thought it was Jelinek. Of course, thinking about it later, he knew the bastard would never do that in public. But what was he doing in private?

As Iris drove through the center of Blue Moon Harbor village and past Island Realty, Julian's nerves quivered and his stomach churned. *This is our secret, Julian.* How many times had Jelinek said that? And here Julian was, a grown man, still obeying him. Even if other boys—

No, he couldn't let himself think about that. He suppressed a groan. When would he be able to leave this fucking island? Go back to the safe world where, most of the time, he could shove the guilt and shame back into the rotten little core of his cowardly heart.

"Julian?"

"What?" His voice came out as an annoyed croak.

"I'm sorry. Did you have an idea for a song?"

"No. God, no. Sorry, did you ask me something?" If he could've found a non-hurtful way of making the request, he'd have asked her to let him out. She deserved far better than his company—and he didn't deserve a friend like Iris.

"I just asked how Antonia is doing."

"Physically frail, but mentally all there, Sonia says. Antonia's not rich, but she can afford a housekeeper and a gardener. The grocery store and pharmacy deliver free of charge to people who can't get out."

"As does Dreamspinner. I haven't seen Antonia in the store for a couple of months. I must get in touch and make sure she knows we'll deliver books." She glanced toward him and then back at the road. "I actually enjoy doing it. A few of the shut-ins are gruff hermit-types, but most are so glad to have company. They ask me in for tea and cookies, and they're interesting to talk to."

Focusing on them, letting them share their stories, would help overcome her shyness, he figured.

Iris turned onto Blue Moon Harbor Drive, which ran along the west shore of the harbor. Some nicely designed low-rise condos and townhouses bordered the road.

"There's been some development in the fifteen years since I first came here," he noted.

"Yes, our population has expanded and needs have

evolved. But development is carefully controlled, in large part thanks to the Islands Trust."

"Islands Trust?"

She shot him a quick smile. "You are *so* not an islander, Julian Blake."

"Very true. Enlighten me."

"Each of the British Columbia Gulf Islands elects two trustees to the Islands Trust. The Trust was created in the nineteen seventies to preserve our unique ecosystems. It has jurisdiction over zoning and community planning, so basically it regulates development. And of course Destiny is very 'green' and opposed to major development."

"Right." That must frost Jelinek's butt, given that he made his living off real estate sales. "Good for the Islands Trust."

Past the condos and townhouses, the land sloped gently down to the left, the waterfront side. Narrow roads, most of them gated, wound off through large, wooded lots, offering glimpses of expensive waterfront homes. On the right side of the road, the homes and yards were regular middle-class ones. A few more minutes, and the road ran closer to the ocean. A park nestled along a beach, beside a marina. Iris pulled into the marina parking lot.

"We're going boating?" he asked.

"Yes." She turned to him, her brow furrowing. "You don't get seasick, do you?"

"Don't think so." He had a strong stomach, except when it came to Jelinek. And he really had to stop thinking of the man, or he'd ruin the day for Iris.

"How can you live on the West Coast and not know if you get seasick?"

"The only times I've been on the water, it was on the ferries. They're pretty stable." Seeing the concern and doubt in her lovely brown eyes, he said, "I've never had problems with motion sickness, so I should be okay."

"Maybe we should do something else."

He'd be happy to go to the old commune, but Iris had planned this outing. "No, this sounds great." He opened the car door and stepped out.

When he'd lived on Destiny as a kid, he'd rarely sought the ocean. He'd felt exposed somehow, standing on a beach or dock by the open water. The secluded commune, a forgotten place of rough grass, gnarled trees, and the ghosts of flower children and sixties music, had appealed to him more. But he wasn't that boy, and the slight breeze with its salty tang felt good on his face. "Fresh ocean air. That'll blow away the cobwebs." He winced internally at using such a cliché. He would never put those words in a song, but it could take hours to craft a single line of lyrics, whereas normal speech was off the cuff.

He extracted his guitar from the back seat, and reached for a turquoise and gray backpack. "This goes, too?"

"Yes, thanks." Iris grasped the handles of a purple tote bag with *Dreamspinner* on it.

Side by side, they walked to the locked gate in the metal fencing separating the parking lot from the marina. While she unlocked the gate, he gazed at the fingers of wooden docking, with several dozen boats tied to them. The craft ranged from small dinghies, power boats, and sailboats through to huge white yachts with black-tinted windows. In the bay, a dozen or more other boats were secured to buoys.

As he followed her down a skid-stripped ramp, he was glad he'd worn rubber-soled running shoes. Walking along a gently swaying dock, they exchanged "good mornings" with two older guys who were loading fishing gear into a dinghy.

The tension was easing from Julian's body. "The commercial fishers all use the dock below the village?" he asked. When he'd flown in and out of the harbor on Blue Moon Air, he'd seen two or three of those craft decked out with sturdy rigging, huge nets, and colorful buoys, but there were none at this marina.

"Yes. That's the commercial marina for fishing boats, seaplanes, whale-watching, and charters, as well as for visiting boaters who want to moor for a night or two. This marina is for island residents and off-islanders who have holiday places here. You pay by the month: pricier on the floats, cheaper at the mooring buoys."

"You have a boat?" That didn't fit the picture of Iris he'd begun to form in his mind, of an introverted book-lover.

"The family does. The ocean's in our blood."

This woman definitely intrigued him. He followed her along one of the wooden docks and recognized the Yakimuras' boat by the name. *Windspinner* was painted in gold on the ivory hull of a sailboat, thirty or more feet long, he guessed. Golden-brown wood gleamed with varnish, brass shone in the sun, and ivory canvas covered the sails. Snugged behind the boat was a dinghy, its woodwork in as perfect condition.

"That's one beautiful boat. It looks like it's vintage." Much more appealing than the three-decker white monstrosity tied up ahead of it, or the faded blue sailboat behind it. In fact, *Windspinner* had to be one of the prettiest boats in the marina.

"We say classic. And yes, she is, isn't she? My grandparents bought her."

"And named her?"

"Yes. When Dad and Aunt Iris opened the bookstore, they chose Dreamspinner to echo the boat's name." She stepped aboard with agile grace.

Julian handed the pack and his guitar case over to her, then clambered aboard, the boat rocking slightly in response. The narrow strips of wood that covered the boat's deck were unvarnished, probably so the surface wouldn't be slippery when it got wet. He raised his face to the sky, again scenting the breeze. A crisp, sunny day, a beautiful woman, and a sleek sailboat. "This was a great idea," he told Iris.

"I hope you'll enjoy it. Sit and relax while I get organized."

The cockpit had padded bench seats and he settled on one as Iris took the bag, pack, and his guitar below deck. She returned with two hooded windbreakers and handed him one. "You may need this once we get out on the water. It's my dad's. He's shorter than you and not so broad through the shoulders, so I hope it fits."

As she uncovered the mainsail, her movements had a graceful efficiency that was the opposite of bustle. She took two harnessy contraptions from a storage compartment and handed him one. "This is a PFD, a personal flotation device. Here's how you put it on." She demonstrated, reminding him of a flight attendant.

He mimicked her, draping the padded band around his neck like a scarf, the ends hanging loose in front until he secured the waist belt. When she told him how the device inflated, he said, mostly kidding but not entirely, "Tell me you're not planning to dunk me."

She gave a soft laugh. "I have no intention of doing that. But the wind and waves are unpredictable, and it's best to be safe."

With the same easy dexterity, she started the engine and then hopped back to the dock, where she untied the boat and, holding on to the rigging along its side, walked it forward and pointed the front away from the dock. Before he could worry about being alone on an unsecured boat, she'd jumped back on board. She steered the *Windspinner* away from the dock and, with the engine putt-putting, they motored out of the marina and into the waters of Blue Moon Harbor.

"Would you take the wheel for a minute?" Iris asked.

"Keep the bow—the front—pointing toward the neck of the harbor while I let out the line on the dinghy."

He rested his hands on the wheel and felt the power and responsiveness of the sailboat as it sliced through the water. Intriguing, but disconcerting. He didn't have his sea legs yet.

As she took back the wheel, a tiny blue-and-white seaplane skimmed out from the commercial marina. Julian recognized the logo. "Blue Moon Air," he said. "The Cessna." Aaron Gabriel's local business had two planes: that four-seater and a larger de Havilland Beaver. Julian knew this from chatting with Aaron when he'd flown to and from the island.

"Did you hear that Aaron's expanding the business?" Iris asked as the Cessna freed itself from the ocean's surface and rose in the air. "Thanks to his and Miranda's inheritance."

"Oh yeah? Good for him. I'd heard about the inheritance, but not about Aaron's plans." Miranda and her brother had inherited a chunk of change when their estranged grandparents—their only relatives—died this past summer.

"He's buying another plane." Iris had turned her attention back to the ocean, which was a good thing as the harbor was busy on this beautiful autumn morning. A couple of largish boats motored toward the commercial marina, a few small power boats zipped around, and a quartet of kayakers paddled closer to shore. "He can hire a third pilot and expand his business."

"That's great. I don't know him well, but he seems like a good guy."

"He is. He and Miranda had a tough childhood. It's so nice that they've made happy lives for themselves."

"Yeah." For the most part, Julian was content with his life—as long as he didn't let himself think about Jelinek.

There were happy times when he was caught up in the world of creation, or he was performing with the band and saw his songs resonate with the audience. But his own guilt put the concept of a "happy life" out of reach.

"The three of you were the ones who stood out," Iris said. "Rebels, I thought at the time. Going your own way, never seeming to care what anyone thought of you. A part of me envied that, though the very idea made me cringe, too." She shot him a narrow-eyed glance. "I know your song, 'Mocking.' About feeling like an outcast and putting on a magic cloak to protect yourself. You and Aaron, acting like bad boys. Miranda, the defiant Goth. All of you were unhappy about being forced to live on Destiny. The island-kids knew each other and you didn't fit. So you had your magic cloaks."

He hadn't realized that about Aaron and Miranda. Hadn't looked beyond his own pain to consider anyone else's. "I suppose we did." Iris had guessed part of his own story but, thank God, she'd never suspect the rest. "But you haven't got it quite right. I wasn't trying to be a 'bad boy.' My magic cloak came from losing myself in my music."

"Ah. Yes, I see that." After a moment, she went on. "No one would have imagined, back then, that Aaron would own his own business, right here in Blue Moon Harbor. That Miranda, a high school dropout, would be getting her certificate in early childhood education, marrying Luke, and planning a life here on Destiny. And that you, another dropout, would become one of Canada's best musicians."

Her characterization was flattering, but hardly accurate. "I wouldn't go that far."

"Two JUNOs," she said firmly. "Plus making the short list for the Polaris Music Prize."

He tried for a diffident shrug, but had to admit to himself that the JUNOs meant a lot to him, as did having the Polaris jurors choose the Julian Blake Band's *Moving* album as one of the ten most artistically meritorious of last year.

Iris flashed a smile. "Ready to fly?"

"Lift the sail, you mean?" He was a bit nervous, but it was the good, excited kind of nervous, like before he performed. "Let's do it."

She let him help, and it was his strong hands that pulled on the rope she called a halyard. The mainsail rose foot by foot. She showed him how to use a winch to raise it all the way to the top of the mast, and then how to cleat the halyard securely. The big ivory sail caught the wind and belled out tautly. She turned off the engine and he marveled at the unfamiliar, exhilarating sensations. The hull sliced through the wrinkled, greenish-indigo ocean with a whooshing sound.

"Sit on the high side," Iris said, "the one opposite the sail. You'll have a better view."

He obeyed and she came to sit beside him, resting a hand on the steering wheel. "Well?" she said, and he knew that this time the flush on her cheeks wasn't from shyness or embarrassment, but from pleasure and the nip of the salty breeze.

"This is great!"

"No motion sickness?"

"It's all good."

"Then"—her dark eyes sparkled and a strand of hair, escaping her ponytail, flicked a black ribbon across her face—"hang on, I'll raise the jib."

Jib?

She gave him the wheel and he watched and learned as she raised a triangular sail to the front of the mast. It had two ropes—lines, she said—attached to it, which she adjusted so the jib sail was on the same side of the boat as the mainsail. And yes, the boat was going faster.

He gripped the edge of his seat. "You promised you wouldn't try to dunk me."

Iris laughed, eyes flashing and teeth gleaming, her usual reserve blown away on the wind. "This is nothing. I'm taking it easy on you, since it's your first time."

That sounded like a challenge, and he found himself laughing, too. Her every move was sure, confident, and he was positive she wasn't a risk-taker. "Do as you will," he told her. "I trust you."

Chapter Five

Julian trusted her. What a compliment. Iris couldn't believe how comfortable she felt with this man. Despite how different they were, they clicked.

He was grinning, his blue eyes sparkling like the glints of sunshine off the ocean's surface. Whatever stresses weighed on him, the wind had blown them from his mind.

Smiling back, she mused that maybe she shouldn't be so surprised by their connection. She'd felt a similar click when she'd met Eden, and again when she met Miranda, two people who were also quite different from her. Eden had been a confident, successful Ottawa lawyer, and Miranda a woman who'd gone from Goth-girl rebel to a carefree single life in Vancouver and then to being a devoted single mom. Yet qualities of their personalities had resonated with Iris, and vice versa. The same as seemed to be happening with Julian.

But Eden and Miranda were women. Iris was more comfortable with women. Add to that, Julian was a celebrity, and so darned hot. Not her kind of man, of course. What she hoped for was someone like Luke: an easygoing guy whose life centered on his family, and who loved living

on Destiny. Not that she'd ever felt the slightest spark of
attraction to Luke, nor, she was sure, vice versa.

She darted a sideways glance at Julian, clad in jeans and
a black turtleneck sweater, his face lifted to the sunshine,
his eyes closed, his longish blond hair tousled by the breeze.
Oh yes, she felt a spark. The kind that with the slightest encouraging breath might easily start a blaze.

What a ridiculous thought. Julian had his pick of women,
ones far more glamorous and exciting than she was. What
he wanted from her was friendship, someone who was easy
to be with, no pressure and no prying. Besides, even if the
attraction were mutual, what could possibly come of it? His
life was on the road, in the public eye, whereas she could
never imagine living away from the safe cocoon of her tiny
island. She yearned for a loving relationship that led to a
lifetime commitment and raising children together, whereas
Julian's "love life," as documented by social media, consisted of hookups with numerous attractive women.

Why was she thinking about this now? Better to practice
mindfulness and concentrate on this moment, in all its
richness.

She eyed the sleek line of *Windspinner*'s hull as it drove
cleanly through the ruffled edges of small waves. The sight
always gave her pleasure, as did the unfurled sails, butterfly
wings taking full advantage of the breeze. Spotting a patch
of dark water indicating a windier area, she asked Julian,
"Would you like to fly faster?"

His eyes opened, their blue dazzling in the sunshine.
"Go for it!"

"Hang on," she warned, "and trust the boat. She won't
tip over." Iris sent the responsive craft into the wind and
their side of the hull lifted high out of the water.

"This is great!" His voice sounded exultant. Free of care.

He had been in pain, from worry over Forbes or from
some other problem, and she'd helped him escape. She

knew how to be a good friend, even if she'd only ever had a few friends.

When they needed to tack, she instructed Julian on how they would "come about," and he followed her directions, ducking under the boom as he moved to the other side of the boat.

After trimming both sails, she settled back beside him again.

"Are we sailing wherever the wind takes us?" he asked.

They were traveling at a more relaxed pace, not so close into the wind, the hull not heeling over as much. "I have a destination in mind. But because of the way a sailboat works, we have to get there by tacking and jibing back and forth." His puzzled expression made her clarify. "We can't sail straight into the wind, so we zigzag, sailing as close to the wind as we can, first one way, then the other."

"What's our destination?"

"I packed a lunch and thought we'd anchor and have a picnic."

"Sounds great, but you should've told me. I'd have brought something."

"Julian, you have enough to worry about. I have very few responsibilities or concerns other than the store. Putting together a picnic lunch is a simple thing."

"You're a generous woman." He leaned sideways, his weight on one elbow, studying her.

His scrutiny made her self-conscious. "What is it?"

"You're a competent one, too."

"Competent?" Of course she tried to be competent, more than competent in fact, at everything she undertook.

"Sorry, that's a pathetic word. Let's say skilled. Accomplished. In Dreamspinner, I watched you handle that obnoxious teenager and her mom. In fluent French. You selected books for me that I'd never have looked at twice, but they're making me reflect."

"I'm glad of that."

"Now, today, I watch you sailing this boat like you're one with it. You don't need my assistance, do you? You'd do as well, probably better, on your own."

Her lips curved slightly. "I thought you'd like to be involved."

"You're right. Do you often sail *Windspinner* on your own?"

"When the weather's nice. On my free days and summer evenings, I go to the commune if I want to relax with a book, or I sail if I want something more active and energizing."

"You do both things alone."

"Yes." Did he guess that, while sometimes she required alone time, at other times she was lonely?

Neither of them pursued the topic and for the next half hour they were quiet. Having grown up an only child in a family of reflective, self-contained members, Iris didn't feel the need to continually make conversation. She guessed that Julian, who spun ideas into music, also often chose silence over chatter.

When they approached their destination, a scenic little bay cradled between two rocky points, she started the engine and dropped the jib, then let Julian help lower the mainsail. When they'd secured both sails, she pointed the boat into the wind, put it in neutral, and went to the bow. She'd anchored here often, knew the depth, and used the winch to lower the anchor and play out the right amount of chain and line. Then, back in the cockpit, she reversed, setting the anchor, and turned off the engine.

Now the only sound was the cry of a few gulls as she pulled the dinghy closer to the boat and secured the line. Sitting down across from Julian, she said, "What do you think?"

He'd been gazing around, but now focused on her. "It's

a pretty spot. I don't think I've ever been here before. This is, uh, the northwest end of Destiny?"

"Yes. Do you know Sunset Cove? There are a few dozen houses, several shops, a pub?"

"Heard of it, but never been there."

"We're just south of it. This is a Destiny secret, a beach you can't find on the tourist maps. I'm sure Luke knows it, and brings the boys here."

"Isn't it private property? There are houses."

A few homes nestled back among trees along the curve of beach, and out on the points that sheltered the bay. One belonged to Kellan Hawke, the reclusive thriller writer, but that was a secret she wouldn't share. "Foreshore can't be privately owned. We could go ashore and walk along the beach, and it would be perfectly legal." The beach came in two parts: a pebbly, log- and driftwood-strewn arc that framed the bay, and inside it grayish-brown sandy flats that were hidden at high tide. The tide was near its ebb now, and the sandy beach filled much of the bay. "There's also an unmarked road and a public access path to the shore, for the islanders who know where to look."

"Are we going to row ashore?"

"If you want. Let's have lunch, and decide afterward." She rose and took off her PFD. "You can take yours off, if you promise not to fall overboard."

As he stood and unfastened the device, she said, "Would you like to see below deck? We have, er, all the facilities, in case you need them."

"Good to know. Yeah, I'd like the grand tour." His teasing wink suggested he didn't think the small cabin could hold much.

Smugly, she led the way below, backing down the three-step wooden ladder and telling him to do the same. When they both stood inside, she realized that the cabin was indeed awfully small. Julian, while larger than her slight

dad, wasn't a huge man, but he had such a physical presence,
with his rangy shoulders, narrow hips, and long legs, and
the contrast of his tanned skin, blond hair, and vivid blue
eyes. Awareness tingled across her skin, even stronger than
before, perhaps because of the intimacy of the cabin or because sailing had stimulated her senses. She took a deep,
centering breath.

"This is cool," he said, his attention on the details of the
cabin rather than on her.

"It is, isn't it? This is the galley, with a small fridge and
a propane stovetop. The door behind you leads to the
head. There's a marine toilet and a sink. No shower, sadly.
We have to use a handheld shower on the deck." Mostly,
she went for day sails, but occasionally she'd travel farther
into the Gulf Islands, anchor, and spend a night or two
on the boat. Sometimes one or more of her family came
with her—she had wonderful memories of trips with her
grandparents—but this was the first time she'd taken a
friend out.

Julian examined everything, including the little dinette
that folded down into a short bed, and the front cabin filled
with a V-berth double bed. "It's all so compact and functional. And beautifully maintained. The wood gleams like
it's received lots of loving. Same above deck."

"Dad does most of the maintenance. He says it's like a
meditation practice, bringing him serenity as well as a sense
of accomplishment. Mom's the same with her garden." Iris's
equivalent was tai chi. "Why don't you go on deck, and I'll
hand things up to you?"

He complied, and a few minutes later they were sitting
in the pale sunlight, drinking sparkling fruit beverages and
eating the picnic lunch she'd prepared. Not knowing his
taste, she had included sushi, sliced ham and smoked
chicken, three cheeses, raw veggies, and a baguette from
the bakery as well as her favorite sesame rice crackers. He

ate everything with apparent relish as she nibbled on tastes of this and that.

His body language now, and when they'd been sailing, indicated that this day was achieving its purpose: to help him unwind. Iris was glad she'd heeded the messages on her calendar, sowing the seeds of friendship and sharing happiness.

After a few minutes, he came up for air. "Sorry, I'm wolfing this down. I was hungry."

"Ocean air whets the appetite."

"It shouldn't make me rude, though." He pulled his sweater over his head and the navy T-shirt beneath it made a determined effort to follow, revealing a tantalizing strip of flat abdomen above the waistband of his jeans. Talk about whetting her appetite.

He pulled down the tee, leaned back on his elbows, and studied her. "You said your grandparents bought the boat, and that the ocean's in your family's blood. Tell me more."

She shrugged. "There are more interesting things to talk about than Yakimura family history. Your musical career, for one. It must be exciting, all the travel and performances." Excitement wasn't something she sought; however, since this was his life, he must enjoy it.

"Exciting, exhausting, it's a lot of things. Which I don't want to think about now. I want to hear about the Yakimuras and the ocean."

"Well, then . . ." If hearing a story would help him de-stress, then she would tell him a true one. "It started with my great-great-great-whatever grandfather, who came to Destiny in the very early days. Coast Salish people lived here, of course, but suddenly people from all corners of the world were discovering the Gulf Islands. My ancestor was a younger son. He sought adventure, and to prove himself, in the New World."

Julian nodded, and she went on. "He and a friend came

to Victoria and were hired by a Destiny Islander as laborers
to clear land and to farm. In Japan, the young men had
been fishermen, and, hello"—she gestured past the boat's
railing—"ocean on all sides. Abundant fish and shellfish.
The ambitious, energetic young men saved money, bought
a boat together, did well as fishers, and sent money home.
Their families found wives for them, and the women immi-
grated here. They raised families, bought a larger boat, and
built a successful business."

"Good for them."

Warm in the sunshine, she pulled her Irish cable-knit
sweater over her head, making sure that her long-sleeved
blue shirt didn't go with it. "They also grew produce and
sold some of it. A few more Japanese came to the island,
so they had a bit of a community, but they also did their best
to be good neighbors and good Canadians. They became
naturalized citizens."

She picked up a celery stick but didn't bite into it.
"There was prejudice in British Columbia. Before the turn
of the twentieth century, Japanese Canadians were denied
the vote. But here on Destiny, they were accepted as hardworking members of the diverse island community. Then
came the First World War." She bit into the celery, the sharp
crunch an outlet for emotion. Tomorrow was Remembrance
Day, so her ancestors' experiences had been weighing on
her mind.

Julian had been grazing on the snacks as she talked, and
now he said, "Yes?"

She suspected that, like many Canadians, he knew little
of this part of his country's history. "Local recruitment
offices wouldn't accept Japanese Canadians, so my great-
grandfather's older brother and another man from Destiny
traveled to Alberta and were allowed to enlist. Sadly, the
other man died in the war, but my relative returned home,

injured but alive." Although humility was ingrained in her, pride made her add, "He received a medal for bravery."

She paused to take a long drink and to collect her emotions, because the next part of the story was even harder to talk about. "Now we get to the Second World War. Pearl Harbor was attacked." She gazed across at Julian, who had paused with a cheese-laden slice of bread halfway to his mouth, a curious expression on his face. Clearly, he hadn't figured out where this was going. "Have you heard of the internment of Japanese Canadians during World War Two?"

Abruptly, he put the bread down again. "Yeah, in general terms. I hadn't thought that—"

"That anyone you knew would have been affected?"

He gave an apologetic frown. "I guess. Sorry, that sounds awful." Leaning forward, he said, "Tell me, Iris."

"The War Measures Act was used to justify the removal of all Japanese Canadians from anywhere around the Pacific coast, on the ridiculous grounds that they posed a threat to national security. Even men who had fought for Canada in the First World War. People who had been honorable, loyal citizens were sent to internment camps in the interior of the province and in the Prairies."

"My God."

She swallowed against a lump in her throat. "Not only that, but their property was seized. The land, businesses, and homes they had worked so hard for. Businesses that made a contribution to their communities—" She broke off, shaking her head, struggling for composure. Injustice drove her crazy, and this particular injustice felt personal.

Julian reached across the cockpit of the boat and took her hands in his strong, warm ones. "That's terrible."

"Can you imagine the humiliation for my great-grandfather's brother, a man who'd been injured in service to his country, and received a medal? He and his family and all the other Japanese Canadians were stripped of their possessions, herded together like criminals, and, basically, sent to prison camps."

"Humiliation," Julian echoed in a low voice. "When they did nothing to deserve that treatment." He swallowed audibly. "No, I can't even imagine what that must have been like."

"I can, because my grandfather told me. He was twelve in 1942, when it happened. He grew from a boy to a man in the Tashme internment camp." She realized that, as she'd been talking, she'd gripped Julian's hands fiercely, perhaps to get her point across or to ground herself. That disconcerted her because, like her family, she was restrained about touching others. Julian had squeezed her hands in return, hard enough to be painful. Iris gently extracted her hands and sat back.

Julian glanced down at his hands almost as if he didn't recognize them, and then spread and stretched his long, graceful fingers. He gazed into her eyes. "I'm so sorry your family went through that. What happened after the war?"

"The government did their best to deport Japanese Canadians, or at least resettle them east of the Rocky Mountains. My family went to the Prairies, but they missed the ocean. Missed their home. They returned to Destiny. They were one of only two families who did so."

"They had to start all over? With no boats, no property?"

"Not exactly." Her lips curved. "Destiny Islanders have always had their own way of doing things, and they didn't like conforming to rules they didn't believe in."

"Forbes says that's why he fits in so well here. So what happened with your grandfather's family and the other family?"

"The Yakimuras had always been such good citizens and generous neighbors, so one of their own neighbors did them a huge, and completely illegal, favor. It only worked because the land title records here were quite disorganized, due to that same antiestablishment thing. Anyhow, when the government seized property, they got my family's fishing boats, but not the land because the neighbors swore it was theirs, that they had rented it to my ancestors."

Julian whistled. "That was a risk."

"Yes, and not one that other islanders were prepared to take. The Yakimura land and house were the only Japanese-Canadian property that was preserved for the proper owners. So my family took in the other family that returned to the island, and they all became farmers. They did well enough that the other family could buy their own plot of land. And my family had enough to finance opening Dreamspinner in the mid nineteen-eighties."

"That's impressive."

Her family's saga finished, Iris spread soft brie on a rice cracker and added a couple of slices of green pepper. "My family has always been industrious. Now, enough of my stories. Tell me one of yours. Anything you choose. Or if you prefer to relax in peace and quiet, I'm happy with that, too." Just being with Julian made her happy.

Nibbling her snack, savoring how the creamy richness of the mild cheese combined with the slightly salty, sesame tang of the cracker and the crisp sweetness of the pepper, she wondered whether Julian would choose silence or conversation.

Julian watched Iris's calm, lovely face as she gazed out at the ocean and ate a cheese-topped cracker. A woman who was content with silence. How often did that happen? Not only that, but when she spoke, she had worthwhile things to say. She didn't babble on about superficial stuff. She wasn't like the groupies, excited by his celebrity rather than interested in him as a person.

That story about her ancestors was amazing. He knew

very well what humiliation felt like. The counselor who'd led the support group he'd attended for several months in his late teens had said that victims of abuse shouldn't feel humiliation, guilt, or shame, because none of the blame lay on them. For Iris's ancestors, that was completely true. For Julian, not so much.

No, he wasn't going there again. Not now.

"Thank you for sharing that story, Iris." She had given him so much. The sailing trip, the picnic lunch, and a tale that gave her both pain and pleasure. What could he offer in return? Knowing she was interested in his career, he asked, "Want to hear about my bandmates?"

Her head lifted, her brown eyes bright with interest. "Very much. I know there are three of them: Roy, Camille, and Andi."

A few wisps of long hair, escapees from her ponytail, fluttered around her smooth-skinned oval face. An impulse made him reach toward her.

She frowned slightly. "Do I have something on my face?"

"No. Hold still a moment." He reached behind her neck and slipped the fabric tie from her hair, freeing a glossy black waterfall. "Okay?"

"It gets in the way when I sail," she said mildly.

"You can tie it back when we get underway." Again he asked, "Okay?"

A slight smile curved her untinted lips. "If that's what you want."

I want to kiss you. To weave his fingers through those silky tresses, cup the back of her head, tilt her face toward his, and press his lips to her delicate ones. To forget about the darkness in his soul and concentrate on the pure light that was Iris. To lose himself in her. To bring heat to her cheeks and arousal to her slender body. To break through her shyness and aura of self-containment and awaken the passion that he guessed—hoped—lurked inside. His body stirred and he suppressed a moan of need.

If he told her all that, would she say, "If that's what you want," and offer herself to him?

Iris liked to please people. But she was a good woman from a good family, and she deserved so much more than a deeply flawed guy like him.

The soft breeze fluttered her hair, sunshine casting a gleam over its inky depths. Beauty and mystery, like the woman herself. Should he try writing a song about that?

Beauty and mystery, shyness and competence, the pursuit of harmony . . . The way her soft brown eyes and subtle changes of expression enchant me. His fingers itched to feel guitar strings.

Her long lashes drifted down and she devoted an inordinate amount of attention to choosing a piece of salmon sushi. "You were going to tell me about your bandmates?"

He took a deep breath. "Right." He reached for a piece of sushi, ate it, and then went on. "Camille, the percussionist, and her husband, Roy, who plays guitar and harmonica, have been with me for ages. I owe Camille a lot. She's Francophone, from Quebec, and it's thanks to her that I brushed up the French I semi-learned as a boy. She helped me create French versions of some of my songs, and write a few solely in French. That earned me a wider audience in Canada, France, and other French-speaking countries."

Iris nodded, silently encouraging him to go on.

"Our other original band member, a guitarist, moved to Australia and we filled his spot with Andi."

"She plays the violin, doesn't she? Or is it a fiddle?"

"A range of stringed instruments. She's great with Celtic music, and her expertise inspired me to add some Celtic-influenced bits to my songs."

"Camille and Roy are older than you, aren't they? And Andi is younger?"

"Yeah, Andi's only twenty-two. Crazy about music and madly talented. She loves being on the road, and picks up odds and ends of work—session work in studios, waitressing, whatever—when we're in Vancouver. She's just being young and having fun."

"What's session work?"

"Filling in with a group that's recording a song or an ad. It's a nice supplementary income for a good musician." When she nodded her understanding, he went on. "Camille and Roy have always been into music. They do session work, too. He also teaches advanced guitar and she, believe it or not, is an accountant."

Iris bit her lip, and he guessed what she was thinking.

"You're wondering whether we make a living from our music, right?"

"It would be rude to ask. I assumed you did, since you're so successful."

"Not that successful, and it's hard to make a living as a musician. I do now, because I'm a songwriter. I get paid when groups cover my songs, or one's used in a TV show or movie or for a ringtone. Or when people buy sheet music. The others do okay, but need additional income."

She nodded. "You're based in Vancouver but do a lot of touring, don't you?"

He grabbed a couple of celery sticks. "Yeah. As well as some local gigs now and then, we usually do a tour in eastern Canada each year, and another in western Canada." He munched, swallowed. "We've toured in the States, Europe, and Australia. Australia in winter, when the weather's bad for touring here. But touring's expensive, so we don't net a whole lot of profit. We're not like the stars who fill the big stadiums. For us, part of the point of touring is to hook and keep fans who buy or live-stream our songs."

"It must be strange, being on the road so much. Are you all friends, as well as being bandmates? Do you hang out together?"

"We're friends and respect each other, but we don't hang out that much. I like exploring, or I work on music. Camille and Roy often hole up in their room. He likes books and video games, and she usually has work to do, accessing her clients' businesses through WiFi."

"And Andi?"

"She often hangs out with local fans." Young, attractive, and bisexual, Andi liked to party and hook up. At first Julian had been concerned, but she'd never once shown up for a performance anything less than professional.

"You're not . . ." Iris was contemplating the two remaining pieces of sushi, a wing of hair partially obscuring her face. "You and Andi . . . ?"

"Do we hook up? No, never. That'd be dumb, for me to mess with a band member. But we're not attracted to each other anyhow."

"Why would it be dumb? You mean if it didn't work out?"

"Whether it did or didn't, it could create weird dynamics onstage and off. But for Andi and me, working out—like, long term—wouldn't be on the table. Neither of us is into serious."

Still not looking at him, she nodded. "Why would you be, when you're young and successful and your career's taking off?"

"Exactly." Too bad those weren't his only reasons. He crunched the last celery stick.

"But," she said so quietly he could barely hear, "what about later? You said you're not a romantic, but don't you envision one day being married? Having children?"

"No."

After a moment, she said, "Oh."

Any other woman would have pushed to know why. The fact that Iris didn't, made him want to give her something more. Some small part of the truth. "I'm not that kind of guy."

"Oh," she said again.

"Not the kind who's built for that level of . . . connection, intimacy, trust. Not everyone is, Iris."

Now her head lifted. "That's true. But your music makes me think you are."

"Don't confuse the creator with the creation."

She blinked, was quiet, and then said, "On this island, I know many artists. Including your father. It seems to me, every good one pours his or her soul into their artistic creations."

"I tell other people's stories."

"Through the filter of your own interpretation and emotions. And in doing so you connect intimately with many people who listen to that music. Do you not agree?"

He realized he was rubbing his left hand over the tattoo on his right arm. Her words made him remember the moment when he decided not to kill himself. He'd been fifteen, living on the street, collecting change playing the guitar on Vancouver sidewalks while he tried to figure out an accessible, reliable way of committing suicide. While he was singing "Ache in My Soul," an elderly woman stopped to listen and when he finished, she gave him a twenty-dollar bill.

Big money, but the true gift came from the tears in her eyes, and her words. "Thank you," she'd said. "My husband of forty years died last month, and I didn't know how I'd be able to go on. But you made me realize I'm not alone. That others go through bad times, too. Your music and your voice also remind me there is still beauty in the world."

As soon as he'd been able to afford it, Julian got the tattoo: a few bars of music from that song. A reminder that he wasn't alone either, and no matter how broken he was, he had value.

"Julian?" Iris said softly. "I'm sorry if I offended you."

"You didn't offend me." His voice came out even huskier than usual. "Just made me think about something that happened long ago."

"When you wrote that song?" A graceful hand gestured toward his arm.

He shook his head, in wonder rather than denial. "You're good, woman."

She dipped her head in acknowledgment. "It comes along with the shyness."

"Your shyness has positive and negative aspects. If you had the option, somehow, of not being shy anymore, would you do it?" His own albatross was one he would shed in an instant if such a thing were possible.

"I wouldn't be me without it, so no," she said calmly. "It's also part of my heritage. My father and aunt are the same, and their father and grandfather were as well. I see no greater intrinsic value to the social whirl Mom enjoys, compared to the things I like doing: reading, sailing, sharing a meal with a close friend. Still, I do sometimes wish I were more outgoing."

She rose and went below deck, which he took to mean that she wanted him to drop the subject. He, too, was alert to people's nonverbal cues, though in his case it came not from shyness but from abuse.

When she returned with a bowl of red seedless grapes, he broke off a cluster and popped grapes into his mouth one by one as she opened a small plastic storage container. "I hope you like chocolate," she said, revealing the contents.

"Nanaimo bars." He recognized the treat: a chewy bottom layer with chocolate, nuts, and who knew what else;

a creamy middle layer; then a topping of melted dark chocolate. "Sonia makes these. I love them."

He took one, bit off a corner, munched, and let out a moan of pleasure. "Man, that's even better than Sonia's."

Iris gave a cat-smile. "It's a Destiny bar. Mom's invention. Pecans rather than walnuts, and Irish Cream flavoring in the filling."

"My compliments to your mother."

Iris, slicing the other bar in half, didn't respond. Julian wondered if she'd told her family she was seeing him and, if so, what they thought. But again, her body language suggested that she'd rather he not ask. When she handed him half of the second bar, he didn't protest, just consumed the treat happily as she nibbled the rest.

"You brought your guitar," she said. "Do you feel like playing it? Or, if you prefer, we could row ashore and go for a walk."

"Actually, I could use your feedback. I did some more work on the lark song."

"I'm flattered."

As she tidied up the lunch scraps, he fetched his guitar and tuned it. Then, sitting in the sunshine with only Iris, a bunch of seagulls, and a man and black dog on the beach as an audience, he played Forbes's song.

Watching Iris's face, intent and responsive, Julian thought that being stuck on Destiny Island just might be tolerable—as long as he could spend more time with this special woman.

Chapter Six

Late that afternoon, Iris was slicing vegetables for beef sukiyaki, her aunt's favorite dinner, a thank-you for covering Iris's normal Saturday shift at the store. From the living room came the strains of the Beatles song, "P.S. I Love You." It was from a 1963 LP album playing on Grandmother Rose's carefully maintained turntable. Rose had loved music and her records dated from the 1940s through until vinyl became more or less defunct. Playing her grandmother's music made Iris feel close to her.

Rose had heard some of Julian's songs. She'd enjoyed them and said he had an old soul. She'd be excited to know that her granddaughter was becoming friends with him.

Iris's phone rang. Seeing the caller display, she lifted it from the charger on the counter. "Hi, Miranda."

"You and Julian Blake? And you didn't tell me?"

"What? What are you talking about?" Had Julian mentioned their outing to his family? Iris hadn't told a soul. She was a private person, and she didn't want anyone blowing it out of proportion. As Miranda seemed to be doing.

"Glory McKenna was driving home from work at Arbutus Lodge and she saw the two of you in the parking lot at the marina."

"Glory knows Julian?"

"We all went to school together, remember? Plus she's a big fan. So, what's up, Iris?" Her tone was affectionate and teasing. "I thought you were this sweet, shy girl who couldn't imagine hanging out with a rock star like Julian."

"He doesn't play rock music."

"Picture me rolling my eyes. I know it's not rock. It's a figure of speech. Don't avoid the question."

She sank onto one of the bar stools at the kitchen island. "Yes, I was that girl. But then I met him and he's amazingly easy to be with."

"Wow. What happened to my girlfriend who can't even look a man in the eyes?"

"It's not what you think. I'm only seeing him as a friend." She brushed her fingertips across her right cheek, as she'd already done a dozen times. Before Julian had climbed out of her car in the community center parking lot, he'd planted a soft kiss on her cheek. She knew he'd meant it as an innocent, friendly gesture, and that he never could have guessed how his touch tingled through her.

"How come? You're attracted to him. Don't deny it, I was right beside you at his last performance. You think he's hot."

"Of course he's hot. Way too hot for someone like me." He was also sensitive and seemed like a fine man.

"Stop with the crazy talk. You're gorgeous and smart and really nice. What more could any guy want?"

"You're a generous friend. And yes, I have some good qualities. One day the right man will come along and view those qualities as special." As had happened for Miranda, with Julian's stepbrother Luke. Iris was thrilled for them, finding a second chance at love. If a part of her was envy green, she would keep that part tucked deep inside her ungenerous heart. "But Julian isn't—"

"You're friends with Kellan Hawke, and he's a celebrity, too."

"A successful novelist isn't in the same category of celebrity as a *rock star*. And Kellan and I aren't exactly friends. We're in a book club together and the store sells his books, that's all." She wasn't sure Kellan had any actual friends, but she refused to gossip about the island's mystery man.

"It sounds like you and Julian get along pretty well, so why not go for something more than friendship?"

Because he was so . . . *much*, and she was so *not*. "We're not a good match."

After a long moment, Miranda said, "Sorry, I guess I wasn't really thinking. I mean, not that you aren't amazingly special, and any man would be lucky to have you, but you and Julian really are very different people."

Iris knew that, so why did Miranda's confirmation depress her?

Her friend went on. "You never want to leave Destiny, and Julian avoids the place like the plague. Luke doesn't understand why he hates it, but he says it's obvious that having to be here makes Julian twitchy. And besides the geography thing, you're looking for a happily ever after, and I doubt that Julian's ever had, or wants to have, a committed relationship."

"Yes, all of that. But we do have an odd connection. I'm almost . . . comfortable with Julian." She gave an awkward laugh. "Maybe we knew each other in past lives?"

"Sure, that must be it. Hey, does he play and sing for you?"

"He plays songs he's working on, and I listen and give feedback, for whatever it's worth."

"Oh man, that's cool. Sexy. Isn't it?"

"It is pretty cool."

"And sexy. Right?"

Trust Miranda to persist. "I . . . I don't want to think that way about him. Not when we'll only ever be friends."

"Don't *want* to means that you *do* think he's sexy.

You're sure you don't want to put aside the big romantic dream for a while and have a mad, passionate fling with Julian?"

"Tempting, but no." Amazingly tempting. At the age of almost twenty-five, she was a virgin. She'd only ever dated one guy, back in her final year at university, and that relationship sure hadn't been a blazing success.

"It'd be something to tell your grandkids about." The cheeky tone was so Miranda.

Iris had to laugh. "Oh yes, I'm sure that's exactly what grandchildren want to hear, that their wrinkly old grandma lost her virginity in a hookup with a *rock star*."

"They'd see wrinkly old granny in a whole new light."

Iris rolled her eyes. She liked this Miranda, with her bubbly high spirits. When they'd first met more than a year ago, Miranda had been, as she'd ungrudgingly labeled herself, a pathetic mess. A single mom, down on her luck, she'd been depressed yet determined to build a better life for herself and her little girl. Which she'd done in a big way, with a new career direction and her engagement to Luke.

Miranda said, "Wait. What? What did you say? You're a virgin?"

Iris wasn't ashamed of that fact. "Yes. I've told you my pathetic dating history. Just when in there did you think I'd had an opportunity to lose my virginity?"

"I didn't," Miranda said, sounding stunned. "Think, that is. Just assumed that, well, any woman your age would have, you know."

"Well, I haven't. And, by the way, unlike you I have no problem saying *had sex*."

"Okay," Miranda said, "I'll shut up now. About virginity and Julian. You'll do what's right for you, I know it."

That's exactly what Iris was doing: fostering a friendship with a special man. "Thanks for the vote of confidence. Listen, it would be nice if you and Glory didn't spread it around that Julian and I are friends. You know I'm a private person, and we should respect his privacy, too."

"Iris, it's Destiny. There's no such thing as privacy."

After making plans to have coffee, they hung up and Iris got back to slicing and chopping. She had everything ready when the door opened and her aunt walked in.

Lily was as perfectly groomed as always, in slim-fitting tan pants, a burgundy top, and one of her lovely scarves, with her long hair pulled back into a neat coil. At fifty-four, her skin was smooth and almost unlined.

After greeting each other in Japanese, Iris continued in that language. "I have rice cooking, ingredients for beef sukiyaki all ready to go, and a bottle of Destiny Cellars cabernet sauvignon. Would you like a glass of wine, or perhaps a bath before dinner?"

"A glass of wine would be nice. Then give me fifteen minutes to change and unwind."

"Of course." Iris poured wine for her and handed her the glass. "Take as long as you need." Her aunt would put on yoga pants and sit cross-legged on a mat by her bedroom window, gazing out and either meditating or simply enjoying the view, the wine, and the solitude.

Aunt Lily had lived with her parents until she was thirty, and then with infinite politeness told them she needed her own space. She'd bought a one-bedroom apartment. When Iris had completed her B.A. at the University of Victoria, her parents assumed she would move back home, but she wanted to maintain a degree of independence from parental oversight. Yet she'd feared that, if she lived alone, she'd be too lonely. It was the paradox of being a shy introvert. She needed solitude to recharge her energy, yet if her shyness led her to avoid people, she became lonely.

Perhaps feeling the same way, Aunt Lily had offered a third option, saying she'd be glad of Iris's companionship. When Iris happily agreed, her aunt had upgraded to a two-bedroom condo, with Iris's rent covering the increased mortgage payments and other expenses. The arrangement had worked out beautifully. They created their private spaces and times as well as their shared ones.

Now Iris poured a glass of wine for herself, and took it into the living room. She turned off the sixties music and put on an album of shakuhachi music, simple and haunting melodies played on the traditional Japanese bamboo flute.

She sat in a chair by the window, near the table that was set for dinner. Most of the furniture was her aunt's, and they had arranged it in a way that satisfied their needs and their aesthetic taste. They both preferred space to clutter, and liked clean, simple lines. They chose neutral colors overall, with a few colorful accents in artwork, vases, and pillows. Relaxing, Iris appreciated the serenity offered by the room, the view, and the pure music of the shakuhachi. This was a far cry from Julian's world of clubs, amplified music, and enthusiastic audiences.

When her aunt emerged from her bedroom, Iris ignited the burner in the center of the dining table, and put the pot of sauce—a combination of dashi, soy sauce, mirin, sake, and sugar—on to heat. She dished hot rice into two bowls and gave them to her aunt to take to the table, then carried the platter of sliced beef and cubed tofu, and the platter of vegetables, to the table. Iris returned for the wine, topped up their glasses, and sat down across from her aunt.

Using chopsticks, Aunt Lily transferred some of the ingredients to the simmering liquid. "Thank you for preparing my favorite meal."

"I'm happy to. Was the store busy today?"

"Yes, quite busy. We did well. Readers are already looking ahead to the holiday season and snapping up the first Christmas novels and coffee-table books. And with *Crimes of Passion* meeting at the store tonight, it should be a successful evening as well."

Iris's parents were working tonight, serving customers

while the book club held its bimonthly meeting in the mystery/thriller section of the store. The club members always ended up purchasing several books themselves.

"How was your day?" Lily asked as she selected a slice of mushroom from the cook pot.

"Very nice. I took *Windspinner* up to Sunset Cove. It was a perfect day for sailing." For her first bite, Iris chose tofu.

"Really?" One simple word, yet there was a pointed quality to the question.

Iris glanced at her aunt. "Yes. Sunny, warm for November, and a nice breeze."

"I see." Again, she heard an odd tone.

Iris watched her aunt select a strip of cooked beef and nibble it. "Is something on your mind?"

Her aunt finished the beef and reached for her wineglass. "Your mother popped out to the pharmacy this afternoon, and she saw you drive by."

Iris stifled a groan. Focused on Julian, she hadn't noticed her mom. "Let me guess." She took a piece of scallion from the pot. "She said I wasn't alone."

"She said there was a man in the passenger seat. She didn't recognize him."

Her aunt hadn't asked a direct question. That would be rude. But to refuse to answer the implied one would also be rude. Besides, as Miranda had pointed out, word was probably already spreading. Adding more ingredients to the simmering pot, Iris said, "Julian Blake came sailing with me. Forbes's son. Sonia's stepson. Luke's stepbrother." Triply credible, in other words.

"The musician?"

"Yes."

"The one who shuns the island, but came after Forbes's accident to help out?"

"Yes."

"I didn't know you knew him."

"We went to school together." It was true, even though

he'd been three years ahead and never noticed her. "He was in the store the other day and we got talking. He's quite stressed, worrying about Forbes. I thought it would be nice to go sailing before the season ends, and thought he might enjoy a break, so I extended an invitation."

"That was kind of you." She didn't add that it was utterly uncharacteristic, but Iris knew she was thinking it.

After another few bites, Aunt Lily said, "You know your parents want to meet him."

Iris reflected for a moment. "We all want things we can't have." As she did, with this silly attraction to a man who would never fit her dream of happily ever after.

"That's the truth." Her aunt's words were solemn and a shadow darkened her brown eyes.

They were both quiet for a minute or two and then Aunt Lily said briskly, "Enough of that subject. I have interesting news."

Relieved and curious, Iris leaned forward. "Is it gossip?" At Dreamspinner, their family overheard many conversations, including some that were intended to be private. They would never reveal secrets outside the family, but even though gossip was unseemly, they were only human and sometimes indulged among themselves.

"No, not gossip. You know the rumor that Walter Franklin doesn't plan to run again when his current term as a trustee comes to an end?"

"Yes, it's been circulating for weeks." Franklin was one of Destiny's two elected representatives on the Islands Trust. "I've heard that people are asking Bart Jelinek to run."

"Today, Melanie Newall suggested to your father that he consider running." Melanie, with her husband and his brother, owned and operated the *Destiny Gazette*, the island newspaper.

"Wow. That never occurred to me." Iris gazed out the

window, not seeing the view as much as considering the notion. "Dad would be terrific." She gave a soft laugh. "Not that I'm prejudiced." Nor was she a particular fan of Bart. No one could fault his accomplishments, but his hearty manner was anathema to her shy personality. His wife, Cathy, Iris liked better. She worked at a credit union and supported her husband's causes in a less ostentatious manner.

"Dad knows everyone on the island," Iris said, "and like Bart he's helped out with so many good causes. Besides, the Yakimuras have lived on Destiny since the very early days." With the exception, of course, of the internment camp years, but that went without saying. "Bart's family doesn't go back far at all."

"No, and I don't think Bart even planned to live on Destiny. He worked as a Realtor in Vancouver for a few years in his twenties, and married Cathy there. Then he came back, *saying* city life was less appealing than the rural charm and community spirit of Destiny."

"*Saying?*"

"There's a lot of competition among Realtors in Vancouver, whereas at the time the only island Realtor was Thelma Sajak."

Iris nodded. Mrs. Sajak, in her seventies now, was still in the business, running Destiny Homes along with her married daughter. Their agency was the sole competition for Bart's Island Realty. "He stood a better chance of succeeding here. That makes sense."

"Plus, Bart likes to be the big fish in a small pond."

The snideness, atypical of Lily, made Iris chuckle. "That's so true, isn't it? Anyhow, to get back to Dad. I bet he said no."

"You're right. He told Melanie he was flattered, but that Bart would do a fine job."

"Was he just being shy and humble, or do you think he truly wouldn't want to be a trustee?"

"The former, I think, plus not wanting to compete with Bart. As you well know, it's the Yakimura way to blend in rather than put ourselves forward."

"Yes, whereas Bart's the nail that loves to stick out," Iris said dryly. Uncharitably, she almost wished that one day the old adage would prove true, and he'd be hammered down. "Perhaps we should remind Dad of what Lao Tzu said, that from humility comes leadership. Responsible leadership."

"True, but Bart is anything but humble and he's done well with the Rotary and the other causes he's taken on. Besides, the rumor mill already has him elected."

Ah yes, the infamous rumor mill.

So far, Iris's aunt, her parents, Miranda, and Glory, not to mention two elderly fishermen, knew about her and Julian. What were the chances that gossip would go no further?

On Tuesday night, Julian was eating dinner with his dad and stepmom. The meal was a chicken, onion, tomato, zucchini stir-fry over rotini, easy for Forbes to manage one-handed. Julian was glad to see him eating heartily. After his surgeries, the pain meds had robbed him of his appetite and he'd had to force himself to take the nourishment his body needed in order to heal.

Julian had never been a cook, but he'd taken over that duty most weeknights and to his surprise enjoyed it. Sonia had a collection of recipes, old family ones and others she'd cut or photocopied from books and magazines, or printed from the Internet. Following directions was like reading music, and he was developing the ability to improvise, too. Homemade sure beat microwave meals and takeout.

If he handled dinner, that freed up Sonia's time after

school got out. She could shop and run other errands—
which meant Julian didn't have to go into the village. It
also allowed her to keep coaching the debate team, which
she'd done this afternoon. Now she was regaling Julian and
his dad with stories of the students' blunders and triumphs
as they debated whether religious and cultural traditions
like Hanukkah, Christmas, and Kwanzaa should be taught
in school.

Forbes's long, ponytailed hair was gray and thinning,
and the character lines that creased his face had deepened
since the accident. But now those lines relaxed as he listened to his wife's stories. His love for her was evident in
his blue eyes, the eyes Julian had inherited. For the first
time since the accident, Forbes looked younger than his
sixty-five years rather than older.

Watching his stepmom, Julian thought that Sonia
Russo really was an attractive woman, with her Mediterranean coloring and black hair. Perhaps her most appealing
feature, though, was her vitality. Her expressions were
animated, and her gestures, too, as she talked about her students. She was there for them, involved with them, trying
to help them achieve their dreams.

When she'd married his father, Julian had seen her as
being absorbed in their love, with no room for anyone else.
Now he realized that, in all likelihood, she'd tried to get to
know her new stepson, but he had been resentful and surly.
Then Jelinek saw Julian's vulnerability and took advantage,
and after that Julian had been too broken and ashamed to
trust anyone.

When Sonia finished a story, he said, "I'm sorry I never
gave you a chance, when you and Forbes got married."

"What?" Her expressive eyebrows winged up. "What
are you talking about, Julian?"

"Listening to you tonight, getting to know you over
the past weeks, I see that you're a caring teacher and a

wonderful partner to my dad. I should've seen that years ago, and not been so hard on you."

Sonia glanced at Forbes and then back to Julian. "Thank you for that, but I wasn't such a wonderful person back then. Not to you. For that I owe you an apology."

He shrugged, said, "Water under the bridge," and then grimaced at the triteness of the phrase.

She reached over and touched his hand, and then drew away again. By nature, she was a toucher, but the two of them only ever gave each other the obligatory, and rather stiff, hugs on occasions that demanded them. "When I met Forbes, I was a mess. Luke's dad had died two years earlier, do you remember me telling you that?"

"Uh, sorry, but only vaguely. Was it cancer?"

"Yes, non-Hodgkin's lymphoma. It was a horrible time. When he died, I was devastated. I barely functioned, what with my depression and the meds I was taking." She squeezed her eyes shut and then opened them again. "I was a terrible mother to Luke."

Why hadn't Julian known all this? Hadn't Sonia shared it, or had he not been listening?

She turned to Forbes, took his hand, and held on. Gazing back at Julian, she said, "Then I met this man. I'd never believed I could love again. I didn't even want to live, but I had Luke, my job, and I had to."

She'd felt suicidal? He'd never had a clue they'd had that in common.

Going on, she said, "But then some girlfriends staged an intervention and dragged me off to Quail Ridge Community Hall to see a band from Victoria that was playing."

"Forbes's band."

She nodded. "My world changed. There he was onstage, playing his guitar and singing, his voice rough-edged but sweet, like a callus on a gentle fingertip. I felt like he was singing directly to me."

A callus on a gentle fingertip. Julian's muse noted that one. He'd long ago learned to live with the fact that, as he lived his life, his muse was taking notes.

"Which I was," Forbes said. "I saw this gorgeous woman, like an Italian movie star, and I couldn't take my eyes off her."

"He was so sexy," Sonia said. Mischief glinted in her eyes as she spoke to Julian.

"Gag," he retorted, and grinned at her.

She laughed. "It was so cliché. There I was, a widow, a single mother, a high school sciences teacher—and suddenly I transformed into a groupie who was infatuated with the lead singer in the band." She nodded. "You know those women, Julian. You have dozens of them in every audience."

"True." He would look out at them, see their flushed cheeks and those dazzled eyes that broadcast, clear as hell, *I want to fuck you.* Once in a while he hooked up with one after a show, for a couple of hours of mindless pleasure. The only time he'd ever seen a woman in the audience who truly captured his interest was back in May. She hadn't looked like an Italian movie star, but like a Japanese flower, a slim and elegant iris amid a garden of gaudy petunias.

"Forbes had lots of groupies, of course," Sonia went on.

"But she was different," his dad said. "I don't believe there's such a thing as love at first sight, but there was sure something. That 'stranger across a crowded room' thing. Thank God she and her friends hung around after the show. I joined them for a drink and then—"

Sonia broke in. "Then all those girlfriends suddenly had other places they needed to be, and it was just him and me."

"We talked for hours." Forbes squeezed his wife's hand. "I learned that that's plenty of time to fall in love."

"For both of us," she agreed. "Of course, the next morning I couldn't believe it had really happened. But he didn't let me forget. We saw each other as often as we could, with me here and you guys living in Victoria. Two months later, Melanie Newall, who's a marriage commissioner, was marrying us in Blue Moon Harbor Park. It seems so crazy, looking back, but it felt right."

"It *was* right," Forbes said. "As proven by the last seventeen years."

"But," Sonia said, "we weren't fair to you and Luke, Julian. Your dad and I were obsessed with each other, caught up in this amazing love we shared. And I was . . ." She paused, searching for a word. "Giddy with relief, too. That I could be happy again, love again, live again. I tossed out the meds and I was high on love. I didn't include Luke in what was going on, and I didn't understand what you were going through, Julian. Your whole life was shaken up."

"I was at fault, too," Forbes said. "You'd always been such a flexible kid, adjusting to whatever came along. I expected you to do that again."

Yeah, he had been able to adjust to anything as long as his dad had been by his side, looking after him. But then Forbes was gone, glued at the hip to Sonia, leaving Julian out in the cold. Luke as well, he realized now, but Luke had had friends. Especially Candace, whom he'd later married. "Guess we all could have done better," Julian said.

"You were eleven," Sonia said. "It shouldn't have been on you to do better. We were the adults and should have been more responsible. But even adults make mistakes. So, again, I'm sorry, Julian." She touched his hand and this time didn't draw away. "I hope you can accept my apology, and that we can be closer now than we have been."

He turned his hand so he could grip hers. "I'd like that, too."

She had such a warm smile. Why had he never noticed that before?

She squeezed his hand and then let go. "Now that's settled, I have a question for Forbes. Honey, are you up to having company for dinner tomorrow? They'll even bring the food."

"Who?" his dad asked.

"Cathy and Bart Jelinek. She called me today. Again."

Julian, who had raised his water glass to his mouth, jerked the glass down.

"You know they've been offering to help ever since your accident," she said.

From what Sonia said, it had been Cathy extending the offers, not her husband. So far, Forbes had, thank God, said he wasn't ready to see them.

"I know," Forbes said, "and that's good of them, but there've been enough people around. I get tired even with the guys from the band, or Randall and Annie. The Jelineks, well, they're more your friends than mine, Sonia."

"I suppose. Bart and Luke's dad were in the Rotary together. I leaned on Bart and Cathy after Hank died. But Forbes, they're such good people. Bart's a community leader and—"

Julian jerked to his feet, almost toppling his chair. Another moment of hearing praise heaped on that sick bastard, and he'd puke. Stomach churning, he said, "There's an idea I need to work on. I'll be out in the studio."

And if the Jelineks did end up coming to the house, he would be far, far away.

Chapter Seven

Iris paid close attention to Julian's reactions as she ushered him into her condo late Wednesday afternoon. This was the first time she'd invited a male friend over to visit. They had the place to themselves; Aunt Lily would be out for the evening. Even so, he didn't repeat the friendly kiss on the cheek and Iris tried not to feel disappointed.

Since Julian had walked in, his movements had been tight and his shoulders high and tense. She hoped he wasn't regretting that he'd come. Yet he was the one who'd initiated this, by phoning in the morning to invite her out for dinner. Was he annoyed that she'd suggested he instead come over to her place?

After handing her a bottle of Destiny Cellars pinot grigio, he walked into the living room and set down the guitar case that she guessed he carried as automatically as she did a purse.

Iris stood by the island that divided the kitchen from the living room, watching Julian gaze around. In black jeans and a charcoal cotton shirt with rolled-up sleeves, he looked very masculine, yet, oddly, not out of place in the gentle, Japanese-influenced room she and her aunt had created.

Tense, though. "We could still go out," she offered. "If you'd prefer."

He glanced over his shoulder at her. "No, this is good. Better."

As he turned and walked toward the sliding glass doors onto the deck, he muttered something. It sounded like, "Even though the village would be safe tonight," but that didn't make sense, so she must have misheard. Tonight was no different from any other night in Blue Moon Harbor. If they ate at one of the several fine restaurants, a number of people would recognize Julian. Some would respect his privacy, but others would drop by to meet him, or to say hi to her. She'd feel anxious and wouldn't relax into that comfortable space she often felt when she was alone with Julian.

He opened the doors. "The sun's setting. Come look."

She followed him onto the deck that ran the full length of the condo, shared by the living room, her bedroom, and her aunt's corner room. There were a couple of zero-gravity chairs that adjusted for sitting or reclining, along with a small table and several potted plants. An Anna's humming-bird whirred toward one of the three feeders, its ruby throat catching the fading light. Another male darted in to chase it off. They faced off, upright in the air, wings thrumming madly as they screeched in hummingbird language at each other.

The birds' antics made Julian chuckle and his shoulders relax. He leaned forward, his forearms resting on the wooden railing.

Iris did the same, a couple of feet away, and gazed out at the ocean. The sun was almost down, painting a few puffy clouds with a peachy-pink glow. A fishing boat and a large pleasure craft were aiming toward the commercial marina at the head of Blue Moon Harbor. A few Christmas-anticipators had already strung lights on a handful of boats and shops, and their twinkle added a festive note. The view was always wonderful but tonight, glancing at Julian's handsome profile, it was spectacular.

"You face east," he said.

"Yes." It was rude to stare at someone, so she turned back to the scenery. "The most we see of the sunsets is a reflected glow, but the sunrises can be dramatic."

"I bet."

"Though sometimes I prefer the sunsets. They're more subtle. Like lyrics that have many levels, the kind of song that's not only pleasing on the surface but resonates deeply on reflective and emotional levels." Without looking at him, she added, "Your songs are like that."

"I write the reflected glow of sunsets, not dramatic sunrises. That's a lovely thought, Iris. Thank you."

She sensed his gaze on her but, embarrassed by how spontaneous and loquacious she could be around him, and how tingly aware she was of his presence, she kept her gaze on the ever-changing sky.

"Tell me why you suggested *The Tao of Pooh*," he said.

"Oh, well . . ." Surprised by the question, she took a moment to consider. "At the commune, and from your music, I sense you have the Tao in you. But I also sense an unrest that leads you to lose touch with it."

His body tensed, and so she hurried to get to the point. "I do that, too, let myself be distracted by complexities rather than focus on what's important. But when I calm and center my thoughts and emotions, then I can perceive things from the appropriate perspective." Thinking of a previous month's quote from her wall calendar, she added, "The individual leaves, the trees, and the forest."

He had relaxed again. "The conventional saying suggests that the forest is what's important. The big picture."

"One must see the big picture, but shouldn't ignore the details that go into making it."

They watched in companionable silence until the last blush faded from the clouds and the sky darkened. Iris, clad in a short-sleeved silk T-shirt her aunt had created, ivory with a pale pink peony on it, wrapped her arms around herself.

"You're cold," he said. "Let's go inside."

"I could get a sweater if you want to stay out."

"No, let's go in." He took her arm, touching her for the first time that night, guiding her toward the door and sending heat rushing through her.

Once inside, she shut the doors but didn't draw the rice-paper blinds. From the dining table by the window, she and Julian could watch the lights of the village and harbor.

"Your apartment's like you," he said.

"Like me?"

"Harmonious, elegant, relaxing."

"Oh!" Flustered, she said, "I'm hardly elegant. If the condo is, then that's due to Aunt Lily. She owned most of the furniture already. I've added only a few things."

"You and your aunt live together?" He followed as she walked to the kitchen, where she set the oven to broil. Seating himself on a stool at the island, he asked in a neutral tone, "Will she join us for dinner?"

Iris felt a moment's disconnect. JUNO-winner Julian Blake was sitting at her kitchen island, his shaggy hair golden under the track lighting, his skin burnished from sunshine, his body lean and masculine in charcoal and black. Did he only ever wear dark colors? If so, was it his professional image or for some personal reason?

Remembering his question, she said, "No, I would never spring something like that on you." She took the filleted salmon from the bowl where it had been marinating, and put it under the broiler. "On Wednesdays, Aunt Lily has an early dinner with a couple of friends, and then they teach a mixed media art course." Iris took the wine from the fridge and handed it to Julian, along with a corkscrew and two glasses.

Working the corkscrew, he said, "Your aunt's an artist?"

"Fabric art." She whisked the dressing she'd made earlier.

"Your blouse," he guessed, putting a glass of wine beside her on the counter as she tossed the dressing onto the cabbage-fruit-nut salad she'd prepared earlier. "The scarf you were wearing in the store."

"Yes. Wall hangings and pillows, too. She takes private orders and also sells some of her things at Island Treasures in the village."

"Her work is beautiful."

"I agree." She raised her glass. "To a pleasant evening."

His lips twisted, a wry smile that gentled. He touched his glass to hers. "I'll definitely drink to that. And to you, for yet again providing me with exactly what I need."

She read a deeper meaning to his words, and sensed he'd prefer she not ask. "I'm very happy to be with you." Her lashes fluttered down as she reflected that those words, too, had a deeper truth she'd rather not reveal. Julian must have spent hundreds of evenings with women, but for her tonight was rare and special. A memory to treasure over the years.

Those dazzling blue eyes of his could be amazingly soft sometimes, as they were now when he gazed at her. "How about you, Iris? I think you have an artistic side, too."

"Me? Oh no, sadly not." A sip of wine made her smile approvingly. "Mm, this is good. Thank you for bringing it. But no, I'm afraid I have no particular talent. I content myself with thinking that the creators like you and my aunt need an appreciative audience. I can certainly fill that role." It was her belief that the gift she'd been given was one of love: to be a generous, loving, loyal friend, wife, and mother. But that was too private a thought to share.

"An appreciative audience is a wonderful thing. When

I'm onstage and things click between the band and the audience, there's an amazing energy."

"I felt it when I saw you in May." She opened the oven and brushed marinade on the salmon, figuring it needed only a couple more minutes.

"You left right after the performance."

"You noticed that?" He really had noticed her?

"I did. That was due to your shyness?"

"In part." She spooned a mixture of grains from the rice cooker into a bowl with a cover, a lovely piece from an island potter. "During your sets, I was caught up in the music. After, I wanted to go home and"—*fantasize about you*—"let the music play over in my head."

"Miranda stayed, though. Did she mention that we met?" An odd note in his voice made her glance up from her task. He gazed at her intently, as if her answer mattered.

"No." Which was strange, after she and her friend had spent so much time gushing over Julian and his music. She put the bowl of rice on the island, beside the salad and two plates.

"It was when she and Luke had broken up, but it was obvious she still cared for him."

"Oh, yes. She was very unhappy. She and Luke weren't communicating well." Iris took the salmon from the oven and transferred it to a platter.

"I realized that when I talked to him the next day. I'm glad they sorted things out. Luke's a good guy. It shattered him when Candace died." He cleared his throat. "I should've been more supportive. But we'd never been all that close."

"That's a pity. I always wished I had a sibling. I envy my dad and Aunt Lily their relationship. When I have children, I want more than one."

"I bet you'll make a great mother."

"I will do my very best."

"Don't be too much of a perfectionist," he teased. "One thing I've seen with Luke and his twins is that kids are messy and parenting's an imperfect art form."

She would love to have her ordered life disrupted by children. "Wise advice. Now, dinner is ready. Please, help yourself."

He slid off the bar stool and topped up their wineglasses. "Everything looks delicious. And beautiful. The food itself, the serving dishes. Don't deny being an artist, Iris."

Feeling herself flush, she said, "It's just dinner."

"That's like saying that blouse your aunt made is just a T-shirt." He served himself.

She followed behind, and then they took their plates and glasses to the living room. She had set the table with woven place mats, sage-colored linen napkins, and a tiny crackle-glazed vase holding a sprig of deep red leaves from the Japanese maple on the deck. "Sit down while I put on some music." Earlier, she had debated what to play for a talented musician, and had selected several of her grandmother's albums. If the first didn't suit his taste, she'd try another.

Now, as she put a record on the turntable, Julian said, "Vinyl?"

"Grandmother Rose adored music and had over two hundred albums. Everything from the Beatles to Cleo Laine to Pete Seeger, Ricky Nelson, and this." Band music began to play, the kind that made Iris imagine a dark, smoky club with men and women in old-fashioned evening dress swaying on the dance floor. A woman sang that she was traveling light.

"Billie Holiday," Julian said.

"Yes. Is that alright?"

"A smoky, sultry female voice singing the blues? You bet."

Relieved, Iris took her seat. "I grew up listening to music with my grandmother."

"I'd love to look through her collection. When I was a kid, Forbes never had a lot of money, but there was always enough for food, shelter, and music. He had eclectic taste, too."

"She heard some of your songs, you know. She said you had an old soul."

"I'm flattered."

Iris waited anxiously as he tasted each dish. Then he grinned. "It doesn't just look pretty, it tastes terrific. I know there's soy sauce in the salmon marinade and the salad dressing, but what else?"

"Soy, sesame oil, balsamic vinegar, honey, and ginger. The vinegar and honey are local."

"And what's the rice pilaf? I've never had anything like this before. Are there nuts in it?"

"No. It's a blend of white rice, brown, wild, and quinoa." Suddenly remembering something, she said, "Oh, would you like butter? I forgot to put it out."

"No, it's great as it is. I love the combination of stuff in the salad, too. The only cabbage salad I've ever had is coleslaw. I like the Asian tang, and the cranberries, cilantro, sesame seeds, and other things you've put in there."

"Thank you. Do you have a favorite kind of food? I imagine you eat out a lot, especially on tour."

"Oh, yeah. Too many fast-food hamburgers and delivery pizzas, but some good meals as well. Everything you can imagine, from sushi to steak to Indian and Mexican food. I like them all. Greek's a favorite. And Italian. Sonia cooks damned fine Italian food, courtesy of a bunch of old family recipes and her own experimenting." He sipped wine and smiled. "She collects recipes. I've never been into cooking, but I've taken over doing it on weekdays. There's pleasure in that, isn't there? Putting together a meal and having folks sit down and enjoy it."

"There is." Her vivid imagination had her coming home

from work to a meal prepared by Julian. That would be almost as incredible as having him play music for her. "You brought your guitar. Will you play something after dinner?"

"Sing for my supper?"

Her cheeks immediately burned, and she pressed her hands to them. "No, of course not. I'm so sorry, that's not what I meant. You should never feel obliged to play for me."

Julian felt a little guilty for flustering Iris, but she was adorable when she blushed. Actually, she was just adorable, period. "Iris, relax. I was teasing."

"Oh. Really?"

Sometimes she was so articulate and so perceptive, yet other times her shyness inhibited her—particularly when it came to male-female stuff. Since he'd met her, he had wondered how experienced she was when it came to men. After a few more bites of the delicious meal, he hadn't come up with a subtle way of asking, so he just said it. "Do you date much?"

Her eyes widened, then she lowered her gaze. Her hair was loose today, so those black wings slid forward to frame her oval face. "No," she said quietly, breaking off a bite of salmon but not raising her fork.

She was beautiful, smart, and sensitive, a highly desirable woman. Gently, he said, "Either you're really picky, or your shyness gets in the way."

She nodded. "I'm awkward with men."

"Maybe a little, but not so much when you get to know the guy." When she raised her head, eyebrows arched, he said, "At least that's how it seems with you and me."

"Yes, but that's rare. You're patient and kind, and for some reason I feel comfortable with you."

"I'm glad. I feel comfortable with you, too, on a level I don't with most other people."

Her lips curved and her eyes glowed. She moistened her lips with the delicate pink tip of her tongue, an innocent yet sensual action that sent arousal thrumming through him. "You give me hope," she said softly. "You see, I've always believed that when the right man comes into my life, he'll value all aspects of my personality including my shyness."

The right man? Did she think—

"No!" she said quickly. "I'm sorry, I didn't mean that I thought you were that man. I know we're just friends. But you see me, strengths and flaws, and you accept me."

Relieved that she wasn't hoping for things from him that he was incapable of giving, he said, "I accept and value you. Never settle for anything less than that, Iris."

"I won't. Besides, that's how it's worked before."

"You mean with past boyfriends?" The idea of Iris sharing her gentle, sensitive soul with other guys gave him an odd pang of jealousy.

"No, I mean that's how it worked for my father and grandfather." Her brow furrowed. "Not for Aunt Lily yet, but I still hope she'll find someone to love and share her life with. Maybe next spring, when we go to Japan."

"You're planning a trip? Have you been before?"

"Yes, she and I plan to go. And no, I've never been. My aunt has, once. Mom's parents have come here, and my family's in touch with the family in Japan. It will be nice to see them in person, and see the country. But it will also be stressful for Aunt Lily and me."

He remembered her saying that shyness was part of her heritage, that her aunt, father, and grandfather all shared the trait. Intrigued, he leaned forward. "How did your father and grandfather meet their wives?"

Her smile told him he'd hit on a subject she was happy

to talk about. "Good things can come out of terrible situations. In the Tashme internment camp, my grandfather Harry wasn't outgoing enough to make friends, but then a Japanese-Canadian girl, Akahana, befriended him. They became inseparable, and as they grew older they fell in love. But after the war, Akahana's family was deported to Japan. The two teenagers wrote, keeping in touch for ten whole years."

Her brown eyes glowed, the romantic in her clearly loving this story. "Her family wanted her to marry a man in Japan, but she refused, saying her heart belonged to Harry. In the mid–nineteen fifties, when Grandfather Harry was twenty-five, he went to Japan. Meeting again, their love was even stronger. Her parents accepted him, and they married and she came back with him. Akahana means red rose. Wanting to fit in, my grandmother anglicized her name to Rose."

Julian shook his head in wonder as his muse seized on an inspiration for a song. "When I hear stories about a love that survives against horrendous odds, it's hard to believe them. But I wonder if sometimes hardship can make people persist when otherwise they wouldn't."

"You mean that if my grandparents had been typical kids who went to high school together and fell in love then, their love might not have lasted?"

"Well, teen love often doesn't, right?"

"I think if it's true love, not merely a crush, it will last. I didn't know Luke and Candace well, but when I saw them together I sensed that even though they were each other's first love, their love was true and would have lasted forever. Don't you think so?"

He felt crappy having to admit, "I'm afraid I didn't know them that well either." Rather than discuss his failings as a stepbrother, he said, "Tell me how your shy dad met your mom."

Her eyes twinkled. "It was facilitated by family. Dad almost never dated, and when he was twenty-five, my grandparents said that he and Aunt Lily, who's three years younger, should visit Japan. The Yakimuras are loyal Canadians, but every generation has stressed the importance of our historic and cultural roots. So Dad and Aunt Lily were sent on a tour of Japan, staying with relatives and friends of the family. Dad was introduced to several hand-picked Japanese women, including my outgoing mom. Despite, or perhaps because, of their differences in personality, they fell for each other."

Was this what Iris's parents had in mind for her? Julian tried to be generous enough to hope that it worked out, and Iris found the love she longed for. "Your parents married in Japan?"

"No, he came home, but they wrote and made long-distance phone calls. Mom came to visit Destiny and to meet Dad's parents. Everybody got along, Mom loved the island and Dreamspinner, and Mom and Dad got married."

"Your aunt didn't meet a Japanese man and fall in love?"

"No, unfortunately. She was introduced to several eligible ones, but nothing clicked. I've always wondered if she should have gone again, when she was twenty-five. Not that I believe in magic numbers or anything, but I have to wonder."

"How old are you?"

"I turn twenty-five at the end of this year."

"Are you going to Japan to meet a man?"

Her long lashes fluttered down and she said quietly, "I'm open to that possibility."

"If it happened, would you move to Japan?"

"No." She gave her head a quick shake. "I can't imagine that. If the man was the right one, I believe he would want to move to Destiny and build his life here, with me. As happened with my mother and grandmother."

She was a romantic, alright. But who was he to judge? Of course he wanted Iris to find the love she deserved, and that person wasn't him, couldn't be someone as broken and flawed as him. He focused on another aspect of her stories. "Does your family really want to, uh, stay Japanese? I mean, not marry someone of another race?"

"No, but none of us ever seems to meet anyone here in Canada."

"I guess there aren't many eligible men on this tiny island. Unless you count tourists, and they're probably not the greatest prospects."

"Some visitors do fall in love with locals and move here, as Forbes did. And Aaron's wife, Eden. And it's not like I've never left the island. I got a B.A. at the University of Victoria."

"Really? You weren't anxious about going away to school?"

They'd been eating as they talked, and now she put down her fork and sipped wine. "Oh yes. But my family's big on education and they were persuasive."

"What did you study? Philosophy?" She was such a deep, thoughtful person.

"Yes, and also English lit, French, linguistics, psychology, sociology, whatever interested me. Dad has a degree in library science, Mom's is in accounting, and Aunt Lily's is in business admin. They taught me everything about running the store, from when I was a kid, so it seemed silly for me to get one of those degrees."

"Did you enjoy university?"

"My classes were interesting but I was uncomfortable being around all those strangers. Thank heavens my long-time best friend was my roommate." She wrinkled her nose. "My only friend, actually. Doesn't that sound pathetic?"

"Well, it's more than I had."

"Really? How awful, Julian."

"When I was little, Forbes and I were mobile, traveling for gigs, moving to different apartments when his finances got better or worse. I changed schools, missed school when we went on the road. But we were a team and I hung out with his musician friends, so it was cool. Then we moved here and—" He hunted for semi-accurate words. "Forbes had Sonia, Luke had Candace, and by then I was pretty much a loner." He had remained one.

"I value my alone time," Iris said thoughtfully, "but I also value people. I've never had many friends, but they matter a great deal to me. Like Miranda and Eden now, and Shelley back in school." Her eyes twinkled. "We were two odd ducks, Shelley and me."

Odd ducks. Iris occasionally used an unusual, but charming, expression. "How so?"

"I was skinny as a reed, tall for my age, and of course looked Japanese. Shelley was short and plump, with frizzy red hair and freckles. I was the academic, reflective type and she was into movie stars and so on. But she was shy, too. We were the kids who never got invited to join others for lunch."

"The other kids teased you?"

"A little. Not bullying, though. Destiny Islanders pride ourselves on our diversity and we don't try to mold everyone into the same shape. But kids will be kids. If Shelley or I had had the spine to stand up to the teasing, we'd probably have been okay. Instead, we just hung out together as BFFs and pretended we didn't care that we were social outcasts."

"Are you still good friends?"

"Only via email and Facebook. She kind of deserted me, our last year at UVic." She grinned. "By which I mean she found her happily ever after. She met this great guy—

the first guy she ever dated, but he was wonderful—and suddenly she was spending every free moment with him. They got married right after they graduated, and now they live in Kelowna and have a baby and a golden retriever." She gave a firm nod. "More support for my belief that there's a man out there who'll find me special."

"Iris, you *are* special. Any man would be damned lucky to have you in his life." The words flew out before he thought them through. What he did register was her expression, the sudden gleam of light, of hope, in her bottomless eyes. Oh damn, did she think he meant that he was romantically interested in her?

Damn again. He was. He wanted her. More than he could remember ever wanting anyone. But it was wrong. He reached across the table and captured her hands. "I wish that man could be me, but it can't."

She shook her head quickly, midnight waves rippling around her face. "No, of course not. I never thought you'd be attracted to me, not as anything more than a friend."

"Iris." He gripped her hands, needing to make her understand. "I *am* attracted to you. Really, really attracted, but—"

"Seriously? You are?" There was that glint of hope again.

"I am. But, Iris, it could never work between us."

Her eyes darkened, the glint dying, which plucked heartstrings he was usually only aware of when he composed and sang. "No, of course it couldn't," she said. "You're a celebrity and I'm plain old me. You're—"

"You're the opposite of plain. You're lovely. I could gaze at you forever. You turn me on, but you also bring peace to my soul." His muse registered the words and filed them away.

"That's . . ." She did one of those head-duck things.

He let go of one of her hands and reached across to raise her chin. Even then, her gaze slipped downward rather than meeting his. He waited until finally her eyes lifted.

"That's the truth," he said. "But it's also the truth that even if you might be a little bit attracted to me, really you're looking for a different kind of man." *A decent one.* "One who'll fit into your life on Destiny. I'm right, aren't I?"

She nodded slowly. "I can't imagine living anywhere else, much less being part of the life you live. Travel, performances, the media, interacting with different people all the time."

"Things that are necessary for my career." He released her chin and her hand, and sat back in his chair. "I do enjoy performing, with the right audience. It's a high like nothing else. Travel has pros and cons; exploring new places is stimulating. The media, well, that's not my favorite part of the job. Interacting with different people can be fun or not so great, but it's often a source of song ideas."

Listening to him, she nodded but didn't speak.

"You'd rather I was just a songwriter," he said. "A guy who hangs out at home writing music and never has to go away."

Her gentle features morphed into something fierce. "No, Julian. I'd never want you to be different from who you are. Of course you must perform. You have a gift to share. The travel and media and all of those things are part of the package, to bring that gift to the world."

"So, I like you just the way you are, and you like me just the way I am, but our two ways are incompatible. Not to mention, I don't buy into that romantic dream of yours. I don't see myself ever getting married and having kids." Julian's brain conjured an image of Luke, Miranda, and their three children, and his heart throbbed in a bass note of regret. Even if he'd been capable of trust and love, he didn't deserve a future like that.

"I'm so glad you like me. But yes, what you say is true. It's important to know one's own nature and respect it."

"As the Tao book says." Reading that, Julian had reflected

on his own inner nature. It consisted of opposites: a creator who brought value to the world and a coward whose failure to report Jelinek had quite probably resulted in the abuse of other boys. Julian hated the dark side, but he'd accepted his brokenness, his guilt, and learned to live with it. Thanks to the old lady in Vancouver who'd changed his life when he was fifteen, he also saw his positive side. That gave him a reason, day by day, to carry on. "If your inner nature has imperfections, do you respect those, too?" No way could he ever do that.

"I think you must. No one is perfect, Julian."

"That's the truth," he said bitterly. But he appreciated the effort she put into trying to help him. "You're a good friend, Iris."

"I'm very happy to be your friend." When she spoke again, her voice was so soft he barely heard it. "I wish . . . there could be something more."

A hot rush of arousal washed away all thoughts of his flawed inner nature. "So do I," he said fervently. "But I respect you. You're not the kind of girl who hangs around after shows, wanting to hook up with a celebrity." He didn't want to insult her, so proceeded cautiously. "It sounds like you're not, uh, very experienced."

She nodded. "I've dated one man. Six whole dates. We kissed and fooled around a little, but it was clear to both of us that it wasn't working."

He swallowed. It had occurred to him, from her bashful manner and serious nature, that she might be a virgin. "So you've never . . ." Used to being with women who engaged in sex as casually as in a coffee date, he now found himself searching for a delicate way of phrasing his question. "Never been with a man?"

Her lips quirked. "What a delightfully old-fashioned phrase. No, Julian, I've never had sex. I'm a virgin. I don't find that fact the least bit embarrassing."

"Nor should you," he said quickly. "I didn't mean to imply—"

Her laugh tinkled like a delicate wind-chime. "It's alright. I know I'm an anomaly, but who wants to come from a cookie-cutter mold?"

"No one would ever accuse you of that. You're unique and fascinating."

The woman who had no trouble admitting to being a virgin now ducked her head and whispered, "Thank you."

"So"—he returned to his original train of thought—"you're a virgin. And you have that big romantic dream." A dream that no doubt included losing her virginity to the love of her life, in some deeply emotional, hearts-and-flowers scene. "A dream that I'm sure one day will come true. But you know I'm not the man for that dream."

Her gaze was on his face again. "I do know. Julian, I may have a romantic dream, but I'm also an intelligent, realistic woman. I have no foolish illusions about our relationship."

Reassured, yet for some inexplicable reason a little disappointed, too, he said, "Good."

"So, given that, I wonder if we might, well . . ." She swallowed and her cheeks took on a pink tinge. "Take things slowly, but, well, let our relationship evolve in ways other than just, um, verbal communication?" Now her cheeks were rosy.

His body heated again. "You mean in physical ways? Intimate ways?" Just how far, *moving slowly*, might she want things to *evolve*? There were many, many things a couple could do, short of actual intercourse.

She pressed her hands to her cheeks. "I feel so forward, even thinking this, much less suggesting it."

"Are you really such an old-fashioned woman?"

"No!" Her hands dropped and her eyes sparked. "I'm a feminist. Yes, I believe in respecting my elders, obeying the law, and treating people with politeness, but those aren't old-fashioned values. They're *solid* ones. I also believe in equal rights for everyone and I don't think it should always be up to the man to initiate a relationship."

Her uncharacteristic tirade made him grin. "Good."

"It's not being old-fashioned," she insisted, "it's my intrinsic shyness. Something that I'm overcoming quite a lot, with you. You're good for me, Julian."

He was flattered. Honored, to use one of Iris's words. "You're good for me, too. And yes, I would love to . . ." She had invited him to move past words to action, so he stopped talking and captured her hand. He explored it with his own, sliding his bigger fingers between her slim ones, running guitar-callused fingertips across her palm, circling her fine-boned wrist and coming to rest there, where he couldn't tell if it was her pulse or his own that vibrated prestissimo— almost as fast as a hummingbird's wings.

Still holding her hand, he rose and came around the tiny table to draw her to her feet. He took her other hand, held both sets of clasped hands down at their sides, and stepped toward her.

She gazed up at him, her brown eyes alive with curiosity and heat.

Chapter Eight

Oh my gosh, is he going to kiss me? Julian stopped moving when their clothing brushed lightly. If she was the modern woman she professed to be, she could seize the initiative. Uncertainty held Iris back.

She'd been kissed before, but only by two guys. Once was in high school on prom night. The school wanted everyone in the small graduating class to attend, and the kids who hadn't already chosen dates were paired up by random draw. Iris had been relieved to be matched with a science nerd who was as reclusive as she. Still, at the end of the evening, he had kissed her. Likely he'd been curious, or thought it more or less obligatory. It had been a sloppy, cringe-worthy kiss, and the next week at school they'd gone back to not talking to each other.

Julian gazed down at her, not speaking, not moving.

Her lips felt dry and she ran the tip of her tongue across them to moisten them, then wondered if he'd think she was trying to be seductive.

She'd participated in just-okay kisses during her fourth year at UVic, when Shelley and her boyfriend had fixed Iris up with a friend of his for a few double dates. He'd been a nice enough guy and Iris had worked hard at overcoming her shyness, encouraging him to talk about himself. Though she hadn't been attracted to him, she'd let him kiss her and touch her breasts, hoping she'd feel something, and tired of being so inexperienced. She mimicked kisses she'd read about in romance novels, but arousal never stirred and she wondered if something was wrong with her. At the end of their sixth date, he'd said, "You're not that into me, are you?"

She'd stumbled over her tongue, apologizing and saying it wasn't him, he was a great guy, but he'd cut her off with, "It's okay. I'm not that into you either."

Iris was into Julian, and he said he was into her. Kissing him would be different. But what was he waiting for?

He bent his head and touched his lips to her forehead.

Now that he'd made the first move, she came up on her toes, enjoying the soft, warm brush of flesh on flesh and longing for more. Next, he kissed the tip of her nose, and she caught her breath, holding entirely still except for the delicate trembling that took over her body.

Now his lips were on hers, the barest whisper of tantalizing sensation.

She ran out of breath and exhaled, air rushing from her nostrils and pushing her lips apart. Julian's parted, too, shaping to hers, and his tongue caressed the sensitive inner lining of her lower lip. But that was as far as he went, just tilting his head to mate their mouths more perfectly but not thrusting inside hers with his tongue.

The delicate touches were the most sensual thing she'd ever felt. She and Julian were barely in contact. Only their lips, their clasped hands, and the fabric of their clothing. Now the quivering that fluttered through her body was a hot pulse of desire.

His hands released hers, his lips slipped away, and her racing heart slowed with a thud of disappointment. She was such a novice, she must have disappointed him. Ducking her head, she tried to frame an apology.

Before she could, his hands were on her again, framing her face, tilting it gently so she met his gaze. What she saw there stole her breath: a heat to match the arousal she felt, and tenderness as well.

"Yes," he said in a low, husky voice, "I want more. But no, I think we should leave it there, a perfect first verse."

"Will there be a second verse?" she dared to ask.

One corner of his mouth tilted up. "With you for inspiration, I'd say that's inevitable."

The next day, Iris's phone rang while she was doing tai chi. Normally, she'd have ignored it but this morning she couldn't resist checking. Her heart raced as she answered. "Good morning, Julian." Last night, she had kissed this man!

"Morning, Iris. Have I caught you at a bad time?"

"No. I'm off work this morning. I'm taking the afternoon and evening shifts at the store. We have a guest author tonight, a mystery writer from Vancouver who's doing a reading, and signing her new release. Forbes has started reading mysteries, hasn't he? Perhaps you might come, and get a book for him?" And she could see Julian.

"Thanks, but I don't think so. Would you get a book autographed for him, though, and I'll pay for it next time I see you?"

"Of course. Uh, when might that be?"

"Luke called me last night."

That was *not* an answer to her question. Puzzled, she said, "Oh?"

"Miranda told him we're seeing each other."

She groaned. "Of course she did. What did he say?"

"Basically, that you're one of the truly nice people, and I shouldn't mess with you."

"Gah!" The sound of frustration escaped, and she clapped a hand over her mouth. "Sorry, that was rude. I appreciate

Luke's concern, but I can look after myself. How did you respond?"

"I told him I think you're great, I respect you, and the last thing I want to do is hurt you."

"Thank you. I appreciate that. Did he back off?"

"Nope. He was under orders from Miranda."

"She's my friend," Iris said indignantly. "She shouldn't try to sabotage our relationship."

"Actually, she told him that if we planned to keep seeing each other, she wanted us to come over for dinner."

"Oh." Socializing with friends as a couple. She hadn't done that since the few times back in university. "I guess that's what people do," she said hesitantly. "At least it's what they do when they're dating. But we're not exactly dating."

"We're not?"

"To me, dating means serious, possibly headed toward a long-term commitment. We agree that's not possible." Despite her regret. "I would say we're seeing each other as friends."

"With a little physical intimacy thrown in for fun." His husky voice had a seductively teasing note that warmed her more than her tai chi workout had.

"Like the whipped cream on the apple crisp," she agreed. Transforming something wonderful into a treat that was even more luscious.

"Make that ice cream, and I'll share your dessert."

A shiver of lust rippled through her. She dared to respond with, "Why don't we be decadent and have both?"

"I'm gonna hold you to that. In the meantime, what do you think about the dinner? Tomorrow night, if that works for you."

Friday. She wasn't scheduled for the evening shift. Though she'd have preferred to spend time alone with Julian, her friendship with Miranda was important. Also,

Iris wanted Julian to have a closer relationship with his stepbrother. "Yes, I think we should accept."

"Maybe it'll get them off our backs."

Her lips twisted in a grin. Did he really not understand the nature of female friendship?

He went on. "I'll pick you up, if you don't mind the old B-B-Zee van."

"Ooh, I get to ride in a band van," she said, only half joking. "You didn't bring a car to the island?"

"I don't own a car. Don't need one in Vancouver. The Julian Blake Band has a van for touring, but it lives at Roy and Camille's house."

She nodded, and wondered whether Julian would take her straight home after dinner, or perhaps find a secluded parking spot, for a little decadent *dessert*. She raised a hand to her mouth, smothering a laugh at thinking like such a teenager. But maybe she was due. As a teen, there'd been no hot, sensitive guy like Julian in her life.

On Friday evening, Julian staggered to the playroom at Luke's house with his four-year-old nephews dragging at one jean-clad leg and little Ariana hanging off the other. He'd been delegated the task of getting the kids settled with a game or video so the adults could clean up the kitchen and then retire to the front room for grownup conversation. The boys were pretending to protest, and Miranda's three-year-old mimicked the twins.

When Julian opened the door to the playroom, two dogs greeted them with happy dances. Both were rescues, by his veterinarian stepbrother. The three-legged, medium-sized female with a blond coat was Cinnamon. Pigpen was a tiny, ancient gray-and-white male that resembled a dust mop. The kids abandoned Julian to hug their pets and he stood back to watch the happy mess of wagging tails, licking tongues, busy hands, and little-kid smiles.

They were great kids, all three of them, and as Julian had watched Luke and Miranda with them at dinner, he'd seen that the adults and kids had already formed a family. Despite Miranda's troubled past and Luke's grief over his wife's death, Julian's gut told him the new family would make a go of it. And what must that feel like?

Some wounds could, over time, make a person stronger, as had happened with both Luke and Miranda. Often, Julian thought that was true for him. But then he'd get a reality check: like when he got nauseous just seeing the storefront of Island Realty. Deep down, he really was like the old guitar pick he toted around: mended, but not truly whole; fragile enough to break again under pressure.

Away from Destiny, though . . . If he never had to face or even think about Jelinek again, might he, like Luke, find happiness and peace and build a family?

No. God, what was he thinking? His story wouldn't have some pretty ending like in Iris's novels. A guy with his rotten core—his damned *complicity* in whatever abuse Jelinek continued to perpetrate—could never find peace and would never deserve true happiness.

"Uncle Julian!" Brandon's demanding voice broke into his thoughts. "Play trucks!"

Julian drew in a quavering breath and forced the darkness aside. Obediently, he lowered himself to the floor, gently moved Pigpen out of the way, chose a blue truck, and tried to figure out the kids' game.

The kids. His nephews and soon-to-be niece. They were his family, like Forbes, Sonia, Luke, and he guessed also Miranda now. If he wanted to be in their lives, he couldn't completely escape Destiny and the ever-present pall cast by Jelinek's existence. If only the asshole would catch a horrendous, agonizingly painful disease and die, so he could never abuse another boy.

A quiet feminine voice said, "Julian?"

He looked up to see Iris in the doorway. The sight of her was like cool water on burned flesh, soothing the pain in his soul. "Hey," he said with a smile. She looked like her namesake flower tonight, in an iris-printed blouse over slim-fitting sage-green pants. Her hair was down, a black silk frame for her lovely face.

She returned his smile. "Ready to come play with the grown-ups?"

He rose. "I could be persuaded." This woman could persuade him to do almost anything.

"You kids and dogs behave yourselves," Julian said, and then closed the door on them. Taking Iris's hand, he said, "Doing okay?"

When they'd first arrived at Luke's house and seen that not only Miranda and the kids were there, but also Miranda's brother Aaron and his wife, Eden, Iris had gripped his hand tightly, her tension palpable. But he'd seen her swallow, breathe deeply a few times, and gradually relax.

Now she dropped her head to brush her cheek against his shoulder, a unique Iris gesture that made him feel special. "Yes. I'm sorry for being so silly earlier. I'm such a coward."

He put his arm around her. "Don't call yourself silly, or a coward. Everyone has fears." He almost went on to say that she was braver than he, but then she'd have asked what he meant. "You're having a good time?"

"I am. Dinner was an experience, having three little kids at the table."

"They have a lot of energy. I admire Luke and Miranda for how well they cope."

"It seems to me each family has its own character. Luke and Miranda and their children are figuring out theirs, and it's high energy. My family meals as a child were much different. We're a quiet family."

"No mealtime conversation?" he asked as they walked down the wide hall with its satiny cherrywood floor.

"Oh yes, but more disciplined. I knew from an early age that there were rules."

"What kind of rules?"

"Politeness, respect, orderliness. Within those constraints, I was encouraged to share my experiences, to ask questions, to offer opinions."

"Civilized discourse," he said. Hard to imagine boisterous Brandon engaging in such a thing, but Caleb, the more reflective twin, would probably be into it. "Growing up with Forbes as a dad, there weren't many rules, but respect was one of them. Opinions and questions were encouraged. Often, we shared meals with other musicians, and it was a varied, interesting group. I learned a lot from those men and women."

"Forbes was a good father."

"Yeah."

Julian and Iris stepped into the front room, a large one with a high, slanted ceiling, an impressive fireplace, and huge windows looking out onto the deck and the ocean beyond. Though the home's architectural design was spectacular, Luke's furniture was modest and practical. Comfortable, too, Julian thought as he and Iris seated themselves on a khaki-colored couch that faced the view. Eden and Aaron, on a two-seater sofa, greeted them. Tonight was the first time Julian had met the dark-haired pilot's wife, and he liked her. Eden was attractive, with walnut-brown hair and amber eyes, and, as he'd learned at dinner, smart and perceptive as well.

Miranda and Luke came into the room, bringing mugs as well as milk and sugar. She handed a mug to Julian. "Full-test coffee, as requested."

The next mug went to Iris and he saw that it was tea, pale yellow-green, with some leaves in it. The scent was nice, more like flowers than a beverage. "What is that?"

"Jasmine tea. I introduced Miranda to it. Want to taste?"

He clung to his mug of dark, strong brew. "Thanks, but I think I'll pass."

She laughed, a melodic sound that braided together with the affectionate gleam in her eyes and the sweet, delicate scent of her tea, creating one of life's rare perfect moments. His muse filed that one away.

"How did I know you'd say that?" she teased.

Yeah, he was predictable, and he did like his caffeine. He grinned at her, had a sip of coffee, and glanced up. Luke had seated himself in a big chair. Miranda, a mug cradled in both hands, was curled up on a cushion on the floor, leaning against his legs. The two of them, and Aaron and Eden, were silent, watching Julian and Iris. Were they judging him, thinking Iris was crazy to let a man like him into her life? Maybe she was, but she was a smart, sensitive woman, and the decision was hers.

Eden cleared her throat. "Every time I come here, I'm amazed by this house."

Miranda nodded vigorously. "Me too. I can't believe I live here. Thank God Annie and Randall approve of me, or they might take back the house."

Julian knew that Candace's wealthy parents had given their daughter and Luke the spectacular waterfront home as a wedding present. "Yeah, it's quite the place," he said. "My home's a basement flat off Commercial Drive, dark and chilly but at least soundproofed." He did okay financially, but only okay, and he wasn't home enough to care about more than having the basics, plus a place to create and practice music.

"Ah, the glamorous life of a star," Luke teased. "But on the other hand, you have the travel and fans, not to mention a couple of those pretty JUNO awards to brighten up your dingy apartment." He shook his head and grinned. "Sure wouldn't trade you. And vice versa, I know."

"That's for sure," Julian said flippantly. The truth was, he *would* trade for some parts of Luke's life, if he could also have his music career.

"Do you two have anything in common?" Eden asked, sounding genuinely curious. "I mean, aside from Sonia and Forbes?"

"Probably not," Luke said.

"That's not true," Miranda said. "You both lost a parent when you were young. Your dad died when you were ten, right, Luke? And Julian, your mom wasn't in your life, was she?"

"No, she ran out on Forbes and me when I was four. I don't really remember her."

"At least I had my dad for ten years," Luke said. "He was a great father. We were very close." If Julian's stepbrother was thinking that at least *his* parent didn't voluntarily leave him, he was kind enough not to say it.

"And then the poor guy got cancer," Julian said. "Non-Hodgkin's lymphoma, right?"

Luke nodded, his greenish-gray eyes as sad as rain-clouds. "It took a year—one utterly shitty year—to kill him."

"I'm sure that was terrible for you, Luke," Iris said sympathetically, and Julian guessed she was thinking about her grandmother's painful battle with ALS. "How long after that," she asked, "was it until your mom met Forbes?"

"Two years."

"That must have been very hard," she said. Her hand slipped into Julian's and it felt like a subtle hint.

He had been so caught up in his own angst back then, he'd never spared a thought for what Luke was going through. "Oh man, yeah. Losing your dad like that, and then Forbes coming along, not a replacement, but . . .

whatever. And him toting me along, a sullen kid who hated leaving Victoria and the life we lived there."

"And hated having someone come between you and your father," Iris said.

In the chair across the room, Luke blinked. "You and Forbes were close after your mother left?"

"Yeah. He was a great dad."

"Then you had to share him with Mom and me."

"Yeah." Julian gave a wry smile. "Though it seems to me the two of them were their own little sunshine-and-rainbows unit, without much room for either of us."

Luke nodded. "They were."

Iris squeezed Julian's hand gently, and he felt compelled to carry on the conversation. This was the first time he and Luke had talked about the past, and he didn't want to lose the opportunity. "And you had Candace and your other friends."

Luke grimaced. "Sorry, I guess we shut you out."

"You had no reason to take me in." With his gaze still on Luke, he intertwined his fingers with Iris's.

"Being stepbrothers should have been enough. But I was an unhappy kid, losing Dad, then Mom being seriously depressed for a couple years. It was Candace who got me through. Her and Viola, the veterinarian. So when Mom got all wrapped up in Forbes, I stuck with my support network and was oblivious to what you were going through." He coughed. "Sorry, man."

When Julian lost Forbes to Sonia, it created a hole inside him. One that Bart Jelinek had been all too willing to fill with his poison. Jelinek had preyed on his vulnerability by making Julian feel important and cared for. Then he'd exploited and corrupted his innocence, even made Julian believe he deserved to be abused. Maybe if Luke and Candace had invited Julian into their circle, he wouldn't have been such an easy victim.

Julian became aware of Iris wincing and flexing her hand inside his, and realized he'd clamped his fingers and hurt her. He loosened his grip and said "Sorry" under his breath. Then, to Luke, he said, "It was a long time ago and we were kids."

"I wasn't fair to Forbes either," Luke said. "I loved my father and no one was going to take his place in my heart. So I shut Forbes out."

"I shut Sonia out because she came between me and my dad."

"Jesus." Luke shook his head, his dark auburn hair catching the light, matching the cherry hardwood on the floor. "What a messed-up pair we were. Thank God we finally grew up."

"You're both wonderful men," Iris said quietly but with certainty.

Julian tensed. She didn't know the rottenness at his core.

She shot him a questioning glance and then addressed the group. "I wonder if we could switch the topic of conversation? I'd love an update on the wedding plans. It must be such a challenge, getting married between Christmas and New Year's."

She'd done that for him. Changed the subject without having a clue why the previous one had upset him. Iris was the most sensitive, considerate person he'd ever met. He sure was going to miss her in the New Year, when Forbes was better and Julian got back to his normal life.

Chapter Nine

When Iris and the other guests said thank you and good night to Miranda and Luke and sprinted to their vehicles in the rain, it was just past nine thirty. Julian helped her up into the van, then hurried to the other side and climbed in, shaking raindrops from his hair.

"My aunt will be home from work," she told him. Aunt Lily would be unwinding after a long day, enjoying her alone time.

"Meaning you want me to meet her, or you're not going to ask me in?"

Iris didn't want to inflict company on her aunt, nor to force Julian into polite conversation with her. His and Luke's talk seemed to have brought them closer, yet she sensed it had been stressful for Julian.

"It's not that I don't want you to meet her. Or my parents," she said as he backed out of Luke's driveway. "I'm proud that you're my friend. But we've spent the evening with others and now I'd prefer to be alone with you." She hurried to add, "Unless of course you're tired and want to go home, in which case you can drop me off and—"

"Iris, stop. No, I'm not tired. I'm a night person like most musicians. And yes, I'd like some time for just us."

128   *Susan Fox*

"Good," she murmured happily. A CD was playing, the volume so low she could barely hear over the rhythmic slap of the windshield wipers. Recognizing the old Beatles song, "Here Comes the Sun," she nudged the dial up. Gesturing toward the player, she said, "Perhaps in metaphorical terms, but not in meteorological ones, I fear."

"I'd say that being with you makes the sun come out for me, but the lyricist in me cringes at the cheesiness."

"God forbid you ever say anything cheesy," she teased.

"Forbes and Sonia are home, but we could go to the studio he built. It's half of the original garage. Though if they notice the van, Sonia might come over to check on me."

"Did you tell them what you were doing tonight?"

"You're wondering if they know I'm seeing you."

"I am." She'd been in Sonia's science classes in high school and had seen her regularly since then, in Dreamspinner. Forbes, she ran into every now and then, mostly when he was in shopping for gifts.

"Seems it's a small island. Yeah, they know. They didn't say much, just that you're a nice person. Subtext, as with Luke, to treat you properly."

Which he would. She was sure of it.

"Thanks again for the mystery novel," he said. "And getting the personalized autograph for Forbes."

"I was happy to." Outside the van's windows, Tsehum Drive was quiet on this rainy Friday night, the darkness brightened by the occasional blurred color of Christmas lights strung around eaves, windows, and trees in yards. A residential street, the homes ranged from old ones that were barely more than shacks, through to even fancier ones than Luke's. "We don't have to go anywhere in particular," she said. "We could just drive. The island's peaceful at night."

"Okay." After a moment, he said, "You enjoyed tonight? It wasn't too hard on you?"

Yes, Julian would treat her properly. She glanced at him,

glad to see that his gaze was fixed on the road. The lighting wasn't good, and nocturnal creatures, not to mention human beings, might be wandering around. She guessed Julian, whose father had been struck by an impaired driver, was well aware of that.

"I did enjoy it," she said, "and it was good for me. I've almost never done that, spent a social evening with a group of friends. I do belong to a book club, with island writers, retired English teachers, and so on, but our discussions focus on the books. They aren't personal."

"You seemed a little stressed when we first got to Luke's place, but you handled it."

"The anxiety manifests physically. My heart races, I have trouble catching my breath, that kind of thing. I try not to let it control me."

He swallowed audibly, suggesting that he identified. Perhaps he was thinking of his interviews with the media. "But isn't it hard for *you* to control *it*?"

"It is if I try too hard. Which sounds backward, but it's true. When I focus internally, on my stress reaction and my desire to control it, I get more upset."

"What's the better approach? To focus on other people, like you do when you think about customers and their needs?"

"Partly. But also to breathe deeply and acknowledge the stress, experience it, accept it."

"You lost me. Isn't the point to avoid experiencing a panic attack?"

"When I simply breathe and accept it, then I'm calm enough that my brain and common sense can kick in and I understand that the anxiety is unwarranted. Then its strength diminishes. It's kind of a Zen thing."

"Hmm. When you recommended that book for me, I thought maybe you were, uh, Taoist. Is that the term? Now I'm wondering if you're Buddhist."

"I'm neither but maybe both." She gave a soft laugh. "That sounds like something from Pooh's 'Cottleston Pie' song, doesn't it?"

"The song about how a bird can fly but a fly can't bird."

"Right. Which, the Tao book points out, is about inner nature. My inner nature is to not practice a formal religion but to have my own kind of—I don't know what to call it— constantly developing spirituality, maybe?"

"I've never been sure what spirituality means."

"I think of it as an awareness of ourselves as one small part of the universe, and a way of trying to understand our part. Of trying to be a good person, a person who does no harm and who contributes something worthwhile." She did a fair job of the first part, and she did help people at the bookstore, but anxiety kept her from participating in activities like volunteer work.

"If that's spirituality, then I wish more people had it," he said grimly.

Oh no, that wasn't the mood she wanted, for this brief time together. "Are we just wandering wherever the road takes us," she asked, "which perhaps would be the Taoist way, or do you have a route in mind?"

"I have a destination in mind. Not as scenic as an ocean view, but it's secluded, the mood's mellow, and I know you like it."

"The old commune? I've never thought of going there at night." But now, imagining that peaceful spot, with rain-drops pattering on worn-out grass, she was intrigued. "Good idea."

They drove past Quail Ridge Community Hall, its out-side lights blazing, the parking lot almost full. Even through the closed windows of the van, she heard a pulsating rhythm. Live music, as was often the case on weekends. Local groups played, from the chamber music quartet to country-and-western bands to Julian's father's group. Off-island bands came too, mostly from the other Gulf Islands, Vancouver Island, and the Lower Mainland.

"You're amazing onstage," she said. "I've listened to your music for years, seen some videos online, but it's nothing like in person. There's a whole different energy. That's why you love doing it, isn't it?"

"It's a high."

Curious, but not wanting to pry, she said, "Speaking of highs . . . I hear that for some musicians, drugs are part of the lifestyle."

"Not for me, nor my band. Well, Andi tokes up from time to time, and Roy occasionally, but no hard drugs. We respect the music too much."

"How do you mean? Don't some artistic people say drugs make them more creative?"

"And maybe that's true, sometimes. But it's playing with fire. Drugs, especially the ones on the street these days, are too damned dangerous. Even if you don't end up killing yourself, you can mess up your health, your brain, your creativity. Not to mention, drugs distort your perceptions, take away your control . . ."

His voice trailed off and she sensed he was reflecting, that there was more he might say, so she kept quiet. The CD was playing Joni Mitchell's "The Circle Game." Julian had said Forbes had made mixtape CDs, and Julian's favorites were from the sixties and seventies.

After a few moments, he said slowly, "I think often people take drugs or drink too much because they want to shut down their brains, to escape from pain, fear, whatever bad shit's in there. But when they sober up, the shit's still there. So, more drugs and drink, and in the end they kill themselves and maybe that's what they really wanted all along."

She guessed he wasn't speaking hypothetically. He had some bad stuff in his own head.

He shrugged, a slow, weighty shrug as if he were lifting a physical burden and then releasing it. When he spoke again, his tone was lighter. "Anyhow, my muse doesn't like marijuana, nor too much booze, so that's that."

"You have to honor your muse." Thank God he did, or Julian and his gift might have been lost to the world.

"If I look after her, she looks after me."

"Why is your muse a *she*?"

"I dunno. She just is." Watching his profile, she saw his lips curve. "Because women are the smart ones?" he said. "The perceptive, sensitive ones?"

"I think you're plenty smart, perceptive, and sensitive. As a musician and as a person."

He put his foot on the brake, steered the van to the shoulder of the road, and stopped. Leaving the engine running, he turned to her. "Iris, you're a bright spot in my life. In a life that right now could sure use one."

It was dark out here in the country with no streetlights or holiday decorations, so she could barely see his face much less make out the expression in his eyes. But she did hear the sincerity in his voice and it touched her heart.

She rested her hand lightly on his jacket-clad sleeve and, choosing her words carefully, said, "I'm sorry your life is rough right now. I know you're worried about Forbes, and I think you also have troubles that run deeper than that. I'll honor your privacy and not push, but please know that if you ever want to talk about those troubles, I would be happy to listen. I may not be able to help, but sometimes just talking, knowing you're understood, can help."

He put his hand on top of hers. "Thanks for that. You're a good friend. But I'm okay, honest. Like everyone, I tote some baggage and every now and then it drags at my ankles. But I'd rather not think, much less talk, about it."

Dragging at his ankles sounded like chains binding him, but he'd made it clear he wanted to keep his secrets. "You could be a Yakimura. We're reserved with regard to what we share."

He got the van back on the road. "Have you told them you're seeing me?"

"Mom saw us when we drove through the village on the way back from the marina."

"Are they hassling you? I'm not most parents' idea of good company for their daughter."

"*Hassling* isn't the Yakimura way. They're more into lectures about what's appropriate behavior and what isn't."

He snorted. "I doubt you've given them much cause for those lectures."

She smiled ruefully. "No. They made themselves clear when they raised me, and what they said made sense. Also, as I'm rather sad to say, life hasn't presented me with many opportunities to rebel. I'm not the person who gets invited on wild adventures."

"Do you crave wild adventures, Iris?"

"To be honest, no, not so much. There's a part of me that wishes I was more adventuresome. When I was a girl, I loved the *Anne of Green Gables* books. She was a spunky child and a part of me longed to be like her, but she was always getting in trouble, while I hate to disappoint people. Anyhow, I realized it's pointless for a tortoise to wish to be a hare rather than enjoying the benefits of being a tortoise. A ridiculous waste of time and of longing."

"Respect your inner nature, right?" He glanced over. "If it counts for anything, I like you just the way you are."

Touched, she said, "It counts for a lot, Julian. Thank you."

"You neatly avoided my question. How do your parents feel about our friendship?"

"They have some concerns, but it's their nature to worry about me. They and Aunt Lily would like to meet you, but that's up to you. You have enough to deal with."

Julian peered through the windshield. "Can you see

where the track to the commune cuts off? In the dark and the rain, I'm afraid I'll miss it."

She squinted, looking for something familiar. "See that big oak tree? Turn just after that."

As he followed her instructions, he said, "If it's important to you that I meet them, then I will. I don't know that there's anything I can do to make them approve of me, though."

"I wouldn't want you to do anything other than be yourself. They'll see the truth about you, as I do."

God, no, the last thing he wanted was for anyone to see the truth at his core.

The headlights barely picked out the almost nonexistent track into the commune, and Julian drove the van at a tortoise crawl. To change the subject, he said, "Forbes and I have had a lot of time to talk. He was telling me about being twenty in Haight-Ashbury, and I finally told him I'd been coming to this place for years. I asked him what he remembered about the commune, and why he didn't stay long."

"What did he say?"

"That it was great for some people but didn't suit others. The leader was one of those charismatic types, and most of the kids worshipped him. Forbes said the guy used that to manipulate them. It pissed him off." Julian pulled to a stop. He turned off the headlights and engine, but left the parking lights on, providing a tiny bit of illumination against the dark, rainy night. "Music on or off?"

"You can even ask?" John Lennon's "Imagine" was playing. "That song should never be turned off. Forbes's mixtape suits the place. The hippies would have played the older songs."

"Yes. Forbes says 'Imagine' was one of the anthems

for him and his friends. A dream that, sadly, has yet to be realized." Because too few people shared Iris's brand of spirituality.

"I know." She sighed. "What happened to the commune anyway? Did the kids grow up and drift away? Does Forbes know?"

"The leader left. The hippies wanted to keep the place going, but no other leader emerged. They couldn't agree on how to run it, so it fell apart. Most of the hippies left, but a few stayed on in Destiny."

If it were summer, Julian would have opened the windows and they might have heard tree frogs—or the laughter of ghost hippies—to accompany his dad's music. But the rain worked, too, a gentle percussive thrum on the roof, a shower-like curtain cocooning them together.

"That's kind of sad," Iris said. "But at least they had that amazing time in their lives, and the lessons they learned from it."

The old van had one feature that he particularly valued tonight: a front bench seat. He slid from behind the steering wheel and put his arm around Iris's shoulders. As she nestled against him, he said, "I feel like we should apologize to the ghosts for disturbing their slumber."

"They won't mind. They know we come in peace."

Her hair felt like satin as he leaned his cheek against the top of her head. Peace. Yes, that was what he felt, being here with her like this. "You seem attuned to the hippies. But if you'd grown up in the sixties, you wouldn't have run off and joined a commune, would you?"

Her wind-chime laugh tinkled. "No. Rebellion isn't in my nature. Though I can relate to their desire for freedom from societal rules that made no sense to them."

He breathed deeply to catch the slight almond scent from her hair, which for some reason made him envision the delicate, blush-pink blossoms on ornamental plum trees in the spring. "You'd like more freedom?"

"It's why I come to the commune and I go sailing. My life is, for the most part, quite ordered. While I think structure is important, so is simply lying in the grass and gazing up at the sky, or letting the power of the wind take *Windspinner* skimming through the waves." She cuddled closer. "It's about balance, and generally I find a balance that pleases me."

"Hmm. You said you're twenty-four, Iris?"

"Almost twenty-five. Why do you ask?"

"You seem particularly mature. Wise."

"Oh, well . . . Thank you."

He'd bet her pale cheeks had flushed with that spring-blossom pink.

"I still have so much to learn," she said. "But what else is life for, if not to keep learning?"

"That sounds right to me." He slid his fingers through her hair, the strands like smooth water flowing around his fingers yet not wetting them. "You haven't asked how old I am."

"You were three years ahead of me in school, so I'd guess twenty-seven. Though you, too, seem more mature than your years." Humor touched her voice when she went on. "Or at least your music does, so maybe it's your muse who's mature."

Liking that she was comfortable enough with him to tease, he said, "It's definitely her. I'm twenty-seven. And you have a birthday soon?"

"Can you believe, New Year's Eve? My parents hoped I'd be the first baby born in the New Year, but, for probably the only time in my life, I was impatient to make my entrance."

"That must be almost as bad as being born on Christmas Day."

"Our family celebrates the New Year on January first, and I get New Year's Eve for my own. We go out for dinner to C-Shell. I suppose New Year's Eve is a lot more exciting in your musician's world."

"Usually we're performing. This year there's a gig in Vancouver at the Commodore."

"Oh." That quiet sound was barely audible above the gentle percussion of rain on the roof, yet it seemed to hang in the air for a long moment. Then Iris said, "Will Forbes be well enough by then so that he and Sonia won't need you?"

"I sure hope so. He's making progress, but it's slow. Painful. He's still determined to play at Luke and Miranda's wedding. I'll hang around for the wedding, of course, then get back to Vancouver for the gig. And to start working with the band to fine-tune the new songs I'm writing. We're scheduled to record the new album at the end of January, and in February we're touring in Australia."

She nodded, her hair brushing his chin. "I'm sure you'll be glad to get back to your normal life."

"Yeah, kind of." Music was his life, and he hated even breathing the same air as Bart Jelinek. Yet he enjoyed spending long hours with his dad and getting to know Sonia better, as well as Luke, Miranda, and the kids. And he loved being with Iris. "But I'll miss you."

Again she nodded. "I'll miss you, too."

They were quiet for a bit, gazing out the windshield even though there was nothing to see but the steady rain, a hazy gold in the light cast by the parking lights. "There was a song we'd just got started on," he murmured. "It could use a second verse."

"I like the sound of that."

He slid his hand up under that raven waterfall of hair and fanned his fingers to cradle the back of her head. She leaned forward with no urging, her lips parting. He kissed her, molding his lips to hers, marveling that anything could feel so soft, warm, and welcoming.

Often when he'd had sex, it had been with a fan, a woman who was excited to hook up with a musician, who was eager, even aggressive. It wasn't about him as a person, because he hadn't let people know much about him, just the filtered information he provided to the media and on social media.

Iris made no bones about being a fan, but she also cared about him. About the man, not just the performer. As he explored and savored her sweet, giving mouth, it dawned on him that in the entire world, this was the person who knew him best. Oh, she didn't know the details of his childhood as his dad did, nor the experiences of his musician life— she certainly didn't know how flawed he was—but he'd revealed more of his true self to her than to anyone.

Would he even have survived being here on Destiny if Iris hadn't been here for him?

He poured his gratitude and his affection into her through his lips and tongue, conveyed it in the brush of his fingertips against her cheek and the delicate shell of her ear. She was so perfect, in so many ways.

Arousal licked through his veins, stole his breath, swelled his cock. His response to her was bittersweet, wanting her more than he'd ever wanted another woman yet knowing he should never make love with her. Her perfection deserved a man who was special, a man who would fulfill her happy, secure, island-based romantic dream, not a shameful coward.

Our song. That was what they were creating now, line by line, with both of them knowing that the song would end in sadness when they had to part ways.

Mostly, he wrote sad songs, poignant ones about loss, fear, guilt. Rarely did they have a "and then the sun came out and everything was wonderful" ending. What he conveyed was reality, that the best you could hope for was coming to terms with your sorrows and achieving a certain peace. Iris knew that. She knew his music and she knew the inevitability of their parting. Didn't she? He rested his hands on her shoulders and eased her away from him.

Even in the dim light, he could see she looked dazed. But she blinked those long lashes and then smiled. "A lovely verse. Does it have to end now?"

Hating to break the mood, he said, "I need to be sure. Sure you don't want more from me than I can give."

Under his hands, her shoulders straightened. "I think you have a lot to give, Julian. But if you mean, am I envisioning a romance-novel ending, no, definitely not. I'm practical and I know our lives could never mesh. But I believe in mindfulness, in fully enjoying the present."

"You mean without considering the future?" That didn't sound practical.

"With an awareness of it, but without letting it spoil the present." She tilted her head, studying him. "In fact, that awareness can make the present even sweeter."

"It can?"

"Like when my grandmother had ALS. We knew her health would deteriorate and eventually she would die. That knowledge turned every moment together into a blessing to be enjoyed to the fullest."

He shook his head wonderingly. "How did you get to be so wise? The things you say make so much sense, yet most people don't think the way you do."

She shrugged. "I like my way. I can throw myself into enjoying each verse, each line, each word of our song as we create it together, and not agonize over the fact that, after the end of the year, I may never see you again."

"No." The word jumped from his lips. "I don't accept that we won't see each other again." It was inconceivable to not have Iris in his life. Feeling almost desperate, he tightened his grip on her shoulders. "We'll stay friends, Iris. Please say we will."

Her eyes widened and her lips trembled into a smile. "I'd like that. I feel as if we're growing close, and I'd hate to lose that."

"So we'll email, Skype, whatever, and when I visit the island, we'll see each other."

"Yes," she said, the simple word calming his anxiety.

He released his tight grip and stroked his hands down her back. "I think I may be visiting Destiny more often. There are more incentives now. You, of course. But also I have a stronger connection to my family."

These weeks had taught him that he could survive for more than a couple of days on Destiny. He wouldn't let his own guilt over Jelinek prevent him from spending more time with the people he cared about. It was progress of a sort.

And with that in mind, he said, "Shall we compose a third verse?"

Chapter Ten

The next Tuesday, Iris was in the office at Dreamspinner, doing a final proofread of their Christmas sale flyer, when her mom popped her head through the doorway. "Eden and Miranda are here, hoping you're free for lunch."

That was no big surprise. Since Friday's dinner, Iris had been expecting at least phone calls from her friends. It seemed they had chosen to conduct the "debriefing" in person. "Is that alright? I can finish proofreading after."

"Of course. Have fun." Her mother's answer was no surprise either. Akemi Yakimura loved seeing her daughter socialize.

Iris collected her tan leather jacket from the small closet and went to find her friends, who were perusing the holiday display of coffee-table books. Eden, a lawyer who worked at a seniors' residential facility, wore a tailored pantsuit in a shade of olive green that went nicely with her walnut hair. Miranda, a blue-eyed blonde who worked at Blowing Bubbles, the children's store in the village, was clad in jeans, a blue cotton turtleneck, and a rain jacket that had seen better days. Iris knew she bought most of her clothes at thrift shops. Even though Miranda had received an advance on an inheritance, her spending habits remained frugal.

After Iris's old BFF, Shelley, married and moved to Kelowna, she'd missed having a close friend to get together with. Then Eden and Miranda had arrived on Destiny. Iris felt grateful to have both of them in her life. Even if today's lunch conversation might be more personal than she was comfortable with. "You decided to kill one bird with two stones?" she joked.

"We're being efficient." Eden's amber eyes twinkled. "You know I value efficiency."

The lawyer was not only smart but organized, focused, and persistent. She was also warmhearted and would do anything for family or friends. Miranda was more spontaneous, but an equally kind, generous person.

"Did you drive in from Arbutus Lodge just to interrogate me?" Iris asked Eden.

"Don't flatter yourself." The twinkle was still there. "I had other business in the village."

"Which she deliberately arranged"—Miranda elbowed Eden—"to give her an excuse to have lunch with us."

It warmed Iris's heart to see the two of them getting along so well. Initially, Miranda had resented her brother's girlfriend, and feared Aaron might move to Ottawa to be with her. But since Eden and her family had instead moved to Destiny, the women were becoming true sisters.

"Well, perhaps," Eden admitted. "So let's celebrate and go to C-Shell. My treat."

"Yes to C-Shell," Miranda said. "No to you footing the bill. I actually do have money now, remember?"

"Then you can pay next time," Eden said.

"And I'll pay the time after that," Iris put in.

C-Shell, operated by Rachelle, a native Destiny Islander, and her wife, Celia, a talented chef, not only had the best food in town but was right on Blue Moon Harbor, with a spectacular view. Conveniently, it was only half a block from Dreamspinner. Not that anything in the village proper was more than three blocks away.

It was brisk out, so they walked quickly, their footsteps matching the rhythm of the cheerful Celtic fiddle music that drifted down the street. Colm, a twenty-something local man, was hanging out in a store doorway, playing. He was talented, and a sizable pile of coins always collected in his instrument case. Iris had to wonder whether, if he hadn't had mental health challenges and had to live with his parents, he might have followed a career path like that of Andi, Julian's bandmate.

The rustically attractive shake front of C-Shell beckoned, and Iris and her friends went inside. Rachelle, who'd been a few years ahead of Iris at school, greeted them warmly. She was stunning, her beautifully styled black blouse and pants an unobtrusive setting for her striking, dark chocolate complexion and her mass of black hair, intricately braided with colored beads. "The ladies are lunching," she said approvingly. "A quiet table where you can chat without being interrupted?"

"That sounds perfect," Eden said, and Iris nodded in agreement.

Rachelle led them across the dining room, only a third full at the beginning of the lunch hour, to an end table by the window where a pillar and a couple of plants offered semi-seclusion. The restaurant décor appealed to Iris, with its simplicity and the authentic nautical touches provided by Rachelle's father, a commercial fisher. The wooden walls and tables suited Destiny's ambience and the large windows gave a light, spacious feel. Rachelle and Celia had added plants, local art, and sprigs of fall blossoms and leaves on each table, bringing beauty and nature into the room without making it cluttered.

As always, Iris took a seat with her back toward most of

the room. Miranda and Eden both chose to sit across from her. *The better to interrogate you, my dear*.

Rachelle said, "Today's special is seafood gumbo."

"Yes," Miranda said, without opening the menu.

"That does sound wonderful," Eden agreed.

"Make it three, please," Iris added.

Rachelle grinned. "You ladies are too easy. Now, what about drinks? Miranda, I know you love the C-Shell cocktail. Eden, Iris, a glass of wine perhaps?"

"Don't tempt me," Eden said. "I'm driving. And working today."

Iris and Miranda also turned down alcohol and they agreed to share a pitcher of fresh-squeezed lemonade.

When Rachelle had departed, Iris, knowing there'd be no avoiding the debriefing, opened the subject. "Thanks again for dinner, Miranda. It was a lovely evening."

Not even bothering with a "you're welcome," Miranda went straight to the point. "You and Julian have a *thing*."

Iris raised her eyebrows and tried not to blush. She hadn't seen Julian since he dropped her at her condo Friday night, because he'd spent every spare moment rehearsing with Forbes's bandmates in preparation for Jane and George Nelson's sixtieth wedding anniversary on Saturday. All the same, he had inhabited her thoughts: his sensitivity, his shadowed secrets, the sensual "verses" they'd been creating for the song of Iris and Julian.

It had surprised her on Friday when he'd stopped kissing her to make sure she understood they weren't building toward a romantic future. As a longtime admirer of his music, she knew Julian didn't write songs with happy endings. Many things in life didn't end ideally, but that was no reason to not revel in the process. Being listened to by a man, being respected, and being kissed the way he kissed her were firsts for her, and very much things to revel in.

"Well?" Miranda demanded.

Iris gave her head a small shake to clear it, and focused on her friend. "I didn't hear a question. And I don't know what you mean by a *thing*."

"A connection. An intimacy. Are you sleeping with him?"

"No!" The exclamation came out too loud, and Iris pressed her fingers to her cheeks. More quietly, she said, "No, we're not. I've only known him a couple of weeks." Though her fingertips felt the heat of embarrassment, she couldn't resist going on. "You sense an intimacy?" Iris knew it was there, but hadn't realized others would notice. "How do you mean?"

It was Eden who spoke this time. "Like between two people who know each other well and care about each other."

"We're friends."

"It's more than what she said," Miranda said. "There's sex, too. Well, maybe not actual sex but sexual chemistry. Don't deny it. I know these things."

Eden shot her an amused look, but didn't contradict her.

"Alright, yes, there's attraction, and—" Iris broke off and lowered her hands from her cheeks as Ellen, one of the C-Shell servers, brought their lemonade and poured three glasses. A middle-aged woman clad in the restaurant's classic black, she wore her blond hair in a thick braid, and moved with professional competence.

When Ellen left, Iris continued, still feeling embarrassed but also a little proud. "And there's caring. The caring of one friend for another. I know it may seem odd to you that a man like Julian would care for a woman like me, but I really believe he does."

"It's not odd that a man would care for you," Eden said.

Miranda nodded vigorously. "You're terrific. And he does." She stopped, wrinkling her nose. "Well, it seems to me he does, but up until Luke, I was actually pretty terrible about distinguishing lust from genuine caring."

"Julian cares," Eden said firmly. "And I can see there's more to him than what I thought when I first saw him."

"Which was?" Miranda asked.

Eden smirked. "A tarnished angel who's playing-with-fire hot."

Miranda laughed. "Yeah, that's good."

A tarnished angel. What an interesting perception. "So far," Iris said dryly, "I've managed not to burn my fingers."

"*So far*," Eden echoed. "I'm glad, but, Iris, where's your relationship heading?"

"Um, into a developing friendship?" she responded.

"Friends with benefits?" Miranda asked.

Iris pressed her lips together. She knew perfectly well what her friend meant, but she wouldn't make this easy for her. "Our friendship has many benefits," she said quietly.

Eden, who was sipping lemonade, almost choked. She coughed a couple of times, her eyes dancing with laughter. But then the sparkle faded and when she found her voice, she said, "Iris, you're wonderful and I believe there's more to Julian than his public image. He seems like a good guy. But I'm worried about you." She reached across the table to touch Iris's hand, a quick, affectionate brush of fingers. "You're not exactly the most experienced at dating. And rather than dip your toes in the water with some nice local man who has a lot in common with you, you've dived off the high board."

"Doing a back flip and some of those fancy twisty things on the way," Miranda added.

"Meaning that Julian's out of my league. Not just in terms of experience, but the fact that he is, to use Miranda's term, a *rock star*. The odd thing is, when we're together, he seems like a . . . well, a special guy but a normal one."

"That's true," Eden said. "I was expecting him to act like, well, a celebrity, but he does seem pretty normal. All the same, I wonder if you've truly considered the pros and cons of your relationship."

Iris and Miranda exchanged eye-rolls. Analytical Eden was fond of her pro and con lists.

Iris believed in considering potential consequences, but as she'd discussed with Julian, she was more Zen or Taoist in her decision-making, opening herself to sensing what the universe intended for her. "In a general way. But a pro and con list sounds so cold-blooded."

"Emotion and intuition come into it as well," Eden said. "But a list helps you focus."

Wanting to oblige her friend, and curious whether she would learn anything useful, Iris said, "Well then, I think the cons can probably all be combined into one overarching one. Julian is a celebrity with a totally different life than mine, and when his father's better, Julian will return to that life and I will stay here. And it will hurt."

Eden and Miranda nodded. "And doesn't that—" Eden started, but stopped while Ellen served three substantial bowls of spicy, fragrant gumbo, and set down a wooden board with a mini-loaf of cornbread and a ceramic container holding butter.

The server told them to enjoy and waited while they all dipped into the soup and exclaimed with pleasure. Iris enjoyed seafood cooked in almost any fashion, and this rich, hearty stew was especially perfect, counteracting the overcast sky outside the window.

After Ellen had gone, the three of them sliced cornbread, buttered it, and ate for a few minutes. Then Eden said, "You seem to believe it's inevitable that you and Julian will part company, and that he'll hurt you."

"No." Iris didn't like contradicting people, but this time she had to. "He won't hurt me. Julian wouldn't do that." She ignored the concerned looks her friends exchanged, suggesting they found her hopelessly naïve. Maybe it was true, but she believed in Julian and the honesty of what they shared. "His leaving isn't something he'll do *to* me, it's simply the inevitability of him returning to his real life."

"And is it so inevitable that you couldn't be a part of that life?" Eden asked.

"I stressed out for four years when I attended UVic, just experiencing a quiet, student life. Can you imagine me on the road with Julian, by his side as fans and reporters mob him and shoot videos?" She shuddered at the thought. "That's not who I am. People can change, of course. Our lives should involve continual growth and improvement. But at heart we have a basic nature. Julian's and mine simply aren't compatible." And yet, as she said that, she thought of the deeply resonant ways in which they did connect. "Or at least," she corrected herself, "not compatible in the ways that would allow for our lives to merge together."

Miranda leaned forward, her elbows on the table. "So why are you doing this, Iris? I mean, I've had plenty of relationships with crappy endings and I've cried lots of tears. But when I got into those relationships, I believed in them. If you know you're going to be hurt, wouldn't the smart thing be to opt out now?"

Iris smoothed back a wisp of hair that had escaped the neat coil at the back of her head. "Pain's part of life, Miranda. It's not such a bad thing to hurt. It makes us more appreciative of the joys in life."

Miranda frowned. "Maybe. But crying sucks. Heartache sucks."

"Maybe it sucks a little less when you know it's coming," Iris suggested. No, she didn't want to think about missing Julian, about lying in her lonely bed and shedding tears. But if that was the price of being with him now, she'd gladly do it. "So I should feel miserable now, knowing that I'll feel miserable later as well, after he leaves? That strikes me as silly. Better to be happy now, enjoying the moments we have together, treasuring each one even more because in a couple of months we'll be apart."

Eden's forehead had scrunched up the way it did when she was puzzled or thinking hard. "You make it sound easy."

Iris smiled. "Making things easy seems to me far better than making them difficult."

"If you can actually do it," Miranda said. "And kudos to you if you can."

Iris turned her smile on the blonde. "You do it, too."

"Nah, I don't think so."

"Sure. Ariana will grow up, eventually she'll move away from home, who knows what her life may bring? But when you're with her, you don't waste time agonizing over all that. You simply enjoy her."

Now Miranda was frowning, too. "That's true. But it doesn't seem the same." She rubbed her temple. "You confuse me, Iris."

"Is that a bad thing? Making you think about life differently?"

"Would you come to Arbutus Lodge, Iris?" Eden said.

"Now there's a change of topic," Iris responded, lowering her soupspoon.

"I think some of our residents would enjoy hearing your perspective. You might enjoy talking to them, too."

"I love seniors. They have so much life experience and wisdom." But tension rose in her body. She breathed in deeply, and out again, feeling her anxiety and accepting it. "But I can't imagine sitting around talking with a group of people."

"You do it with your book club," Eden pointed out.

Her book club had met last night, in fact. "We talk about books. I'm good at that."

"Seniors read. Why not choose one or two books you think might interest them?" Eden suggested. "Ones that deal with the same kind of philosophy you've been sharing with us."

Maybe the same books she'd convinced Julian to buy . . . Could she handle this?

"I think some of the seniors would really benefit," Eden said.

Iris thought of what she'd told Julian, about spirituality and the desire to do good in the world. How could she be so selfish as to focus on her own anxiety rather than on the needs of her elders? Besides, she would no doubt learn more from them than they could possibly learn from her. "So we could structure it like a book club discussion," she said, thinking it through. "I'd relax more if we started out talking about the book, with everyone joining in. Then, if the themes in the book resonated with them, we could move into a broader discussion of their personal experiences and their opinions on issues that are relevant to them."

The seniors would enjoy the Pooh stories, which most would remember reading to kids and grandkids. And *The Tao of Pooh* could lead to discussing any number of topics, like aging, illness, the loss of loved ones, or contemplating the future.

"Maybe your aunt or one of your parents could participate, too," Miranda suggested. "That would make you feel more comfortable, right?"

"It would." As with her and Aunt Lily's prospective trip to Japan. "I promise to think seriously about it." She dipped a chunk of cornbread into the spicy gumbo.

"Iris," Eden said gently, "lots of people get anxious in

certain situations. Fear is natural. Fear of new experiences, of pushing yourself, of what people will think of you. But you don't have to let it hold you back."

Eden seemed like such a confident person. "Have you ever been afraid of doing something new?" Iris asked.

"Moot court in law school," she answered promptly.

"What's that?" Miranda asked.

"A mock trial. We had to prepare cases and present them in front of real judges who volunteered their time. I was terrified. Not of the prep part, I had that down cold. But I'd never done any public speaking, and to have my first experience in front of a real live judge . . ." She shuddered. "I had to do it in order to graduate. So, though I barely slept for nights before, and I threw up that morning, I managed. Not well, but I got through it. And it got easier."

"Food for thought, Iris," Miranda said. "Right?"

"Yes, it is."

"Great," Miranda said. "Now, back to our previous topic. Intimacy." Her grayish-blue eyes sparked with mischief. "Of the physical sort. Specifically, between you and Julian. Yeah, you haven't known him long, and you're the opposite of slutty, but the guy's hot. Seems like it'd be a pity to not check out all the *benefits* of being his buddy."

Though Iris's instinct toward privacy made her squirm, this was a novelty, being the center of interest in a guys-and-sex conversation with two girlfriends. "I admit the thought has occurred to me," she confessed. "Yes, he's hot, and he's also really nice, and here I am, almost twenty-five and my knowledge of sex comes from books." She glanced at Eden. "I assume Miranda told you I'm a virgin?"

"I suspected you were," Eden said, diplomatically not answering the question. "It seemed in character. Though I wouldn't have said dating Julian was in character."

"We're not dating. To me, dating means moving toward a future together, or at least considering that possibility."

"Yeah, I get that," Miranda agreed. "So d'you figure you'd only go all the way with a guy you're seriously dating, or are you waiting for marriage?"

"I would definitely want to ensure my mate and I were sexually compatible before I'd contemplate a lifetime commitment. As for whether we'd need to be seriously dating . . . I'm not sure. The subject—the possibility—has never come up." It hadn't yet with Julian and her, but in verse three he had lifted the bottom of her blouse and caressed her bare back, and she'd dared to unbutton a couple of buttons of his shirt and press her cheek against his hard, warm chest. Being with Julian was so sensual and sexy. A few more verses, and who knew where their song might lead?

"I kind of wish I'd been a virgin when I met Aaron," Eden said. "It would have been so special if he was my first." Quickly, she went on. "Though the fact that I'd had sex before meeting him makes me realize how truly wonderful it is with him. What I do regret is having wasted my virginity on a boy I didn't love. We were in twelfth grade and we'd gone out for a while, and he really wanted to and I was curious. It didn't seem like a big deal, so we did it. And no, it wasn't a big deal. Sadly. We repeated the experience and I hoped it would get better, and the physical part kind of did but it still felt flat. So I broke up with him."

That did seem like a waste. Iris had always hoped her own first time would be special, physically and emotionally.

"Ha," Miranda said. "For once slutty me has a better story than good-girl you, Eden. I was fifteen, the first time. And I did love the guy. He was the musician in Vancouver, the one I fell for and left the island to move in with. The sex was pretty good for kids our age, and my heart was really into it." She wrinkled her nose. "Of course it turned out my heart had lousy judgment and the guy was a loser, but when I lost my virginity, it was with love."

"It seems," Iris said slowly, "it's rare for the first time to be with someone you love, who also loves you."

Eden cocked her head. "Maybe that's too much to ask for. But if there's a lesson to be learned from Miranda's and my experience, perhaps it's that it's important to be sure you know what you want, the man respects you, and you won't have regrets after."

Julian respected her. The more time she spent with him, the more she wanted him—in all possible ways. A future together wasn't possible, but intercourse was. If she lost her virginity to him, would she regret it after he was gone? Or when the true love of her life finally came along?

If that man did ever come along . . .

No, she'd think positive thoughts. Visiting Japan at the age of twenty-five had worked for her dad and granddad, so maybe it would for her. If not, there was still loads of time.

Iris sliced the remaining cornbread into three chunks, took one, and mopped up the remains of her gumbo. Eden and Miranda did the same, and when they'd all finished, Ellen stopped at their table to collect the empty bowls.

"Tell Celia we totally hated the soup," Miranda joked.

"I'll be sure to," Ellen said. "Dessert or coffee, ladies?"

"Wish I could," Eden said, "but I need to get back to work."

"Me too," Iris said.

"Me three," Miranda agreed.

Ellen left the bill on the table and as Eden pulled out her wallet, Miranda said, "Oh damn, please don't let him come over. Nope, of course he will."

Iris, with her back to the room, didn't know who Miranda was talking about. Tension tightened her muscles.

A moment later, Bart Jelinek's voice boomed, "Three lovely ladies, hidden away behind a pillar. Now I call that a true shame."

Iris swallowed and forced a smile as the Realtor came up to their table, though as usual she had trouble meeting his gaze. A glance up from under her eyelashes told her he was dressed as usual in business casual attire: nice but not dressy pants, a sports jacket, and a tie. The gray streaks in his blondish hair, and the tortoiseshell horn-rims gave him a somewhat professorial air, but that impression was counteracted by his broad smile. That smile seemed to live on the man's face almost like a painted-on mask. She had no reason to believe he wasn't sincere, yet his heartiness exacerbated her reticence.

"Hello, Bart," Eden said.

Miranda echoed the greeting, her tone unusually flat.

Iris murmured, "Hello."

"It's nice to see all of you," he said jovially, "although I confess you disappoint me."

"How so?" Eden asked a little warily.

"Here I'd hoped you would move to Destiny Island and buy a house, Eden, but instead you moved in with Aaron. And your parents used my competition when they bought their home. As for Miranda"—he turned to her—"I doubt you'll ever be a client, not with that architectural dream of a house Luke owns. And, Iris, I keep hoping one day you'll leave your aunt's place and buy something of your own."

"I'm happy living with my aunt," she murmured. Iris was in fact saving her money for the day when either she or Lily met her special man—but when Iris was in the market for a new home, she intended to give her business to the mother-and-daughter Destiny Homes. Thelma Sajak came from a longtime Destiny family, and she and her daughter were laid-back people.

"Then, ladies, I'll just have to hope for your support in another matter," Bart said. "I'm seriously considering running for the position on the Islands Trust that Walter Franklin is vacating. A number of people have asked me to do it."

"Oh, has Mr. Franklin definitely decided not to run again?" Eden asked.

"That's certainly what I've heard," Bart said.

"Well then," she said, "I'll have to study up on island governance."

Iris held back a smile at her lawyer friend's noncommittal answer. Miranda kept silent, and so did Iris. Her father had told the family that he would only consider running if no one else did. Miranda hoped someone she liked better than Bart would throw her or his name in the hat, though it seemed unlikely.

"I'm glad that Forbes's condition is improving," the man said to Miranda.

"Me too," she responded. Iris got the feeling that Miranda wasn't keen on the guy.

Bart touched the bridge of his glasses, seeming to push them up though they already sat firmly in place. "It's kind of Julian to take time to help out. I haven't run into him, but I hear you've been seeing him, Iris. I'm sure your parents have warned you of the perils of getting involved with someone like him."

Iris's mouth fell open and Miranda asked in a challenging tone, "Someone like him?"

"You know," Bart said. "He was always a little, well, unstable. Brilliant, I'm sure, in his way. An imaginative mind, but moody, erratic. Not quite . . . normal."

Yes, Julian was moody, but he was sensitive, warm, creative. Wonderful. Bart Jelinek was a fool for not seeing that.

"Thank God for creative types," Miranda said. "The

world would be awfully boring if everyone was *normal.*"
She didn't add, *like you, Bart*, but her inference was clear.

Before the man could respond, Ellen came over with the debit/credit card machine, and Bart took his leave.

A few minutes later, as Iris and her friends walked toward the door, they saw him talking to a middle-aged couple at another table.

"He's such a schmoozer," Eden whispered.

"I do not like that man," Miranda stated.

"A fact you weren't at pains to hide," Eden said as they went out into the rain and she raised her umbrella. "Personally, I don't know him well enough to decide."

Miranda snorted. "It's gut instinct. You know how sometimes you take a disliking to someone on sight?" She'd pulled up her jacket hood so it hid her profile, but her voice emerged clearly. "It's like negative pheromones. Iris, what do you think of him?"

"I don't like how he spoke about Julian." She wished that she'd had the guts and presence of mind to speak up the way Miranda had. "And I think he's awfully hearty." Iris hadn't bothered to bring an umbrella, and she lifted her face to the refreshing drops, glad she never wore makeup and that her hair was coiled back. "That's not a personality style I'm comfortable with. But he has done a lot of good for the island."

"Well, I'm not voting for him," Miranda said as they walked down the street. "So there."

"He's likely to be the only one who runs," Iris told her. "He's one of those people. Not charismatic, but persuasive. And persistent. When he wants something to happen, people tend not to stand in his way."

"People ought to have more guts," Miranda said.

They exchanged hugs and parted ways, but as Iris entered Dreamspinner she reflected on her friend's words.

Miranda had been forced to develop "guts" as a child, she and Aaron fending for themselves when their addict mother ignored them and failed to provide. The circumstances had damaged Miranda, but they'd also given her a strength that Iris, with her loving, sheltered, upbringing lacked.

Fortunately, life on Destiny didn't require her to be particularly brave.

Chapter Eleven

Driving Forbes's van the next Friday evening, after picking up Iris, Julian had mixed feelings about this dinner with her family. Although she'd assured him he shouldn't feel obliged to meet her parents and aunt, he knew it was important to her, and he was curious. Besides, this was a day of celebration for them, and he was honored to be included.

Mostly, he was nervous. He wasn't the kind of guy most parents wanted their daughter to date. Foregoing his usual jeans and tee, he wore a long-sleeved, button-up shirt and had borrowed a pair of black dress pants from Forbes, hoping to create a decent first impression.

"Labor Thanksgiving Day," he said. "You have to know that, to a Canadian like me, that sounds pretty weird."

"Oh, we observe the regular September Labor Day, too, and Canadian Thanksgiving. But November twenty-third is a special day in Japan, and Mom grew up with it. The holiday is about celebrating the labor and rights of workers, and basic human rights."

"Hard to argue with that. You're sure I shouldn't have brought something more than a bottle of wine and the orchid?" He tipped his head toward the green-flowered plant Iris now held carefully in her lap. When he'd asked her to recommend a gift, she'd told him green was her mother's favorite color, and she loved orchids, then she'd even volunteered to pick up the plant for him so he didn't have to make a trip into the village.

"No, that's perfect. It's not a big deal, just a time to appreciate each other."

Yet they closed Dreamspinner on a Friday night, when it would normally be open. To him, that suggested the holiday was kind of a big deal.

"Besides," she went on, "it's nice to have a celebratory dinner midway between Canadian Thanksgiving and Christmas."

As Iris directed him to her parents' house, he discovered it was in the outskirts of Blue Moon Harbor village, within walking distance of the bookstore. "Your family no longer has the farm you told me about?"

"No. Dad and Aunt Lily grew up there, but neither wanted to farm. Mom and Dad bought this house and Aunt Lily bought a condo. When Grandfather Harry died, Grandmother Rose was alone at the farm. When she was diagnosed with ALS, she moved in with my parents and me. There was no point to keeping the farm."

In this neighborhood, each home had a distinct character. The Yakimura one was smallish and attractive with simple lines, wooden walls stained grayish-green, and cream-colored trim. The front yard didn't have a lawn like most of the neighbors' houses. Instead, the ground was bark-chipped and planted with grasses, colored-leaf shrubs, and late autumn flowers. Unlike several of the neighbors' houses, this one had no holiday decorations.

"Nice place," he commented as he parked at the curb.

"I remember you saying that the garden is your mom's special thing, like *Windspinner* is your dad's."

"Yes. Nature is highly valued in Japanese culture."

"Your family likes to incorporate elements of Japanese culture into your Western life?"

She nodded. "We appreciate having two heritages. We can draw the best from both worlds. For example, we're all fluent in Japanese and in French, and speak both when we're alone together."

"There aren't too many Western Canadians who speak French fluently."

"No, but after the Official Languages Act was passed in 1969, my grandparents believed that good Canadians should speak both."

Good Canadians. She'd told him about how the government had interned her ancestors because of their connection to Japan, even though they'd been loyal, hardworking citizens. He wondered if the Yakimuras' desire to be "good Canadians" might contribute to the shyness factor. If you were concerned about being judged, perhaps it fostered timidity.

"By the way," he said, "I did some research online on Japanese-Canadian history, and wondered if you had a book in the store that gives a more complete story."

"I own a couple of books I'd be happy to loan you. But, Julian, why are you interested?"

Wasn't that obvious? "Because that's part of who you are. I want to understand what your family and other Japanese Canadians have gone through."

"If you're sure. When you drive me home, remind me to give them to you."

"Thanks." He climbed out and went around to open her door, and take the orchid plant from her. She accepted his hand to assist her in getting out, but then let go, saying, "Let's avoid PDAs. I've told my family we're friends."

She'd picked *now* to tell him he couldn't even hold her hand? He was about to ask for clarification, but the front door of the house opened to reveal a slender Asian man in dark brown pants, a tan shirt, and a brown cardigan. Having lost his opportunity, Julian muttered, "Got it."

He took the wine bottle from the back seat, and Iris collected a Dreamspinner bag with something in it. Then, side by side as the older man watched, they walked along the path and up the steps.

"Hello, Daughter." Mr. Yakimura extended his hand. "Welcome to our home, Julian."

Julian shook his hand. "Thank you for inviting me, sir." The *sir* slipped out without thought. "Especially on Labor Thanksgiving Day."

A petite Asian woman dressed in green and gold—a long, patterned skirt, a simple green top, and a gold necklace and earrings—stepped up beside Mr. Yakimura. Her face was rounder than Iris's and her sleek black hair was coiled up and decorated with a dragonfly pin. "We're always happy to have a friend of Iris's at our home, and to share our celebration," she said. "Welcome, Julian. I'm Akemi and my husband is Ken."

Iris's parents must be in their fifties, but neither one's black hair showed any gray, and their faces were virtually unlined.

Julian offered the orchid to Iris's mom. "I appreciate the welcome."

"Ah," she said, smiling as she took it. "How lovely. You're most kind. Please come in."

Julian handed Ken the wine and Iris gave her dad her tote bag, murmuring, "Here's dessert." Then Julian and Iris followed her mother to a sitting room with furniture made of rattan with bamboo-patterned cushions. A bookcase lined one wall, plants flourished, and three watercolors of island scenery were artfully displayed. A glass-topped coffee table held a tray of sushi, small ceramic bowls, chopsticks, a teapot and cups, napkins, and an orchid plant with purple and white blossoms. Akemi whisked the purple orchid away and replaced it with the green one, saying, "That's much nicer."

At least it seemed everyone was going to be polite.

Ken returned, empty-handed, along with another middle-aged woman. Julian saw the family resemblance among her, Iris, and Ken, in their reed-like slimness and fine features. She wore tan pants and a stunning, peach-colored blouse with a flower pattern. "You must be Iris's aunt Lily," he said, smiling.

"And you are Julian Blake." Her gaze didn't quite meet his.

"I'm pleased to meet you. You're a talented artist. That blouse is beautiful."

Her lashes flicked up as she darted him a surprised look. "Why, thank you. How did you know I made it?"

"I recognize your art from some things Iris has worn. Like tonight's blouse." Under a dark green cardigan, Iris wore a blouse with a pattern of spring blossoms.

"Why are we standing?" Akemi said briskly, and Julian remembered that Iris had said her mom was, unlike the rest of the Yakimuras, an extrovert. "Please, sit, be comfortable. Julian, Iris assured me you like sushi. I hope that's true."

"Yes, I do." He chose a seat on one of the couches. "This looks delicious, but almost too pretty to eat." Sesame-seed-coated rice rolls containing orange and green ingredients, dark green cones of sushi, and curls of pickled ginger were artistically arranged on a pale green platter.

After the others had seated themselves—Iris beside him but several inches away—and Akemi had poured tea, he realized everyone was waiting for him to start in on the sushi. Using chopsticks, he mixed soy sauce and wasabi in one of the little bowls, then chose a colorful roll, dipped it, and ate it. When he'd given his sincere compliments, the others served themselves.

"How is your father recovering after that horrible accident?" Akemi asked.

"It's a slow and painful process," Julian said. "Forbes is impatient, but he's doing his physical therapy and he's determined to play at my stepbrother Luke's wedding, just after Christmas."

"I'm glad to hear he's coming along," she said. "I notice you call your father Forbes."

"Always have. I guess it was a hippie thing. And after my mother left, he and I . . . well, of course he was my dad, but we were kind of like two buddies hanging out." He sipped tea. Though he was more of a coffee drinker, this fragrant, herb-scented beverage suited the sushi.

"Surely it's a parent's job to be a parent," Ken said quietly, his tone so nonjudgmental that Julian knew he was working at it. "To teach and guide, so his child understands the rules of the world and how to behave in it."

"Forbes Blake is a different man from you, my dear," his wife said. "He's a good man and a creative one, but I would say he walks to the beat of his own drum. Or is it drummer?"

"The original is from Thoreau," Iris said. "It's that he hears a different drummer. As I recall, Thoreau goes on to say that he must follow that beat."

"Provided it doesn't lead him to harm anyone, or to harm nature," her aunt Lily said. Her gaze was on her niece and she'd yet to meet Julian's eyes. "And certainly Forbes is a peaceful man who respects others and the environment."

"As does Julian," Iris said. "His upbringing may have

been unconventional, but you only have to listen to his music to know he has strong values."

He smiled, appreciating her support even if it embarrassed him to have her defend him.

"And he has—" her mother started, and then she turned to Julian. "Forgive me for speaking as if you're not in the room. *You* have achieved success in a challenging field." She glanced at her husband and then back to Julian. "We looked you up on the Internet. It's quite a life you lead. An exciting life compared to ours here in Blue Moon Harbor."

"I suppose that's true." Although the woman's tone was neutral, Julian was pretty sure his wasn't a lifestyle she admired.

"You put aside this exciting life for several months," she went on, her gaze on the sushi cone she was picking up, "to look after your father and help out your stepmother."

"Yes."

"Until Forbes's accident, you rarely visited Destiny Island."

It was a statement of fact but felt like a judgment. "That's also true." He wanted to leave it at that, but if he had any hope of winning Iris's family's approval, he had to be more forthcoming. "When I lived here as a kid, I was unhappy. The island has some bad associations for me. It's always been easier to stay away."

Beside him, Iris nodded encouragingly. She would assume he was talking about the family issues he and Luke had discussed.

Akemi turned her gaze on him, and this time when she spoke her voice was gentle. "I'm sorry to hear that. Childhood wounds can cut deep and leave scars."

Somehow, her understanding made him want to go on. "Yes. I keep hoping the wounds have healed, but each time I come back to the island it's like ripping off scabs."

Iris spoke quietly. "Maybe some wounds never heal completely."

He turned to her. "I think that's true." His voice grated. His deepest wound never would, not as long as Jelinek was alive and quite possibly abusing another victim. Nausea rose in his gut and he took deep breaths, forcing it down.

Iris's eyes were soft with concern. "We need to accept the wounds as part of ourselves," she said. "And look for positive aspects."

Appreciating that she was trying to help, he said, "Hmm, maybe so." There was no positive aspect to his cowardice. But perhaps the abuse itself had fueled the power of his music, given it the depth and perceptiveness that spoke to so many people.

As they'd been talking, the five of them had almost polished off the sushi. Akemi rose. "Please excuse me. I will put the finishing touches on dinner."

Lily got to her feet, too. "I'll help."

When the two women had left the room, Ken spent an inordinate amount of time preparing a piece of sushi for himself. Was his silence due to shyness, or was he formulating another tough question or comment?

Julian seized the initiative. "Ken, it's great what you've done with Dreamspinner. Tell me how you decided to open a bookstore."

His choice of topic was a fortunate one. The man's enthusiasm, and Julian's interest, made Iris's dad almost verbose.

Akemi appeared in the doorway. "Dinner is on the table and I've opened the wine."

They all rose and followed her to the dining room, where Lily was fussing with the arrangement of platters and bowls of steaming, aromatic food. There were a couple of stir-fries, a tureen of something that looked like yellow curry, and a big bowl of rice.

"Julian, please sit here, beside Iris," Akemi said. "We are shifting from Japanese food to Thai for the main course. In Japan there's no traditional dinner for Labor Thanksgiving Day, not like turkey for our Canadian Thanksgiving. Each year we choose a different country's cuisine."

"It looks and smells wonderful."

When they were all seated, he was beside Iris, with Lily across from them. Iris's mother was to his right, at one end of the table. Her father sat at the other end, to Iris's left.

"On this special day," Akemi said, "before we eat, we take a moment to thank each other for the work we do. I will start. I thank my family for their contributions to this household and for continuing to make Dreamspinner what I like to think is the heart of Blue Moon Harbor. I thank Julian for providing support to his father and stepmother, and for the music he brings into the world."

Her husband and sister-in-law went next, and then Iris, all of them giving similar thanks in simple words.

When it was Julian's turn, he said, "I thank the Yakimura family for creating a store that provides education and entertainment for Destiny Islanders. I thank Ken and Akemi for their hospitality tonight. I thank Lily for creating beauty in the world. And I thank Iris for her wisdom and generosity. I couldn't ask for a better friend."

Akemi gave a nod of approval, and then said briskly, "Time for dinner. Julian, we eat family style, so each person may choose exactly what he or she wishes. Please help yourself."

They all served themselves and he tasted everything, finding the food as good as anything he'd had in a restaurant. After he passed on his compliments, Akemi asked him about his music and his life as a musician. As he talked, Iris chimed in, and occasionally the more reserved Ken and Lily interjected a comment or question. Clearly, her family wanted to get to know him.

He weighed each response, being honest without sharing the more unsavory details.

He was very aware of Iris, at his side yet a foot away. She said things that subtly encouraged and supported him, but her body language reinforced the no-PDA request she'd made. So he resisted the temptation to touch her arm or rest his hand on her thigh.

Over the scrumptious apple pie Iris had made for dessert, he managed to shift the conversation, asking about Yakimura family history both on Destiny and in Japan. He learned how badly Iris's parents wanted her to visit Japan, to see the country and spend time with relatives. They were too polite to say *And to find a more suitable husband than you*, but he sensed they were thinking it. He wasn't convinced they bought Iris's "just friends" message.

Iris breathed in the crisp air tinged with a whiff of wood smoke and then let her breath sigh out slowly, relaxing as she and Julian walked side by side—but not hand in hand—away from her family home.

When he opened the door of the van for her, she waved to her parents, who stood on the porch. They remained there despite the brisk November air, until Julian pulled away from the curb.

A tape was playing, Bob Dylan's distinctive voice singing "Don't Think Twice, It's All Right," but for once she didn't feel like listening to music so she clicked it off. "Whew." She let out another sigh, releasing more tension. "I think that went as well as it possibly could."

"Everyone was polite," he said, "but I didn't get a read on what they thought of me."

"Ah, that inscrutable Japanese thing," she joked.

"Sorry, was I stereotyping? I didn't mean to."

"No, you're right, my family is restrained rather than

expressive. I've become good at translating." Finally, she allowed herself to touch him, resting her hand on his warm thigh, which felt unfamiliar in wool pants rather than his usual jeans.

At a stop sign, he gave her hand a squeeze and smiled at her. "Dare I ask?" He made a left turn, heading toward the main road.

"Okay, here's how things stood before they met you. The fact that you're Forbes's son and Sonia's stepson carries weight. Family is important to my parents and they respect Forbes and Sonia. That's counteracted by the fact that you're a musician, and not the classical symphony kind. When they Google you, they find pages of search results, including photos at flashy clubs, and of you with loads of women . . . well, you get the picture."

"Mm."

"The fact that you're my friend has both positive and negative features. It does mean you have excellent taste."

Watching his profile, she saw his grin. "Can't argue with that," he said. "What's the negative side?"

"Despite my many wonderful attributes, they wonder why you want to be my friend. I'm not the sort of person you normally spend time with. You're worldly and experienced and I'm far less so, so they worry that you may be trying to take advantage of me in some way."

He frowned and glanced at her. "You know that's not true."

"I do." Realizing he'd stopped the van, she said, "You probably want to get home. After all, you have the Nelsons' anniversary party tomorrow night."

Was that a grimace? Yet he said, "No, it's still early. I'd like to spend some time alone with you. But then, when your aunt drives back to the condo, she'll know you're with me."

That did trouble Iris. But being with Julian outweighed

the concern. "She'll go to bed and not know when I come in. I'll say we talked for a while before you dropped me off. It's true."

"You don't like to lie outright," he commented as he pulled back onto the road. "But you're selective about what you say."

"Lying is disrespectful. But full disclosure isn't always necessary." Reflecting on the evening's conversation, she pointed out, "You find a similar balance."

"Another thing we have in common," he said dryly. "But let's get back to what you were saying. How do you think your family feels about me now?"

"They're reassured that you're not some drug-addled rock star or egotistical jerk celebrity, and—"

"Now who's stereotyping?" he teased.

She didn't deny it. "My family has no experience with people in your line of work. Island musicians like Forbes are as close as they've come, which is far different from a musician who's achieved national, even international acclaim. Anyhow, the way to shatter stereotypes is for prejudiced people to meet individual members of the stereotyped group, don't you think?"

As she spoke, he nodded slowly. "Yeah, that's true."

"So my family will see that while your life experiences are different from ours, you're a decent person." She considered whether to go on, and then went for it. "They are concerned about the wounds from the past that you still carry."

Julian's entire body seemed to tense, so she hurried to finish. "On the other hand, they can relate. We carry the wound of the internment camp, even though it happened to our ancestors and not to us. We are also aware something similar could happen again. That affects us. It's part of the reason we keep our heads down and try to be respectable, contributing citizens who don't make waves."

"Jesus. You don't really think it could happen again?"

"Julian, I want to believe in the good in people, but I see a world where people are hated and attacked, even killed, for their religion, the color of the skin, or their sexual orientation. Even their gender. Yes, horrible things can happen when people get scared."

"Horrible things can happen for all sorts of reasons," he muttered.

She nodded. "It's not a reason to live in fear, but perhaps a reason to live with caution. Which, I think, is a sad thing. I do feel blessed to live on Destiny, though. For the most part, our citizens are decent, kind human beings."

He didn't respond, and his body had locked up again. What had she said to trigger that response? Feeling his tension creep into her own body, she took deep, deliberate breaths. "Let's talk about something more pleasant."

The van was now bumping down the track to the commune. "If you'd been born in your father's times," she said, "and been a hippie like him, would you have worn those wide bell-bottom pants? Maybe orange ones, or printed all over with peace symbols?"

He rotated his shoulders for a few seconds, the tension relaxing. "Peace symbols, for sure. And hair down to my waist, with a leather thong around my forehead."

"I'd have worn floaty long skirts and bells around my ankles." Mischief sparked. "And gone braless, of course."

He sucked in a breath. "I like the thought of you braless."

Was this really her, flirting with a sexy man? Daringly, she said, "That's easily achieved." Her body longed for the touch of his hands. Imagining it made her nipples tighten and sent pulses of need throbbing between her thighs.

"Easily, eh?" He stopped at their usual spot and shut off the engine and lights.

Tonight it wasn't raining, but without even parking lights on, it was quite dark. She could barely see Julian, but when he slid toward her on the bench seat, she went unerringly into his arms. "This feels so good," she said.

"It's been a long evening, not being able to touch you." He smoothed her hair back from her face, kissed her temple, and then his lips were on hers.

Julian's kisses were like a box of excellent chocolates, each one delicious and slightly different, so she never knew quite what to expect—only that she'd savor the luscious treat. With him, she'd learned to experiment. Her tongue became wanton, seeking to give and receive pleasure. Her teeth learned that tiny nips could make Julian groan with need.

She loved how much he aroused her. She also loved that he got so turned on, yet respected their initial decision to take things slow. But now, rather than simply repeat the previous verses of their song, she was ready for them to compose a new one.

The bench seat, while better than bucket seats, inhibited their movements. When they broke for air, their warm breath panting against each other's cheeks, she whispered, "How uncomfortable is the back of this van?" Everything behind the front seat had been torn out to allow for the transportation of musical equipment.

"There are some padded blankets, like movers use. It's not exactly romantic, though."

Just being with Julian was plenty romantic. "We have so few opportunities to be alone someplace private. Let's take advantage of this one."

"Where did shy Iris go?" he teased.

Embarrassed, she said, "Am I being too forward? It's good for the woman to make the first move sometimes, isn't it?"

He laughed softly and she caught the gleam of his teeth in the dim light. "Of course it is. And you could never be too *forward*." The slight emphasis told her he thought the word was another quaint term she'd picked up from a book. "I love how you've relaxed with me, Iris. Seems to me you're being yourself. Don't start second-guessing yourself now. Please?"

"I'll try not to. And now? I recall making a suggestion . . ."

"Yeah, let's move into the back. Music?" he asked.

"Yes, please." She turned the player back on and there was Bob Dylan again, telling her not to think twice.

She and Julian had to get out in order to climb into the back, and the night air was cold. Once inside again, he spread a couple of the padded blankets on the floor and, feeling awkward, she lay down. The song rang out clearly, such a simple one, just Dylan's unusual voice, some beautiful guitar-picking, and that twangy harmonica. A song about a man leaving a woman who hadn't given him what he needed. It made Iris wonder what Julian really wanted from her, and whether she was capable of giving it. She sat up again and peeled off her jacket and then her cardigan. The van's heater had been running and the air remained comfortably warm.

Julian tossed his jacket aside, too, and lay down beside her. On their sides, they gazed at each other in the barely there light. Her hair, which she'd worn loose tonight, slipped forward across her cheek. He slid it back over her shoulder, and then stroked her shoulder, down her bare arm. "I seem to remember," he said, "some promise of bralessness."

Though a ghost of the reserved Iris whispered through her body, she liked the woman she was becoming with Julian. "I could use your help. This blouse zips at the back." She'd worn one of her aunt's creations, most of which featured patterns on the front that would be spoiled by buttons. A zipper ran all the way from the top to the bottom of the slim-fitting blouse.

Julian reached under her hair, his warm fingers teasing her nape, and then the zipper slid down. He did it slowly, stopping along the way to caress the skin he'd bared. By the time he reached the bottom, her nipples were diamond-hard inside her bra.

The blouse fell open down the back. She resisted the urge to cross her arms over her breasts and hold it in place. Instead, she freed herself from it, one arm at a time. Holding the delicate garment, she gazed around to find a safe place to lay it, and hoped the folded blanket she chose was free of grease.

When she turned back, she wondered how he would react. Her size Bs were hardly impressive and her bra wasn't one of those padded underwire "shaper" types, but a simple silvery-gray bralette in a silky fabric. There was no fancy lace or trim, because her skin was too sensitive.

Julian's gaze was heated, and he whispered, "Every inch of you is stunning."

She almost said there weren't very many inches, but bit back the self-deprecating comment. "Thank you." She couldn't help but wonder how many *inches* he was hiding beneath the fly of those dress pants. Her hand ached to stroke him, and when she thought of pressing her tongue and lips against his hard shaft, saliva filled her mouth. Squeezing her thighs together against the delicious ache of arousal, she said, "But I did promise braless."

"Not yet," he breathed.

He didn't want to see her naked breasts? But—oh!—he ran a callused fingertip along the top edge of her bra and each cell stood to attention. As did her nipples, which so badly wanted to feel that raspy caress. Then he did touch them, through the silky fabric, brushing across the beaded peaks. She caught her breath, her body straining toward him, wanting more. Gently, he pushed her back so she was

lying down, and he bent over her. His tongue flicked the
fabric, and then he sucked.

Her body arched involuntarily. "Oh, so good." Heat
spread through her, as rich and thick as warm honey. "But
please, take off my bra. I want your lips on my bare skin."

He reached behind her, found the clasp, and pulled off
her bra. The air was cool against her damp nipple, but only
for a moment because his mouth returned to work its
magic.

She wanted to lose herself in the amazing, unprece-
dented sensations, yet she also wanted to touch him. With
fingers made clumsy by need, she fumbled to undo the buttons of his long-sleeved shirt, and then stroked his back. He
was so hard, so taut, all lean muscle over bone. So totally
different from her; so utterly male.

He made an impatient sound, paused in his caresses to
yank off his shirt, and then returned to her breasts.

She ran her hand down the long line of his back, from
shoulder to waist, feeling that tempting dip at the base of
his spine. Hesitant to delve past the belted waist of his
pants, she slipped her hand around to explore his rib cage
and his chest, where she found a scattering of soft, curly
hairs. When she brushed his nipple, it was as hard as hers.
Gently, she pinched it between her thumb and index finger.

He groaned and shifted position, hooking one leg over
her body. Against her thigh, she felt the rigid length of his
erection. The achy pulse between her thighs urged her to
twist her body, to match her pelvis to his, to grind against
him. And so, because she could and because she doubted
he'd protest, she did it.

Though she'd never had sex in any form, she'd read a lot
of books, both nonfiction and fiction. She knew the inven-
tive things two people could do to find pleasure. She'd
thought she was familiar with her own anatomy and phys-
iology, and she occasionally masturbated to climax, but

never had she felt this kind of sensuality, this intensity of sensation. Now that her body had come alive, she wanted to experience everything.

His hips thrust, driving his erection against her thigh so forcefully that it hurt and she couldn't help but wince.

"Damn." He pulled away, dragging a hand through his long hair as he sat up. "I hurt you."

"No, it's okay," she said on a long, shaky breath as she panted for air. Her bosom was actually heaving, like the cliché. "We got carried away and—" And it felt wonderful and she wanted more, she was about to say, but he spoke first.

"You can say that again." His voice was sandpaper over raw wood. "We have to stop now or I'm going to embarrass myself."

"Oh." Or they could go on, all the way. Was she ready to do that? Her body said yes, but did she really want to lose her virginity to a man who would never make a romantic commitment to her? Yet she truly cared for Julian, and with him it would be special. Just as Eden and Miranda had said it should be.

"We need to go," he said, turning away. He handed her blouse to her.

She could change his mind. But the heat of the moment had fled. Goose bumps pricked the sensitive flesh he'd abandoned. And she knew that she did need to think twice, in the cold, rational light of day.

Chapter Twelve

The next day, Saturday, Iris was off work, thanks to having worked a couple of double shifts over the past week or so. By the time she emerged from her bedroom, her aunt had left for the store. Though Iris was curious to hear what Lily would say about Julian, it could wait until later in the day. When her mom didn't call, Iris guessed that Aunt Lily would deliver the family's verdict when she returned home.

With some notion of good karma, Iris decided to prepare two of her aunt's favorites for dinner: Greek roast chicken and chocolate hazelnut cake.

She had a relaxed day, catching up on email and Facebook, where she admired the latest photos of her friend Shelley's baby boy and tried not to feel too envious. She Skyped her mom's parents in Japan, where they were having breakfast, and spent a half hour catching up, though she didn't mention Julian. She did, though, have a quick phone call with him, to wish him luck with the performance at the Nelsons' anniversary party that night.

Iris had just finished setting the table and putting on some soothing flute music when her aunt came in. Rather than heading to her room to change and unwind, Lily slid onto a stool at the kitchen island. In French, she said, "I heard something interesting today."

"About Julian?" Iris asked warily.

"What? No. About Walter Franklin." She sniffed the air. "Greek chicken? That smells so good."

Iris took a bottle of Destiny Cellars pinot gris from the fridge. "I read in the *Gazette* that Walter confirmed the rumor that he'll resign at the end of his term with the Islands Trust."

"He was in the store, Christmas shopping for relatives in Australia. Bart Jelinek came along to talk to him, and I happened to overhear Bart tell Walter that he plans to run."

Iris sighed. That meant her dad definitely wouldn't do it. "That's not a big surprise."

"Walter said it was a terrific job and he'd loved doing it. And"—Aunt Lily leaned forward—"he said he had planned to run again, but a rumor got started that he was stepping down, and it seemed people were ready for a change. He felt he should stand down." She picked up her wineglass and took a sip.

"That's too bad. I thought he did a great job."

"As did I. Anyhow, Bart said he'd believed the rumor, otherwise he wouldn't have let people persuade him to run. He said he could withdraw his name, but then he'd let down all those people. And Walter quickly said that no, of course Bart should run, and I heard some manly backslapping."

Iris sipped her own wine. "I wonder who started the rumor?"

"It might have been Bart."

"Wow. You really think he'd do that?"

Her aunt shrugged one slim shoulder. "He doesn't let anything stand in his way when he wants something. And he does like being the big fish."

"But that would be so sleazy."

"One tiny hint can turn into a rumor, and rumors take on a life of their own."

"True."

Her aunt put her glass on the island and patted the second stool. "Sit down, Iris."

Ah, here it came. Clutching the stem of her glass, she seated herself.

"The islanders know you're dating Julian."

"Seeing each other as friends," she corrected.

"The gossips don't recognize that distinction."

"Then they're wrong." She wanted to say that people shouldn't gossip, but that would be hypocritical given that she and Lily had just been doing exactly that.

"You dating anyone is news. As for being just friends, I would point out that you and your *friend* left your parents' house shortly after nine and he didn't bring you home until almost midnight."

Iris had been as quiet as possible when she'd snuck into the condo, given Julian the books he wanted to borrow, and then gone to bed. "I'm sorry if I woke you. We were talking and time got away from us."

"I don't need to know what you were doing. What matters is that you care for Julian. I saw it in your eyes last night."

So much for avoiding physical demonstrations of affection. Walking the familiar balance of being honest yet selective, Iris said, "I know there'd never be a future for us. But that doesn't mean we can't be friends and care for each other. He does care for me, Aunt."

"I saw that, too. But it's dangerous."

Iris arched her brows. "Forgive me, but I'm not sure you're qualified to give relationship advice." If her tone was the slightest bit tart, well, her aunt deserved it.

Iris assumed that Lily would take the hint and drop the subject. Instead, after a long drink of wine, her aunt said, "I can give advice on how to fail at a relationship."

"You've never been in love," Iris said, puzzled. "So what do you mean?"

Those brown eyes, so like her own, gazed into a distance that only Lily could see. "I was. Once. A very long time ago. It was all wrong. He was married and—"

A gasp of shock escaped Iris. "What?" No, it wasn't possible.

"We did nothing . . . sexual." Lines grooved Lily's usually smooth face. "But in other ways we betrayed his wife."

"Aunt Lily, I can't imagine it. You, being the other woman."

"It's the last thing I expected of myself."

Clearly, her aunt was still deeply troubled by her long-ago behavior. Perhaps Iris should leave this topic alone, but she was baffled, and her aunt *had* started the conversation. "Tell me how it happened." Iris cast her gaze downward, hoping she didn't seem too pushy. "Please?"

A deep sigh made her look up, to see her aunt's shoulders slump. Given how perfect Lily's posture always was, that tiny sag spoke volumes. "I was at university," she said, fingering the stem of her glass. "You know I studied business administration, because that was the practical thing to do, with your father and me opening Dreamspinner. But I also took a few courses in subjects that nourished my soul. The man was my creative writing teacher."

This aunt she'd thought she knew so well was full of surprises. "You were—are?—a writer?"

"I never wrote again, not after that year. I turned my creativity into art instead."

"I'm sorry I interrupted. Tell me about your professor."

"He asked me to come to his office to discuss my first assignments, and was complimentary. We talked about the power of words, the craft of writing. We connected in a way I'd never imagined experiencing. It was intellectual, yes, but much more than that." She ducked her head, studying the straw-colored wine. "Despite my shyness, I bloomed in his company."

Yes. It was exactly like that for Iris, with Julian.

"He was a brilliant man," Lily said, "and an attractive one. A quiet man, an introvert like me. A scholar who admired great writing but said he lacked that talent himself." She glanced up, grimacing. "I'm afraid it was the old 'my wife doesn't understand me' story, but I do believe that in their case it was true. They had married young, then their interests and personalities developed with adulthood and diverged dramatically."

Iris barely breathed, so compelling was it to hear this previously untold story.

"We didn't intend to fall in love," Lily said, "but we did. Through words, written and spoken. Through gazes. Through touch, but never through sex." She blinked. "He said he would leave his wife. He asked me to marry him."

Iris gasped again. "But . . . you didn't."

Her aunt swallowed. "They had two children."

"Oh," Iris breathed.

"I would not be the cause of a broken family."

Iris reflected, rotating her wineglass. "But," she said slowly, "if this man and his wife were unhappy, then the family was already damaged, wasn't it? I don't think children are ever oblivious to, or uninfluenced by, their parents' unhappiness."

Her aunt sighed. "You think I made the wrong decision."

"No, no," she hurried to say. "I would never presume to second-guess you."

"Well, *I* think perhaps I made the wrong decision."

"Oh. Well . . . Wow. That's . . . I'm sorry, Aunt Lily."

"He's the only man I ever loved. The only one I ever felt connected to on an intimate level. All the clichés—magnets attracting, jigsaw pieces interlocking—they were true. And so, since then I've been alone. And always will be." The sadness and resignation in her eyes confirmed that she believed that. And if she wasn't open to love, how could it find her?

"Do Dad and Mom know about this?"

"No. Only you."

"I'm honored that you trusted me. But why did you tell me?"

"Because I recognize the expression in your eyes when you talk about Julian."

Iris bit her lip. "You're warning me off. But there's no need. I know it can't work."

"I told myself it couldn't work with Fredrick, too. I have spent decades wondering if that was true, or if I was simply not brave enough to risk all that would be involved. Leaving Destiny Island, my safe place, to live with him in Victoria. Facing censure. Feeling guilt. Having to deal somehow with his ex-wife and his children. And what if our love didn't stand the tests of reality and time, but proved to be only a romantic dream?"

"Yes, that's a lot to consider," Iris agreed. They were both quiet for a minute or two, and then she asked, "Have you ever looked him up on the Internet?"

"No."

"Aren't you curious?" What if Fredrick was divorced? Might he, too, still dream about his long-ago love? If the two reunited and found that the romantic connection still existed, perhaps they'd have the courage to put their love to the tests of reality and time. Her aunt could have a happy ending, just like in a romance novel.

"I think it's better not to know. We had a short but wonderful time together. I made my decision then. Best to leave it at that."

If her aunt had held on to a romantic dream for decades, and because of it not been open to falling for someone else, then that was a tragedy. And yet, was it possible to

experience that kind of truly intimate connection twice in
a lifetime?

And once you'd known it, could you ever settle for less
than that?

As Julian adjusted the *Windspinner*'s course, the wind
tugged at his hair and made his cheeks tingle. It was
amazing that they could be out on the ocean so late in
November.

"You're getting pretty adept," Iris said.

His hands resting lightly on the wheel, he grinned at her.
"Thanks to my excellent teacher."

Forbes's friend and bandmate Christian had volunteered
to keep Forbes company and drive him to his therapy ses-
sions, and Iris had taken the day off work. They would sail
for a while, then maybe go back to her place, but dinner
would be at her parents' house. As a thanks for the Labor
Thanksgiving Day dinner, Julian had offered to treat them
to dinner—one he prepared and brought to their house,
since he still avoided going out in public. They had accepted, and the lasagna and pineapple upside-down cake
he'd made last night from Sonia's recipes now sat in the
Windspinner's fridge, along with salad ingredients.

On deck, wearing a shirt and a heavyweight brown
sweater-jacket he'd borrowed from Forbes, Julian was
toasty warm, all but his face and his hands. He'd forgotten
to bring gloves, and the ones Ken Yakimura kept on the
boat were too small.

He didn't mind the cold. Not when he was flying across
the ocean, hearing gulls cry and bull seals bark at one another, filling his nostrils with the most bracing scent in the
world, and sharing the experience with the woman seated
to his right.

Though Iris, who wore a multicolored knitted hat, had started out with her hair ponytailed, he had, by distracting her with a kiss, tugged off the twister. As he tucked it in his pocket, she'd tried to grab it, but when he said, "Please don't. I love to see your hair blow in the wind," she had smiled and surrendered.

He knew it annoyed her to have those long ribbons whip across her face, and he appreciated that she'd done this for him. She was far too good for him, and that knowledge created a dilemma. Up until now, having sex with a woman he'd just met was typical, and often that sex was shorter than a one-night stand because it rarely involved waking up together in the morning. He'd always been honest up front, and if he sensed that the woman wanted more than casual sex, or if it seemed like she was under the influence of booze or drugs, he walked away. It was crucial to him that his partner not only consent, but that it be full, informed, unimpaired, enthusiastic consent.

Now, there was Iris. A mature woman, but sexually naïve. Well, not exactly naïve, because she'd read a lot, and was applying her knowledge in ways that startled, charmed, and thoroughly aroused him. *Inexperienced* was the more accurate word. And, though she made it clear she knew they had no long-term future, she did have that romantic dream—which surely must include losing her virginity with the man she loved.

Yet she threw herself enthusiastically into their sex play. He loved how beautifully responsive she was, and the way she shared her body unreservedly. The last couple of times they'd been together, he'd brought her to climax with his fingers and tongue. He also loved the way she seemed to revel in his body, touching and tasting more boldly each time. Two nights ago, at the commune, she'd gone down on him and not pulled back even when he told her he was going to explode. Coming in her mouth, feeling the movement of her tongue and throat as she swallowed, seeing her smile afterwards as if it was he, not she, who'd bestowed the gift . . .

Oh man, he was hard as a rock now, as he piloted the boat and she raised her closed-eyed face to the wind and sun.

Her eyes opened and she caught him staring. "What?" she asked.

"Just watching. You're so beautiful, Iris." So desirable, so generous, so insightful.

"Thank you. But," she teased, "you're supposed to be watching the wind, the water, the sail." Pointing ahead, she said, "That's SkySong, the serenity retreat."

A large, lodge-like wooden building and several log cabins were nicely spaced amid natural, attractive landscaping, set above a curve of sandy beach. On the lawn, a few bundled-up people were exercising. "Hardy souls," he said.

"Tai chi warms you up. I do it every day, myself."

No wonder she was in good shape if she did tai chi as well as walking to and from the store. "SkySong," he said. "This is the place Di and Seal own."

"Yes. You've met them?"

"They've dropped by the house. They're friends of Forbes's, dating back to the commune days."

She flashed him a smile. "You know who else they are? Eden's aunt and uncle. Since Eden is married to Aaron, and Miranda is his sister, and she's marrying your stepbrother, then you'll be related to them, too."

"Huh." It reminded him of what a small island Destiny was. And how lucky he'd been, managing to avoid hearing about, much less seeing, one of its prominent citizens. His worries about the Nelsons' anniversary party had been for nought. Jelinek hadn't attended.

"We should head back to the marina," Iris said. "It's too cold to stay out much longer."

He nodded, called "Coming about," and turned the wheel. They both scrambled to adjust the sails, him handling the mainsail and her the jib.

She let him sail all the way to the entrance of the bay, where they dropped and secured the sails and fired up the engine. With the ease of experience, she steered through the fingers of the wharf and brought the boat into its mooring slip, where Julian jumped to the dock to tie it up. With numb fingers, he tried to wrap the lines around the cleats.

Iris hopped out to help, teasing, "Fumble-fingers."

"Numble-fingers. I can barely feel them, much less make them cooperate."

After securing the lines, she stripped off her gloves and examined his icy hands. "No frostbite, thank heavens." Cradling them in her warm hands, she said, "Honestly, Julian, if you were this cold, you should have stuck your hands in your pockets and let me do the sailing. Please tell me you'll buy gloves, or at least borrow them from Forbes."

"There are benefits to not having them," he pointed out.

She gave his hands a squeeze, which, sadly, he barely felt. "Shall we have lunch and hot chocolate below deck? I'll turn the furnace on and we can warm up."

"Sounds good." He and Iris had come to *Windspinner* a few days ago, seeking a cozy sanctuary on a wet, wild day. Of course they couldn't sail, but with the furnace on and the hull rocking gently, the cabin was a warm, intimate place.

Now, as soon as they went below deck, she clicked on the furnace. He wrapped his arms around her, both their bodies bulky in their outdoor clothing. She met his kiss eagerly and then pulled back, saying, "That's not going to warm your icy hands."

"It's warming the rest of me."

"Sit down." She unzipped her windbreaker and tossed it onto the V-berth. "You need a mug of hot chocolate."

He sat on the dinette bench that faced the galley, and rubbed his hands together.

"I guess you're too frozen to play?" Iris asked as she poured a tin of soup into one pot and milk into another, and lit the elements on the propane stove.

"Sorry, yeah." His guitar case was cushioned in the V-berth where it couldn't bang around with the boat's movement.

"What are you working on?" She took cocoa powder from the cupboard.

He'd been trying to compose a song about Iris, but it eluded him. He'd found a few phrases, in both music and lyrics, that felt right, but he couldn't seem to figure out what story he wanted to tell. He was pretty satisfied with another piece, though, and would love her feedback. "I'll play you one when I thaw out." He shook his hands, which tingled painfully as they warmed up. "I've been reading those books you loaned me and I've written a song that's loosely based on how your grandparents met at the internment camp."

"That's fantastic. I can't wait to hear it."

After stirring cocoa into the hot milk, she poured the brew into two mugs and brought one over to him. "Wrap your hands around this," she instructed, and then walked the couple of paces back to the miniature galley to cut slices of French bread and cheddar cheese.

He cradled the mug, wishing the heat under his fingers was that of her naked skin. Though if he touched her now, she'd shiver, and it wouldn't be the good kind of shivering, the kind she usually did when he caressed her silky flesh . . .

His hands might still be cold and semi-numb, but another portion of his anatomy was feeling the heat, and he removed the borrowed sweater-jacket. The last time he and Iris had been on the boat, they'd ended up in the V-berth naked, and he'd discovered the disadvantages of that cramped space.

"What are you thinking about?" she asked, coming to the table with two bowls of soup. "You have this funny smile."

He cocked his head in the direction of the V-berth. "The last time we were here."

"Oh." Her cheeks, flushed from the sun and wind, then the heat of the cabin, turned a deeper shade of rose. She turned back to the galley, and returned with two side plates and a cutting board with the sliced bread and cheese. "Not an elegant meal, but a hearty one." She took the seat across from him.

He let her change the subject. For now. "It suits the day," he told her, inhaling the tomato-basil aroma of the soup.

The dinette was small enough that their knees bumped companionably under the table as they ate with fresh air– fueled appetites. When she finished her soup, she hoisted her legs up onto her seat so she sat on it lengthwise, her back against the wall, her mug between her hands. "There's something I wanted to talk to you about," she said.

"Uh-huh?"

"Eden works at a seniors' residential and care facility. She asked me if I'd arrange a book club for the seniors."

"Sounds like a good idea, and right up your alley." He used a thick slice of bread to mop up the last trace of soup in his bowl.

"Yes, well, she wants me to not just set it up and provide the books, but to attend and facilitate." She swallowed. "I would choose books with subjects the seniors could relate to. Then we could talk about the books themselves, but also move into subjects that are relevant to the seniors' lives, and perhaps their concerns about their health and the future."

He nodded, trying to imagine it, and saw the doubt in Iris's dark eyes. It seemed to him that she—along with her dad and aunt—used shyness as a security blanket. An excuse. Not that there was anything wrong with being shy; it sure beat pushiness. But it held her back from doing things she'd otherwise enjoy.

Not that he could judge, not when he avoided even looking at photos of Jelinek. Trying to be supportive without pressuring her, he said, "That's a nice idea."

"I think so, too." She sighed. "I've become complacent."

It seemed her thoughts might have paralleled his. "Tell me more."

"Each person's inner nature has weaknesses as well as strengths, and I believe that one should either attempt to overcome the weaknesses or turn them into strengths."

What if you were too weak, too cowardly, to overcome your weakness, and there was no possible way of turning it into a strength?

This is our secret, Julian.

But this wasn't about him; it was about Iris.

"For me," she went on, "I've focused on how my shyness is not just a weakness but also a strength, in making me more sensitive to others."

"I hear a *but* coming."

"That's led me to be complacent in avoiding pushing myself out of my comfort zone. Well, I do sometimes, like when I went to university, but my first reaction is to steer clear of situations that make me anxious. And so, even though I believe in doing good in the world, I only contribute within my own small comfort zone."

He nodded. "Would you be more comfortable if you

focused on the seniors rather than yourself? And on the benefit they'd be getting?"

Her lips twitched. "Eden used that argument. Yes, I think that's true. She also told me that everyone experiences fear. It's how you deal with it that shows who you really are."

Exactly. That was why Julian knew that, in his core, he was not only broken but rotten.

"I want to be a better person," Iris said softly, "so I think I may do the book club." Her lashes fluttered down and then up again. "Miranda suggested that my aunt might come along."

Focusing on Iris rather than his dark thoughts, he said, "Mutual support. Good idea."

"It is." She pressed her lips together, thinning their fullness.

He topped another slice of bread with cheese. "There's something you're not saying."

"Oh." She fidgeted with her mug. "It was a crazy idea, just something that crossed my mind, not even worth mentioning."

"Spit it out."

"You. I thought about you. Instead of my aunt."

Him? In a seniors' book club?

"If you brought your guitar and sang a couple of songs, they'd love it. And for the first books, if I do this, I would choose the ones I convinced you to buy. So you could participate in the discussion."

"You'd choose them so I could participate?" She was trying to organize his life for him? That didn't sound like Iris.

"No, no. I said that badly. I mean, I thought those books would be good for the first meeting. *Pooh* would be fun and bring back pleasant memories. And *The Tao of Pooh* isn't a heavy read, but it's thought provoking and the concepts

are relevant to whatever's happening in a person's life.
Then, thinking about how Pooh's a songwriter, and how
you and I have talked about the books, it popped into my
head that you might come. But as I said, it's a crazy idea."

Thinking it through, he said, "I'm kind of flattered.
But . . ." But he didn't go out in public on this island.

"Why would you want to waste your time discussing
books with a bunch of old folks?"

Did she think he was ageist? "I like old folks. I have fans
who are in their eighties. For some reason, my music ap-
peals to people from all generations."

"Your themes are universal and your tunes are distinctive and resonant."

"Thanks. You know, I've never discussed books, except
with you. And Forbes, recently. He wasn't a big reader, but
now it fills time and distracts him from pain." Julian enjoyed those discussions, and he enjoyed thinking about how
authors crafted their creations as compared to how he, as a
songwriter, crafted his.

Iris would like him to do this. It was something they
could share, another memory to sustain him in his basement flat in Vancouver, or in some nondescript hotel room
on tour. Bart Jelinek wouldn't be there. He wasn't a senior,
and his parents were dead. Jelinek had told him that, and
that he and his wife couldn't have kids. Later, Julian had
realized it had been a manipulative tool used to deepen the
bond between them.

"Honestly, Julian," Iris said briskly, sliding off the bench
seat. "Don't think twice about it." She began to stack the
dishes.

"I'm up for it," he said. "As long as we can fit it around
my schedule with Forbes."

"Really?" She stopped, hands full of plates and bowls. "If
I do decide to go ahead with it, that would be wonderful."

He'd never before seen a face glow with pure pleasure the way Iris's sometimes did.

But when she said, "Aunt Lily's at work this afternoon. Let me tidy up the dishes, then why don't we go to my place where it's more comfortable?" he figured it was his face that was glowing. With pleasure, anticipation, and more than a little lust.

Chapter Thirteen

Once they were at her condo, she and Julian stripped off their jackets and sweaters, and put the dinner stuff in the fridge. Iris stepped into his arms, marveling at how comfortable she felt doing this. Not that he didn't still excite her in every way, but it was incredible that their relationship felt so natural.

Did she love Julian? She'd read about love in everything from academic texts to pulp fiction. The term could mean many different things. She felt love for her family and, to some degree, for her girlfriends. Her feelings for Julian were multifaceted: lust, admiration, an odd sense of being kindred spirits despite their differences, and a deep-in-her-soul caring.

If she turned off her brain and simply *felt*, every instinct told her this was her man, the one she had always believed would come into her life. Her brain said that was impossible—so how could being with him feel like destiny? Mindfulness told her not to agonize over it, but to relish the moment and lose herself in this kiss that went on and on.

A deep sense of certainty seeped through her. This, with Julian, was right. She'd deal with the future once it became the present. Now, she wanted to lose her virginity, to make love, with this man. She eased away from him, took his hand, and led him to her bedroom. After closing the door, she leaned back against it. "Now I have you where I want you," she teased.

"Handily, it's exactly where I want to be. Well, actually, over here would be better." He pulled her toward the bed.

Standing, they worked the fastenings of each other's clothes—shirt buttons, jeans snaps, zippers—doing it slowly, in an almost ceremonial way. Fabric rustled as, item by item, pieces of clothing fell to the floor, until they were both naked.

The room was comfortably warm and Iris had come to feel at ease being naked with him, so she didn't pull back the covers. Instead, she lay on top of the duvet, sinking into its softness as if she were reclining on a cloud.

Despite his fair hair, Julian did not look like an angel. His body was lean, all muscle and sinew as he stood gazing down at her, an erection rising. The black notes and bars of the music tattoo twining around his arm sang of sorrow, not joy. The expression in his vivid blue eyes was a complicated blend that included affection, desire, need, and—again—wasn't that sorrow? Julian's unhealed wounds, whatever they might be, were an intrinsic part of him. She wished he would share that part with her, but doubted it would ever happen.

Would he share another gift? Reason told her that romance authors exaggerated when they wrote about intercourse in terms of bodies shattering, the earth moving, the sky bursting into dazzling fireworks. That wasn't what she craved anyhow; it was the emotional intimacy. If she lost her virginity with him, he would always be part of her soul.

"Come lie with me," she said, moving over and rolling onto her side, facing him.

He joined her, lying on his own side, and reached out to stroke her. She caught his hand, rose to her knees, and flipped him onto his back. Then she straddled him, one knee on either side of his hips. As she bent forward to kiss him, her hair streamed down around her face, getting in the way. "Such a nuisance," she murmured, scooping it back with one hand.

"So lovely," he said just before their lips met.

She lost herself in the bliss of their mouths mating slowly and sensually. Julian was like a drug in her blood, slowing some of her reactions, speeding others, making her hyperaware of every sensation. The moist fullness of his lips, the warmth of his breath, and the lingering hint of chocolate. The pillowy smoothness of the cotton duvet under her knees, the firmness of his muscled legs, the tickle of curly hair against her breasts and inner thighs. And, most of all, the hard thrust of his erection against her belly.

She edged forward to rub against that firm shaft, and he groaned against her mouth.

Freeing the hair she'd scooped back, she let it fall in a curtain around their faces. She eased back, turning the kiss from a deep meeting of tongues and breath to tiny kisses that nipped across his lips and then over the hint of blond stubble on his chin. When he reached out for her, she said, "No, Julian. Lie back and let me." She wanted to caress every inch of him, tease every erogenous zone, savor every reaction, and to make him hers.

In leisurely fashion she stroked, kissed, licked, tickled, sucked here and there, memorizing each breathy gasp, each moan, each surprised laugh. The jut of a hipbone proved to be ticklish, the inside of an elbow an erogenous zone. It awed her that he was so responsive to her, that she controlled his arousal. And her own, because turning him on was as much an aphrodisiac as when he teased and caressed her body.

When she finally made her way to his center, when her hair brushed his stomach and her lips surrounded his shaft, he moaned. "God, Iris, I can't believe how good you make me feel."

The last time they'd been together, she had brought him to climax with her hands and her mouth. But now she wanted more. She wanted everything. Sitting back on her heels, she gazed into his eyes. "Julian, make love to me. All the way."

"What?" His body jerked under her. "No, Iris, I can't do that."

A possibility occurred to her, one she hadn't thought of before. "Don't you have a condom?" Didn't sexy guys keep condoms in their wallets, or was that only in books?

"It's not that. You're a virgin, and the first time should be special."

Didn't he think their lovemaking would be special? He couldn't really mean that. She must be misunderstanding. "I care about you, and I know you care about me. Yes, one day I hope, I believe, that I'll find true love, a man to build a life with, but that's in the future. Now, with you, I want this. I want you, my dear friend, to be the one. I want us to share this."

He propped himself up on his elbows. "Jesus, Iris, that's . . . I'm honored. By your trust in me and by your caring. Yes, I care for you, too. How could I not? You're an incredible woman. But it wouldn't be right, you and me doing this. I don't . . ."

When he didn't finish, she said, "You don't want to?"

He groaned. "Yes. No. I mean, physically, yes, of course. But no, I don't." His wilting erection confirmed that. "You should wait for a man who deserves the gift. A man who loves you deeply and truly, who wants to share his life with you."

Hurt and a little annoyed, she was starting to feel kind

of ridiculous, naked and straddling him. "I didn't know you
were so old-fashioned. Sex isn't that big a deal in this day
and age."

His brow creased. "Not usually. But sometimes maybe
it should be."

"There are different kinds of big deals." How could she
make him grasp this? "I'm a feminist, a modern woman.
The fact that I've never had sex isn't because I hold archaic
views of sexuality, it's that I've almost never dated. I've
never even enjoyed kissing a man until you. Now, I feel so
close to you, and I know we're not going to share our lives,
but why can't we share this now? You've given me so much
already, so why won't you give me this one thing I want so
much?" How pathetic was she, begging him to make love
to her?

Julian squeezed his eyes shut as if he was in pain. "You
know I have a dark side, Iris. Wounds that won't heal. If
you knew who I really am, you wouldn't ask for this."

Who he really was? Okay, that was it. He'd ruined what
she had hoped would be one of the sweetest experiences of
her life. She clambered off him and retreated under the
covers. "What are you talking about?"

Shaking his head, he rose from the bed and bent to pick
up his boxer briefs.

He wouldn't tell her. Of course not. He might care for
her, but he would only let her get so close, and then he
slammed the door. It seemed, though, that he wasn't so
much rejecting her as putting up a defensive shield to
protect himself. Out of fear? The fear that if she knew his
secrets, *she* might reject *him*? He didn't trust her to understand.

What if he was right? It was hard to imagine that Julian
could have done something so awful she'd reject him. But
she'd only known him a few weeks. His music conveyed pain,
regrets, anger sometimes. What events had left those scars?

Feeling vulnerable, she tugged the duvet up to her neck. Looking away from him as he dressed, her gaze caught on the arrangement of photos on the wall beside her dresser. She'd put them together herself, some with pale green matte and dark purple frames, some with mauve matte and forest-green frames. Her gallery consisted of her grand-parents as young teens at the internment camp; her dad and aunt in front of Dreamspinner on the day the bookstore opened; her parents on their wedding day; herself and her BFF Shelley with their university diplomas, an engagement ring sparkling on Shelley's finger. She should add a photo of Eden and Miranda.

As for Julian . . . She'd snapped a few pictures of him with her phone, including a couple of selfies of the two of them on *Windspinner*. Would she add one to her display? That depended on what happened next, between them.

"I'm sorry, Iris."

She turned her gaze on him. He'd finished dressing and was dragging his fingers through his tousled hair. "The last thing I want is to hurt you," he said. "Please believe that I care about you and respect you. Can we go back to the way things were? Forget that this happened?"

Go back to how things were? With him fully dressed, halfway across the room, and her huddled in bed, her body throbbing with unfulfilled desire and her heart aching with the knowledge that there would always be a barrier between them?

She took a deep breath, calming herself, seeking bal-ance, hunting for her inner truth. Her gaze sought the wall calendar with its message about sharing light and hap-piness. She had wanted to do that with Julian but now, because she'd asked for something he wasn't prepared to give, they were both in pain.

"I'm sorry if I pushed," she said slowly. "No, it's never possible to go back." Or to forget, but Julian, of all people, knew that. She remembered October's calendar message, about sowing seeds and being patient. "But I hope we can go forward. As friends. I don't want to lose your friendship."

He walked toward the bed, stretching out both hands. "I don't want that either."

After securing the duvet under her armpits, she took his hands. "Then we'll move forward." She had no idea what that would be like, but all they could do was take one step at a time. "I'd like to take a quick shower before dressing to go over to my parents'." Warm water and scented soap always soothed her when she was troubled. "Would you still like to go?"

Uncertainty clouded his eyes. "As long as it won't be too awkward for you."

"Of course not." They'd have to stumble through those first new steps sometime anyhow. The polite, restrained atmosphere of her family home might not be a bad place to do it. "While I'm showering, why don't you tune your guitar? Once I'm dressed, I'd love to hear the song about my grandparents. If you're still willing to share it."

"I'd be happy to." He swallowed. "I only wish . . ." But then he shook his head and left the room, leaving her to wonder what he wished.

Julian gazed around the Yakimuras' living room as he strummed the closing notes of his new song, "From Dust, a Rose." Iris's parents sat side by side on the couch, leaning forward, clasping hands. Tears sheened Ken's dark brown eyes—a high compliment from that reserved man. Akemi smiled gently, nodding. Lily sat in an upholstered chair, her posture perfect, unmoving—but her lips were parted and her expression rapt.

Iris, who'd first heard the song that afternoon at her

apartment, stood leaning against the doorway. She had asked him to play this song for her family after dinner—a dinner they'd all complimented him on—but she hadn't sat down with them. She'd remained slightly removed, as she had for the past few hours.

When she'd offered him her virginity, he'd been stunned by her trust, her honesty, by the fact that she'd chosen him. He'd hurt her by turning her down, but what else could he do? She might profess to be a modern woman who didn't think sex was such a big deal, but he wanted her to share her first time with a man who deserved that gift.

He hated that he'd hurt her, and he hated the distance between them. He'd only seen her drop that delicate, invisible shell of reserve once in the past hours: when she first listened to the song. She had cried as he'd sung a love story that was born out of adversity and flourished bravely despite the obstacles of racism, time, an ocean's distance, and family pressures.

Now, as the echoes of the final notes faded in the Yakimuras' living room, Akemi said, "It's beautiful, Julian. You have a rare talent."

"Thank you for telling this story," Lily said quietly.

"My parents would be honored," Ken said.

Only Iris was silent, but from her post by the doorway, she sent Julian a smile.

"I'm glad you like it," he told them all. Inside his jeans pocket, his phone pulsed. "Sorry," he said, drawing it out, "I need to check that it's not Sonia. She's alone with my dad."

The display said it was his bandmate Roy, so he let it go to voice mail. A few moments later, Roy rang again. It was a signal between them: if something was important, they called twice. "I really am sorry," Julian said. "This seems to be urgent."

"No problem," Akemi said. "Please, take it. We'll tidy up the kitchen while you do."

All the Yakimuras left the room, leaving Julian feeling like a rude guest. He accepted the call, saying, "Roy, this better be good."

"Yeah, man, it is. Your dad's still doing okay?"

Julian was in touch with his band members two or three times a week, so he didn't hide his exasperation. "Yes. Did you call just to ask that?"

"No, to see if you could leave him and your stepmom for an overnighter. We got offered a gig in Victoria on December first."

"This Saturday? That's late notice."

"You know Dak Spencer of Big Bad Blood? He broke his frigging wrist this afternoon."

"Ouch. Poor bastard." Dak was a drummer.

"The band manager called to see if Camille could fill in."

"That's fine with me, if she wants to."

"She doesn't. Says it'd be too difficult to learn their music, fit into their groove. So then the manager asked if we could fill in for the band. What do you say?"

"Maybe. I need to check with my family."

"Big Bad Blood needs to know right away."

Resigned, Julian said, "I'll get back to you in a few minutes."

He called his stepbrother, explained the situation, and said, "Forbes is improving, but if Sonia's worried about not having a strong guy to assist during the night, could you sleep over?"

"Sure. The whole family could. We'll all watch a movie in our pj's, eat some popcorn. The boys and Ariana will love it."

"Thanks. I owe you."

"Nope. I owe *you* for putting your life on hold to help Mom and Forbes."

"Not a problem." As Julian ended the call, he remembered how he'd hated the thought of being stuck on Destiny Island for months. But, despite his angst over Jelinek, he was glad for the new closeness with his family and for his friendship with Iris.

He called Roy back, then he went to find the Yakimuras and apologize for his rudeness.

They were all in the kitchen, dealing with dishes and leftovers. Iris noticed him and came over, stepping out into the hall and asking, "Is everything okay?"

He filled her in, then asked, "Want to come? We could take the ferry Saturday morning. While the band practices in the afternoon, you could hang out and listen, or sightsee, shop."

Her delicately arched brows drew together.

"Then we'd grab a bite with the band, and you could watch the show. And after—" He broke off when she shook her head.

"No, Julian. Thank you, but no."

"Is it because you're upset with me?"

She glanced toward the kitchen. "I'm not upset with you. A trip like that would be very difficult for me."

But she knew Victoria; she'd gone to university there. And he would be with her. Was her shyness really that crippling, or was she keeping him at a distance? He wished he could make her understand that he hadn't rejected her, he'd protected her. But in order to do that, he'd have to reveal his dark secrets—and then she'd be the one rejecting him.

Chapter Fourteen

A couple of days after Julian had refused to take her virginity, Iris was still trying to view it as a gesture of respect. She knew he meant it that way, so it was ridiculous to let it sting. Better to be grateful that she'd be able to share that special intimacy with the love of her life when he came along.

On this Friday morning, Dreamspinner was quiet. She'd just finished putting together packages to deliver to shut-ins, something she'd do tomorrow. While Julian was traveling to Victoria to meet up with his band members. She'd hated to see the disappointment in his eyes when she'd turned down his invitation to go with him, but surely he must realize that just the notion made her break out in a cold sweat.

Deliberately, she forced herself to shift focus to a more cheerful subject: the upcoming holiday season. It was always so much fun decorating Dreamspinner and setting up special displays. Her spirits received another boost when she saw Eden and Miranda enter the store and stride toward her. Eden looked tailored and businesslike, wearing a pant-suit under a trench coat, her walnut hair neatly ponytailed. Miranda was more casual, in jeans, a coral-colored sweater, and her old rain jacket, her wavy blond hair pulled back with dragonfly clips.

"Hey, you two," Iris said. "It's good to see you."

"I just finished some business in town," Eden said, "so I dragged Miranda out for coffee. Can you join us?"

"We're not busy now, so yes, please. I'll just tell my dad. Meet you in the coffee shop."

A few minutes later, she got a cup of coffee and an approving smile from her mother, who was working behind the counter, and joined her friends at a four-top table by the window. "This is a pleasant surprise," she said as she sat across from them.

There was no reason to be depressed about her relationship with Julian. He was her friend, these terrific women were also her friends, and she had an amazing family. For some reason, she thought of the saying on the November calendar, about sharing light and happiness. The same principle also applied to friendship, and to love. Light, warmth, and love were meant to be shared, not hoarded.

And suddenly she knew it was time to stop waffling about the seniors' book club and to push past her comfort zone. When she thought about how her shyness had cost her opportunities in life, it wasn't social activities like parties that she regretted, but doing things that—even if just in a tiny way—made the world a better place.

"Eden, I want to go ahead with holding a book club at Arbutus Lodge," she said.

She'd done it and there was no going back. Nerves brushed scratchy fingernails against her skin, yet she also felt a sense of relief and rightness as Eden exclaimed with pleasure, and Miranda beamed approval.

"Wonderful," Eden said. "Will Lily join you?"

"I was thinking we might have a variety of guests. Like, don't you think it would be fun to read one of our local romance writer's books and have her attend the discussion?"

"That's a great idea," Miranda said. "I love local authors."

"So does my mom," Eden said. "Any chance of getting Kellan Hawke, I wonder?"

It was possible Iris could twist the arm of the reclusive thriller writer, who was a member of her own book club. But that was something to check into down the road. "I wouldn't count on that. However . . ." She took a quick swallow of coffee, and said in a rush, "I thought the first guest could be Julian."

"Julian?" Eden and Miranda cried, loudly enough that the heads of neighboring coffee shop patrons turned.

Iris ducked her own head and took a long breath. She looked up again and said quietly, "He could play a couple of songs and participate in the book discussion. It might be interesting for the seniors to hear his perspective, and I imagine there are things he could learn from them."

"Have you talked to him about this?" Eden asked.

"Yes. He's in."

"It would be cool," Miranda said. "All the women will be madly infatuated."

"And the men will tell stories about the days when they were young and handsome," Eden said dryly, "and charmed all the ladies—which in most cases would be total faulty memory." She frowned slightly. "But maybe that would distract from the purpose of the club."

"Hey, if it gives the seniors some fun, why not go for it?" Miranda asked.

"If we offer a variety of experiences and perspectives," Iris said, "it will keep people's minds stimulated."

Miranda nudged her soon-to-be sister-in-law. "Can't argue with that, Eden."

Eden smiled. "I wouldn't dare. Alright, let's do it."

"I'm surprised that Julian agreed," Miranda said. "He's not exactly Mr. Sociable. He just hangs out with family, and of course with you, Iris." She gave an exaggerated wink. "Since you have that *connection*, and all."

Not as much of a connection as Iris would have liked, but she wasn't about to share the saga of offering up her virginity and being turned down. "Julian's busy with Forbes," she said. "And he's a private person. When he has spare time, I don't think he wants to be . . ."

"Mobbed by adoring fans?" Miranda said. "No, he's not that kind of guy."

Iris smiled, glad that her friend shared her perception of Julian. "You're right, but I know he appreciates each and every fan. He loves performing for a live audience and feeling the interaction with them. And he loves knowing that people listen to his songs, identify, maybe find a respite from their worries, or find solace in songs about other people whose lives aren't easy either."

"Then he'll be perfect for Arbutus Lodge," Eden said. "Thanks for getting him to agree, Iris." She took her phone out of her pocket and tapped the screen. "Let's set up a meeting to plan the book club. You, me, and Glory. You know Glory McKenna, right?"

"Of course. Not at school, really, because she was a few years ahead." And Iris had barely spoken to anyone in school other than her best friend Shelley. "But she's in the store a lot, with Gala." Glory and her partner, Brent, had an adorable three-year-old daughter. "She mentioned that she's now assisting you with programming, and loving it." Right after high school, Glory had gone to work at Arbutus Lodge as a receptionist. Recently, Eden had increased her responsibilities.

"Let's try to set it up soon," Eden said. "Before all the Christmas activities get going in full force."

After arranging a time to meet, Eden put her phone away again. "This is going to be an amazing winter," she said. "It's Aaron's and my first Christmas as husband and wife, and Mom is cancer-free, which is the best gift any of us could get. On top of that, rumor has it"—she put on an innocent expression—"that there's a wedding happening before too long."

Iris turned to Miranda. "How are your wedding plans coming along?"

"Really well, except that I can't find a dress that feels like me." She heaved a sigh. "I mean, it's only a dress, right? The important thing is that I'm marrying Luke, and we're crazy about each other, and our three kids are wonderful. I shouldn't obsess over the dress."

"No," Eden said, "but all the same, every bride wants that special dress on her special day."

Iris wondered if by any chance her aunt might be able to help Miranda. She'd talk to Lily and see what she thought, before mentioning it to her friend. "When I first met you," she said to Miranda, "you were so determined to be independent. And now here you are, getting married."

One corner of Miranda's mouth kinked up in a wry smile. "I've come to realize independence is an illusion. Everyone needs other people, and it's stupid not to admit it."

Eden grinned at her.

Miranda smiled back. "Now there's a body-language *I told you so* if I ever saw one. But anyhow, I know marriage is this archaic institution, rooted in all sorts of chauvinistic crap, and sometimes I think I'm crazy that I actually want to do it, but I do."

"Inconsistency, thy name is Miranda," Eden teased.

"Why do you want to get married?" Iris asked, not challenging, just curious.

Miranda took a breath and her light blue eyes took on a grayish tone, as they did when she was sad. "The way I grew up made me insecure. I kept chasing after love, never finding it, and deep down inside I didn't believe I deserved it."

"Of course you do," Iris said. "You know that, right?"

"A bunch of good people, like you ladies and Luke, are convincing me of it. And marriage, that stupid old institution, is a formal recognition that Luke loves me and wants to spend his life with me."

A formal recognition. Wasn't it the essence that mattered, not the formalities? Not that Iris would ever dispute her friend's beliefs, but now she was even more curious. "Eden, why did you and Aaron get married?"

Eden gave a soft laugh. "Besides being madly in love? Well, he was the one who proposed, so you'd have to ask him why he did. As for why I accepted, it's due to Mom and Dad. Their marriage is wonderful and I always dreamed of having the same thing." She cocked her head. "Your family's pretty traditional, Iris. I'm guessing you and Mr. Right will be saying wedding vows?"

Iris had reflected on this subject over the years, as she contemplated her ideal future. "Maybe, maybe not. I like the idea of a personalized commitment ceremony."

"Like Aunt Di and Uncle Seal," Eden said. "Theirs was on the beach."

An image flashed into Iris's mind of her and Julian at the old commune. A crown of wildflowers adorned her hair and they held hands, gazed into each other's eyes—

"Iris?"

She came to with a jolt, to see her friends studying her with curiosity.

Eden went on. "You wouldn't care about that formal, legal recognition?"

"Not from a religion I don't believe in. As for a civil ceremony and an official certificate of marriage . . . Well, you're right that my family's quite conventional, but common law partnership is widely accepted now. I think the decision of how to make a lifetime commitment should belong to the individuals who are making it."

"You sound really secure," Miranda said. "More than I am, that's for sure."

"I'm quite secure in knowing who I am," Iris said, "and knowing my own value. My family always made sure I knew I was loved and valued for exactly who I am." Her lips twitched. "Of course it helps that I wasn't inclined to be anything but a good girl."

Eden chuckled. "That makes two of us."

"A lot of people don't really see me," Iris said. "My shyness and reserved nature have always made me prefer to stay in the background. Some people interpret that as aloofness and others think I'm boring. That's fine. The few people who do see past that are the ones who matter." She sent a grateful smile across the table. "I'm glad to have you as friends."

"And don't forget Julian," Miranda said.

"Yes. Him too."

"He's still 'just a friend'?" Miranda put quotations around the term.

There was no controlling the heat that rose to Iris's cheeks, but she tried to keep her tone neutral when she said, "There's no possibility of a future together. That doesn't mean we can't enjoy each other's company until he leaves in December."

"You'll miss him like crazy," Miranda said.

"Of course." She squared her shoulders. "That's a reason to value this time together rather than stop seeing him and start missing him right now."

"That sounds so logical," Miranda said. She glanced at Eden. "How come she's always so reasonable and wise, like she's a decade or two older than us?"

"She's an old soul?" Eden suggested with a smile.

"Julian is good for me," Iris said. "The fact that someone like him—a sensitive, interesting man and also a fairly big celebrity—truly sees me and values me, that boosts my confidence. It supports my belief that one day another man will come along, one as special as Julian"—surely such a thing was possible—"who loves me. A man who wants to build a future here on Destiny with me. To have babies together, or maybe to adopt because I hate the idea of there being unwanted children in the world."

"Of course that will happen," Eden said. "And in the meantime, I'm glad that Julian's good for you. Just please guard your heart a little, and don't get too emotionally invested in him." She glanced at her watch. "Oh gosh, I need to get back."

They all rose, Eden and Miranda put on their coats, and they exchanged hugs.

As Iris walked back to the bookstore, she mused on Eden's last comment. Yes, it was unwise to get too emotionally invested in a man who would never be more than a friend. But, when that friend was Julian Blake, how could she stop herself?

Chapter Fifteen

Late on a Friday afternoon, two weeks after he'd brought dinner to Iris's parents' house, Julian again sat at the kitchen table. Akemi was showing him how to construct sushi rolls, Iris was making an orange cake for dessert, and Ken was preparing chicken *karaage*. Dreamspinner was closed for business tonight. Iris had told him that a regular customer had booked it for a combination bridal shower and Christmas party. Lily was at the store making sure everything ran smoothly.

In the Yakimuras' kitchen, they were all speaking French. Knowing that the family used either that language or Japanese at home, Julian had told them he'd be happy to speak French. The fact that they accepted his offer, and that Akemi was teaching him to cook rather than serving him, made him feel like a friend rather than an outsider.

Iris's mom placed a bamboo mat on the table and spread a sheet of nori seaweed on it. As she worked, she peppered him and Iris with questions about the seniors' book club meeting they'd attended that afternoon.

Julian was glad he'd gone. The songs he'd chosen to perform had gone over well and his presence had helped Iris cope with her anxiety. He'd enjoyed the seniors' insights and sense of humor, and found it thought-provoking hearing about their experiences and their issues. His muse had been taking notes.

Akemi looked up from spreading rice on the sheet of nori. "There's much to be learned from the wisdom of your elders. I'm glad to see you young people learning that lesson."

Iris laughed. "Mom, I've been taught to respect my elders since I was in your womb."

"And you, Julian?" Akemi arched her black eyebrows.

"I never knew my grandparents, but Forbes's musician friends were men and women of all ages. They were interesting, diverse. I learned to listen and not mouth off. So, yes, I learned respect." Maybe he should leave it at that, but he wanted to be honest with these people. "My dad and his friends thought for themselves, though. They didn't conform just because their elders told them to. They challenged authority when they thought it needed to be challenged. That was another lesson I learned."

"There's value to conformity," Akemi said evenly. She unwrapped a package of bright pinkish-orange salmon, took a cucumber from the fridge, and picked up a knife. "Watch. You slice the fish like this. Long, thin strips." She demonstrated and then gave him the knife. "Carry on. And the same with the cucumber."

While he got the feel of the knife, she went on. "I see value to fitting in. To respecting social institutions without necessarily agreeing with all of them."

"Forbes says you need to pick your battles," Julian said. "It's a matter of what your conscience can live with."

This is our secret, Julian.

He swallowed hard and his voice rasped when he added, "And of whether you're brave enough to fight the battle."

"One must have principles," Ken put in quietly, as he

stood by the stove. "Sometimes, though, the principle is the value of compromise."

Iris turned from the kitchen counter, raising the back of her hand to her brow to give it a dramatic swipe. "I love philosophical discussions, but that's what Julian and I have been doing all afternoon. Could we please talk about something a bit less mentally challenging?"

Akemi, who had spread mayonnaise on the rice and was now lining the salmon and cucumber down the middle, said, "Julian, I imagine the seniors enjoyed your music?"

"They loved him," Iris said. "So did the staff. Including Eden and Glory, who are big fans of Julian's."

He remembered Glory's starstruck eyes, huge in her elfin face, when she stuttered out a request for his autograph. She and Eden had participated in the book club as well, and he'd been happy when Glory got over the fangirl thing and showed her introspective side. She and Iris had had an interesting exchange about identity, Iris saying that hers included her Japanese heritage and Glory saying that she completely rejected her Chinese one. She'd been born in China, abandoned by her birth parents during the one-child era, and then adopted by a Destiny Island couple of Scottish background. Glory said that, despite looking Chinese, she rejected the country that had rejected her, and identified entirely as Scottish. Julian envied Glory her ability to simply reject a part of her makeup. If only he could do that with his shame and guilt.

"Did you play songs you wrote yourself?" Akemi's question brought him back to the cozy kitchen.

He watched her roll the sushi into a long tube, thinking that her fingers were as deft in the kitchen as his were with guitar strings. "A couple. I also played snippets of songs from each decade, back to the nineteen thirties." He'd enjoyed the reminiscent smiles on the seniors' faces. "When Forbes is better, I'm going to suggest he go over with his guitar now and then. They'd love it, and I think he would, too."

"That's a nice idea," Ken said. "It would be generous of Forbes to give them that gift."

"Speaking of music," Akemi said, "how did your band's performance in Victoria go? You must have been missing that life, spending so much time here on quiet little Destiny Island." She cast a sideways glance at her daughter.

Iris, pouring the cake batter into a pan, didn't seem to notice.

"It was great," he said. "Fun to be with my bandmates again. The audience was terrific. Really involved." He only wished Iris had been in that audience. There'd been the usual groupies, including one persistent and very attractive redhead who'd come on to him. But having meaningless sex would have made him miss Iris even more and, for some not entirely logical reason, have felt like a betrayal.

"I'm sure you have many fans," Akemi said. "A talented musician like you, and such a handsome young man." Wielding the sharp knife, she cut the roll into symmetrical slices.

"Uh, thanks. Yes, fortunately the band is pretty popular." He truly appreciated the real fans. But loads of people said they loved him, loved his music, when in fact they only wanted something from him. To have sex with a celebrity and get their photo on social media with him. To get hired on as a singer or musician with the band, or to have him sing and promote songs they'd written.

People always wanted something from you. His dad loved him and was thrilled about his career, yet wanted his son at home more often. Even Iris wanted him to somehow become a homey guy, an island boy. Oh, she never said that, perhaps didn't even acknowledge it to herself, but he knew it.

Of course *he* wished that *she* could overcome her anxiety

about social situations, and become part of his life outside
Destiny Island.

"Now," Akemi said, arranging neat slices on a glazed
plate, along with a couple of other varieties of sushi she had
prepared earlier, "everything is ready. Let's move to the
dining room."

Iris took a salad of thinly sliced cucumber from the fridge
and Ken brought a bowl of delicious-smelling *karaage*. Once
they had seated themselves and used chopsticks to serve
themselves, Akemi said, "Do you realize, it's only ten days
to Christmas? In two weeks, the year will be over."

And he would be back in Vancouver. He avoided looking at Iris, who was as aware of that fact as he was.

"Blue Moon Harbor is so pretty at Christmas," Iris said.
"It's a wonderful time of year."

Julian had never been big on Christmas, but in the past
years Luke's boys had livened up the day. He needed to get
started on his gift shopping.

"I phoned Melanie Newall," Ken said, "and thanked her
for the great job the *Gazette* did on our holiday ad. We've
had a wonderful response to it."

Books were perfect gifts. Everyone in his family read—
even Forbes now, with his current fascination with thrillers.
Sonia, she loved anything scientific . . . He smiled, thinking
of Iris's knack for selecting the perfect book. She could
help with his Christmas shopping.

His mind was only half on the Yakimuras' conversation
as Iris asked her dad if Melanie had given him a hard time
about not running for some position.

Ken shrugged, and Akemi said, rather sharply, "I do
wish you would have."

"So do I," Iris said. "But I'm also sorry to see Walter
Franklin step down. He's been an excellent trustee. It's a
shame that a stupid rumor kept him from running again."

"At least there's a good man stepping in," Akemi said. "And it is uncontested, so we already know the result."

"Yes," Ken said, "Bart will do a fine job."

"Bart?" The name came out of Julian's mouth in a dry croak. He put down the forkful of *karaage* he'd been raising to his mouth.

Akemi turned to him. "Bart Jelinek? The man who owns Island Realty."

"Yeah, right," Julian managed, fighting a surge of nausea. He slipped his hand into his pocket and gripped the mended guitar pick. Curiosity drove him to ask, "He's running uncontested for what?"

"A trustee position on the Islands Trust," Ken answered.

Julian struggled to control his racing heart, churning stomach, and desire to flee. Iris had said that if she breathed deeply and accepted her anxiety, then her brain would understand that the panic was unwarranted and it would diminish. He sucked in air and let it out. "The Islands Trust is one of the governing bodies? They handle"—unable to think of the French word for "zoning," he switched to English—"zoning and development?"

"That's right," Ken said, speaking in English now, too.

"It's one of the most influential leadership positions on the island," Akemi said, also in English. "Since my dear *retiring, humble* husband refused to run, I suppose we should be glad it'll go to such a capable, respected man."

Respected.

This is our secret, Julian.

Yeah, Jelinek was *respected*. That was how he'd controlled Julian, by saying no one would believe a kid like him over a community leader. Since that time, the man's "star" had only risen. Now he would become even more prestigious. He would use that to manipulate other boys. So much for deep breathing and calming the anxiety; Julian's gorge rose and he took shallow breaths in an attempt to quell the nausea.

For years, he'd tried to box up the past and keep from thinking about it. From letting himself realize that he wasn't a *special boy*. That Jelinek wasn't just *his abuser* but a fucking *pedophile*. That over the past decade and longer, Jelinek had victimized other boys. And Julian had done nothing to stop him.

He shoved back his chair, its legs grating across the ceramic tile floor, and jerked to his feet. Nausea, dizziness, cold sweat; he couldn't even breathe. If he stayed here a moment longer, he'd throw up or pass out. Possibly both.

"I can't . . ." He gulped air. "Sorry, I . . ." Somehow, he managed to get his body coordinated enough to stride toward the door, and then he was running.

Iris stared after Julian, her mouth gaping. Then she was on her feet, too, rushing after him.

"Iris!" her mother called.

Iris, who never raised her voice, shouted, "Sorry, Mom," and kept going.

The front door of the house was wide open to the late November cold, and she slammed it behind her, flying out into the rain, down the steps, and toward the street. She caught up to him at the B-B-Zee van as he tried to jam a key into the driver's-side lock. Shivering, her light sweater absorbing the chilly rain, she tried to remain semi-calm. Taking the key ring from him, she said, "You can't drive. Julian, come back inside. Whatever's wrong, we'll talk about it."

He shook his head, tremors racking his body. "Can't."

Tension and cold made her tremble. His agony was obvious, and somehow she had to help. "Go around to the passenger side." She unlocked the door, hoisted herself into the driver's seat, and reached over to unlock the passenger door. Julian hauled himself in and sat, hunched into himself, quaking.

She turned on the interior light, levered the seat forward, and put the key in the ignition. Studying the diagram on the gear shift, she pressed down the clutch pedal and ran through the gears. Thank heavens Grandmother Rose had driven a stick shift. When she turned on the ignition, Janis Joplin's voice blared out, singing that a woman could be tough. Iris flicked off the CD player. She located the headlight and wiper switches and then, in first gear, pulled away from the curb. "I'll drive you to Forbes and Sonia's house." She made a jerky shift into second.

"No."

It was too cold for the commune and they couldn't go to the boat because her keys were in her purse, back in her parents' living room. Her apartment, then—provided Mrs. Wong, the neighbor who had a spare key, was home as she almost invariably was.

Visibility was nasty. Iris leaned forward, peering out the windshield. Beside her, Julian was like a child with night terrors, curled trembling in a fetal position. She'd seen him exhibit minor versions of the same symptoms before. Was he physically ill, or was it a panic attack?

Hands tight on the wheel, damp and shivering herself, she tried to think of possible triggers. A discussion about the Islands Trust and zoning? What could be more harmless?

When she stopped at the village's one traffic signal, the lights from holiday decorations were a colored blur through the rain, incongruously cheerful in contrast to Julian's state of mind. She clicked on the heater, was blasted with cold air, and turned it off again.

She passed Dreamspinner, Blowing Bubbles, and Island Realty, and turned onto Blue Moon Harbor Drive.

"Stop!" Julian cried in a choked, frantic tone.

Heart racing, she slowed and pulled toward the curb. Before she got there, he jumped out. She jammed her foot down on the brake pedal, forgetting to depress the clutch, and the van stalled and lurched to a halt. After shifting into first, she got out, too. The headlights and streetlights didn't provide much illumination through the heavy rain, and she didn't see Julian. Gazing around, she shivered as cold water beat against the top of her head and her shoulders. She had parked beside a row of townhouses, the property set off from the road by a low hedge.

She heard the sound of retching, over by the hedge. She followed it, to see Julian kneeling, his back to her. She touched his shoulder.

He jerked as if she'd struck him. "Go away!"

She wanted to help, but how could she if her touch upset rather than soothed him? Helpless, she stood in the rain as he vomited again.

Eventually, he rose slowly. When he turned to her, his face was white in the dim light, wet hair plastered to his forehead. "Sorry," he said grimly.

"It's okay." Again, she yearned to reach out but she didn't dare. "What can I do to help?"

He shook his head, which seemed to her to say that he didn't think anyone could help.

Trying to sound firm and competent, she said, "We'll get hypothermia. Come back to the van and we'll go to my place. We'll take off our wet clothes and I'll make ginger tea. It'll warm us and help settle your stomach." Maybe this was merely a tummy upset, but she doubted it. If the pain he suffered was emotional, how could she help if he wouldn't share with her?

"Okay." He said it with resignation, not hope, but he did accompany her to the van and haul himself inside.

This time, he didn't hunch over but flopped back in the seat, not bonelessly like a rag doll but taut and trembling, like he was exerting iron will to hold himself together but not quite succeeding.

She was shaking, too, from cold and tension, and could barely manage to drive. But she got the van into a guest parking spot outside her building. After they trudged through the rain to the front door, she crossed her fingers and buzzed Mrs. Wong. Fortunately, the seventy-something widow answered.

"It's Iris and I've forgotten my keys. Can you let me in?"

The door released and Iris and Julian took the elevator to the third floor. Mrs. Wong stood in the open doorway of her apartment, dressed in burgundy sweats. She held out a key, her sparse gray eyebrows climbing her forehead as she stared at the drenched pair.

"It's a long story," Iris said.

She unlocked her door and ushered Julian inside. "Go into my bathroom and get out of those wet clothes. Toss them outside the door and I'll put them in the dryer. Have a hot shower. There are a couple of new toothbrushes in the cabinet under the sink."

He said nothing, but walked down the hall.

Like her keys, her phone was in her purse, so Iris used the land line to call her mom.

Akemi answered promptly. "Iris, what's going on? Where are you?"

"Julian's sick. I'm sorry to run out like that, but I didn't want him to drive. We're at the condo." It would feel like a betrayal to say she suspected that the scar had ripped off his emotional wound. "I don't know what's wrong. I hate to ask this, but do you think Aunt Lily might stay at your house tonight? Julian didn't want to go home, and just seems to want to be alone. If she came home, it could be awkward for everyone."

"Yes, I see. We will do what we can to help Julian. Do you want me to call Lily at the store?"

"Thanks, Mom. That would be great. I need to get out of my wet clothes."

"If you need anything, you'll let us know." It was an order, not a question.

"Absolutely."

Iris went to her bedroom, stripped off her clammy clothing, and slipped into a plum-blossom yukata. She hung up her blouse, bra, and wool pants to dry. A shower would be nice, and she could use her aunt's bathroom, but she wanted to be available when Julian emerged, so she settled for toweling her wet hair. He had, as requested, tossed his pants and shirt outside her bathroom door. She cleaned out his pockets and put the clothes in the dryer in the laundry closet, and then put the kettle on.

Rubbing her arms to warm up, she stood by the stove. When the kettle whistled, she made a pot of ginger tea—no strong black coffee for Julian's stomach tonight—and took the teapot and two mugs to her bedroom. The bathroom door was still closed. The shower no longer ran. "Julian?" She tapped on the door. "Are you all right? Can I help? Your clothes should be dry soon, but in the meantime why don't you come get under the covers?"

He didn't respond, but after a minute the bathroom door eased open and he came out, clad in black boxer briefs. His face was pale and strained, his blond hair wet and tousled.

She dared to reach for his hand and this time he didn't jerk away but let her lead him to the bed. When she pulled back the duvet, he obediently slid between the sheets, sitting up with two pillows behind his back, the duvet pulled to his waist. He took the mug she handed him and she stood by the bed, not knowing what to do next.

"Look at you," he said, his voice even huskier than usual. "So pure and lovely. Like springtime on this dark, dirty winter night."

This wasn't the time to tell him about the kimono tradition of wearing a pattern that reflected not the current season but the upcoming one, hence her plum blossoms. Besides, she sensed he was talking about more than just clothing, using an analogy she didn't grasp.

Clasping her mug, she went around the bed and curled up on top of the duvet, facing him. "Julian, please tell me what's wrong. Let me help."

He stared down at the mug, took a sip of tea, and then gazed back to her face, his expression bleak. "If I tell you, you'll know how . . . *contaminated* I am." He spat out the word with disgust.

She didn't believe that, or at least didn't want to. She thought she knew Julian's soul, yet might his unhealed wound be something so horrible that she'd recoil? There was only one way to find out. "Tell me. Keeping this secret is tearing you up inside."

Chapter Sixteen

Iris was right. What she didn't know was that revealing his secret would also tear him apart. Not only that, but it would shatter Forbes and Sonia.

This is our secret, Julian.

"No," he muttered in a rasp that tore at his throat. "No longer."

"Julian?"

He took another sip of tea, his motions slow and deliberate. From here on in, everything would change. He noted the delicately curved line of the mug, the cream and rust ceramic glaze. He savored the ginger flavor on his tongue, unusual and a little exotic. Rather like Iris, with her wisdom and a rare beauty that went soul-deep. He put the mug on the bedside table beside a sage-green glazed bowl holding a half dozen pretty shells and rocks, and then turned back to Iris.

He knew the words he had to say. They'd been hidden in his soul for more than a dozen years, though he'd done his shameful best to bury them. "Bart Jelinek is a pedophile."

She blinked, frowned. "What? What did you say?"

He waited. She'd heard him; she just needed to process.

Her eyes narrowed in concentration. Slowly, she turned away from him.

Crap, I've lost her. She won't even allow for the possibility.

She put down her mug and turned back to him. Her lips quivered and her eyes were wide and glazed with moisture. "You?" she whispered. "He abused you when you were a boy?"

"Yes."

"Oh, Julian." She leaned forward and put her hands on his shoulders. "I'm so sorry."

She believed him. Still wanted to touch him. Didn't censure him. But that was only because the truth hadn't truly sunk in, with all its ramifications. Even so, the fact that she believed him was like one stone lifting from the heap that weighted down his heart.

"Tell me," she said as tears slipped down her pale cheeks.

"You don't want to hear the details." Yet now he'd ripped off the scab, more poison spilled out. "I was eleven when we moved to Destiny. A pissed-off kid. I'd lost my home and friends, lost my dad to Sonia. I had a stepbrother I didn't know, and the kids in school were his longtime friends. There was no place for me. I was vulnerable and I was weak."

"He preyed on you?"

Julian nodded. "He was a friend of Sonia's and Luke's. He visited the house, sometimes with his wife. He . . . recognized what I was. Flawed, weak. He befriended me, invited me to"—he gulped, remembering—"this outbuilding on his property. His man cave, he called it. His house wasn't far from ours, an easy bike ride. The man cave had cool stuff: a wide-screen TV, video games, snacks. He paid attention to me when no one else did. Enjoyed my company." He swallowed, a sour taste in the back of his mouth. "It felt like he was the one person on the island who saw me. And wasn't I an idiot to not realize what he really saw, this pathetic little victim?"

As he'd been speaking, he and Iris had adjusted their positions so now she was nestled against him with his arm around her shoulders. She stroked his bare chest in slow circles, and he didn't know whether she was trying to soothe him or herself.

"Julian, you were a child. You had no reason to suspect he was anything other than he appeared to be. He was a friend of your stepmom's and stepbrother's, so—" She sucked in a breath. "Luke? You don't think . . . ?"

"That Jelinek abused him, too? No. There were no signs of that. *Luke* was better adjusted than me, not so vulnerable."

"It was his island, his home, his support network with Candace and their friends."

"Yeah. So, anyhow, Jelinek said he'd always wanted a son but his wife couldn't have kids. He said I was a special boy, said he cared about me. Cared *for* me." Julian choked out the rest. "Said he fucking *loved* me. And I was flattered, needy, he knew all the buttons to push."

"My God," Iris said slowly. "It's so hard to comprehend. He's a criminal, yet everyone thinks he's a total good guy." Her eyes narrowed. "Every time you've gone strange, looked like you might be having a panic attack, it's because something reminded you of him."

He nodded. "Just being on the island has always been hard. I don't even read the *Gazette* for fear some article will mention him, or I'll see his real estate ad with his picture." Hoping to rid himself of the sour taste in his mouth, he reached for the mug and drank. His stomach had settled a little, thanks to the tea or maybe to spewing forth the truth to this amazing woman.

"He said we needed to keep my visits to his place a secret, because others would be jealous. He gave me attention, approval, affection—and God knows, maybe it was genuine. Maybe he's so fucking perverted that he actually equates abuse with love. He seduced me, like the salesman he is. Not with a hard sell, the kind that's so blatant even a stupid kid like me might've been able to recognize and resist it. But with a subtle, smart, persistent soft sell, exploiting all my weaknesses and fears and breaking me down until I was putty in his hands."

Iris's hand kept up that soft, repetitive stroking. "Go on."

"You know where this is going. He touched me, got me to touch him. Little stuff at first, and then . . . everything. A part of me was sure it was wrong, but here was this respected adult telling me it was good."

He squeezed his eyes shut and admitted another horrible secret. "Sometimes it felt good, Iris. Sometimes it hurt like a bastard, but other things felt good. That made me think I was a total perv. Made me question my sexuality. A few years later, when I went to a support group, I learned that even if it's abuse, it can feel good. Physically and emotionally."

He didn't dare look at her, but she hadn't stopped smoothing her hand over his chest. That gave him the courage to go on. "On the one hand, I felt loved and I experienced pleasure. But on the other hand, there was pain and the conviction that it was wrong. I was so conflicted and there was no one to help me sort it out."

"You didn't feel like you could talk to your dad?" she asked quietly, nonjudgmentally.

"I felt ashamed, guilty, but I was also mad and hurt that Forbes was so caught up in his new love that he didn't notice how miserable I was. In a way, being with Jelinek was like, *That'll show my dad*, which makes no sense at all."

"How could anything possibly make sense in a situation like that? I'm so sorry there was no one who could help you."

"Sometimes I'd get mad at Jelinek, tell him he was a bad

man and I was going to report him." *This is our secret,
Julian.* "He'd say we loved each other and nothing between
us was wrong, but others wouldn't understand. But there
was also this cold, hard edge. He'd remind me I was a trou-
blemaker kid, new to the island, and he was a community
leader. He said no one would believe me, that I'd get in
trouble and people would hate me."

Exhausted and depressed, Julian added, "Which was
true." And still would be, in all likelihood. But he couldn't
remain silent.

"That was why you left the island?"

He nodded. "I was fifteen. I couldn't take it any longer.
I hated him, hated the island, actually pretty much hated
my dad and Sonia. At school, I felt the other kids watching
me and was sure they could see my broken, filthy soul. At
home I'd curl up in bed in a fetal ball, utterly miserable, and
hear Forbes and Sonia laughing, singing along to music,
like I didn't even exist."

He shook his head. "I hated that room. After I left the
island, I wouldn't come back to the house until I persuaded
them to convert it to a home office for Sonia."

From down the hall, something buzzed. They both
jumped.

"Dryer," Iris said. "I wish I'd known, Julian. I could have
offered you friendship."

He caressed her shoulder through the soft cotton of her
kimono. "Ah, Iris, I doubt I'd have accepted the offer. I was
too messed up."

He took a long breath and let it out again. "The abandoned commune was my sanctuary. I'd cry, scream until my
throat was raw, punish my poor guitar by playing out all the
fear and shame and anger and hatred. But slowly the serenity
of the place would seep into me. Sometimes my muse would
venture out from hiding and my fingers would find different
notes, notes of pain still, but more expressive. Screaming

conveys a message, but meaningful words wrapped around haunting music can convey the story better."

"Yes, that's exactly what you do. I'm so glad you had one sanctuary. But it wasn't enough, I guess, and you had to leave?"

Speaking of leaving, his clothes were dry now. He could climb out of this cozy bed, get dressed, and drive away. He didn't have to tell her the rest. Except . . . she was Iris and he cared for her. He couldn't deceive her any longer. Even though, if he revealed himself to her in his full wretchedness, she might well reject him.

He was an onion, peeling himself. This next layer would be difficult, but beneath it was an even fouler one, and ripping it off would feel like flaying himself raw. But first things first. Thrusting her away gently, he held her shoulders and gazed into her eyes. "I left because I intended to kill myself."

Her body clenched and her eyes went huge. "Julian, no!"

"Jelinek had turned me into something I hated, something I had to destroy. But I didn't want Forbes to know I'd committed suicide. I was mad at him, but I still loved him. I didn't want him to blame himself. I decided to run away and disappear, become some nameless street kid in the Downtown Eastside. So when I died, I'd be a John Doe in a morgue. Forbes would wonder where I was, but as time went by and he didn't hear from me, he'd get over it. Forget about me."

"He never would have forgotten," she said, her expression uncharacteristically fierce.

He curved one corner of his mouth. "I know that now. Then, I had no perspective."

"Did you try to kill yourself? Or did you change your mind?"

"An old lady changed my mind. She, my muse, and the music. I'd been in Vancouver a few days and was trying to figure out how to kill myself: jump off the Lions Gate Bridge, buy some drugs and OD, steal a knife and slit my wrists."

Iris shuddered, and he said, "Sorry. Anyhow, of course I was driven to play my guitar, so I'd hang out on a downtown street corner, guitar case open to collect change. One afternoon, I was singing an early version of 'Ache in My Soul.' This white-haired woman came along, all hunched in on herself as if she felt as shitty as I did. But she stopped, listened, and her shoulders straightened a little.

"Tears trickled down the grooves in her wrinkled face and I felt bad for making her cry, but when I stopped playing, she put a twenty in my guitar case and she thanked me. She said her husband of more than forty years had died and she was feeling so alone, not knowing how she'd survive without him. But she said my song made her realize that she wasn't the only one who suffered horrible pain and felt afraid, and that realization made her feel better. She also said that my music was a reminder there was still beauty in the world."

Iris's eyes were luminous, her own smooth cheeks tear-streaked again. "You gave her a reason to live, and she saved your life with her words. Oh, Julian, I'm so grateful to her."

A little choked up himself, he cleared his throat and went on. "She made me understand that I wasn't alone either. And that, no matter how broken I felt, I had something to contribute to the world. So I kept playing and singing. As soon as I'd scraped together enough money, I got the tattoo. It's the first bars—the original ones—from that song. Long before I reworked it and recorded it."

"Wow." It came out hoarse and sniffly.

She reached over to the bedside table and his gaze followed her graceful hand. His wallet, keys, and phone lay there, along with—thank God—the old glued-together guitar pick. His possessions looked utilitarian next to the bowl of shells and stones, her silver-and-gold alarm clock, a hardcover novel with a feminine cover, and a tissue box with a pattern in mauve, blue, and green. Trust Iris, even when she bought something as mundane as tissues, she showed her aesthetic flair. His soul felt a moment's peace.

She took one of those tissues, wiped her damp cheeks, blew her nose, and then stroked the tattoo on his arm. "That's an amazing story. You know, when I saw you back then in school, I imagined one of two things happening to you: that you'd self-destruct or you'd do something incredible. I am so, so glad you didn't commit suicide." She blotted her eyes. "So there you were, a street musician who had decided to live. What did you do after that?"

"Slowly hauled myself out of the pit of despair," he said wryly, choosing a cliché he'd never use in a song. "Steps forward, steps back." Big steps back when it dawned on him that Jelinek wasn't just his abuser but a pedophile who had most likely found a fresh victim.

"The music kept me going, and the memory of that old lady. I did open-mic nights, got a few gigs at coffee shops and bars—just for tips, but it was something. I made some casual friends. Then I got in touch with Forbes, apologized for running out. I told him I didn't want to go to Destiny, so he hopped the ferry to Vancouver now and then, and we hung out. Played together on the street. That was a kick."

"I bet. He must have been so relieved and happy. But you never told him about Jelinek?"

He shook his head. "Just let him figure I was a troubled teen who was sorting himself out. And I did. Sorted out my sexuality, too. Slept with a couple of my casual female friends. Then I overheard a stranger talking about a support group for victims of abuse, so I asked him about it, and I went for a few months. Finally, I got to the point that I could come back to the island for a day or two, as long as I stuck close to home and avoided Jelinek."

Iris's dark eyes glowed. "You're a strong person, Julian."

He'd been feeling kind of okay, remembering how he'd pulled himself together, but her words socked him back like a punch to the gut. Literally, because now he was sick to his stomach again. He swallowed against the nausea. "I'm not." She hadn't seen it yet, the rest of the horrendous story.

Iris was amazing. Having her in his life felt like a blessing, and *blessing* wasn't a word he was in the habit of using. Since he'd first met her, she'd been serenity, sanity, and acceptance. So far tonight, she'd listened to everything he'd said and been on his side. But now . . . When he shed the final layer and revealed the rot at his core, what would she think of him?

Knowing that he might well lose her, he still had to reveal the truth. "A strong person would have reported Jelinek as a pedophile."

Staring at him, she blinked a couple of times and then said slowly, "I'm not surprised you didn't. As he said, it would have been your word against his, and he was the credible one."

"Yeah, probably. But I should have tried. Because it wasn't just me."

Her eyes widened again and now he saw it, the dawn of horror in their brown depths.

"I wasn't the first," he said. "That man cave had stuff for boys in it, and it wasn't set up just to seduce me." The words dropped like stones on a coffin. "I'd bet anything that after me, he raped other boys."

As had happened at her parents' house, a toxic mix of anger, loathing, and nausea jolted through his blood, making it impossible to stay still. He jerked away from her, thrust himself out of bed, and paced a few steps. He turned, his hands clenched into fists, his body vibrating with tension. "I'm a selfish, gutless bastard. As long as I stayed away from this fucking island, I did okay. I felt okay. Normal. But normality was a scab over an unhealed wound. Iris, the wound isn't so much that I was abused, it's that I didn't stop him from doing it to other boys."

Her lovely, gentle eyes were glassy.

"I tried to tell myself that I was the only *special* one, but deep down I knew there'd be others. It wasn't like he'd shown remorse. He didn't acknowledge that what he was doing was wrong. It was fucking *love*, to him. That's my wound, the one that never healed. That knowledge. And each time I came back here, the scab started to crack. I'd feel sick, scared, guilty. So I'd run back to my real life and the scab would heal over again. All I let myself care about was that I was okay. I couldn't go further than that, to imagine other boys suffering through what I had. Because if I did . . ."

Tension made him turn and pace a few steps away. With his back to her, he said, "I'm almost as guilty as he is."

"Maybe it was just you." Her voice was soft and uncertain. "Maybe he did love you in some bizarre, perverted way, and it was a unique thing. He's married, after all."

Julian turned, seeing that her arms were wrapped around her waist as if she, too, felt nauseous. "Don't make excuses for me not reporting him."

"The boy—or boys—before you didn't tell. Nor the ones after. I've never heard a whisper."

Which didn't excuse Julian, and she knew it. "He intimidated them, too, broke them down. Or maybe one or two did tell a parent, but no one believed them. Everyone thinks Jelinek is such a great guy."

He turned away again and walked to the sliding glass door. Iris hadn't pulled the blinds. The rain had stopped. Julian stared out at blackness dotted with lights. Not only were the stores and restaurants lit up, and the giant tree in the oceanfront park, but the commercial fishing boats also had colored lights strung in their rigging, and one had a big Santa Claus on its deck.

Blue Moon Harbor decked out in holiday style.

Blue Moon Harbor, a place that Jelinek virtually owned. "He keeps adding to that reputation," he said. "The more power and status he accumulates, like with this Islands Trust thing"—he turned—"the easier it is for him to violate another boy, to intimidate him, to get away with it."

Iris was hunched over, arms tight around herself, looking almost as miserable as Julian felt. "Yes, I see," she whispered. "Oh, Julian . . ."

Staring at her in her pink-blossomed kimono, so innocent and beautiful and springlike, he steeled himself to say what had to be said. "When it happened, maybe I had an excuse for not reporting him. I was a terrified, guilt ridden, powerless kid. But since then, I hid from the truth. I enabled the abuse of other boys." The burden of culpability made his throat ache. "That makes me a shitty person."

She was still looking toward him, but her eyes were unfocused. She was reflecting, consulting that spirituality of hers. Deciding whether to kick him out of her life. She dropped her face into her spread hands, rested it there for a long moment, and then gazed up at him. "I understand your feelings of guilt." Her body straightened, her crossed arms dropping. "Reporting him would have been the morally correct thing to do."

No shit.

She slid off the bed and walked toward him. "But you didn't, and even though you said you've mostly healed, I know how wounded you were. Avoidance was your psyche's way of protecting you. I know that sometimes doing the right thing can feel impossible." She stood in front of him, a foot away. Her shoulders rose and tightened and then she took a long breath and dropped them again. "What are you going to do?"

That foot of distance felt ambiguous—so easy to close, but unless she was the one to do it, it might as well have been a hundred miles. Tears ached behind his eyeballs. Unable to face her any longer, he turned again to stare out at the night, his vision blurring as the tears welled up and overflowed.

"Go to the RCMP and tell them everything." His gut twisted. "First, I have to tell Forbes and Sonia. And Luke. If there's an investigation . . . that's not how I want them to find out."

Chapter Seventeen

A shudder rippled through Iris. She felt raw and shaky, so could only imagine how wrecked Julian must feel. But she was glad he'd finally told her. Trusted her. She was glad he intended to do the right thing—but oh, how hard it was going to be for him.

She stretched her aching neck and gazed at Julian's naked back, reading his tension in his locked shoulders. Beside him, on the wall beside the patio door, hung her calendar. The December saying, from Horace, was particularly appropriate for Julian's situation. It was about keeping your mind even, during tough times. Much more easily said than done, of course.

"I can't imagine," she said tentatively, "don't want to imagine what you've gone through." Her eyes welled up again and a tear overflowed. "You survived, that's the most important thing. Not only survived but brought beautiful music into the world." She remembered how Eden had described her first impression of him: a tarnished angel.

Iris dared to rest a hand on his bare shoulder and felt his muscles twitch. "You're going to do the right thing. As for not reporting him before, you shouldn't blame yourself but forgive. You're human, Julian, and you suffered a terrible trauma." For years. That *bastard* had abused a vulnerable boy for years. Though Iris didn't believe in violence, she felt an overwhelming urge to punch Jelinek, to castrate him, to somehow make him feel an iota of the pain he'd caused the man who hadn't moved since she touched him.

"Julian . . ." She rested her damp cheek against his back. "I'm here for you. I want to help but I don't know what to do."

He remained still for a long moment, then began to turn and she lifted her head. She raised her tear-sodden eyes to him, and held out her hands.

Tears streaked his face, too, and when he reached out to take her hands, his own were trembling. "Thank you," he said shakily, clasping her hands and drawing her to him. "For not rejecting me. It's more than I deserve, but I'm grateful for it."

She put her arms around him and his came around her. They held each other loosely as she gazed up into his face.

"As for helping," he went on. "This helps. So much. You being with me, listening, trying to understand. Touching me rather than stepping away."

If her heart hadn't already broken for him, it would have done it then. She managed a wobbly smile. "I would never step away."

And she knew, this was the time. Their time. Blinking tears from her lashes, she summoned the courage to make her request for the second time. "Make love with me, Julian. Join with me, fully." They both needed it, to help heal tonight's pain, to get past the tragic stories and write a verse that was warm and loving.

His blue eyes were starry, tears glazing them and tiny drops dazzling his lashes.

She swallowed. "Please. I want you. Don't reject me now."

"I would never reject you."

Did he realize how his words paralleled the ones she'd just spoken to him? "Good."

"But, Iris—"

"No." She broke in with calm firmness. "No *buts*. Don't deny me this." Momentary doubt seized her. "Unless of course you don't really want me."

His head went back as if he were in pain. His Adam's apple bobbed as he swallowed. "Want you?" His arms tightened around her and he lowered his head again. "I want you more than anything, Iris."

"Then come to bed with me." She stepped away and pulled the blinds. Then she untied the sash of her yukata and, without ceremony, slipped out of it. Underneath, she wore skimpy panties, and she slid those off as well.

An erection was rising, stretching the clingy cotton of his underwear.

She tugged his boxer briefs down his legs and he kicked them free. Then she pressed her body lightly against his, her breasts flattening against his hard chest, his erection cradled between their lower bodies. What she felt included physical arousal but went beyond that. It was about honesty, nakedness of the soul. It was about need, and the desire to give and share and merge. To become an irrevocable part of each other.

She stepped back again and skimmed her fingers, light as butterfly wings, across his cheeks, brushing away the tracks of his tears. Down over his shoulders, all bone and muscle and sinew, shoulders that had carried such a burden yet not broken under the strain. Along the outside of his arms, the arms that held his guitar, his other half, the instrument that had saved him. Finally, she caught his hands, the fingers that sent music flying into the air to touch hearts, to change lives and—she had no doubt—to even save them.

Stepping backward, tugging him gently, she moved toward the bed. He came with her. Not letting go of his

hands, she sat on the edge of the bed and then eased up
to lie diagonally across it, pulling him along until he lay
sprawled half over her.

He freed his hands and adjusted his position so he lay
between her spread legs, his forearms on the bed framing
her face and taking some of his weight. Gazing into her
eyes, he said, "You are a lovely woman, inside and out."

She had always hoped, wanted to believe, that one day a
man would see her that way.

"I'm honored you want to give me this gift," he said. "I
don't deserve it, but no—"

No! He couldn't turn her down again.

Perhaps he saw alarm flare in her eyes because he gave
a slight, rueful smile. "Let me finish. No, I won't refuse
your gift."

Relief washed through her and then his lips were on hers
and, as they kissed, she felt a softness inside her. A yield-
ing, a readying.

Before, when they had fooled around, she'd learned
from him but sometimes taken the initiative, trying out
things she'd read about. This time, she lay back and left it
all to him, letting her reactions tell him how much pleasure he gave her as he explored her body with gentle, slow
caresses that teased and aroused every inch of her.

When she was a flushed, damp, nerve-tightened mass of
need, he took a condom from the wallet she'd placed on the
bedside table and sheathed himself. She bent her knees,
expecting him to enter her, but instead he lifted her lower
body, bending down and bringing her to his lips.

She was so ready that it took only a few strokes of his
tongue for her to come undone.

As she quivered with aftershocks, he came up the bed,
his hips between her bent legs, and slipped into her, easing
in bit by bit as her trembling body adjusted and opened
for him.

She wrapped her arms around him, readying herself for pain.

His thumb pressed her clitoris, startling and distracting her, and with a quick, decisive thrust, he broke the barrier. One heated burst of pain, and she was no longer a virgin. He paused then, his only motion the gentle rub of his thumb across that tiny, taut bundle of nerves. "Okay?" he asked, the intense blue of his eyes dazzling her.

"More than okay," she responded, knowing she would never be the same. And glad of it.

His face lit, just tiny movements around his eyes and mouth, but she read affection, need, and a touch of humor. "This is when the fun begins."

He stroked slowly, smoothly, and her body learned this new sensation. There was still a little residual pain, yet sex felt like dark chocolate, the slight bitter edge only making the sweetness more luscious. He dipped his head to kiss her, his tongue mimicking the thrusts of his penis, and she welcomed it with her tongue.

His eyes were open and so were hers because this was Julian, this was her making love for the first time ever, making love with Julian, and she wanted to experience it with all her senses. The concentration on his face; the wet slap of their bodies as he withdrew and then thrust back into her; the harsh sounds of their breath; the scent that was salty, musky, headily erotic. And of course there was touch, the best sense of all. The gentle abrasion of five o'clock shadow against her chin; the flex of his buttock muscles under her fingers; the seductive in-and-out pumping that aroused her in a way she'd never imagined.

Her body tightened again, reaching, preparing for orgasm and clamoring for it. It was a stronger, sharper, more all-consuming sensation than she'd ever experienced.

Julian's eyes glazed and his strokes lost their rhythm,

becoming fast and uncontrolled. His thumb again found her clitoris. "Iris, come with me," he gasped.

That tipped her over the edge. "Oh, Julian!" she cried as she experienced the glorious sensations of climaxing all around him, and feeling his orgasm take him deep into her center.

Saturday morning, waking with Iris spooned in his arms, Julian felt surprisingly good. It was the Iris effect. Telling her about Jelinek had physically and emotionally drained him, and yet her acceptance and generous love-making had refilled his reserves.

He raised his head to check her alarm clock, seeing that it was just past seven. The motion was enough to make her stir and stretch. She made a purry, feminine sound. "Julian," she said in a satisfied tone, wriggling her butt against his rising wood.

"Good morning."

"It feels very good." She wriggled again, then lifted her head to look at her alarm clock.

"Do you have to work today?"

"I'm supposed to. Aunt Lily did handle the party at the store last night, but she probably wouldn't mind filling in for me. She'd want to come home and get fresh clothes, so—"

"Iris, don't change your plans. I'll get out of your hair. I need to arrange a family meeting, for tonight if I can." His body clenched at the thought. "I think I'll see if Sonia and Forbes can spare me for the day. I could use some quiet time, just me and my guitar."

"You can use *Windspinner*. I have spare keys here. You know how the furnace works, and the stove. There's hot chocolate, soup, crackers."

A haven on a cold winter day. "That would be great.

Thank you." His erection was full and hard now, urging him to thrust against her warm, curvy butt, but he resisted. They'd made love a couple of times last night, and likely she was sore.

She gave a suggestive wriggle. "We have lots of condoms."

He'd had one in his wallet, and she'd surprised him by getting a box from her bathroom cabinet. Somehow, Iris had found the nerve to shop for condoms. "Are you sure? I bet you're tender. I don't want to hurt you."

"Sometimes a little pain is worth the pleasure."

He hated the thought of bringing her even a small amount of pain, but he wanted her and knew she wanted him. So he rolled her onto her back and then slipped under the covers, kissing her gently and caressing her with soft fingertips, working his way down her body until, between her thighs, he licked and teased her. Her fingers gripped his head, holding on for the ride as he coaxed her to orgasm.

Then, when she was all soft and warm and wet, he sheathed himself and slipped into her, moving in and out in a slow, easy rhythm. Her slim, graceful body was perfection under his, silky and warm and womanly. Her arms curved around his back, holding him securely, and her long, flexible legs wrapped around his waist, pulling him close. She smiled at him, her eyes glistening pools of melted chocolate, her lips pink and a little swollen. Irresistible lips, and so he kissed them and she kissed him back, and he felt like he was home.

They kept the pace slow, rocking together, until her breath quickened and her body tightened. He speeded up, being careful not to thrust too forcefully, and they climaxed together.

After, when their breathing slowed, she said, "I hate the

way it came about, you and me getting together like this. But I'm so glad we have."

"Me too." He lifted himself off her and dealt with the condom.

She slid out of bed. "Tell me we'll do this again," she said, pulling on her robe.

"Yes, please."

Her back to him, long and slender in the flower blossom kimono, her hair shiny and tousled on her shoulders, she cast a glance over her shoulder and smiled. Then she walked over to the patio doors and opened the blinds. "It's nasty out there today."

Naked, he came over to see. He was greeted with the slap of rain against the glass doors, driven by a fierce wind. "Oh, great. Weather that matches up with the tasks ahead of me." The pretty Christmas lights were almost obscured by the storm. "I'm going to ruin Christmas for my family," he realized.

"No. Your family will be stronger for knowing the truth." She took his hand and tugged him over to stand in front of her wall calendar. "Julian, read this month's message."

He'd noticed her calendar before but never taken a close look. Now he saw a photograph of a dark pond with a path of asymmetrical stones crossing it, and green grasses growing alongside. A quotation attributed to Horace said that when your path in life was steep, you needed to keep your mind even.

"Even," he said. "That's not exactly crystal clear."

"That's one of the things I love about this calendar. There's always lots to muse on, over the month." She leaned against his side, tipping her head onto his shoulder.

He put his arm around her as she said reflectively, "I think it means not worrying about the obstacles to come, nor getting sidetracked by distractions. Finding your balance, your quiet place deep in your soul, and focusing on that when the going is tough."

Iris was the quiet place deep in his soul. "I'll try to do that." Feeling a little foolish, he said, "Will you give me something?"

She looked up at him. "If I can. What do you want?"

"Something of yours. A token, like . . . I know, one of those beach stones by your bed."

Arms around each other, they walked over. The pretty bowl of shells and stones was partially obscured by discarded condom wrappers. "Something I can put in my pocket, that I can touch and feel connected with you." A pebble would also remind him of the calendar's message.

"I love that idea. Choose whichever one you want."

He cleared away the wrappers, considered, and picked a satiny smooth oval stone with delicate green veins running through it. Though Iris hadn't asked for anything of his, he wanted to reciprocate. He wanted her to have a tangible reminder of their bond.

He wanted her to have a part of him. And so he slid the old guitar pick off the edge of the table and rubbed it gently between his thumb and index finger. How many times had he done this, over the years? "It's just an old pick. Twelve years old, in fact. I'm really glad you found it in my pocket and didn't put it in the dryer." He handed it to her. "I want you to have it."

She took it gingerly and examined it, then ran a fingertip along the crack. "A dozen years old? You had it when you were fifteen, when you left Destiny."

"It's the one I was playing with, the day that old lady stopped."

Her head jerked up. "Oh, Julian."

"It's just a cheap one, and it broke a couple of days later. But I was alive. I couldn't throw it away, so I glued it together and I've carried it ever since." That pick was a lot like him, broken but glued together and still surviving.

"You can't give this away."

When she held it out to him, he took it, tucked it into her palm, and curled her fingers around it. "Then keep it for me, in case I ever need it again." His lips curved. "And don't worry if it breaks. It's been re-glued more times than I can count."

Her expressive eyes were limpid with tears again. "I will treasure it."

Chapter Eighteen

Julian had called his family on Saturday morning, saying he wanted to schedule an "adults only" gathering as soon as possible. Everyone had consulted and decided to get together after dinner at Sonia and Forbes's house. Luke said he and Miranda would find a babysitter.

Julian had stayed on the boat all day, napping, fooling around with the guitar, heating tinned soup but not having the stomach to eat more than a few spoonfuls.

Now here he was at seven thirty, driving the B-B-Zee van into the familiar neighborhood. Every day there were more Christmas lights and decorations, though not at his dad and stepmom's house, because nobody'd had the time. Again he had the thought that he was about to spoil the holidays for the family he'd grown increasingly close to over the past weeks. The family he'd come to Destiny to help, not hurt.

Even though Julian's view of the family home was partially obscured by blustery wind-blown rain, he felt as if he saw it through fresh eyes. Vaguely, he remembered what it had looked like when Forbes and Sonia married, sold her old house and bought this one, and they all moved in. The house had been a mediocre rancher, run-down, with barely enough room for all of them, on a lot that was more wilderness than landscaping. It was situated on a dirt and gravel road that at the time was in the middle of nowhere. But Forbes saw the potential and could do the fixer-upper work, and Sonia had starry-eyed faith in her new husband.

Her faith had been well placed. Over the past decade and a half, Julian's dad had not only converted the old garage into a workshop and music studio, he'd expanded and renovated the house into an attractive two-story. He had strategically felled some big evergreens and he and Sonia had planted flowering trees and shrubs, and put in flower borders.

Although Destiny was into protecting the environment, controlled development was ongoing and had affected this area. The road was now paved, putting the neighborhood within a ten-minute drive of the village and making this a popular area. The property must be worth four or five times what his dad and stepmom had paid for it, not that they planned to sell.

Julian parked in the driveway beside Luke's SUV.

No, the place barely resembled the house he used to cycle to and from on his trips to school, the old commune, and Jelinek's house. And Julian wasn't that same kid, broken and ashamed, harboring suicidal urges. That didn't mean he felt strong, though. In fact, a large part of him would rather run away again than face what he needed to do.

But that wasn't an option. He climbed out of the van and rain attacked him. The pale gray Henley he'd worn to Iris's parents' house last night had been soaked so many times he'd lost count. But what was a little physical discomfort compared to his emotional turmoil?

He trudged along the path that led around the house to the back door.

This would have been easier if Iris was by his side,

holding his hand, brushing her cheek against his shoulder in that way of hers. She was so slender and delicate compared to him, but hers was the strength of a stalk of bamboo, a reed, a willow tree. The winds might buffet her and she would bend, but she wouldn't break.

He put his hand in the pocket of his black jeans, which were also getting wet again, and rubbed his thumb over the green-veined stone. If he'd asked her to come with him, she would have. But that hadn't seemed fair to her nor to his family. Instead, he had this pebble: tossed by the ocean, ground against other stones, then collected and treasured by a special woman who saw the beauty in its history as well as in its smooth surface and subtle colors. This was his connection to Iris, his way of borrowing some of her strength. His reminder of her interpretation of the quote from Horace about keeping his mind even.

The lights were on in the kitchen and no one had closed the blinds. Miranda and Luke sat side by side at the table, with Forbes in his usual seat at one end and a plate of cookies in the middle. At the counter, Sonia poured water from the kettle into the teapot.

With his hand in his pocket, curled around the stone, Julian opened the door. Four heads turned toward him, expressions of greeting and curiosity on their faces as everyone said some version of "hi."

"Julian," Sonia said, "you're soaked. Where's your jacket?"

"I forgot it."

"Go change into dry clothes," she ordered. "I'm making Earl Grey. Do you want some, or would you rather have a beer or a cup of coffee?"

Beer, definitely. But that would be a dumb idea. And caffeine was the last thing his jangled nerves needed. "Tea sounds great, thanks. I'll be back in a minute." When he'd thought about how he was going to do this, changing his clothes hadn't entered the picture. But he was pretty sure his stepmom wasn't going to listen to him until he did as she said. So he hurried upstairs, toweled his hair, and changed into an old sweatshirt and clean jeans, transferring Iris's pebble in the process.

Back downstairs, Sonia had taken her place opposite Forbes. In front of the chair across from Luke and Miranda sat a mug of tea. He picked it up, blew on it, and took a sip. The tea was hot, his clothes were dry and should be warming him, but still he felt chilled. Rather than sit, he went over to the counter. With his back against it, he said, "Thanks for coming. I'm sorry to wreck your Saturday night, but—"

Miranda interrupted. "You're not wrecking anything, Julian."

"Just wait," he said grimly.

That clearly got through to them. The cozy kitchen vibrated with tension.

"You need to leave, don't you?" Sonia said. "To go back to Vancouver and work on those new songs with your band."

"It's not—"

She cut him off. "Your dad and I have talked about this and he's a lot better. We'll be able to manage with a little help from some friends."

"Sonia, that's not it." Although they might want him to leave after he said what he'd come to say. "It's, well . . ." He took a deep breath, the familiar nausea in his gut.

He swallowed hard, and went on. "What I'm going to tell you will sound pretty awful. You're going to be shocked. You're going to want to stop me, to ask questions. To protest. But would you do something for me? Just listen. Let me get through it, all the way to the end, and then we'll talk about it. Will you do that?"

Eyes widened; they exchanged glances; questions formed on lips and went unspoken. Before any of them figured out how to respond, he went on. "Everything's going to change. I'm really sorry about that. It's going to mess up your lives, this stuff I'm going to tell you. But I have to say it. I have to do"—he swallowed hard again, thinking of telling his story to the police—"what I'm going to do. After you've heard me out, I hope you'll understand why." He fingered the pebble and took a deep breath. *Stay even.* "I hope you won't hate me."

Again, they exchanged shocked glances.

Forbes was the one to speak. "We won't hate you, Son."

Julian only hoped that proved true. He took a long swallow of tea, not registering the flavor, and then set the mug on the counter. Barbed-wire tension quivered through his nerves.

Staring out the window into the darkness beyond their heads, he said, "When I was eleven, Bart Jelinek raped me for the first time."

Ignoring the gasps, not looking at their faces, he went on. When he'd told this story to Iris, he'd felt so raw that he'd relived parts of it, but now he'd had time to prepare himself, and he recited the facts more dispassionately. As he spoke, he heard stifled gasps, a sob. But he couldn't look at their faces, because what he saw there might stop him—be it disgust, blame, or pity.

When he told them about running away from the island, he didn't mention his plan to commit suicide. He said he'd gradually pulled himself together, gone to a support group. Guilt clogged his throat and he could barely keep talking. "A part of me knew I wasn't the only kid, that he was doing it to other boys. And I let it happen. But now I can't keep quiet any longer. He's a pedophile and I have to try to stop him. I'm going to the police on Monday, but I wanted you to know first." He squeezed his eyes shut.

And then, because he had to, he dared to look at their faces.

His dad looked like he'd been sucker punched. Sonia

was blotting her eyes with a tissue. Luke was frowning. And Miranda stared at him with a fierce, angry expression.

She jumped to her feet like a spring that had been released, and rushed over to him. "The bastard. The utter bastard!" She clutched his forearm. "Julian, I am so, so sorry that happened to you." Usually, her eyes were the soft shade of well-washed denim, but now they were a storm-cloud gray, the kind of storm that threatened lightning.

"You believe me," he said. Even though they barely knew each other. He'd wondered about having her here tonight but had known Luke would only tell her afterward. Besides, she was already part of this family. For better or worse, tonight being the worse.

"You would never lie about something like that," she said with certainty. "I never liked that man. I always thought there was something wrong with him."

Sonia came to his side next, moving more slowly. She didn't touch him, just stared at him with a sad, baffled, tear-stained expression. "I'm stunned. I never had the slightest idea. He's always been . . . I mean, he *used to be* such a friend. Of my first husband's and mine, and then after Hank died, he was there for Luke and me." Her brown eyes widened and she swung around. "Luke! You went to his place, too. Did he—?" She broke off.

Luke still sat at the table, his fingers now gripping his temples. He stared across the room at them, but his eyes looked unfocused. "No, but . . ." He shook his head. "I know that man cave, the video games. Popcorn." His focus sharpened and his raised eyebrows asked Julian a question.

"Yeah. Popcorn." Oh crap, had that bastard abused Luke, too? "One bowl to share. Both of you dipping your fingers into it."

Luke nodded.

"It was a way of touching you," Julian said. "Seemingly

innocent, the kind of thing you'd do with your dad. But he was testing, to see how you reacted."

Another nod.

"Luke?" Miranda let go of Julian's arm and went over to her fiancé, leaning down to hug him. "Tell me he didn't."

He shook his head. "No. But now I see it all in a different light. After Dad died, Jelinek said I needed an older man in my life, someone to talk to and hang out with. He said I was a special boy—" He broke off when a choked growl escaped Julian.

Staring at Julian, Luke said, "He told you that, too, didn't he?" Not waiting for a response, he went on. "He said he'd always liked me." He swallowed. "He saw how much I missed Dad, how lonely I was. He was ready to exploit that." His troubled gaze was steady on Julian. "He said he wished he had a son like me. It seemed like he was trying to take Dad's place. It pissed me off, so I shoved him away."

"Thank God," Sonia said from where she stood beside Julian.

Forbes was the only one who hadn't said anything, the one whose opinion most mattered to Julian. His dad had been staring at Luke as he spoke, his expression saying it was all too much to comprehend.

Finally, he looked at Julian. He made a fist and slammed it down on the table, making the mugs and the plate of cookies jump and rattle. Then he pushed his chair back, the legs scraping across the floor. His crutches rested against the table, but he ignored them. In a lurching gait, he bee-lined toward Julian. "The fucking bastard. I'll kill him."

With both arms extended, he caught Julian in a bear hug. His momentum and unsteadiness on his feet would have toppled both of them if Julian hadn't been braced against the counter. With his dad's weight almost crushing him, Julian hugged him back.

They believed him. Every single one of them. Without

question. It was more than he'd allowed himself to imagine. Grateful beyond words, he fought against the lump in his throat and managed to croak, "You're a pacifist, Forbes."

"Not when it comes to this. I'll rip off his fucking balls."

"I'll hold him down while you do it," Miranda said.

"I'll help, dragon girl," Luke said, referring to the vibrant tattoo on her left forearm.

"I am so very, very sorry," Sonia said, her voice thick with tears. "It was because of me that he had the opportunity."

"You didn't know," Julian said. "There's no way you could have."

His father dropped his arms and stepped back, losing his balance. Julian braced him and Luke rose to bring him the crutches. Forbes wedged them into his armpits. "Son, you should have told me. I'd have believed you."

"Jelinek had me brainwashed. And you were . . . you and Sonia were in love and . . ." How could he say this without sounding as if he blamed them?

Luke said, "You were unavailable. Mom, Forbes, I know you didn't intend to shut us out, but you were so wrapped up in each other that you weren't there for Julian or me."

Sonia let out a sob and buried her face in her hands. "You're right. I'm so sorry."

"Crap," Forbes said.

"I had Candace," Luke said, "and Viola and the vet clinic. But Julian . . ."

"I was in a new place, didn't know anyone," Julian agreed. "I was uprooted and unhappy and I never tried to fit in."

"And I never helped," Luke said grimly. "This is partly my fault, too."

"This isn't about placing blame," Julian said. "If we're gonna do that, it lies on me. I was vulnerable and he saw it. He manipulated and exploited me, and I let him do it."

"You were *eleven* freaking years old!" Miranda said. "Look, people, something awful happened and there's only one person who's to blame. Okay?" She narrowed her eyes and glared at each of them in turn.

Sonia gave a shaky laugh. "Son, you did well when you chose this one." She went to get a tissue from a box on the counter and blew her nose. "Let's go sit in the front room and drink our tea and, well, I guess Julian will tell us how he plans to handle this, and how we can help."

She came to stand in front of him and put her arms around him loosely, tentatively. "I know I'm not your mom and I was a pretty bad stepmom, so I have no right to be proud of you. But I am."

Proud of him. He'd made it clear that due to his silence, God knows how many boys had been abused. But she was proud of him. He returned the awkward hug. "Thanks."

A few minutes later, they had regrouped in the front room with its comfy, well-worn furniture. Forbes and Sonia were on the couch, and Luke on an overstuffed chair with Miranda perched on its arm. Julian took the matching chair, sitting on the edge rather than sinking into it.

Forbes said, "When you ran away, I was scared and hurt. Now I know you did it because you were scared and hurt. I wish I'd been there for you to talk to."

"Me too. I should have tried harder. I was too messed up to think straight."

"You didn't even let your dad know you were alive," Sonia said softly. "Why not, Julian? Were you so very mad at him?"

He shook his head. "I was just too messed up."

"So messed up," his father said, "that even when you'd escaped Jelinek, you still couldn't contact me?"

"Oh hell, I don't know what to say."

"You've kept enough secrets," Miranda said. "Can't you

see, whatever you're hiding, no one here's going to judge you for it?"

"It's not me I'm worried about."

"Just tell the story, Son," Forbes said heavily. "Don't worry about us and our feelings. We want to know all of it."

Julian stared at his father, sitting on the couch with his good arm around his wife. Despite the faded tie-dye T-shirt and scraggly ponytail, his old man had an air of dignity. His blue eyes, an older version of Julian's own, telegraphed love and sincerity. Deciding to respect his dad by doing as he'd asked, Julian said, "I wanted to disappear. Become an anonymous street kid. And then I was going to kill myself."

Sonia gasped, Forbes gulped, and Luke said, "Jesus, Julian." Only Miranda was silent.

He told them the same thing he'd shared with Iris, about trying to figure out how to do it. How the old lady stopped to talk to him, and her words saved his life. Sonia cried again, and there were tears in his father's eyes. "That's the song I got tattooed on my arm," Julian finished.

Miranda rose and came over. Dropping to her knees beside him, she rolled up her left shirtsleeve and then peeled up the right sleeve of his sweatshirt to reveal his tattoo. She placed her forearm next to his, the fire-breathing dragon and the bars of lifesaving music. "It's about control, isn't it?" she said.

"I'm not sure I understand."

"Not the tattoos. They're just the symbols. But what saves you, it's control. When you feel like you don't have control over your life, it's a horrible, desperate feeling. When I was thirteen . . ." She sent a quick glance in Luke's direction. "No one knows this but Luke and Aaron. I used to cut myself with a razor blade."

When Sonia made a sound, Miranda quickly went on. "Not to commit suicide but because, with the lifestyle our addict mom created, I felt like I had no control over anything. But that blade gave me control. Over my skin, my blood, my pain, my life. I had control over those."

Her eyes were clear blue now, focused intently on Julian. "Aaron caught me cutting, and he told me I had control over far more than that. I had survived our mother, I'd survived everything life had thrown my way. He said I was strong and fierce and smart, like a dragon."

"You got the tattoo so you'd never forget that."

She gave a rueful smile. "That was the idea. I've faltered sometimes, as Luke well knows, but I've survived. So for you, it's the same, right? The bastard pedophile took away your sense of control over your life, but that old lady gave it back. She showed you that you had something incredible, a gift that could make other people feel better. Improve their lives."

"Yeah. That's it. Thank you for understanding." First Iris and now Miranda. To have people actually *get* him felt like a gift.

As she rose and returned to sit by Luke, Julian said, "I guess that's why I didn't get in touch for so long. I needed to feel like I was in control of my life before I could let anyone else in." He shook his head, refocusing. "Let's move from the past to the present. I don't know what the police will do after I tell them. They may question you. Sorry about that."

"I hate to ask," Luke said, "but is there a statute of limitations or anything like that?"

"No," Sonia said. "Not for the sexual abuse of a minor. And Julian, we're the ones who are sorry." She squeezed Forbes's hand. "We failed you in the past. All of us except Miranda. We want to be there for you now."

Julian had managed to hold it together through their tears and angst, but now emotions threatened to swamp him. Relief, gratitude. "Thanks," he said gruffly. "Thank you, all of you."

"You're welcome," Miranda said brightly, "but hey, enough about you, okay? Luke and I have our own minor crisis. It's only ten days until Christmas, and we've been so busy with wedding plans that we haven't got a tree up, or lights or anything." She tossed Julian a flash of a smile and he realized she'd deliberately rescued him.

She turned to Luke. "So, we could use some help. Right, fiancé of mine?" A wordless message passed between the two of them.

"Right," Luke said. "Tomorrow afternoon. Who'll come?"

"You can have my hands," Forbes said. "One of them isn't as functional as it used to be, and I won't be climbing any ladders, but I can untangle strings of lights, that kind of thing."

"Really, he just wants to boss us all around," Sonia said, her voice quavering despite her teasing words.

"Count me in," Julian said, suspecting Miranda and Luke had manufactured the family activity on the spot, to give them all something positive to do together.

"Invite Iris," Miranda said. "She has an artistic eye."

"She does," he said. "I'll ask. That'd be nice." He would love to have Iris be part of his family's holiday preparations. He hoped her shyness wouldn't lead her to refuse the invitation.

"So this is really a thing, you and Iris?" Sonia asked.

"Yes." The word popped out of his mouth.

Miranda made a funny snorty sound. "Yeah, but what kind of thing?"

"Why?" he asked. "What's she said?"

"That you're good friends and will remain so after you get back to your musician life. Is that how you see it?"

Good friends. It felt like so much more. They were lovers now—and his brain did a sidetrack wondering if Iris would share that information with her girlfriends—and yet the basic truth hadn't changed. No matter how important Iris had become to him, he had to respect her personality and her needs. Including her need to find love with a man who'd be content within the boundaries of her little world. "Sure." He tried to sound casual. "She's a terrific person and I really like her, but what more could it ever be?"

Miranda gave him one of those untranslatable female cat-like smiles. "I'm not the one to answer that question, Julian."

Chapter Nineteen

It was Wednesday evening and Iris was with Julian. But, sadly, not alone in her apartment exploring the new physical and emotional intimacies of their developing relationship. Instead they were in her car, on their way to Miranda and Luke's house.

She was driving, both hands on the wheel as always, but Julian's hand rested on her leg. They were both silent. She'd been unusually silent with her family as well, these past couple of days, anxious not to inadvertently reveal Julian's secret.

On Monday, Julian had filed a report at the island's tiny Royal Canadian Mounted Police detachment. The male officer had been professional, but Julian said it was obvious he was skeptical. He'd said he would investigate the report—and he did talk to Forbes, Sonia, and Luke. This morning, the officer had phoned Julian and said that so far they'd found nothing to support his allegations, but they would continue to investigate.

Iris had suggested getting a lawyer's opinion, and Eden had agreed to stop by the condo on her way home from work today. She'd done her best to assist but, sadly, had no miraculous solution to offer.

After she left, Iris had set out a light dinner, but neither she nor Julian had done more than pick at the food. She knew he was frustrated and pissed off, and so was she.

The village, as they drove through, was postcard picturesque on this crisp, clear evening, but she wondered if she'd ever view Blue Moon Harbor in the same way. Despite island gossip and the occasional feud, she'd believed her home was a safe, warm, wonderful place. Now, the sight of Destiny Realty with its festive cedar boughs and holly put a sour taste in her mouth.

She averted her eyes, to refocus them a few doors down, on the display in Dreamspinner's window. Mr. and Mrs. Claus sat in rocking chairs reading to several elves, while a couple of reindeer eavesdropped.

It was the holiday season, a time for optimism and hope. Iris refused to believe that Julian's courage would be for naught. She would, as the December quotation said, keep her mind even, and she'd keep her spirit strong. "It's only the first skirmish," she said. "In the end, he will not prevail. You have a whole team on your side. We'll come up with a strategic plan." That was the purpose of tonight's get-together.

Julian squeezed her leg. "You're right. I refuse to let him win."

A few minutes later, as she drove down Tsehum Drive, she gestured toward Luke and Miranda's house. "We did a great job on Sunday."

The waterfront home was an architect's dream, in the very best way. All wood, huge windows, and unusual angles, it blended with its environment and was designed for energy efficiency. Now, the various angles of rooflines and windows were strung with multicolored lights, and white fairy lights sparkled in a couple of trees in the front yard.

"All it needs is snow," Julian said, "to really look like Christmas. Not that it's likely to happen."

"We've had a couple of years of unusual snowfalls. I wouldn't bet against it happening again." It was nice to talk about something as normal and mundane as the weather.

When she'd parked, Julian touched her shoulder. "Thanks, Iris. For everything."

She leaned toward him and their lips met in a tender, lingering kiss. They separated only when headlights flashed behind them, another car pulling up to the curb.

She and Julian climbed out of her Chevy Volt, to see that the new arrivals were Sonia and Forbes. Julian went to pull his dad's walker from the trunk. Though Forbes was okay on crutches in the house, it was still safest for him to use a walker outside.

As Julian helped his dad get out of the passenger seat, Sonia linked her arm with Iris's. Previously, their relationship had been one of bookseller and customer, but that had relaxed on Sunday amid the happy chaos of setting up Christmas decorations with the "assistance" of three kids and two dogs. Their affection for, and support of, Julian also bonded them.

Luke greeted them at the door, and there was the usual flurry of discarding boots and shoes by the door and getting coats hung in the closet. He led them through the house to the living room on the ocean side. The curtains were drawn across the view windows, and the big Douglas fir they'd erected and decorated on Sunday dominated one corner, but the room was large enough to still feel spacious.

A wood fire burned in the stunning, rough-stone fireplace. Plates of sliced Christmas cake and brownies sat on a round wooden coffee table. "Miranda's upstairs getting the kids settled," Luke said, "and the dogs are shut in the family room. Coffee's brewing and the kettle's on. What would everyone like?"

They all made their requests, and Iris went to the kitchen to help Luke. In a few minutes Miranda joined them; giving Iris a warm hug. "How're you holding up?"

"I'm not the one to worry about."

"Sure, you are. This is stressful stuff. But we're a bunch of smart people and we'll figure it out."

On that reassuring note, they took the drinks into the front room where the others were talking rather stiltedly about the village's Christmas festivities. Julian sat on a two-seater sofa and when Iris slipped into the seat beside him, he clasped her hand. Forbes and Sonia occupied the couch, and Luke, after adding more wood to the fire, took one of the chairs. Miranda curled up on the floor, leaning against his legs.

It all seemed so cozy and festive with the scent of fir in the air and the pretty lights and decorations on the tree. This should have been a relaxed social evening.

"Okay," Julian said, "I'm going to dive in. The cop says the RCMP take all allegations of sexual abuse very seriously, and they'll keep investigating, but so far they've found no evidence, not even a rumor, that Jelinek abused me or any other kid."

Iris took a sip of jasmine tea, the flowery scent a soothing contrast to the painful grip of Julian's fingers.

"Bottom line," he said grimly, "it's like Jelinek said all those years ago: it's my word against his. And he's the one with credibility."

Silence, a heavy silence, filled the room.

"Iris thought it would be a good idea to get Eden's opinion," he went on, "and we talked to her today. At first, she wasn't sure whether to believe me."

"That," Sonia said, "is because she doesn't know and love you the way we all do."

Iris's heart jolted at Sonia's phrasing, though the other woman didn't seem aware of what she'd said. But it was true. Iris did love Julian, as a friend and lover and . . . Well, that was all she'd allow herself. There was no point yearning for the impossible.

"To clarify," Julian said, "Eden said she knew that I believed it had happened, but she raised the issue of false memories."

Iris remembered exactly how Julian had responded. He'd leaned forward, his gaze locked on Eden's face, and said, "Don't you understand? All I've done, all these years, is try to *forget*!" He'd rubbed his hand across his forehead. "I remember how he'd always take off his horn-rims before he . . ." He swallowed. "I remember the expression in his pale gray eyes, like a predator." He paused. "I remember the disgusting mole on the inside of his right thigh. Tell me that's a false memory."

He'd continued, raking up memories as Iris, one hand interlocked with his, had trembled and tried to steady her breathing—to stay *even*—so she could support Julian. She hated that he had to relive these horrible things.

Now he told his family, "I gave her enough specifics to satisfy her. Then she mentioned something that Jelinek said one day. Right, Iris?"

"Yes. Remember, Miranda, when we had lunch at C-Shell?"

"Yeah, the asshole said Julian had always been unstable, erratic, and imaginative."

"Eden figures he was trying to undermine Julian's credibility," Iris said. "In case he ever did speak up."

"I'm glad she had the sense to believe you, Son," Forbes said. "But did she offer any practical advice?"

"Well," Julian said, "she said it's not her field of expertise and she could find me an expert to consult. But she did say that a criminal charge isn't the only route. I could bring a civil suit for sexual assault. The burden of proof is lower,

and it forces the accused to testify. But I'd have to hire a
lawyer and sue for damages."

"Damages?" Miranda asked.

"Things that can be monetarily quantified," Iris said.
"Eden mentioned medical expenses, lost income, pain and
suffering."

"But that's not what this is about, for me," Julian said.
"It's about stopping him. Besides, it's not like money could
compensate for what he did. As for lost income, what the
hell, maybe the angst made me a better songwriter and gave
me more income-earning potential."

"I know," Iris said. "But according to Eden, if you want
to sue and get a judgment against him, which means a
public record that he's an abuser, you have to claim damages and quantify them in dollars."

"You can sue for a dollar, right?" Miranda said. "Like
Taylor Swift did, against the jerk who groped her and then
sued her when he lost his job."

"That's an idea," Julian said.

Forbes, who'd been silent until now, said, "I have another
idea."

When Iris turned to the ponytailed man, she saw a gleam
in his eye, the kind of fire that she guessed he'd only rarely
displayed since his horrendous accident.

"There's an advantage to having an old hippie in the
room," he said, rubbing his hands together and looking
almost gleeful. "We didn't have a lot of respect for the law
back in my day, and we found ways of being effective. Civil
disobedience, protests, sit-ins."

"Uh, okay, Forbes," Julian said, a hint of lightness in his
voice for the first time since they'd all sat down. "You're
suggesting I stage a sit-in or protest at Island Realty?"

"We could all do it," his father said. "Picket outside the
door with signs saying 'Stop the Pedophile.'"

"Much as I love that idea," Sonia said, "we'd be arrested within ten minutes. Besides, most of the islanders would think we were crazy. Yes, it would stir up gossip, but they'd take Jelinek's side and nothing would come of it."

Forbes gave a wicked grin that took ten years off his age. "Not if the media's there. It's a classic strategy. Try it in the media rather than in the courts."

Iris winced. The media? Wasn't that the last thing Julian would want, having his painful story dragged into the public eye?

"Could we do the media thing," Sonia asked, "and skip the being arrested part?"

"Spoilsport," grumbled her husband. "Getting dragged off to jail is the fun part."

"Remind me why I ever married you," she joked.

He pulled her into a hug. "Later, babe."

"Count me in," Miranda declared.

Iris turned to Julian, her eyes wide with an unspoken question. Could he imagine doing what they were suggesting?

"I appreciate the thought," he said slowly. He squeezed her hand and then released it, stood, and walked across the room to stand in front of the fireplace, facing them. "But you're members of this community, with businesses and jobs here, friends here. If you stand up against one of the island's most respected leaders, it could hurt you."

"That's the point," Forbes countered. "Jelinek's relying on his reputation in the community for his credibility. Well, if you put all of us together, the people in this room, we have a hell of a lot of credibility ourselves."

"No, you—" Julian started, but Luke's voice overrode his.

"That's the key," Luke said. "Together. Yes, we each have

something to lose, but stopping Jelinek is more important than any personal cost."

"And if we stick together," Sonia said, "there'll be . . . well, not exactly safety in numbers because there'll still be risk for each of us. But it'll be less risk than if one or two people do it. And far more impact."

"No," Julian said again, his voice louder this time. He waited until everyone else was silent, looking at him. "Thanks, all of you, but no. I'm not going to let you risk your livelihoods, your reputations, your friendships on this island."

"It's not up to you, Son," Forbes said. "This is bigger than just you."

"Yes, but it's my responsibility. So, let's talk about what I can do. I have a bunch of media connections." He drew a ragged breath. "I can set up an interview somewhere high profile. CBC Radio. Tell the fucking story, for all the world to hear." The painful rasp in his voice indicated how difficult that would be for him.

Iris shuddered. "You shouldn't have to do that. There must be some other way."

Sonia cleared her throat and said quietly, regretfully, "It seems to me that whatever happens, unless Jelinek actually confesses, which he shows no signs of doing, Julian is going to have to tell his story and it will become public knowledge."

"No, surely not," Iris protested. "Isn't there a way of revealing the truth about Jelinek without . . ." She trailed off, seeing Sonia bite her lip.

"Think about it," Julian's stepmother said. "A civil or criminal trial would likely end up in court, with Julian on the witness stand. Testifying as to every horrible detail. Being cross-examined by Jelinek's lawyer, who'd try to rip him to shreds. And all that testimony would become public knowledge."

"Fuck," Julian said. He looked so alone, standing by the fireplace.

Iris never swore, but just this once she felt like echoing his sentiment. Or throwing up. She put her tea mug on the side table and wrapped her arms around her roiling stomach.

"But if Julian does what he just proposed," Sonia said, "one significant interview, then he can control the details he reveals."

"Other media and social media will jump on it," Forbes said with satisfaction. "It'll spread like wildfire. A prominent musician like you, Son."

Iris felt a strong urge to bolt, to run down the hall to the bathroom and hug the toilet, but purging the nausea in her stomach wouldn't clear the images of a media frenzy from her brain. She also remembered something else Eden had said, a consideration Julian hadn't yet mentioned.

"What if he sues you, Julian?" she asked. "Eden said your defense is that it's the truth, but that brings the whole thing back to it being your word against his. You might lose."

"I don't care," Julian said. "As long as people are warned about him."

"Julian," Sonia said, "if you do an interview, be sure to address any other victims who might be out there. If they're willing to go to the police, then it's more likely that charges will be laid against Jelinek."

"Okay, this is all good," Forbes said. "But we need to do something else, too."

More? When Iris had suggested talking to Eden, she'd hoped for some formal, legal solution. Now she was hearing a cascading snowball of publicity-oriented strategies. Her fragile emotions felt battered and pummeled, and she wished she could cling to Julian's hand, but he was all the way across the room. Standing alone, and yet the core of this circle of brainstorming support.

"What are you thinking of, Forbes?" Luke asked.

"Something to show we all support Julian." The older man winked. "Since no one else wants to picket."

"What about a dinner at C-Shell?" Miranda said. "After Julian's interview. All of us dining together at the island's best restaurant at Christmastime. It's more subtle than a picket line and it won't get us arrested"—she grinned at Forbes, her future father-in-law—"and because it's so respectable, it would get the message across."

"You're a good strategist," Forbes said. "We could have used you, back in the day."

"No, it's not a good idea," Julian said. "You're going to suffer consequences after the interview, just by being associated with me. I don't want to drag you in any deeper than that. This is my battle."

Forbes began to struggle to his feet and Sonia rose with him, putting her arm around his waist to support him as they walked over to Julian. Forbes in turn put his arm around his son's shoulders. "*Our* battle. We weren't there for you when you were a kid, but we're here now."

"Me too," Luke said, and Miranda chimed in with, "That bastard needs to be put away."

Which left Iris. These people had all, to varying degrees, become her friends. The notion should have given her a warm sense of security. Instead, she felt terrified. But this was the right thing to do and she must find the strength to do it. She tried to force down the panic and nausea that threatened to swamp her. *Breathe, center yourself, stay even.* "Yes," she choked out.

She'd have to tell her family, the family that believed in living a principled life but also believed in blending in, not making waves. Going up against one of the most powerful, respected men on the island wasn't just a wave, it was more like a tsunami. "I'll be at that dinner, too."

Julian could only guess what that gesture had cost Iris. She was so pale, her face looked like a white mask. This was too much for her. He shouldn't have asked her to come, but, selfishly, he'd wanted her—no, maybe needed her—at his side. And he hadn't wanted to shut her out of his life, though on reflection that would have been more considerate.

He smiled at her, trying to convey his apology and thanks. "Iris and I should go now." He came over to her and held out his hand. "I've taken up enough of everyone's time and I think the two of us could use some peace and quiet."

Peace and quiet. Once he spoke to the media, that'd be the end of any peace in his life.

Iris's hand, when she put it in his, was icy and trembling. He helped her to her feet, and the perennially graceful woman stumbled. As Sonia'd done with Forbes, Julian put his arm around her, steadying her—and himself as well.

"Thanks, everyone," he said. "It's such a small word in the face of what you're doing for me, but I don't know any other way to say it. Guess the next thing I need to do is tell my bandmates. And our label. Before the shit hits the fan. God knows how this'll affect our careers."

"They say there's no such thing as bad publicity," Forbes said, sounding unconvinced.

"Yeah, well." There'd been lots of examples where that wasn't true. "I'll let you know when I set up the interview."

He sighed, feeling almost as shattered as he had back when Jelinek was abusing him. In exposing the pedophile, he'd be exposing himself as well. Some people would say he was lying or his memories were false. Those who believed him would stop seeing him as a semi-successful musician, and instead as a battered, bleeding, emasculated kid. A coward who'd not only allowed himself to be abused, over and over, but had hid the truth, facilitating the abuse of other boys. And he deserved it. All of it.

What he didn't deserve, but treasured immeasurably, were the hugs and pats on the back that followed him and Iris to Luke's front door.

Outside, the night was clear, Luke's yard and several neighbors' creating a holiday mood. It was less than a week until Christmas. What would his life look like by then? And how much would his revelations affect his family's lives, and the upcoming wedding?

Iris was silent until they reached her little car. So quietly he barely heard her, she said, "Are you able to drive?"

"Sure." He took the keys she fumbled out of her purse, unlocked the passenger door and helped her in, and then climbed behind the wheel. Adjusting the seat for his taller frame, he said, "I'll drive you home and call a cab to get back to Forbes and Sonia's."

"Oh," she said dully. "I can . . ." She raised her slender hands, which trembled. "No, I really can't drive." She shook her head. "I'm sorry. This is so pathetic, so stupid. You're the one going through trauma, and I should be strong for you, but I'm falling apart."

He reached over and caught one of her hands. "I shouldn't have brought you into this. I'm sorry, Iris. When we . . . became friends, I had no idea that I'd . . ." He shook his head. "You should distance yourself from me."

She didn't respond and her hand rested quietly in his, almost as if she wasn't aware he was holding it. He didn't start the car engine.

Finally, she turned to look at him. "It's human nature to seek to be comfortable. We focus on the areas of life we can control. Like you with your music, once that old woman gave you her gift. Me, with my family and the store. Outside of the realms we can control, we often feel powerless, and so we avoid venturing there. Jelinek rendered you powerless. It's no wonder you tried to shove all of that into a little box in the past, all locked up. You tried to throw away the key or forget where you'd hidden it. But now you've unlocked the box and this time it's you who's seizing power and putting yourself in control."

He nodded. As usual, Iris's wisdom resonated with him. "Yes, I'm trying to."

"You're a strong man, Julian." Her shoulders rose and then dropped. "I feel very weak compared to you."

"This isn't your battle. You can walk away now, before it gets really bad."

She sighed and the smile she gave him was slight, sad, and resigned. "How could I live with myself if I did that? A friend supports a friend." Now, finally, her hand moved in his, giving him a gentle squeeze. "All I ask is that you understand my frailties. I will give as much as I can, but my strength has limits."

"I don't want to push you. I don't want *you* to push you."

"No." That smile again. "Of course you don't. Because you're a good, caring person. Do you remember how, in the *Tao of Pooh,* he talks about courage coming out of caring and compassion? Well, I'm trying to remember that, and find my courage." She let go of him and raised both hands to press them against her forehead. "But I'm afraid that tonight I truly have reached my limit. I need to go home and rest."

"Of course." He started the engine. "Just one more thing. I need to tell your parents and aunt. Before any media interview."

"I can do that. Not tonight, but tomorrow."

"Thanks, but no. They should hear it from me." He tried to think. "Maybe you could ask them to come to the store half an hour before opening tomorrow. Hopefully, that wouldn't be too much of an inconvenience. And we'd have privacy."

"You hate being in the village."

A rough laugh grated from his throat. "That's the least of my worries right now."

Chapter Twenty

It was Christmas Eve, and Julian's nerves were as jagged as barbed wire. Iris, seated beside him at C-Shell, facing the ocean-view window, gripped his right hand as if it was the only thing holding her together. He knew how hard this was for her, but she was by his side. Her hand was as much his lifeline as his was hers.

The past week had been the roughest of his adult life. After Wednesday evening's strategy session, he'd Skyped with his bandmates, an emotional but—thank God—supportive call. Thursday morning, he had notified his label, who'd said they'd consult their lawyer, and he'd told his story to Iris's family, who'd been shocked. When he called CBC Radio, the promise of an exclusive got him a Vancouver studio interview on Friday morning. Aaron had flown him over and back in his Cessna, a private flight he refused to let Julian pay for.

The CBC host had been excellent. She was gentle about not pushing too hard for details, but sincerely troubled, enough that at one point she'd choked up.

No, the interview hadn't been the worst part. Nor, even, was the social media firestorm that followed. What Julian truly hated were the phone calls Forbes and Sonia received

from islanders, berating them for letting their son tell such
dreadful lies. And the fact that media had camped out in
front of the house.

When Miranda had talked to the owners of C-Shell—
Rachelle and Celia, a married couple she knew fairly
well—about this dinner, she'd warned them that media
might appear at their door. They were not only willing to
take the last-minute group reservation, but Rachelle said
she'd ensure no paparazzi made it inside.

She had kept that promise. Shortly after the appetizers
arrived, there'd been a commotion at the entrance. Turning,
Julian had seen Rachelle, a stunning, chocolate-skinned
woman dressed in black, firmly refuse entrance to several
people. "Fucking media," Forbes had muttered.

Iris told him that Rachelle had rearranged the restaurant,
squeezing tables closer together in order to give their group
a semi-private long table in the prized location by the wall
of windows. The windows were unscreened, and the view
was a harmonious blend of lights from the boats in the
harbor, and reflections of the restaurant's candles and holiday lights. Fishing nets draped down from the ceiling,
studded with glass floats and colored bulbs, and the tables
had centerpieces of red-berried holly and gold-sparkled
cones. If only this meal were simply a Christmas Eve celebration.

Forbes said they mustn't cringe under the storm of
gossip and media attention, but stand proud and stand together. His dad, who couldn't even stand solidly on his own
two feet without crutches, had rallied this amazing group.
The gratitude Julian felt for the people surrounding him
would, if he were standing, have brought him to his knees.

His dad and Sonia were across from him, then Luke and
Miranda and also Luke's in-laws, Annie and Randall. Not
only were Eden and Aaron there but also her parents and
younger sister. Also her aunt and uncle, Di and Seal

SkySong, the old friends of Forbes's. Glory, his fangirl from the seniors' facility, who was a friend of Eden's and Miranda's, had come. Christian and Jonathan from B-B-Zee were here, and Jonathan's wife. And so were Camille, Roy, and Andi.

Julian's bandmates had, after conspiring with Forbes, taken him by surprise last night when they'd arrived on the ferry, complete with luggage, instruments, and the van the band used for gigs. None of them had family in Vancouver, but all the same they'd walked away from whatever holiday activities they'd planned. They said they were not only rallying around to offer support, but they figured it would be a good opportunity to work on music. Camille and Roy were staying in the grandkids' room at Forbes and Sonia's house, and Andi was camping out in the music studio.

On Iris's other side were her dad, her aunt, and then her mom. To associate themselves with him, and the public censure aimed at him, was a huge thing for the Yakimuras, who valued fitting in. But, like Iris, they were people of principle.

All the people at this table believed him and supported him, at substantial personal cost. Whenever he thought about it, he had to fight back tears.

The mood at the table was odd. The islanders knew each other and chatted about everything going on in their lives: Forbes's recovery, Luke and Miranda's wedding, Sonia's students, and the commune video game Luke's mother-in-law was developing. The B-B-Zee guys talked music with Camille, Roy, and Andi. The conversations were determinedly cheerful, with an underlying aura of tension. It was an "in your face" to the islanders who condemned Julian.

Julian's salmon was delicious, but he had little appetite these days and only managed to fork up an occasional mouthful. To his chagrin, Iris was barely eating either, and through their linked hands he felt tremors of anxiety quiver through her.

One day, he would write a song about tonight.

Of course, it remained to be seen whether he'd even have a career left.

Forbes had told Julian, Iris, and her family to sit with their backs to the room, so they could ignore what was going on elsewhere in the restaurant. A spot between Julian's shoulder blades itched and he knew they were under constant scrutiny. He overheard an occasional loud comment: "That's him, that's Julian Blake." "He should be ashamed of himself." Even worse, "What's Ken Yaki-mura doing with that scandal-monger?" Every now and then he was aware of someone approaching the table and of Rachelle or one of the servers warding them off.

Now, behind him, he heard Rachelle speak quietly but firmly to someone, no doubt another ill-wisher or jour-nalist. The response was equally quiet, male. Across the table, Julian saw his dad scowl and then a man came up behind Julian and said hesitantly, "Excuse me?"

Steeling himself, he turned his head to see a skinny older guy with thin gray hair, a lined, brown-skinned face, and a troubled expression. Not accusatory, though. "Yes?" Julian asked. "Can I help you?"

The man swallowed audibly. "You didn't lie, did you?"

How about that? Someone who was willing to give him the benefit of the doubt. "No, sir. I didn't. Every word was the truth."

"I was afraid of that, when I saw all these good people here with you." His voice broke and, to Julian's astonish-ment, the man's faded brown eyes filled with tears. He looked as if he was about to collapse.

Julian jumped to his feet, still holding Iris's hand. "Here, have a seat," he told the man, turning his chair and offering it. He heard whispers, not just among his own group but all around the room as people became aware of what was happening.

The man sank into it as if his body weighed much more than it did. With tears trickling down his cheeks, he stared up at Julian. "I think maybe I should have believed my son."

"Your son?" It was Julian's turn to gulp. "He was abused by Jelinek, too?" Julian tried to use his body to block the distraught man from the view of curious diners. Iris's fingers dug fiercely into his hand.

"Maybe so. He was twelve. He told me and his mom, but we didn't believe him. He'd been getting in trouble, acting out. We thought this was just another thing, you know?"

Classic symptoms of abuse, but Julian didn't say that.

"Making up stories," the man said. "We thought the school gave him the idea, telling the kids about 'inappropriate touching.' Adults touch kids all the time, to show them how to do stuff or to be affectionate." He grimaced as if the last word left a foul taste in his mouth.

It did in Julian's.

The older man said, "We couldn't believe it was more than that. I mean, Bart was . . ."

Grimly, Julian finished for him. "A respected community leader. How old's your son now? Is he doing okay?" He had to wonder whether the boy might come forward and tell his story, or would that be even more traumatic for him?

"Al would have been twenty-two in January." Tears slid unchecked down his face.

"Oh crap." The words slipped out, and he heard Iris gasp. Looking down into the man's bloodshot, tear-drenched eyes made Julian's heart clench, and he couldn't ask what happened. Instead, he rested his free hand on the guy's shoulder in silent sympathy.

"He was fourteen when he killed himself," the man said.

"My wife and I blamed ourselves. Not that we believed his story about Bart, but we blamed ourselves for not being better parents. Our marriage had been troubled. She said I spent too much time at work, and it was true. I said she was too lenient on Al, she let him run wild. Maybe that was true, too, I don't know. Anyhow, we never got over it. We divorced a year after Al died."

"Jesus. I'm sorry." Julian squeezed his eyes shut. If he'd told the truth all those years ago, maybe he could've convinced Forbes. Maybe they could have stopped Jelinek. Saved Al. "It's my fault." The words grated past the ache in his throat. "My fault for keeping quiet."

The man studied him, looking dignified despite his obvious agony. "Yours. Mine. My wife's. We can never make up for that."

No one was more aware of that than Julian. "No."

The man surprised him by holding out his right hand. "My name's Jorge Martinez."

Iris freed Julian's hand so he could shake Mr. Martinez's. "Thank you for telling me your son's story. Again, I'm so sorry."

"Me too. Tomorrow—no, that's Christmas. On Boxing Day, I'll go to the police and tell them."

It would bolster Julian's accusation against Jelinek, but he had to warn the man. "If you do, there'll be negative attention. From islanders and from the media."

The older man bowed his head. "Yes, but Al deserves to have the truth told. Finally."

Julian nodded. "If you ever want to talk, just let me know."

"No, wait." The quiet, urgent voice was, to his surprise, Iris's. When he glanced at her, she said, "I'm not sure you should discuss what happened. If Jelinek's charged, I think it might weaken the case against him. Remember the Ghomeshi trial?"

"Ghomeshi," he echoed. Yeah, he remembered. The guy had been a celebrity, the host of a popular national radio show; he'd interviewed Julian a few times. Ghomeshi had lost that job when he was accused of several counts of sexual assault, but at trial he'd been acquitted. The witnesses had lacked credibility, Julian recalled, in part because they'd communicated before the trial and discussed details of the alleged assaults. "I think she's right," Julian said.

"Here!" This time the urgent voice was his dad's. "Look at this." He held his phone out.

"Forbes," Julian said, "this isn't the time—"

"Look at it," he insisted.

Iris leaned closer as Julian took the phone. A headline blazed from the screen: "Second Victim of Julian Blake's Pedophile!" His eyes widened as he scanned the first couple of paragraphs. A thirty-three-year-old high school teacher in Victoria—Sam Gupta, a married man with a child—had come forward to say he, too, had been abused by Bart Jelinek as an adolescent and a young teen.

Iris let out a quavering breath and Julian passed the phone to Mr. Martinez. The man read slowly and then said, "Now the police will have to take us seriously."

Hope bloomed inside Julian, some of the stress of the past week falling away. "Yes. Yes, they will."

To Iris's relief, Rachelle and her staff's persistence eventually wore down the reporters, and when their group left C-Shell, the street was quiet. Julian gave subdued but sincere thanks to everyone and then Iris hugged her mom, her dad, and her aunt. "Thank you so, so much for being here tonight," she told them.

Her father said, "We're glad to stand with Julian. I'm only sorry that we've supported Jelinek over the years."

She noted that it was no longer "Bart," but "Jelinek."

Aunt Lily clasped Iris's hand in hers. "I know we never exchange Christmas gifts."

Iris nodded. The Yakimuras instead donated money and books to a literacy foundation.

"So this isn't a gift," her aunt went on. "Just another act of support from all of us. I'm going to stay at your parents' house. I think you and Julian could use a sanctuary where you can escape the world and be alone together, until he returns to Vancouver."

Which he would do in less than a week. His band had a New Year's Eve gig.

But Christmas Eve wasn't the time to think about him leaving, or about missing him. After thanking her aunt, she returned to his side and stretched up to whisper Lily's offer. "Do you want to spend the night tonight?" Always before, when she was stressed to the max she had sought solitude. But Julian was so easy to be with; in some ways his presence was even more soothing than being alone. If she woke with him on Christmas morning, it would create a memory to treasure forever.

He studied her for a long moment, and she hurried to say, "I know you're an introvert, too, and if you need privacy to unwind, I'll completely understand."

"I'd love to be with you, but I was wondering if that is what you really want."

"Trust me, it is. Forbes and Sonia don't need your help at night anymore, right?"

"No, he's pretty self-sufficient now. Besides, Roy and Camille will be there."

He went to have a quiet word with his dad and stepmom, and then he took Iris's hand. In peaceful silence, they strolled through the gaily lit village and then along the oceanfront walk to her condo. Almost every boat in the harbor was strung with colored lights, and trees along the path had sparkly white mini-lights. If there'd been snow, it would indeed have been a winter wonderland, but so far this year Blue Moon Harbor had seen nary a flake.

Even when they got home, Iris felt no need to speak, and it seemed Julian didn't either. The evening had been so full and intense, but she felt as if the two of them shared their perceptions and feelings without needing speech. After they undressed and got ready for bed, they slipped under the covers, both naked, and made love. Slowly, silently, with an intimacy that touched the deepest part of her soul.

Christmas morning, though, was a whole different matter. They made love again, but couldn't linger in bed because they'd been invited to join Julian's family at Luke and Miranda's house to watch the three kids open gifts. The adults had decided to forego gifts for everyone except the kids. Instead, they donated money, and any gifts they'd already purchased, to charities that supported victims of abuse.

Iris loved watching Miranda's little girl and Luke's twin boys down on the floor by the tree, tearing into their presents and squealing with joy. She so hoped to one day be sharing this holiday magic with children of her own. And when she noticed Julian gazing at the kids, she thought she saw the same sentiment in his eyes. But of course that was just her imagination; he'd made it clear he didn't want a long-term relationship or a family.

From his stepbrother's house, Julian and Iris went to her parents' for a Yakimura Christmas lunch that reflected their own blend of traditions: roast turkey, wild rice pilaf, stir-fried Asian veggies, and maple syrup pie for dessert. They all spoke in French, and her dad and aunt were almost as gregarious as her mom, making Iris feel as if they'd truly accepted Julian.

After lunch, Iris and Julian had a couple of free hours and they drove to the old commune, where they wandered around, holding hands.

"This is where it all started," Julian said. "If I hadn't met you here, I'd have hated every day on Destiny. God knows, I might not have found the perspective to get closer to my family, nor the courage to report Jelinek." He stopped walking and put his arms around her. "I'm damned sure I wouldn't have written the songs for the new album. I owe you so much."

"I owe you even more. Thanks to you, I've become more courageous myself and my horizons have widened. Not to mention, I've learned what it's like to make love with someone I care very much for."

"When we said we wouldn't exchange Christmas presents," he said, "at first I felt kind of weird about it. Then I realized, we've shared so many things, wonderful times and tough ones. Giving a material gift would almost trivialize all of that."

"I agree. The gift of your company, your honesty, your trust, that's everything I could possibly want." She swallowed, and made a silent revision: *That's everything I could realistically want.* Because, of course, in her heart of hearts, she wanted a future with him. She wanted to spend every Christmas with him, and every other day of the year as well. She wanted them to have, or adopt, kids together, to build a family, a life, a future together in Blue Moon Harbor.

"The time's getting on," he said. "We have more turkey waiting for us."

"Yes, we should go. It would be rude to be late."

They climbed back in the van and she said, "I guess it's no surprise that Sonia and Forbes would do turkey."

"Nope. She foregoes her Italian roots at Christmas. It's all the classic stuff: turkey, mashed potatoes and gravy, stuffing, cranberry sauce, brussels sprouts. Mince pie and Christmas pudding."

"I'm glad Forbes is feeling up to it. And to having so many unaccustomed guests." Julian had told her that the holiday dinner was usually just three generations of family, from Sonia's mother down to the twins. This year, not only were Miranda and Ariana included, but also Iris, Camille, Roy, and Andi.

Julian reached over to touch her hands, which she'd clasped in her lap. "You okay? Is it too much for you, all this socializing?"

"No, it's not too much. The quiet time at the commune recharged my energy. I'm looking forward to dinner."

And even more than that, she was looking forward to going back to the condo after, when it was just her and Julian. What better way to end Christmas day than to cuddle up in bed together?

Late Thursday morning, a couple of days after Christmas, Iris was sitting on a battered leather couch in Forbes's music studio, listening to Julian and his band work on his new songs. Iris was so glad his bandmates had come to Destiny. Thanks to them, Julian could spend hours every day focusing on the positive, creative part of his life.

And, thanks to her parents telling her to take the day off work at Dreamspinner, she got to witness the band collaborating to refine the tunes he'd worked on over the past couple of months. It was also deeply flattering when they asked for her input.

These three people were Julian's other family, a family that had pulled together to support him. Roy, with his neatly trimmed ginger hair, beard, and mustache, freckles, and big smile. Camille, who with her silver-streaked, curly long hair, looked like an aged edition of Carole King on the cover of Grandmother Rose's *Tapestry* album. Andi, with her spiky, green-streaked black hair and multiple piercings and tattoos. All of them with huge hearts as well as huge musical talent.

A key clicked in the lock of the studio door, and Miranda, toting a couple of reusable shopping bags, pushed the door open. The band, in the middle of a number, kept playing, but Iris rushed over to relieve her of one of the bags. Forbes hobbled inside on his walker and Miranda closed and latched the door behind them. Miranda had this week off work to prepare for the wedding on Saturday, and today she had offered to drive Forbes to and from his morning physical therapy session, in exchange for Sonia babysitting the three kids for the day.

Iris put down the bag and lent Forbes a supportive arm as he transitioned from his walker to the couch.

The band wound up their number and Julian said, "Must be lunchtime."

"We brought it with us," Miranda said.

Julian and his bandmates rose from the stools they'd been sitting on, put down their instruments, and stretched. He went over to the window that faced the driveway and peeked through the closed blinds. "No media?"

"Nope," Miranda said. "Looks like they got the message about no interviews."

Julian, his family, and his bandmates had consistently told reporters that they had nothing to add to what he'd already said in that radio interview.

He came over to Iris and hugged her. Despite the Yakimura avoidance of PDAs, she wouldn't pass up an opportunity to melt into his arms and hug him back. It felt a little surreal, though. On the one hand, this was her friend and lover, a man whose body she knew intimately. But he was also the center of a growing media firestorm. And, as this morning's music session had clearly demonstrated, he was also Julian Blake, JUNO winner.

She rested her cheek against his T-shirted chest, feeling the hardness of his pecs, the heat of his skin burning through the fabric. She loved the intimacy of this embrace, and she loved that everyone else in the room accepted it—her and Julian, like this—as perfectly normal.

"Have you guys checked social media recently?" Miranda asked.

Julian shook his head. "I'm not sure I want to know."

Iris didn't. She'd rather exist for another few hours in this lovely cocoon.

"Yeah," Miranda said. "You do. That awesome video of Iris has gone viral."

"Oh no," Iris moaned, burying a burning cheek against Julian's chest.

"You did great, Iris," Forbes said. "It's a beautiful thing."

Yesterday morning, Boxing Day, she'd walked to work and found a half dozen journalists in front of Dreamspinner. She turned to go around to the delivery entrance, but one of them spotted her and she was mobbed. Phones and faces invaded her space; questions flew at her so fast they created an insane babble.

Animals reacted to danger by fighting, fleeing, or, like rabbits, freezing in place. *If I don't move, you can't see me.* Iris was a bunny. When she had an anxiety attack, her muscles locked, like she'd been cast in concrete. Even her brain shut down. The only parts of her that remained alive were her thready, racing pulse and the nausea churning her stomach.

It would have been a really good time for that oft-threatened "big one" earthquake to finally happen, for a fault line to open and suck her in. But of course that didn't

happen, and she did her best to breathe. If she fainted, this
horde would probably trample her to death.

Breathe. Center. Stay even.

Her frozen-bunny imitation did, surprisingly, calm the
flurry of questions. The reporters stared at her, looking
baffled.

Maybe if she continued to play statue, they'd get bored
and go away. But it seemed that was wishful thinking. One
woman, phone held high, said, "I'm with Julian Blake's
girlfriend, Iris Yakimura. Iris, what can you tell us about the
accusations Julian has leveled against Bart Jelinek?"

She had to support Julian. Silence wasn't going to do it.
*Stay even. It's not about you, it's about Julian. Breathe.
Breathe again.* She straightened her shoulders and swallowed. Her muscles were working again, but she wouldn't
use them to turn tail and run, no matter how badly she
longed to.

"I believe Julian." She spoke quietly, and the reporters
were silent. "I believe *in* Julian." She considered, but what
else was there to say? There was no point quibbling over
the term *girlfriend*. "Please let me go to work."

To her surprise, the crowd parted.

Her legs were stiff, but she managed to walk toward
Dreamspinner, where Mr. and Mrs. Claus cozily rocked
and read in the window. More questions came, bashing her
from all directions, but she ignored them. She unlocked the
door, seeing the display tables and shelves of amazing
books, the festive holiday touches honoring the traditions
of various religions and countries. It would be sacrilege
to have the horde of paparazzi invade this wonderful space
her family had created, a sanctuary to be shared with other
book-lovers, not with sensation-seekers.

There was no way she could stop the reporters. But she
had to try. So she would try the same technique she did

with little kids when they explored the board books and picture books. She'd let the paparazzi know she expected good behavior. In the doorway, she turned to face them. "This is my family's store. You will not dishonor it by seeking interviews inside."

Pulse racing, she stepped inside and closed the door. She did not turn the latch. And not a single person followed her inside.

What they did do, though, was upload videos of her to social media. She had refused to look, but her friends said she'd been poised, succinct, and highly effective. Amazing how being scared spitless could come across as all those other, far more desirable, qualities.

Sadly, she'd found it impossible to maintain that same equanimity over the course of the day. Boxing Day was always a busy one, as Dreamspinner, like most of the shops in Blue Moon Harbor, had a sale. But this year, the islanders who came into the store were less interested in buying books than in asking her how she could be so gullible as to believe some drugged-out rock musician over wonderful Bart Jelinek, and berating her for her part in bringing the nasty paparazzi to the island—as if she'd have ever chosen to do that.

This was tough on her parents and aunt, too. Her family trusted Iris's judgment, wanted to trust Julian, and had strong moral principles, yet facing censure from their neighbors and customers made them cringe. But what could you do? Only the right thing, no matter how difficult. In her family, there was no other option.

Now Forbes said, "Iris's words have become a mantra. There are T-shirts. People have made signs, and pickets are starting." There was smug satisfaction in his voice.

Iris lifted her head. Pickets?

"Pickets?" Roy said, pulling out his phone. Andi and Camille were already on theirs.

Life had been so much easier when Iris was a little girl, before everyone seemed to require a 24/7 digital link to the entire world. She was happy to have her hands on Julian's warm back, not on an electronic device, and even happier that he seemed content to hold her and wasn't reaching for his own phone.

"Yeah, in front of the RCMP detachment here," Forbes said. "People have come from the other Gulf Islands, the mainland, and Vancouver Island. The signs—"

Roy broke in with a loud whistle. "Oh man, yeah. The signs say 'I Believe Julian,' 'I Believe in Julian,' 'Throw Jelinek in Jail,' and—"

"'Lock Up the Pedophile,'" Andi said. "This is fantastic. Julian, you gotta take a look."

"Honestly, I'd rather not," he said, not letting go of Iris. "I mean, I'm happy for the support, but I never wanted this to turn into a circus. I just want him stopped."

"And punished," Forbes said, his gaze on his own phone's screen. "Sometimes it takes a circus to make sure justice gets done."

Miranda shoved aside the clutter of magazines on the coffee table, to reveal the beautiful, intricate woodwork Forbes was known for. She delved into one of the reusable bags and set out food. "Sandwiches and wraps from the deli, fruit, and Destiny Bars, courtesy of Iris's mom."

The band members dragged chairs over and made their selections. Iris hated to step out of Julian's arms, but he needed to eat. She sat at the end of the couch, giving him the seat between her and Forbes, and selected half of a shrimp croissant-wich. Julian took a roast beef sandwich.

Miranda selected half of a tuna sandwich and sat in a battered leather chair. "There are still a bunch of islanders who are defending Jelinek." She wrinkled her nose. "And saying nasty things about Julian and all of us. But they're not as vocal as yesterday. With Mr. Martinez and that teacher, Sam Gupta, going to the police, people have to wonder."

"A lot of other folks are getting their five minutes of fame," Forbes said, leaning forward to pick up a ham and cheese wrap. "Other musicians saying Julian's a good guy, women who've dated him saying nice stuff about how well he treated them and stupid stuff like how they just wished he'd let them be the one to heal him. Psychologists all too happy to share their wisdom. Some blogger ranting about how it's not right that sexual assault's almost always viewed as a women's issue."

"Damn right it isn't," Andi said, through a mouthful of corned beef on rye. "It's a *people* issue. There are male victims, not just female, and women abusers as well as men. Not to mention spouses who turn a blind eye when their partner commits abuse. Which, by the way, makes me wonder about Jelinek's wife."

"Cathy," Forbes said. "Sonia and I have talked about that. If she's innocent, this must be hell for her. But it's hard to imagine she never had a clue. She's always taken a back seat to Bart, but she's a smart woman with a good job."

"All the same," Iris said quietly, "there have been cases where the spouse was genuinely innocent. Let's not condemn Cathy when there's no evidence against her. Bart is a highly persuasive, manipulative man."

"Good point," Forbes said.

"I wonder if she'll leave him or stick by his side?" Andi said. "I hate it when women stand by husbands who are assholes."

"His lawyer will sure hope she does," Forbes said.

Camille had been quiet, sitting on a hard-backed chair

across from them, eating the other half of the shrimp croissant-wich with one hand and manipulating her phone with the other. Now she said, "Julian, I've been going through your email."

"You know how much I appreciate that, right?" He'd told Iris that Camille had volunteered, to save him from having to deal with hate messages from trolls as well as steamy ones from women who wanted to have sex with him. She'd promised to send "thank you" responses to those who supported him, and filter out any business stuff for his attention.

"I do," Camille said. "Here's one you'll want to see." She passed the phone across.

Julian juggled it one-handed, still holding his sandwich. "Shit."

"What's wrong?" Iris asked.

"It's another one. A grad student at McGill. Jelinek abused him." He put down the sandwich.

That would support the case against Jelinek, but Iris felt Julian's pain. The student was younger than him. Julian was thinking that he might have been able to prevent what happened. She rubbed his jean-clad thigh in silent sympathy.

"Poor bastard," Forbes said gruffly. "Is he willing to go to the cops?"

"Yeah, he says he will. After he tells his family and his boyfriend."

"What's his name?" Forbes asked.

"Henri Bellefontaine."

Iris gasped. "Oh, poor Henri."

"You know him?" Julian asked.

"He used to come into Dreamspinner. He's an introvert, likes to read poetry. His mom, Thérèse, buys a lot of self-help books. He has a teenage sister who's always fighting with her mom over what kind of books she's allowed to read." She glanced at Julian. "You saw them in the store."

"The father, Pierre Bellefontaine, is a chef," Forbes said. "He works at camps—mining exploration, oil sands—in Northern Alberta. They fly him in for two, three weeks at a stretch, then he's home for a bit, and then away again."

"Was he doing that when Henri was a boy?" Julian asked.

"Yeah, he's always done that kind of work. He likes the wilderness, the adventure, not to mention the money. He says one day he'll quit and open his own restaurant, but I don't know if he really means it." Forbes cleared his throat. "So Henri might've been open to Jelinek trying to mentor him, act like a father figure. Same thing as with Sam Gupta after his parents split up and his dad moved to Surrey, remarried, and started a new family. And Al Martinez, when his dad was at work all the time and his parents were fighting."

Julian nodded. "Jelinek's a predator. He weeds out the weak ones in the flock."

"Not weak," Iris protested.

"No," Forbes said, his voice grating. "Vulnerable. Because your damn parents weren't doing their jobs. And we will never, ever forgive ourselves for that."

Julian gave a tired sigh. "For what it's worth, if there's any forgiving to do, then I forgive you. If you'll forgive me for being so self-centered that I didn't see that, even if you were in love with Sonia, you still loved me, too. That you'd have been there for me if I'd told you the truth."

"Son . . ." Forbes couldn't seem to find words but instead reached over to catch Julian in a rough one-armed hug.

Iris brushed her fingers under her eyes to flick away tears and noticed Andi, the brash young member of the band, doing the same. Andi gave her a wry smile and Iris smiled back.

In the past year, Iris's life had changed in so many ways. Yes, she had unwanted media attention, but she also had an amazing lover and her social circle had expanded by leaps and bounds. Had *she* somehow changed or could she have done this all along, rather than cocoon herself away like a hermit within the protective shell of her shyness?

Chapter Twenty-One

Thursday night, finally alone with Iris after an intense day working on music with his bandmates, Julian drove them back to her condo.

It was stormy out, the temperature hovering around freezing. He wouldn't be surprised if it snowed, and he hoped the weather wouldn't mess up Luke and Miranda's Saturday wedding. Inside, Iris stripped off her gloves, knitted hat, and coat. "Sometimes I wish I lived in the Caribbean," she said.

His own outer clothing off, he hugged her tight, rubbing his hands down her back to warm her. "You'd miss winter. Not to mention Blue Moon Harbor."

She laughed and acknowledged, "Okay, you're right. I can't imagine living anywhere else. And I do enjoy having real seasons. Weather like this makes me appreciate so many things. Electric heat, for one. Hot chocolate. And summer. On stormy nights, I lie in bed and remember sunny days at the old commune, lying on the grass, gazing up at the clouds, and dreaming."

Her brown eyes glowed as she spoke. He could've looked into them forever. It would be nice to imagine a future of lying in bed beside her on stormy nights. Lots of women yearned to be a part of his world. Why couldn't he have fallen for one of them?

Because none of them was Iris. His arms tightened around her. He *had* fallen for her, even though he'd always believed he was incapable of trusting and loving. He'd also believed no one who knew his foul secrets could love him. But Iris did care. Maybe it wasn't love, but it was a deep caring. Was it possible that, unlike most of his songs, theirs might have a happy ending? Perhaps once the Jelinek thing was resolved, when life got back to normal . . . But of course *normal* for him meant a life away from Destiny Island, whereas for her it meant the opposite.

No wonder he couldn't find the right ending for the song he was writing about Iris.

"On those nights," she went on, "I also remember my afternoons on *Windspinner*, skimming the waves without a care in the world."

"Wouldn't that be nice?" he said wryly. "To not have a care in the world?" The moment he said it, he wished he hadn't, because her dreamy expression changed to one of concern.

"Oh, Julian. When Henri goes to the police, that'll make four reports. Surely that will give them enough to charge Jelinek."

"I hope so. But then there'll be years of legal crap: motions, delays. You hear the news, you know what it's like. And if it does eventually make it to trial, we'll all have to testify. It'll be . . ." He swallowed. *Agonizing*.

"I know." Her expressive eyes said she got it. "It's unfair that the four of you can't talk together and support one another. Do you think the other men have gone to support groups or had counseling? They should, if they haven't?"

"I'll ask Eden or the RCMP if I can suggest that, without jeopardizing the case."

"I know the process is painful, but when it's all over, the

four of you will feel better. A weight will be lifted." She said it with a certainty that reassured him.

"Thanks, Iris." He released her. "Let's change the subject to something more pleasant."

She smiled up at him. "Let's switch from verbal to non-verbal communication." She made a zipping-her-lips motion and then used those very same lips to kiss him senseless.

He replied in body language of his own, by hoisting her into his arms and carrying her to the bedroom, where he stripped off her clothes and then his own. Once they were under the covers, he forgot that anything else in the world existed except making love with Iris.

Being with her like this was the perfect tonic: the silkiness of her skin, her sweetly pebbled nipples, the salty moistness between her legs, her short-nailed fingers caressing his back and then digging into his shoulders, her breathy moans and little gasps. The way she whispered, "Oh yes, Julian, so good," after he brought her to climax with his mouth. And then her sigh of pleasure when he sheathed himself and entered her.

This, right here. This was paradise. The tiny enclosed world of her bed. The woman in his arms, her sleek limbs intertwined with his, the black silk of her hair framing her exquisite face, her hips rising to meet his slow, deep thrusts. The knowledge that the intimacy between them was emotional as much as physical. He prolonged the experience as long as he possibly could, but finally they both surrendered to orgasm.

After, lying on their sides with him spooned around Iris, he felt so boneless and drained he could have fallen asleep. But, not wishing to waste a moment of this precious time, he concentrated on every sensation. A month from now, he'd be alone in his studio apartment in Vancouver with only memories of her to keep him company. To help him through the stress of whatever might be going on with the police and Jelinek by then.

Perhaps he tensed, because she stirred. "Julian? Are you okay?"

"Can't turn off my freaking mind."

She stroked his forearm, a sensual whisper of touch. "You and Forbes were talking about forgiveness. You've really forgiven him and Sonia and Luke for their role in what happened?"

"Yeah." He used his nose to push silky hair from her nape, inhaling that delicate almond scent, and then kissed the sensitive spot. "I admit I was carrying some anger, trying to shove it deep down for all those years. But I've let it go. They're good people. We all focus on our own stuff, right? Luke had his own crap. Sonia's emotions were a mess. Forbes had so many changes to deal with. I'd been a self-sufficient, flexible kid. It wasn't on his radar to worry about me. And if I turned into a sullen, rebellious teen . . . well, he'd been a rebel himself at that age."

"I'm glad you've reached a place of understanding." She took a deep breath; he felt it move through her body. "Can you imagine ever forgiving Jelinek?"

His muscles tightened. "No. I don't think so."

She nodded, a slow movement that sent her hair sliding against his cheek. "Do you think he was abused as a child? I've read how that's often the case."

"He didn't talk about his parents, just said they were dead." Julian swallowed. "Even if he was, that's no excuse. I was abused, and the last thing I'd ever do is hurt or pressure someone else."

"I know that."

"Do you think it's wrong of me not to forgive him? When I went to that support group, some victims said they'd forgiven their abusers. Some said it was part of their religion. Others said they needed to do it in order to heal.

But I can't imagine forgiving him." Julian was almost scared to admit this to Iris, with her evolving spirituality. But he wouldn't lie to her. "It's not like it was an accident," he said, "or a one-time thing. He's been a pedophile for a long time. I'd bet you there's some broken, terrified kid out there that he's abused in the past year or two. I can't see ever forgiving him."

She was quiet, a warm curve of woman nestled against the front of his body. "Maybe he has a brain abnormality," she said, "or was abused himself, but you're right, there are no excuses. I can't find it in my heart to forgive him either. I don't think that makes me a bad person."

"You couldn't be a bad person."

"You know something? We shouldn't have to wrestle with whether or not we can bring ourselves to forgive him. This shouldn't be on us, any more than the fact of the abuse should be on you, Al, Sam, Henri, or any other boy. Or their parents. Bart Jelinek committed crimes. Many crimes. That's on him. Period."

He hugged her tighter. "Thank you. I've had so much baggage dragging at my ankles all these years, and you just lifted a bit more of it."

She hugged her arms over his where they crossed her chest. "I'm glad. But here's another question for you. Have you forgiven yourself?"

He blew out air gustily. "That's a tough one. I think I've forgiven myself for letting myself become a victim, and for not telling anyone back then. I was a boy, up against a powerful, experienced adversary."

"I'm glad you see that. But how about for not reporting him later on?" she asked quietly. "I know how much it troubles you, that he abused other boys since you."

"That's for sure. And now, putting names to some of those boys, it's awful. And yet there's Sam, who came before me. If he'd spoken up, maybe he could have saved me. But I don't blame him. How can I? I understand."

Iris nodded. "By understanding and forgiving Sam, can you forgive yourself?"

"Maybe," he said slowly. "It's not, like, a sudden revelation. It's a slow sinking in, and a feeling that a darkness that's shadowed my soul is beginning to lift." He hadn't actually realized it until now. "Another few pounds of baggage, gone."

"I'm so glad." He couldn't see her face, but heard the sincerity in her voice. "You'll write *that* song one day, Julian. A song with, if not exactly a happy ending, an uplifting one."

He smiled against the back of her neck. "I think you're right."

Iris had never learned to dance, but when she was in Julian's arms at Quail Ridge Community Hall, it didn't matter. He had such a strong sense of rhythm and was so physically confident, she just let him guide her. Besides, the dance floor was so packed at Miranda and Luke's wedding reception, it was hard to do much more than shuffle around and laugh as people bumped into one another.

Just four days after Christmas, the big wooden hall still sparkled with multicolored lights. Wreaths made of pine boughs, cones, and holly scented the air. Shimmering silver tinsel, colorful ornaments, and bunches of mistletoe hung in every available spot.

Onstage, B-B-Zee was performing for the first time since Forbes's accident. He sat in a wooden chair with his bandmates, Jonathan and Christian, on either side of him. Jonathan had also served as the officiant, performing the short, very moving marriage ceremony.

When Miranda and Luke, with their children beside

them, had gazed into each other's eyes and spoken the vows they'd each written, simple words revealing the depth of their emotions, Iris had realized something. She really, truly loved Julian.

When had it happened? Was it when he'd summoned the courage to expose Jelinek and they'd made love fully for the first time? When he'd written the song about Grandmother Rose and Grandfather Harry? Or was it that first day at the commune, when she woke from one dream and found herself in the middle of another?

It still seemed amazing that she, an introverted bookseller, had even met Julian Blake. Yet her love for him felt inevitable and right. Even though he'd leave Destiny tomorrow.

Tomorrow. December thirtieth. The day before her twenty-fifth birthday. Some birthday it would be, with her life, her heart, feeling so empty without Julian.

They would remain friends, stay in touch, but that was just so inadequate.

She took a deep breath. *Center, stay even, practice mindfulness.* Right now, she would throw herself into every remaining moment together. Later, when he was gone, she would cherish the memories and their friendship.

She'd been given an amazing gift. A gift, she thought as she smiled against his shoulder, that was still giving. Who'd have ever thought she'd be swaying in the arms of a handsome, sexy guy, a man thousands of fans lusted after? But Julian was so much more than that.

He rested his cheek against the top of her head, seeming as content as she. He didn't pull her too tight, didn't grind against her. She'd have been uncomfortable if he had, in this public forum. Even so, a sense of sexual awareness hovered in the air. A promise of *later*.

"You're doing okay with this?" Julian murmured in the lull after one song ended.

She raised her head from his shoulder to look at him. "With what?" With the knowledge that he'd be leaving?

"Being in a crowd."

Oh, that. It seemed kind of minor, in comparison. "As long as I'm in your arms." There were maybe a hundred people in the hall, but she felt surprisingly relaxed.

When the next song started up, he said, "That's my signal." He released her from his arms and took her hand. "This is the last song in the set and we're up next."

With Roy, Camille, and Andi here on the island, Miranda had talked the Julian Blake Band into performing.

Fingers entwined, Iris and Julian threaded their way among people, tables, and chairs. Their seats were at a large table with Eden and Aaron, Eden's parents and sister, her aunt Di and uncle Seal, and Iris's own parents and aunt. Iris had seen her parents dancing earlier, which was pretty cool. Almost as cute as the bride and groom's three little kids, happy-dancing in a circle together.

Now Iris took her seat beside Eden and across from Aunt Lily, who was talking to Di.

Julian gave Iris a quick kiss. "See you after our set. Don't dance with anyone too sexy."

"I'll be too busy fangirling you," she said with total honesty.

Her gaze followed him as he made his away across the room. A few people spoke to him, many smiled, some touched his arm. There were no scowls or angry words. And no paparazzi. She turned to Eden, who looked lovely in a dress in shades of cream and amber, her walnut hair glossy on her shoulders. "I was afraid the Jelinek thing might make for some awkwardness."

Eden smiled. "Most of the islanders who supported the bastard are eating crow."

Six victims had now come forward, and yesterday afternoon Jelinek had been charged with numerous counts of sexual assault. Island Realty was closed and Bart and Cathy were rumored to have left the island for Victoria. He'd no doubt be consulting a lawyer there.

Aaron turned from the conversation he was having with Iris's dad and touched Eden's shoulder. "Hey, haven't you ladies heard, this is a wedding?"

"You're right," Eden said. "We shouldn't let Jelinek throw a damper on the celebration. Speaking of which, I think Julian's up now." She nodded toward the stage.

Forbes, Jonathan, and Christian had stopped playing and were nodding and smiling to acknowledge the applause for their last number.

Then Forbes spoke into the microphone. "It's time for B-B-Zee to take a break, but—"

The audience groaned and booed, but that was because they didn't know what was coming. Julian's band's participation had been kept a secret, otherwise nothing would have kept the paparazzi from invading the hall.

Raising his voice, Forbes cut through the noise. "But you won't go unserenaded. We all get a special treat. Please welcome the Julian Blake Band."

To whistles, cheers, and loud applause, Julian and the three members of his band walked onto the stage carrying their instruments and exchanged greetings with the older musicians. Julian gave a hand to his dad, helping him rise from the chair. Jonathan and Christian put supporting hands under each of Forbes's elbows.

But Forbes didn't let go of his son's hand, nor relinquish the microphone. "It's been a true pleasure to get to know Camille, Andi, and Roy. They're not only great musicians, but terrific people. And I'm deeply grateful to my son for moving back home to look after his injured old dad. Despite my failings as a father, Julian's grown up to be a fine man, a man I'm very proud of."

"Aw," Miranda murmured, slipping into the empty chair—Julian's chair—on Iris's left. "How totally sweet."

"It is." Iris sniffled back tears as she smiled.

As Forbes hobbled off the stage with his friends' help, Julian's band started to tune up.

Iris turned to the bride. "You look utterly stunning."

"I know," Miranda said complacently. Raising her voice so Lily could hear, she said, "All thanks to your aunt's wonderful gift."

Aunt Lily gave her a smile of acknowledgment. When Miranda had complained to Iris that she couldn't find a dress that "felt like her," Iris had talked to her aunt. Lily had consulted with the bride and then created a designer dress as a wedding present. Although her aunt normally used flower motifs—like the boat-necked silk dress Iris wore, with a peony pattern—for Miranda she'd created a dragon. A dragon that managed to be fierce and tender at the same time, and ineffably feminine. The three-quarter-length sleeves displayed the bride's dragon tattoo, and the knee-length skirt was full and flirty, perfect for dancing. The turquoise cowgirl boots Eden had loaned the bride for her "something blue" were the perfect complement and, as Miranda had noted, much more comfortable than the spike heels she wore back in her city-girl days.

"It's not just the dress," Iris said, "it's you. You're glowing."

"I have never in my entire life been happier."

For some reason Iris was reminded of the moments at the commune just before she met Julian. She had enjoyed being there, yet regretted that winter weather would soon restrict her visits. She had mused about how so many moments in life contained elements of yin and yang, of dark and light. That was how she felt now: totally happy for her dear friend, glad to have been given the gift of Julian's friendship, and yet sad that, unlike Miranda, she wouldn't be finding her happily ever after with the man she loved.

And speaking of that man, Julian's voice now came through the mic, rough-edged, laid-back, confident. "We'd like to start off with a song that'll be on our new album. It's dedicated to the amazing bride and it's called, 'You're Better than You Think.'"

Miranda nudged Iris. "Déjà vu all over again, right? Us in the audience, and you drooling over Julian."

Iris didn't remind her that, last June, Miranda had been drooling, too.

"Go find your hubby, Miranda," Julian said from the stage, "because you two are going to want to dance to this one."

Miranda laughed and hurried over to where Luke was standing with his mom and the three kids.

Then Julian played the first notes, ones Iris was familiar with, and she was barely aware of Eden and Aaron getting up to dance. She feasted her senses on Julian. A man who would always be in her heart.

The only time she'd seen him onstage before, he'd been all in black, a ripped tee and jeans. In every picture she'd seen of him performing, he'd worn similar clothing. Today he stayed with his trademark black, but rather than a T-shirt that hugged his tautly muscled torso, he wore a long-sleeved cotton shirt with the collar open and the sleeves rolled up far enough that the lower part of his tattoo was visible. His burnished golden hair gleamed and he looked like a more sophisticated version of a bad boy.

After Miranda's song, he announced "Your Reality." She, Iris Yakimura, was the person whose words had inspired this song, the first day she and Julian met. Each of their realities had changed so much over the past weeks, and the two had braided together. But, as of tomorrow, that braid would have to unweave itself, or at least loosen.

She listened to the rasp of his husky, low voice as he sang about the lark with its broken wing and its struggle to cope and to heal. Somewhere in this room, Iris figured Forbes had his arms around Sonia and tears in his eyes. But she didn't shift her gaze from Julian.

The lark story had been written about Forbes, but it applied equally to Julian. He'd been broken, too, he'd fought his own battle, and he had triumphed.

He might look like a bad boy, but he wasn't bad at all. He was one of the most sensitive, gentle people she had ever known, and she had the great good fortune to have known a number of them. And tonight Iris heard a difference in his music. There was still darkness and pain, and there probably always would be in his songs. The stories that resonated with him, the ones he wanted to tell, were about suffering. But now, in the music and the lyrics, there were threads of light, of optimism and joy and love. They were there in part, she knew, because of her.

Something warm and soft touched her hand where it rested beside a half-finished glass of now-flat champagne. She glanced down to see her aunt's hand, and then looked across the table. The tender sympathy in Aunt Lily's eyes brought tears to her own eyes. She turned her hand over to clasp her aunt's, and then refocused on Julian.

Chapter Twenty-Two

After Julian's band finished their set, he joined his dad's band for a couple of numbers. When Julian had first heard the extent of Forbes's injuries, and the medical prognosis, he'd feared that his father might never play again, that they'd never again share a mic, but now here they were. After the band bowed for the final round of applause, Julian hugged his father and felt those reassuring arms hug him back. Forbes wasn't whole yet, nor was Julian, but they were both on their way, and they were emotionally closer than they'd been since he was a boy.

When he climbed down from the stage with his guitar, a bunch of islanders attempted to talk to him, but he politely brushed them off and made his way straight to Iris.

Onstage, he'd had a revelation. The certainty, and the hope, had been building in him for a long time, like when his muse teased him with almost-there notes or lyrics, just out of reach but tantalizing and unforgettable.

He had begun to imagine—had allowed himself, for the first time, to imagine—what it might be like to have a life like his stepbrother's, one with not only a fulfilling career but a loving home. Julian imagined himself in a house with a music studio, a real home that he shared with the woman he loved and their children.

Because yes, he loved Iris. Last May, he'd performed on this same stage and seen a stranger in the audience, a hauntingly lovely woman. Tonight, that woman was even more lovely, but she was no stranger. He knew her better than anyone else in the world, and she knew him the same way. Weaknesses and strengths, they saw each other, *got* each other, supported each other. He wanted a lifetime of that. He wanted to create that lifetime with her as his partner.

When he reached her side, he said, "I'm ready to go. How about you?"

She rose from her chair. "I'm ready, too."

They murmured goodbyes to the others at the table, and made for the exit.

In her car, they exchanged a few comments about the evening, and then fell silent. He returned to imagining the future. He'd grown so much in the past months, mostly thanks to her. But she'd grown as well. When he first met her, she'd had trouble even meeting his gaze. Earlier this month, she'd stood up to a pack of reporters and done it with grace. Iris could do anything, if she set her mind to it.

Would she set her mind to shaping the future with him?

They'd make Blue Moon Harbor their home base, but hopefully she'd also want to spend some time on the road with him. It was great that she got along so well with his bandmates. He'd cut back on touring, though, when they had kids. He could be a good father. Iris was so wise, so great with kids, she'd make sure he didn't screw things up too badly. He let out a soft laugh.

"What?" she asked.

"Tell you later." This was hardly the right setting to declare his love and to ask her to consider a future with him.

As he drove through the village, lights glittered around

the windows and eaves of the stores and restaurants, and the holiday window displays were lit. Except at Island Realty.

"I wonder what Jelinek and his wife are doing?" he mused. It gave him considerable satisfaction to say, "Bet they won't have a very happy New Year." Would Cathy stand by her husband? Did she believe in his innocence? Julian didn't know whether to view her as complicit, or as a victim herself.

"My New Year's wish is that he admits his guilt and that you and the others don't have to go to court."

"That would sure be nice. Especially for the other guys. For me, if I have to testify, it'll be okay. I've come to terms with all of it now. With what I did, and what I didn't do."

"You survived something horrible, and became an amazing man."

"Thanks. I always thought I coped pretty well, and I guess in my career I did. And emotionally, too, as long as I had music as an escape and a safe way of releasing my pain." He reached over to squeeze her ungloved hands, which were clasped in her lap. "This is where I was screwed up. Not letting myself get close to people."

He took his hand away, to turn into the driveway that led to the underground parking in her building. "I felt like everyone I'd ever trusted had betrayed me. My mother, my dad, and then Jelinek. And with him, the concepts of trust and love and loyalty got so messed up." He clicked the remote fob and the security door slowly rose.

"But now?"

"People aren't perfect," he said as he drove inside. "Not me, not Forbes. We screw up. That doesn't mean we can't love, forgive, move on."

"And keep the lines of communication open. If you'd felt like you could trust your dad when you were a boy, you'd have talked to him. I'm sure he'd have believed you, and he'd have done something to stop Jelinek. Like picket his business."

Julian chuckled. "Yeah, he'd have done that. But anyhow, it's all in the past. I'm a different guy from the one who came here back in October."

They climbed out of the car and took the elevator to her condo.

Once inside, she said, "Want something to drink? I could make tea or coffee. Or do you just want to go to bed?" She didn't step into his arms, and in fact seemed a little restrained. Was she thinking about him leaving for Vancouver tomorrow, and wondering how their relationship would be affected?

He shook his head. "Come sit with me. There's something I want to talk about."

They went into the front room and the view drew them both to the window. Side by side, they gazed out over Blue Moon Harbor. The holiday decorations were still up, though he suspected they'd be coming down in the next couple of days.

A scattering of white flakes drifted down.

"Oh, look!" Iris said. "It's started to snow. I hope it sticks. The children will be so thrilled if they wake up to snow on the ground."

"I'll be thrilled to wake up to you beside me." Tomorrow and, he hoped, for innumerable mornings to come.

She turned from the window and he turned, too, to face her as she smiled up at him. "That can be arranged."

If only she meant the same thing as he did. His lips were dry with nerves, worse than the time he performed for a charity fundraiser with Prime Minister Trudeau and his wife in the audience. He moistened them. "I said I'm a different guy from the one who came to this island a couple of months ago." He swallowed. "I feel whole, or at least on the way to being whole."

She touched his forearm, where his black shirt covered his tattoo. "I'm so glad."

"Whole enough that today I spent a lot of time envisioning a completely different future than I'd ever let myself imagine before."

"What kind of future?" she whispered.

He swallowed again. "Not being alone."

Her brown eyes were huge. Did she guess where he was going with this?

"I love you, Iris."

"Oh!" It was a soft, startled gasp. Her hands flew to her cheeks, her eyes glowed, and pink tinged her delicate skin. "I love you, too, Julian."

Yes. Maybe he should've been ecstatic, done some Snoopy-dancing, but instead he felt a deep sense of peace sink into his soul. Peace, and the certainty that this was right. He pulled her gently into his arms and felt her arms circle his back. He captured a kiss, but only a quick one because there was more he needed to say.

"I feel as if my life up until now," he said, "was all preparing me for you. For finding you, for being mature enough to understand what an amazing treasure you are, for becoming a man who could come anywhere near to deserving you."

He might feel certainty, but what he saw flicker in Iris's eyes was doubt. "Julian, I—"

"No, wait. You know how I said I was writing a song about you, but I refused to play it because it wasn't coming together right, and I couldn't find the ending?"

"Yes." She was still in his arms but her body no longer felt relaxed.

"It's because I hadn't been honest with myself about my feelings for you. And now, now that I know I love you, I still don't know the ending. I know what I want it to be, but . . ."

"What is that? Because I . . . I don't understand."

"I want us to be together."

Hope flashed in her eyes, but then she frowned and shook her head. "How could that be possible?" Her eyes widened again, brightening. Her arms tightened around him. "Would you move here? But what about your bandmates? And touring?"

"I haven't thought this all the way through," he admitted. "I just hope there's some way we can reorganize our lives and make it work. I could make Destiny my home base. I'd still need to spend a fair bit of time in Vancouver, working with the band and recording. And yeah, we'd still tour, though at some point we'd cut back on that. Especially if—when—we had kids."

Her beautiful eyes were open wider than he'd ever seen them.

"I know you're anxious about new people and situations," he went on, "and I know you're really close to your family, and you love Dreamspinner and Blue Moon Harbor, but . . . could you imagine coming with me sometimes?"

What he saw in her eyes now was fear, and that made him afraid. "Iris, I've come a long way these past months, and so have you. Look at the way you dealt with the paparazzi."

She stepped back, shaking her head. "I was terrified."

"But you handled it. You've handled everything that's come along." He wanted to reach for her again, but she had crossed her arms, a symbolic wall to hold him back.

"Yes, but I don't want to *have* to. I've hated a lot of the things that have happened lately." Her gaze was focused intently on him, but her shoulders hunched and her body curved inward as if she was protecting herself. "Having reporters virtually assault me. Knowing my picture's out there on the Internet for all time. Being censured by people who've known me all my life, even if most did end up

SAIL AWAY WITH ME 309

apologizing later, or at least looking hangdoggy." Her lips trembled. "I loved my peaceful life. If you know me at all, you know that's how I need to live."

Damn. Damn it. Rather than curse, he tried to sound reasonable. "I thought, hoped, you might change your mind. That we could find a compromise, so we could be together a lot of the time, yet you'd still find the peace and privacy you need and I'd still have my career. Love often involves compromise, doesn't it?"

She pressed her lips together, and delicate lines of strain bracketed her mouth. When she spoke, he saw the pain in her eyes. "It does. I wish I were capable of what you're asking. But I'm not the right woman for you."

"You're the only woman I could ever imagine loving."

"Oh, Julian . . ." she whispered, her dark eyes sheened with tears. "No, I'm sure one day you'll meet someone very special, a woman who deserves you."

"Deserves? What do you mean by that?" *He* was the one who'd struggled to be a man who deserved *her*.

"You are so brave and you've overcome so much." She straightened again, speaking intensely. "You rose out of a horrible dark place to create works of insight and beauty, to build a successful career. You faced down your demons and you're bringing your abuser to justice. You are a brave, amazing man, and you deserve an equal partner to stand by your side."

"You're that partner."

She shook her head. "I'm a coward."

"Iris, you say I'm brave as if that's some attribute I possess, like having blue eyes. But I'm no hero, just a normal guy. And it's been so hard, sometimes a struggle minute by minute."

"A struggle that you've had the courage to take on. I don't have that courage."

He considered his next words. Maybe he'd piss her off,

but he had to tell her what he believed. "I think you do. You've shown that, over and over. You had the courage to support me when the world was censuring me."

She ducked her head so that her hair fell forward in black wings, reminding him of how she'd behaved when he first met her. "I had to do the right thing. But it cost me, Julian. It's not a cost I can continue to bear."

Was he a horrible, selfish bastard if he pursued this? But he had to know for sure. "Not even to be together?" he asked gently. "To love each other and share our lives?"

Gazing down rather than at him, she shook her head. "The time we've spent together has been amazing, but I've always known it would end. I thought you realized that, too."

He blinked, taking that in. Then he placed a finger under her chin and raised her head so she could no longer avoid his gaze. Trying hard not to sound accusing, he said, "You gave up on us without ever giving us a chance." He released her chin.

She sighed. "There was never meant to be an *us* in the sense you mean. The *us* that I hope for is to be two loving friends who stay in touch and are there for each other."

"That's not enough. We could have more. Things change, Iris. When we met, I never imagined I could love a woman, be loved by someone like you, have a partner at my side to share my life. To have kids with one day."

She gave a soft moan.

"Now everything's different," he said. "I'm different. You say I need an equal partner, and that's who you are. I've learned from you, and your support's helped me confront the truth. We've talked about inner nature. Well, you've helped me realize that mine isn't rotten at the core. You've helped me become a better person, not to mention a better songwriter. You're more than my equal. You're wise and gentle and generous and . . . just incredible, Iris. And I bet that if you peel off that *shy* label that you and your family have plastered on you, and look deep inside, you'll find that your inner nature is more open and confident than you've let yourself see."

She had lowered her head again as he spoke, and didn't respond.

He took a breath and tried again. "You know how everyone, Pooh included, says he's a Bear of Very Little Brain?"

Now her head came up, curiosity in her eyes.

"Yet somehow," Julian went on, "he's often the one who finds the solution to the problem. Well, you keep saying you're a Woman of Very Little Courage, but really you have so much strength and bravery."

Her lashes fluttered down and she shook her head.

"Damn it," he said. "Why won't you see the truth?"

Huge, soulful eyes, swimming with tears, stared into his soul. "Why won't *you*?" she asked softly.

He thought of one of the first things she'd said to him, the line that gave him Forbes's song. *I do not like your reality*. No, he didn't like her "truth" one bit. But Iris had made up her mind. Because he respected and loved her, he had to accept that.

All these years, he'd walled off his heart from the possibility of love. Now, when the rocks in that wall had finally crumbled and he'd learned to love, his only reward was heartache.

The children of Destiny Island might wake to snow tomorrow, but Julian wouldn't be waking up with Iris in bed beside him. Not ever again.

Chapter Twenty-Three

The next day, Sunday, the thirtieth of December, Iris was behind the counter at Dreamspinner ringing up a sale when, if Blue Moon Air was on schedule, Julian would be boarding his flight to Vancouver. After he left her place last night, she'd texted him:

> I'm sorry, Julian. Sorry if I hurt you. Sorry I can't be who you want me to be.

His reply was brief:

> You are.

In other words, he rejected her point of view. That annoyed her, and yet she wouldn't believe that this was the end. The friendship they shared was stronger than that. She'd give it some time, and then try again.

The store's front door opened and Eden entered, followed by Miranda.

Miranda? The day after her wedding? The pair strode side by side toward her like an invading army determined to take no prisoners.

"I know you and Luke are saving your honeymoon for spring," Iris said to Miranda, "but didn't you at least get today to be alone together?"

"Until a dog broke its leg," she said, sounding philosophical. "I married a vet. Animals come first."

"Of course they don't," Eden said. "You and the kids come first. It's just that the dog had a more urgent need."

Miranda rolled her eyes. "I actually do know that. Doesn't mean I'm not above whining." To Iris, she said, "I called Eden and told her she had to take me for lunch and buy me a C-Shell cocktail. And now I'm telling you, you have to join us. Bride's prerogative. Since I can't have Luke right now, I get whatever else I want."

Usually, Iris enjoyed her friends' banter, but today she was too darned tired and depressed. She was about to find an excuse, when Aunt Lily came over, stepped behind the counter, and nudged her aside. "Go with your friends for lunch. I have this covered." Her manner was brisk and professional, but her soft eyes conveyed concern.

"Fine," Iris muttered, and then gave herself a mental whack upside the head. She should count her blessings for having such an understanding aunt, and wonderful friends. *Practice mindfulness. Live in the moment. Celebrate all the positive things life has to offer.*

Feeling maybe an iota better, she summoned a smile. "I'll get my coat."

"And umbrella," Eden said. "It's slushing out."

Oh, great. Iris liked snow, so rare here and so crystalline and pure. Having grown up on the West Coast, she also quite enjoyed the rain. But that in-between mixture was depressing. A perfect match to her mood. No, wait, she was supposed to be looking at the positives. "I'll be back in a minute."

She went to the office to gather her things. Julian's guitar pick was safely tucked inside a zipped pocket in her purse.

Maybe she should return it, but she couldn't bring herself to part with it.

Outside, she and her friends unfurled their umbrellas and dashed down the block and across the street, dodging puddles and clumps of melting snow. Inside C-Shell, Rachelle showed them to a window table and gave them menus. "Today's special is cream of mushroom soup, with a blend of wild mushrooms and herbs. It's classy comfort food."

Iris, who had no appetite, didn't open the menu, sipping water while the others perused theirs. Their server, Jonah, a university-student cousin of Rachelle's, came over. Iris ordered the mushroom soup and so did Eden. Miranda stifled a yawn and ordered a crab-and-cheese-melt panini, along with a salad. And a C-Shell cocktail.

After Jonah had gone, Eden said, "Miranda, that's a lot of food. Did you skip breakfast?"

"No, I just seem to be starving all the time these days." She yawned again.

Eden studied her intently. "You aren't pregnant, are you?"

Iris watched curiously as Miranda frowned and said, "I just got married."

Eden snorted. "And the relevance of that is . . . ?"

"Uh, yeah, you're right. But . . . pregnant . . . I mean, we'll probably have another kid or two. We've talked about it but figured we'd wait awhile."

"Birth control?" Eden asked.

"I have an implant."

"No method's one hundred percent reliable," Eden said. "Except, of course, no fooling around at all, which I know doesn't apply to you and Luke."

"Things have been so crazy this month," Miranda said. "I lost track of when my period's due." She rubbed her fingers across her forehead. "No, wait . . . When we picked the wedding date, I calculated timing so my period would be over by then, but I never got that period. So I'm overdue by almost two weeks." Her blue eyes widened. "Oh, wow. I could be pregnant."

A pang of envy made Iris wince. What must it feel like to be in a secure, loving relationship and have a baby on the way? Would she ever have that experience?

Julian had mentioned having children . . .

"Are you okay with that?" Eden asked.

Iris jerked in her seat, and then realized Eden's gaze was on her sister-in-law's face.

"Yeah." A grin took over Miranda's mouth, bit by bit. "Yeah, definitely. Luke will be, too, if it's true. I'll buy a test at the pharmacy."

Jonah arrived and placed a frothy peach-colored cocktail in front of Miranda. She gazed longingly at it and then, after he left, shoved it away. "Eden, Iris?"

Eden raised both hands. "Wish I could, but I'm driving."

"Iris, please? Let me at least enjoy watching someone drink it."

Iris pretty much only ever drank wine. But today . . . "Why not?" She raised the martini glass and took a sip. "Wow, I see why you like these." Mostly, the drink tasted of mixed fruit juices, but there was an herbal undertone and a subtle alcoholic bite that warmed her tummy.

"If I'm not pregnant, I'm so going to regret that," Miranda said. "Okay, now I don't want to think about it anymore, not until I know one way or the other." Another yawn had her raising her hand to cover her mouth. "Change of subject," she said. "It's nice to see Island Realty shut down. I sure hope Jelinek confesses and gets sent to jail for life."

"I talked to the Crown Prosecutor," Eden said. "She's committed to getting justice. She thinks Jelinek's lawyer will advise him to plea bargain. If so, this could all be over soon. She said she'll insist on at least five years in prison, which—"

"Five years?" Iris broke in. "That's not long enough."

"It sure isn't!" Miranda said.

"I know," Eden agreed. "But it's in line with sentences for similar offenses."

They all sighed. Then Eden said, "If there's a plea bargain, the victims won't have to testify. And they won't have this hanging over their heads for months, if not years. So there's the bright side."

"True," Miranda said. "Though I'd liked to have seen Jelinek take the stand and try to explain how he thought that abusing boys was an act of love."

Iris grimaced, and Eden said, "The strange thing is, he seems so normal."

"Which is how he got away with it all these years," Iris said. "That and his stellar reputation and influential position in the community."

"I know," Eden said. "He actually has done a lot of good for the island. He was the driving force behind a number of initiatives, like the medical clinic, new equipment for the fire department, bringing the Al-Khouris here from Syria. I guess it's rare to find a person who's totally evil."

"Yes, he's leaving a mixed legacy," Iris said. "A number of good things, but also horrendous damage to the boys he chose as his victims. And their families." She pressed her lips together. "He'll be a model prisoner. He'll start up some great programs among the inmates. He'll get out early, for good behavior. And the first thing he'll do is look for some innocent, vulnerable boy." She grabbed her glass and took a healthy slug of the cocktail.

"Crap," Miranda said. "I'm afraid you're right."

Eden said, "Bear in mind, he'll be on the National Sex Offender Registry, so he'll be required to report regularly to the police."

"Where he'll snow them with his charm," Iris said cynically. "There's never a happy ending to a situation like this, is there?"

"If he's declared a high-risk sex offender," Eden said, "one who's likely to reoffend, then a public warning may be issued. And there'll be restrictions on his release, like not being allowed near places where kids hang out."

"Someone should just castrate the bastard," Miranda said. "Hey, maybe that'll happen in prison."

They stared glumly at each other until Jonah brought their meals and wished them *bon appétit*.

Eden picked up her soupspoon. "On a happier note, Glory's been getting loads of feedback on the book club, Iris. The first meeting was such a big hit, a lot more seniors want to sign up. Glory wanted me to ask if you can handle another half dozen."

Iris tried to summon the energy to be happy about this development. "Sure. I think that'll work. If we get too much bigger, though, we might need to break it into two separate groups."

"They do know," Miranda said, pausing in attacking her crab melt, "that Julian won't be there, right?" Before Eden could answer, she went on. "And speaking of Julian—"

Iris broke in before she could finish the thought. "How's Glory? Did she have a good Christmas?" She'd enjoyed working with Glory and getting to know her a bit better.

Eden exchanged a meaningful glance with Miranda and said, "She's okay. Going through a bit of a post-Christmas letdown, though."

"That's too bad." Obviously, her friends knew something that she didn't, and she respected that they'd guard Glory's privacy. She was concerned, though. Maybe one day she'd invite Glory for coffee, or offer to babysit Gala so Glory and Brent could have a date night.

"Speaking of letdown," Miranda said, "how are you feeling, Iris? With Julian back in Vancouver?"

It wasn't nosiness; it was concern, just like Iris felt for

Glory. So yes, she'd tell her friends. She could use a little commiseration and a couple of sympathy hugs.

"I miss him already, but I knew that would happen. What really bothers me is that we parted on a sour note, after a disagreement. So I'm not sure how things will go, from here on."

"A disagreement?" Eden said.

"Well, first we confessed that we love each other"—a fact that still amazed her, but evoked knowing expressions from her two friends—"and then Julian said he'd like us to be together. Really together. But I can't. I'm not strong enough to handle the lifestyle that being with Julian would entail."

Miranda stopped eating but didn't put down her fork. "You know the title of the song Julian dedicated to me? 'You're Better than You Think'? Well, in my not-so-humble opinion, you're stronger than you think, Iris."

"When you and I first got to know each other," Iris said, "I remember telling you how brave I thought you were. You said that when I fell in love, I'd find out I was braver than I think. But you were wrong, Miranda. I'm still a pathetic mess of quivering nerves."

"Sure."

Her quick agreement raised Iris's brows. "Then I don't know what you're getting at."

"I mean that we're all, sometimes, a pathetic mess of quivering nerves. Like Eden said about that mock trial thing in law school."

Eden put down her soupspoon. "Yes. And with Mom's cancer. Every time she sees the doctor and gets blood tests, I'm terrified. But whatever happens, we'll face it as a family. We'll be weak together and strong together and we'll get through it."

"Which is what courage is really about," Miranda said.

"It's not about being fearless, it's about sucking it up and dealing."

"You know that *Tao of Pooh* book we read for the book club?" Eden asked. "There was something in it about courage that stuck with me. That it comes from caring and compassion."

"I know," Iris whispered.

"That fits perfectly, with my family," Eden said. "And for you, too, Iris, standing up for Julian when he told the truth about Jelinek. Miranda's right, you sucked up your fear because you cared for Julian. And you cared about what might happen to other boys."

"So if you want to be with him, then go for it," Miranda said. "And if you don't, well, you need to do what feels right for you."

"I agree," Iris said. "And that's what I'm doing."

"Really? It feels right to be separated from Julian?" Eden queried. "When Aaron and I fell for each other, and I was in Ottawa and he was here, it felt all wrong to be apart."

Nothing felt right today. This morning, Dreamspinner'd been a bright and happy place with tons of customers, but Iris had felt removed from it, like she was going through the motions. The store might be cheery and wrapped in festive trappings, but her mind and heart were smothered by a fog of melancholy. Even this lunch with her girlfriends, something she'd normally revel in, felt like another task she needed to get through before she could eventually go to bed and dream of Julian.

She was trying to follow the December advice on her calendar and keep her mind even, but in fact she felt seriously out of balance. More so than ever before, even in the stressful years at UVic.

Staring down at her barely touched soup, she said, "I was always content with who I was. I would read my romance novels and believe that one day a man would come along who saw me as I see myself, not perfect but special in my own way, and he'd fall in love with that person."

Flicking a glance upward she saw her friends watching her intently. Their expressions told her there were things they wanted to say, but they were holding back, giving her an opportunity to go on. So she did. "Julian did that. To my amazement."

Miranda's firm nod almost made her smile, but her lips didn't have the energy. "In a good romance story," Iris said, "each lover faces almost insurmountable challenges. Challenges that test them, that make them examine their fears and frailties. They find courage they'd never known they possessed and they forge ahead, they grow into stronger, better people. People who deserve and win love. Eden, Miranda, that's what happened in your relationships, isn't it?"

Miranda nodded, and Eden said, "Yes, but isn't that also what's happened with you and Julian? I can't think of a much bigger challenge than him coming to terms with the abuse he suffered, and bringing Jelinek's crimes to light."

Iris nodded emphatically. "Exactly. Julian had to be strong to survive, and then he had to be strong again when he ripped the scar off the old wounds and told the world that a highly respected man was in fact a pedophile. Julian has faced the challenges life's thrown him, and grown stronger." She closed her eyes for a moment. He had overcome his deep-seated mistrust and learned to love, and look how she'd responded. "He's a hero and he needs a true heroine, not a wimp who's scared to talk to strangers."

"You *are* his heroine," Miranda said. "Have you seen that video of you?"

Iris shook her head. "You see? I don't even have the guts to watch it."

"Watch it," Eden said. "See yourself the way others see you."

Iris narrowed her eyes, trying to figure out what they meant.

"You're fierce," Miranda said. "In a totally classy way. Fierce and strong. You should have your own dragon tattoo."

The very notion of having her body inked brought another almost-smile.

"Not a dragon," Eden said. "An iris. A flower that looks delicate, but in fact stands bravely on its narrow stalk, maybe bending with the wind but not breaking, always showing that lovely, serene face to the world."

Miranda nodded.

Iris was flattered that they saw her this way. But they were wrong. Weren't they?

"Before I forget," Aunt Lily said that night, "your mother is working on next year's calendar for the store." Lily, in yoga pants and a long-sleeved tee, was curled up in a chair in the living room of their apartment, her feet tucked up under her. Iris, dressed similarly, was on the couch, her bare feet up on the coffee table.

Lily had worked the evening shift, and now they were relaxing with a glass of wine. Music played softly, Grandmother Rose's favorite old LP on the turntable: Ricky Nelson, a singer who'd been a teen heartthrob in the late 1950s and early '60s.

"She wants to book our trip to Japan," Aunt Lily went on, "so she can schedule around it. Not during spring break or over a holiday weekend, of course."

"Right." Iris's voice came out flat, which was exactly how she felt about life in general. Flat, gray, too apathetic to focus on the positive. Definitely too flat to be enthusiastic about a trip she'd once hoped might lead her to repeat her dad and grandfather's experience of finding love there at the age of twenty-five. She'd already found love, for all the good it had done her.

Iris knew she should look forward to the opportunity to visit her mom's parents, meet other relatives in person, and enjoy the scenery and culture of Japan. She also should be glad, right now, to be in this serene apartment, enjoying the loving, undemanding company of her aunt. And she was, except that the two of them had spent, and would spend, too many evenings this way. Two lonely old maids.

No, two self-sufficient, well-rounded single women. She had to view it that way. And be positive about the upcoming trip. "Sure. Let's sit down tomorrow with a calendar."

"Fine." Lily sounded no more excited than she did. "How was your lunch outing?"

"Good." Iris took a deep breath and forced herself to be more upbeat. "I'll tell you a secret if you promise not to share it, not even with Mom and Dad."

"I always enjoy a good secret." She picked up her wine-glass.

"Miranda's pregnant." Her friend had texted to say she'd bought a pregnancy test and taken it as soon as she got home. "She just found out."

"Oh my. That's sooner than she and Luke intended, isn't it?"

"Yes, but she's thrilled. I know he will be, too."

"I'm sure he will." Aunt Lily smiled. "I'm so happy for them." Her smile softened at the edges, becoming reflective, wistful even. "She's so alive, your friend Miranda."

"Alive?"

"She lives her life, really lives it. Remember when she first came into the store, newly arrived on the island to stay with Aaron? So unhappy, depressed even, yet she was depressed in such an animated way. I saw her browsing through the board books with Ariana, and then Miranda gave this huge, exasperated huff and muttered, 'I can't even afford a book for my precious little girl. I'm so freaking *pathetic*!'"

Iris smiled fondly. "That sounds like Miranda. She's certainly not pathetic now."

"No. And I knew, when I heard her that day, that she wouldn't remain pathetic for long. She loved her daughter too much, and she had too much spirit."

"She's fierce like her dragon."

Aunt Lily nodded. Head lowered, gazing at her wineglass, she said, "You were alive like that, Iris. When you were with Julian. You were fierce in supporting him. Now you're subdued."

"I'm sad he's gone. I miss him. But I knew it would happen. I'll bounce back." Especially if she and Julian got over this awkward patch and resumed their friendship.

"But will you ever be fierce again?" Her aunt was still staring at the ruby-red wine.

"I doubt it. Not unless there's another situation where a friend needs me to be fierce."

"You think Julian no longer needs you to be fierce?"

Iris squeezed her eyes shut. "I can force myself to do it short term, but I can't live that way."

Her aunt didn't speak for a long moment, as Ricky Nelson sang about being a poor little fool for falling for a girl who lied to him. Then Lily said, "Perhaps not. Only you can know that."

"I feel as if I let him down," Iris confessed, thinking about that teasing, deceiving girl in the song. "Not intentionally, of course. But somehow I must have given him the impression that I was, well, a person he could let himself fall in love with."

"Iris, you don't *let* yourself fall in love. It happens, regardless of whether or not you want it to." She sighed, and then asked, almost too quietly to be heard over the music,

"Perhaps the question to ask is whether you feel that you've let yourself down."

Iris remembered the conversation she'd had with Julian on *Windspinner*, when she'd confessed to becoming complacent. She had then forced herself out of her comfort zone and had facilitated the seniors' book club, and despite some anxiety she'd had a good time. She'd enjoyed the seniors' stories and wisdom, had loved seeing them become so animated, and had believed that some of them had even gone away with helpful insights.

But an occasional book club get-together with some engaging, easily entertained older people was a far different thing from being part of Julian's musician life.

Her aunt didn't press her for a response and the two of them were quiet for a while, listening to the music.

"You remember what my mother said about Ricky Nelson?" Aunt Lily asked.

Glad of the change of subject, Iris replied, "Grandmother Rose said that when she came to Canada as a bride in 1955, she devoured all those family-oriented American TV shows. She said she learned from them, tried to model her behavior after Donna Reed, Margaret Anderson on *Father Knows Best*, and Harriet Nelson. She loved the Nelson family on *The Adventures of Ozzie and Harriet*, and when Ricky Nelson grew up, picked up the guitar, and began to sing, all dreamy eyed, she said he was"—Iris smiled, remembering—"a dreamboat. I have to admit, he is pretty sexy on the album cover."

"Yes, I understand what she saw in him. His voice is appealing, too, and his songs are romantic." One track ended and Aunt Lily, who knew the album by heart just as Iris did, said, "This next song, she said it was the story of her and my father's love."

The song was titled, "I Will Follow You." Iris nodded. "It

could have been written about them." Grandmother Rose would have loved Julian's song, "From Dust, a Rose," just as much.

They were both quiet as the singer vowed that he would follow his true love, follow her anywhere. That she was his destiny. As the last notes faded, Aunt Lily uncurled her legs and stood, picking up her half-finished wine. "Please excuse me. There's something I need to do."

"An inspiration for a design?" As with Julian, and probably all creative people, ideas could tease her aunt's mind at any moment, and Lily didn't want them to slip away.

"An inspiration. Yes, that's right."

Iris gazed after her aunt as she walked from the room, so slim, graceful, and lovely. A woman with a brilliant talent and a generous heart, a woman with so much to give. A woman who did just fine without a man, yet who, Iris knew, longed as she did for a loving relationship. Would her aunt find that love in Japan, or was her heart irrevocably bound to the one man she'd ever loved?

Iris blinked, because of course that question applied to her just as it did to her aunt.

How could she fall in love again? How would she ever find a man who measured up to Julian? What other man would view her as he did, would care for her as deeply as he did?

Now she truly understood why her aunt had remained single all these years.

Like Iris, Lily had been the one to reject the offer of a future. What if . . . Iris rose slowly. Was there any chance Fredrick was now widowed or divorced? A single man who—was it possible?—still held in his heart the memory of the lovely woman he had once asked to share his life?

Iris grabbed her wineglass and hurried to her bedroom. There, she propped herself on the bed, pillows behind her, computer on her lap. Her aunt hadn't told her Fredrick's surname, but the Internet could work magic. Iris held her breath as her fingers flew on the keyboard: *Fredrick professor creative writing university of vict . . .* As she typed, search results assembled on the screen and by the time she was halfway through typing *Victoria*, she had him.

Fredrick Magnusson. Still at UVic, and now the chair of the English Department. She clicked a link and gazed at the picture on his faculty listing. *Ooh, Aunt Lily, you have good taste!*

He looked to be around sixty. The poetic type, not unlike Julian. Not as handsome, perhaps, but striking with an aquiline nose, a sensual mouth, and gray eyes that, to Iris, looked intense. Sandy hair, kind of wavy, on the longish side, with lots of silver at the temples. The silver made the gray in his eyes even more dramatic. Though it was a head-and-shoulders shot, so she couldn't be sure of his build, he looked rangy, on the tall side.

She imagined this man thirty years ago, gazing with intensity and adoration at her beautiful young aunt. And Lily looking back, losing her shyness in those incredible moments of connection with the man she loved. Oh yes, she could see it.

Marriage was supposed to be forever, yet the reality was that so many couples, even ones who'd loved each other with all their hearts, grew apart as they got older. Divorce was common. Was it more moral to stay with a wife you no longer loved, and the children you'd created together, or to be honest and seek a new future?

Fredrick had chosen a new future, but Aunt Lily had denied him that option.

How had things turned out for him? Now that Iris had identified him, it was easy to track him on the Internet. In ten minutes, she knew that he was divorced and there was no hint of a new spouse or partner. The two children were adults now, and the daughter had a scarily open-to-the-world Facebook profile. There she was in a selfie of herself, Fredrick, and his granddaughter, all three of them grinning widely.

He was happy. He and his family were close. He was still teaching the subjects he loved. He hadn't remarried.

Iris copied the Facebook link and pasted it into an email. She did the same with the faculty listing and a couple of other interesting links. She addressed the email to her aunt and deliberated over the subject line and message.

A tap sounded on the frame of her open door and her aunt said, "May I come in?"

"Of course." Would Aunt Lily be offended if Iris sent this email? Upset? Or might this be the stimulus she needed to take a second chance at being happy with her professor?

Iris put her computer aside as her aunt seated herself on the side of the bed. She held an envelope with a purple ribbon tied around it. "What's up?" Iris asked.

"In an hour, it will be your birthday. So this is an early gift." When Lily handed over the envelope, Iris noticed a slight tremble in her usually steady artist's fingers. "You may choose not to use it."

Puzzled, Iris slipped off the ribbon. The envelope wasn't sealed, so it was easy to pull out the contents: two pages of white letter-size paper, folded together in thirds. She unfolded them and found herself staring at an e-ticket for Blue Moon Air, for a flight to Vancouver tomorrow afternoon. Why on earth would she leave Destiny and miss the traditional birthday celebration with her family?

Her breath caught. Already guessing what the next sheet might be, she turned to it and, yes, found a ticket to the Julian Blake Band's New Year's Eve performance at the Commodore Ballroom. An aqua Post-it note was stuck to the page, with Aunt Lily's beautiful handwriting: *Your grandparents' love story had a happy ending.*

What was that supposed to mean? Mouth open, not knowing what to say, Iris looked up—to see that her aunt had silently left the room.

Iris thought about her grandparents' love story. Meeting in an internment camp, being separated and living in different countries for ten years, facing parental opposition, and then her shy granddad traveling by himself to Japan to reunite with the girl he had always loved. And Rose leaving her home and family, leaving everything she knew, to come to Destiny Island—all because of her love for this man. Both of them had been brave enough to risk so much.

Iris was their granddaughter.

And Aunt Lily was their daughter. Iris pulled the computer back onto her lap. Her aunt had issued her this challenge and she was going to reciprocate.

Chapter Twenty-Four

On the afternoon of December thirty-first, Julian and his band were at the Commodore Ballroom in Vancouver, working with the venue techs to set up their equipment. They would run through a few numbers, do a sound check and make sure everything was working okay, then have a relaxed dinner before the night's show.

The four of them fell into a familiar routine, each knowing his or her tasks, joking back and forth as they moved around the big stage and discussed venue specifics with the tech people. The chatter was a little buzzed because, after all, it was New Year's Eve. This kind of gig was always special, with the audience in the mood to party. And the Commodore, on the second floor of a lovely old brick building on Granville Street, was a favorite venue: a grand old lady restored to her art deco elegance with her huge arched windows, coffered ceiling, and chandeliers, not to mention her colorful history as a speakeasy during Prohibition.

Julian was trying to psyche himself into a celebratory mood. So many things in his life were good. Being with these great musicians who'd become close friends in the past weeks. Preparing for an audience that was bound to

be upbeat. And, last but most important, coming to terms
with the burden of guilt and shame that had weighed him
down for so long. Not shedding it, because he couldn't
make up for those years when other boys were abused, but
knowing he'd finally done what needed to be done. He
was learning, in large part thanks to Iris, to be at peace
with that.

Iris . . .

If he'd never met her, he wouldn't feel as if he'd left a
chunk of his soul on Destiny Island. Yet he couldn't regret
their time together. He was glad she was in his life—and
he wouldn't let their quarrel ruin that. Eventually, his heart
would come to terms with the fact that she would be only a
friend, rather than a loving partner. He still carried her
green-veined pebble, often sticking his hand in his jeans
pocket and running his fingers over its smooth surface,
feeling the ache of longing.

He had phoned her this morning, but she hadn't answered. Maybe she wasn't ready to talk to him, or perhaps
she was just busy. He'd left a voice mail wishing her a
happy twenty-fifth birthday and happy New Year. She had
texted back not long after. Texted, not called. Her message
had been short:

I hope you have the best New Year's ever.

As if. Didn't she know she'd peeled back the shell
around his heart, captured it for her own, and then shredded
it with her graceful fingers? His muse stirred, flagging
those words. Maybe he'd found the elusive ending to his
song about Iris.

He and Roy were fiddling with a speaker when his phone
rang. He pulled it out, saw Iris's name, and felt a poignant
mix of happiness and regret. "Hey. Happy birthday."

"Thanks, Julian. Uh, where are you?" Her voice was

higher pitched than usual. Nervous. After all, it was the first time they'd spoken since the heart-shredding.

"At the Commodore, setting up for tonight's concert. How about you? At the store?"

"No, I'm standing on the wharf waiting for Blue Moon Air to load."

That made no sense. "Uh, why?"

"Because I'm booked on the flight over to Vancouver." Her speech was fast and breathy. "I have a ticket for the concert."

"What?"

Roy was gaping at him, so Julian walked to the side of the stage, phone to his ear. "Seriously? Iris, I'd love to see you, but there'll be a thousand people here." He stared out at the huge room with numerous tables, the mezzanine, and mostly the huge dance floor that would, tonight, have hundreds of bodies on it. "I'll get you a backstage pass. You can watch from there." His brain was racing; his heart, too. "Wow, you're coming to the show." But why? What did this mean? "I'll pick you up at the seaplane terminal here. We can talk."

"You need to set up and rehearse, don't you?"

"More than that, I need to see you." How could he concentrate on anything until he knew what was going on? "I'll pick you up, we'll talk, you can watch us rehearse. No, wait a minute. You're not coming alone, are you?" She wouldn't travel by herself. She hadn't even dared go off to university on her own.

"All alone." The quiver in her voice told him she was anxious about that.

"I'm definitely meeting you. When does the flight get in?"

"Around three. Aaron has a couple of drop-offs and pickups along the way."

"I'll be there. If you get in early, or I get tied up in traffic, wait for me. Will you do that?"

"Yes, Julian. I'll wait for you."

He couldn't think straight. His brain kept repeating *What does this mean?* Earlier, her text had wished him the best New Year's ever. She must've known then that she was coming. Was this a test? Could she actually be considering a life with him, and using tonight's concert to gauge whether she could handle it? He wished she'd chosen a smaller event, something midweek in a little town.

"Julian, are you still there?"

"I, yeah, sorry. I just . . . well, we'll talk when you get here."

"Is it alright that I come? Maybe it's inconvenient. I don't want to impose if—"

"Iris! Goddammit." He took a breath, calmed himself. "Yes, I want you to come. Get on that plane and I'll see you in Vancouver." He ended the call before she could have any further second thoughts.

As he turned around, shoving his phone back in his pocket with a shaking hand, he was so hyped he felt as if pure caffeine ran through his veins. The venue's people were still working, but Roy, Camille, and Andi had all stopped and were staring at him. He realized they'd listened to his side of the conversation. Andi spoke first, sounding jazzed. "Iris is coming?"

He nodded. "I don't know why, but she's coming."

"Because she loves you," Camille said with certainty, beaming at him.

If only it were that easy.

Julian tried to get back to work, but after a few minutes Roy said, "You're more hindrance than help. Drive down to the terminal and pace. We'll do what needs doing here, then go for coffee. Give me a call when you want to come back to rehearse." He grinned, white teeth flashing between his neatly trimmed ginger mustache and beard. "And if you don't make it back to rehearse, we'll still be okay. Just don't be late for the show."

"Thanks, guys."

Julian wasn't sure he was fit to drive, so he was extra careful as he negotiated the downtown streets. He parked near the Vancouver Harbour Flight Centre, and went into the terminal building. The view from the big windows was stunning, of North Van and the North Shore Mountains, the busy harbor, the giant green space of Stanley Park. But rather than wait inside, he strode along the seawall walkway, barely noticing the scenery or the chilly, damp wind blowing in off the ocean. Nerves—and hope—kept him warm.

What seemed like hours later, but was probably less than an hour, he saw the blue and white de Havilland Beaver sporting the logo of a plane flying across a blue moon. It took its sweet time dropping altitude, landing on the ocean, and then motoring to the dock. Because he wasn't a ticketed passenger, he wasn't allowed down on the dock, so he waited impatiently at the gated entrance above it as Aaron jumped out, secured the plane, and opened the passenger door.

He assisted two older women down the metal stairs, and then a young couple, and finally Iris. Graceful Iris almost stumbled as her feet met the dock. She wasn't looking where she was going; instead, her gaze scanned the shore. Julian waved madly.

He loved how her face lit up, a light he could see even from here, like a shaft of pure sunshine on this gloomy, gray afternoon. She waved back and started to walk along the dock. Her hair was loose, black silk tossed by the wind, and she was slim and elegant in a belted beige trench coat and black boots.

Aaron laughed and said something, which she seemed to

ignore as her steps quickened. She was almost running as she
came up the skid ramp, and then she was in Julian's arms.

His world tilted on its axis and then settled again into a
brand-new position, one that felt absolutely right.

They clung to each other for ages, her face buried in the
shoulder of his jacket, his nose deep in her almond-scented
hair.

She pulled back enough so she could look up at him,
and when he saw her face he had to kiss her. It was a
breathless, laughing kiss, one of sparkling brown eyes and
pink-tinged cheeks.

When they finally came up for air, he said, "I can't believe you're here."

"Me either. But I am. With a nudge from Aunt Lily."

"Really? Tell me."

"Not here, with everyone around."

The other passengers from the Blue Moon Air flight came
up the ramp toting their luggage, and Julian and Iris moved
aside. Aaron followed the group, carrying a weekend-sized
bag, and said, with a wink and a smile, "Thought you might
want this, Iris."

"Oh! I forgot my bag."

"Understandable." He passed the bag over to Julian.
"Have fun, you two."

Julian hoped they would. "Thanks." To Iris, he said,
"How about we put your bag in the van and go park in a lot
by the ocean in Stanley Park? I'd take you to my place, but
it's a bit of a drive there and back and—"

"And you're supposed to be rehearsing. I didn't mean
to take you away from that. When I called, I only wanted to
give you a heads-up that I was coming. And a chance to tell
me not to, if you didn't want me here."

"Why would I not want you to come?"

She did that head-ducking thing. "If you had some other woman attending the show."

He caught her chin and raised it. "There is no other woman. There's only you. Screw it. Scrap the van, the park. I need to know now. Why did you come, Iris?"

"Because I love you and I want to be fierce. If I had the guts to stand by you when you told the world about Jelinek, then I can be brave enough to be with you when you perform. And when you go on the road. Just as long as . . ."

Julian could barely breathe. His heart was pounding in his throat; he was choking on hope. "As long as what?"

"As long as we can go back to Destiny Island sometimes. So I can rest, recharge my energy. Be with my family. Go to the store, the old commune, go sailing."

He needed those things, too. "Yes, Destiny should be our home." How ironic that the island he'd once hated was now the place he most wanted to be, with Iris at his side. "Close to both our families. I want to sail *Windspinner* with you. I want to compose music at the old commune and get your input. I want us to make love there in spring, under the apple blossoms. In summer, when there are daisies in the grass. And in autumn, when the nip in the air makes you shiver and cling to me."

"Hello again," an amused male voice said. It was Aaron, carrying luggage down to the dock. Julian and Iris remained silent as a cluster of passengers followed him.

Then Julian said, "I want us to be together, and I want you to be happy. You have to talk to me, let me know if something's too much for you, tell me how I can make things easier. We'll work it out. If we need to spend some time apart, when I'm on the road and you need a Destiny break, then we'll do it. I won't ask you to promise me the future. Not now, when you don't know what that future's going to be like. But I will ask you to promise one thing."

Her eyes were huge, intent. "What's that?"

"That you'll be honest with me. I love you so much, Iris. I think that, together, we can do anything. If we trust each other and we're honest."

"I think so, too." She smiled up at him. "You are the best birthday present ever."

Chapter Twenty-Five

When Iris had seen Julian's name on the screen of her phone that morning, she let the call go to voice mail. She hadn't wanted to talk to him until she stood beside the plane and knew she had the courage to board.

And now here she was, in a setting she'd never imagined herself in: with nine hundred and ninety-nine other people, in a huge room filled with noise and flashes of light. A few months ago, the notion would have terrified her, and she'd had some anxious moments in the beginning, as the room started to fill. But she'd breathed through it, accepted the anxiety, and realized that there was nothing to fear.

She even felt a sense of kinship with these strangers who loved Julian's music and had chosen this concert as the perfect way to end a year and bring in the next.

Also, it turned out that, sitting at a table on the mezzanine of a stunning restored ballroom, she was more of an "island" than on Destiny, where everyone minded one another's business. In this room, people were in pairs or groups. If anyone even noticed her, they would assume she was waiting for a friend to return from getting a drink or visiting the restroom.

She'd worried she might be recognized, from the video that had gone viral. But Vancouver had a huge Asian population, and she was just one slim, black-haired young woman among many. A few guys and a couple of women had asked her to dance or offered to buy her a drink, but when she'd said, "Thank you, but no," they'd gone away.

Her attention was focused on the stage, on Julian. He looked fabulous, in the typical tattered black jeans and tee he wore to perform, his tattoo twining along his muscled forearm. He sounded amazing and had a crazy kind of energy—fed, no doubt, from the spirited mood of this New Year's Eve crowd and also, she hoped, from knowing she was here.

He'd told her where to sit, so she'd have a good view of the stage. She doubted he could see her, what with the stage lighting focused on him and the band, but his gaze often seemed to rest on her.

He loved her. She loved him. They were a couple. She didn't know the details of how things would work out, but she and Julian would figure it out together, day by day. She was an iris and she might bend when the winds blew hard, but she would hold up her head and blossom for Julian.

The band had been playing for an hour and a half, some of their old songs and some from their upcoming album, all equally well received, when Julian announced a fifteen-minute break.

Iris wriggled her shoulders, realizing she'd been so absorbed in the music that she'd barely moved. A glance at her watch told her it was just past eleven. The next set would cross over into the New Year. What would the band do as midnight approached? A big countdown, a thousand people sharing the moment? The new Iris, the woman who loved and was loved by Julian, felt a pleasant anticipatory thrill.

She pulled out her phone and texted her aunt, her parents,

her girlfriends on Destiny and her old BFF, Shelley. Then she people-watched, relaxed in her anonymity. Much of the crowd were twenty- or thirty-somethings, but there were a number of middle-aged people and even some with gray hair. Clothing varied from minuscule skirts and cami tops to cowboy boots and hats to evening dress. Hairstyles and makeup were just as varied.

She was about to reach for her glass of ginger ale with soggy lime and melted ice when a young woman with chopped-short hair and huge earrings, dressed in a figure-concealing black top and black leather pants, handed her a flute glass filled with sparkling liquid. "You're her," the woman said, "aren't you? Julian's girl. Iris. The 'I believe in Julian' woman."

Iris's heart skipped. "I, uh . . ." *Breathe. Stay even. You can handle this.*

"I won't give you away. I just had to tell you what an inspiration he is. And you."

"An inspiration?" Curiosity chased her anxiety away.

"My uncle abused me when I was a girl. For two years, and I didn't tell. Then every time there was some family gathering and he was there, I felt like a victim all over again." Her chin came up. "This year at Christmas, there he was again. And I thought of Julian and of how you supported him. So I went to the police."

"Oh my. I'm so sorry that happened to you, but congratulations on your bravery."

A smile trembled. "Thank you. Doing something like that, you sure find out who your friends are."

Concerned for her, Iris said, "You do. And I hope that . . ."

The smile firmed. "Yeah, turns out I do have some. Like Julian, I'm lucky that way." She glanced over her shoulder and wiggled her fingers at someone. "And I'm here with them tonight, so I better go. But thank you. Okay?"

"I didn't do anything. But you're welcome. I'll tell Julian. He'll want to know." Iris rose, saying, "What's your name?"

"Marianne."

Iris, who was shy with strangers, who didn't believe in public displays of affection, gave the young woman a hug. "Happy New Year, Marianne."

Marianne hugged her back. "Thank you. Again. So much. Happy New Year to you, too, Iris. You and Julian."

When she had gone, Iris raised the flute glass in a toast to Julian, Marianne, and all the survivors, and then sipped the bubbly wine.

A few minutes later, the band came back onstage, quickly tuned up, and began to play again. They alternated upbeat tunes, ones that got the audience jumping around on the dance floor, with slower ones, songs that had couples melting into each other's arms. Iris didn't even envy them because, when this concert ended, she'd be going home with the hot singer onstage.

She and Julian would spend the early hours of the New Year in each other's arms, making love with not only their bodies but their hearts and souls, creating the next verse of their love song and promising each other a future.

Watching and listening to the band, Iris lost track of time. But it seemed Julian didn't, because after the band finished one song, he exchanged a few quiet words with Roy, Camille, and Andi, and then he spoke into the mic.

"In five minutes, it'll be a New Year. This wasn't how the band had planned to end the old one, but there's something I want to do. To share. And my bandmates are kind enough to indulge me."

He plucked a couple of notes, no tune that Iris recognized, and then he went on. "I'm going to play this next one on my own because it's brand-new. So brand-new, my band hasn't even heard it yet. I've been working on it for a while, but I could never figure out the ending. Not until today. So bear with me if I fumble a little."

He paused, looked down at his guitar, and looked up again. "It's the end of a year, and most of you know that the past month's been tough for me. The fact that you've come here tonight, and many of you have supported me online, means a lot to me. Anyhow—"

A call from the audience interrupted him, a female voice shouting, "We believe in you, Julian!"

Others joined in, those who were sitting coming to their feet as a huge roomful of people chanted, "We believe in you, Julian!" over and over. His bandmates joined in and Iris was on her feet, too, but not calling out because tears clogged her throat.

Julian looked stunned and uncharacteristically ill at ease on the stage he'd owned for the past hours, as noise and energy came at him from all corners of the room. Then he held up his arm, the tattooed one, and spoke into the mic. His voice didn't cut through the chanting, but gradually the audience stopped so they could hear him.

"Thank you," he said. "That means more than you can possibly know." He paused and then said, "As you can imagine, I'm looking forward to the New Year, and to moving forward now that I've done my best to exorcise the demons from my past."

He glanced down at his guitar, played a couple more notes, looked back up. "This past year has also been the best year of my life, because of something that happened to me recently. I think you'll understand what I mean when you hear this song."

He lifted his head and gazed straight toward where she sat.

"It's called 'Iris,'" he said.

If you enjoyed *Sail Away With Me*, be sure not to miss
all of Susan Fox's Blue Moon Harbor series, including

COME HOME WITH ME

*It may be a dot in the Pacific Northwest, but tiny
Blue Moon Harbor always has room for love . . .*

Miranda Gabriel has finally hit rock bottom. As a high
school dropout, she fled Blue Moon Harbor and her
shattered family life, and chased after love in all the
wrong places. But now, as a single mom, her priority is
her two-year-old daughter. Her only choice is to swallow
her pride and return to the island she's always hated.
At least between working and studying, she'll be too busy
for romance—especially when the prospect is a nice guy,
exactly the kind she knows she doesn't deserve . . .

The island veterinarian, Luke Chandler is a widower
raising four-year-old twin boys. In high school, he found
bad girl Miranda fascinating—and though life has
changed them both, he's still intrigued. Luke has known
true love, and something about Miranda makes him long
to experience it again. Yet he's wary of opening himself,
and his boys, to hurt. But his heart may not give him
a choice. And together, maybe he and Miranda can give
each other the courage to believe in themselves,
and to embrace a promising new future . . .

A Zebra mass-market paperback and eBook on sale now.

Turn the page for a special look!

"Guess what?" Miranda Gabriel's brother cried, raising his girlfriend's left hand like a boxing referee proclaiming the champ. "We're engaged!"

Diamonds sparkled on Eden's finger, and when Miranda stared from the ring to Aaron's face and his fiancée's, their excitement was no less dazzling.

Miranda's heart sank like a heavy, cold stone.

She had been peeling sweet potatoes in the big kitchen at SkySong when Aaron and Eden burst into the room. Tonight's dinner at the serenity retreat was planned as a celebration of Eden's tidying up all the details around the sale of her family's home in Ottawa now that she, her parents, and her sister were becoming Destiny Island residents. Aaron, owner of Blue Moon Air, had flown over to Vancouver in his Cessna seaplane on this chilly, early December day to pick Eden up after her Ottawa flight. Now it seemed the celebration would be a dual-purpose one.

"He proposed on the dock," Eden said, her voice bubbly, neither she nor Aaron seeming to notice that their wet jackets were dripping on the terra-cotta-tiled floor. "Right there in the middle of Blue Moon Harbor." She laughed up at him, her amber eyes glowing with happiness and love. "In the rain, and it was the most romantic thing in the world."

Engaged.

Eden's aunt and uncle, Di and Seal SkySong, who owned this rustically lovely retreat on four acres of waterfront, rushed over to the happy couple, offering hugs and congratulations. Miranda's two-year-old daughter remained in her booster chair at the kitchen table, still absorbed in the tea party game she and Di had been playing with one of Ariana's cloth fairy dolls. And Miranda herself stood rooted at the teal-topped kitchen counter, her feet as leaden as her heart.

Of course she'd known where Aaron and Eden's relationship was heading. In truth, the depressed, pessimistic, defeated spot in her soul, the one she hated to surrender to, had known ever since that day back in June. The day when her pride had hit an all-time low. Evicted from her tiny apartment, without the funds to rent another, she'd felt worthless and powerless. For the sake of her precious daughter, she had phoned Aaron and admitted she had no choice but to accept his offer of help. There she'd been, more pathetic than ever before in her life. She'd had no strength left, no option but to leave Vancouver and drag herself and Ariana to Destiny Island, a place she'd always hated, to shelter under her big brother's roof.

But Aaron, the one person who'd always been there for her, was away in Ottawa, visiting a woman he'd just met.

Sight unseen, Miranda—selfish bitch that she was—had hated Eden Blaine for threatening the one bit of stability in her and Ariana's lives. But then she'd met the smart, sensitive, beautiful Eden, seen her with Aaron, listened to what her brother said and didn't say. She'd seen that despite the huge problems the two lovers had faced, Eden made him happy. And Aaron's happiness was the second-most important thing in the world to Miranda. Only the welfare of her daughter ranked higher.

Now, realizing she'd been silent too long, she forced herself to walk across the kitchen. Normally she found this room so warm and welcoming, with its white-painted wood and brick walls and cabinets, accented by a hodgepodge of vividly colored chairs, kitchen accessories, and artwork. But today her heart was a frozen lump in her chest and it would take a lot more than Di and Seal's cheerful, eclectic décor to warm it.

Throwing her arms around the happy couple, she squeezed both of them, but Aaron a little harder. Her handsome, dark-haired brother, her best and only real friend for all their lives, now belonged to someone else. "I'm so happy for you guys."

It wasn't a lie. Honestly, it wasn't. It was just a truth that jostled uneasily side by side with her selfishness and her envy. The guy who'd been so cynical—or, as he called it, realistic—about love had had, for the very first time, the guts to throw his heart into the ring. And what did he get? A freaking happy ending. As compared to her. She truly did believe in love and she'd been brave enough to go for it, to love and lose and try again, over and over. She'd been doing it ever since she was a tiny child hoping against hope that one day her mom would love her and be there for her. And yet here she was, twenty-seven years old and still alone.

So many times, as the children of a cocaine-addicted prostitute, she and Aaron had been the kids left outside, looking in windows at happy families eating together, at stores full of shiny new toys and games, at grocery shelves stocked with more food than anyone could possibly eat in a lifetime. Wanting, always wanting, but not getting.

Now Aaron had crossed over and he was on the inside. And she was left outside, no longer shoulder to shoulder with her big brother but all by herself.

She drew in a long breath, trying to flush the sour gray tang of depression and self-pity from her mind and heart. The fact was, she wasn't alone; she had Ariana. Having a daughter made life so much richer and more wonderful but also created pressures so heavy that a few months back, Miranda had almost cracked under them. Because it was one thing to be strong and resourceful enough to look after yourself. It was quite another when you were responsible for a small, fragile human being who deserved so much more than you'd ever been able to give her.

Miranda went over to the table where her beloved black-haired fairy princess of a daughter had stopped playing with her doll and, it seemed, belatedly come to the realization that everyone's attention was focused elsewhere than on her. Her cute face had gone pouty, a warning that a TTT—terrible two tantrum, as Miranda called them—was threatening to explode, as so often happened when the toddler felt neglected or thwarted.

"Sweetie, this is so exciting," Miranda said, hoisting her mocha-skinned daughter, so unlike her own fair self, into her arms. The familiar weight and warmth, the delicate scent of the baby oil Di made from the petals of wild roses, soothed Miranda's nerves.

Forcing enthusiasm into her voice, she brought the little girl over to the newly engaged couple. "Uncle Aaron is getting married." She glanced at his fiancée, the walnut-haired lawyer who'd given up her entire life in Ottawa to move to Destiny Island. "I guess that's going to make you Aunt Eden?"

Eden beamed, her happiness so vivid that, if Miranda had been a normal woman rather than a seething mess of insecurities, she'd have found it contagious. "I can't think of a bigger honor." She took Ariana's small hand gently in hers. "What do you think, Fairy-ana?" The nickname had been bestowed by Aaron a few months before, when his niece became obsessed with fairies. "Will you let me be your aunt Eden?"

Now that the attention was back on her, Ariana was happy. "An-te-den?" she ventured.

"That sounds so good," Eden said, turning to put her arm around Aaron, as if she couldn't bear to go more than a moment without touching him.

"It sure does," he said.

Oh God, Miranda's big brother, the guy who'd taught her to shoplift and pick pockets as necessities of survival, had gone all schmaltzy. With a reluctant grin, she had to admit it was actually pretty adorable.

And it was high time she stopped being so freaking pathetic and looked on the bright side. Aaron's happiness proved he'd been wrong to say that love wasn't in the cards for either of them. She was right: they *could* find true love. They could beat their track record of being unloved by their mom, their two dads—because, in truth, she and Aaron were half siblings—and their grandparents.

But right now wasn't the time to muse about love. She had to think about her and Ariana's immediate future. They couldn't keep living in the guest room at Aaron's small log home. That arrangement wasn't fair to him and Eden.

Resting her right hand on her shirtsleeved left forearm, she summoned the power of the tattooed dragon that lay beneath the faded blue cotton. The dragon that symbolized her strength and ability to cope with whatever life tossed her way.

Eden's aunt and uncle got back to the dinner preparations, Seal taking over the sweet potatoes Miranda had abandoned. Eden and Aaron went into the mudroom to take off their jackets and boots, then returned, pulled out chairs at the table, and sat down side by side, hands linked.

Bouncing Ariana gently in her arms, Miranda listened to

the conversation with half an ear while she formulated a plan for finding a new home for herself and her daughter.

"Eden, you've told your mom and dad?" Di asked.

"Yes, we stopped at their cabin first." Eden's parents and younger sister were living in one of the eight scenic log cabins at SkySong, though Helen and Jim planned to buy a house on Destiny Island in the spring. "Mom and Dad are thrilled to bits. They'll be over for dinner shortly. Kelsey was out for a run, so she doesn't know yet."

Eden went on, gushing about how she couldn't believe how wonderful the past year had been, finding her long-lost aunt Di, discovering this wonderful island, and best of all meeting the love of her life.

Helen and Di had been separated since their teens, when Di, the older sister, had run away from their Ottawa home along with her new, secret boyfriend, a member of the Mi'kmaq First Nation in Nova Scotia, who was also a teen runaway. They'd traveled west, all the way to Destiny Island, where they'd joined the Enchantery commune. Last summer, a long-lost letter had provided a clue that brought Eden here, and the rest was history. A family reunion, not to mention a new love.

Di, who'd been emptying glass canning jars of chopped tomatoes into a large pot on the stove, glanced over her shoulder. "Have you two talked about a wedding date?" The serene woman in her mid-sixties looked a bit like the hippie she'd once been, wearing one of the woven Guatemalan tops she loved, with her walnut-and-silver hair gathered into a long braid.

"Soon," Aaron said.

"But Aaron," Eden said, "I start my new job at Arbutus Lodge after New Year's. There'll be so much to do, and I need to concentrate on that rather than giving them short shrift."

Yeah, that was Eden. Superresponsible and organized.

"Do *not* tell me we're going to wait a year," Aaron said, sounding a little panicky.

"No, no, of course not. It's just, this is such a surprise. I need to get my head around it, and planning a wedding does take some time and effort."

He groaned, and Miranda gave him a sympathetic smile. Just wait until the poor guy found himself being dragged into discussions about flowers, music, and catering.

The scent of cooking tomatoes and herbs drifted across from the stove, stirring guilt in Miranda. She always tried to pull her weight and really should be helping with the meal. But right now something else was more important. She plunked down on a sky-blue chair across from Aaron and Eden, with her daughter in her lap.

Eden, gazing at Aaron, said, "How about the spring? April or May?"

"I guess I can live with that. After all, we'll be living together anyhow."

And there was Miranda's cue. "Ariana and I will clear out of the house as soon as I can find a place." She'd been in denial, should have done this back when Eden decided to move to the island.

Cuddling her daughter, she said, "I'll talk to Iris at Dreamspinner. She and her family know everyone on the island." The Yakimuras' bookstore and coffee shop were the heart of Blue Moon Harbor village. "I bet some of the summer folks would be willing to rent their place at least until May or June, and by then I'll have found—"

"Whoa," Aaron said, casting a quick sideways glance at Eden.

"That's for sure," his fiancée said. "Miranda, Aaron's place is your home, yours and Ariana's, just as much as it's mine. We don't want you to leave."

Even as she appreciated Eden's generosity, Miranda's

heart gave a twinge at the *we*. Already, Aaron and Eden were a *we* who made decisions together.

"Besides," Aaron said, "if you pay rent somewhere, you'll have to increase your work hours, and that won't give you as much time for your studies."

For years he'd been urging her to further her education. As an eleventh-grade dropout who'd never done well in school, she'd had no desire to go back to the books. And she'd been busy, what with the waitressing and retail jobs she'd held, and her pre-Ariana active life as a young single woman in a dynamic city. But then she'd gotten pregnant and life had changed.

Last summer it had sunk in that, if she was going to give her daughter the kind of life she deserved, she needed higher-paying work. So she'd worked her butt off for the past few months and almost finished her GED online. Turned out, she wasn't all that bad at schoolwork if she applied herself. In the new year, she'd start the online courses to get certified as an early childhood educator. Even if she busted her butt on those, too, which she fully intended to do, it would take her more than a year. "I'll still study," she said grimly.

"Are you sure?" he asked.

She'd have snapped at him for his lack of faith, except he had plenty of reason to doubt her. But now she was committed to building a better future for herself and the precious girl whose weight and stillness now indicated she'd dozed off on her mom's lap. "Yes, I'm sure." Somehow she'd find the time.

"And you guys need privacy," she said firmly. "Stop being so nice and generous and all that good stuff and be realistic." She managed a one-sided grin for her brother. "Isn't that what you've been telling me all these years? To be realistic?"

"Yeah, but—" he started.

"I have an idea." The calm voice was Di's, reminding Miranda that she and her brother had an audience.

Miranda glanced over her shoulder to see that Eden's aunt had turned away from the stove, where a pot of spicy tomato sauce now simmered. "Stay here, Miranda," Di said warmly.

"Here? At SkySong?"

The teen runaways had been together forever now. Never married, they'd rechristened themselves, changing the first names their parents had given them and taking the surname SkySong, and over the years they'd created this retreat by the same name. In addition to the lovely old wooden two-story home where Di and Seal lived, the scenic property included log guest cabins and a huge organic garden.

"We'd be happy to have you," Seal agreed, looking up from spreading something on a loaf of homemade French bread. Garlic and herb butter, from the delicious smell of it. He, like his partner, showed his hippie roots, clad in faded tie-dye and wearing his graying black hair in a ponytail secured by a leather thong. His deep brown eyes were sincere behind wire-framed glasses.

"I can't take your charity."

"It's not charity," Di said firmly. "Nor is having Helen, Jim, and Kelsey in a cabin."

"No, of course it's not, with them," Miranda said. "I mean, they're your family." Not to mention the SkySongs were assisting in Helen's recovery after surgery and treatment for a recurrence of breast cancer.

"You're family, too," Seal said.

"No, I'm not." Aaron and Ariana were her only family.

"Of course you are," Di said, coming over and resting a hand on her shoulder. "Aaron's about to be our . . . uh, nephew-in-law and you're his sister. Besides, you sure can't accuse Seal and me of being sticklers for convention, can you?" Her bright blue eyes danced.

Miranda's lips twitched. "I wouldn't dare."

"For us," Di said, "it's the family of our hearts that counts. You and Ariana most definitely have a place in our hearts."

"It's the truth," Seal said.

Miranda swallowed, trying to clear away the lump that had formed in her throat. If she could believe them, she might cry. It was more acceptance and support than she'd had from her own grandparents, not to mention the unknown father who'd knocked up her mother. Or the mom who'd put her next fix or her current boyfriend ahead of her children's welfare.

"We're never full up in winter," Di went on. "You and your sweet girl can have a cabin for the next four or five months at least. You'll have lots of able babysitters, so—"

"It's no problem for me to take Ariana to the store." Blowing Bubbles, where she worked part-time, sold children's toys, furniture, strollers, and so on. Kara, the owner, brought her own little one along with her and encouraged Miranda to do the same. There was a fenced playpen for their toddlers and the kids of customers, and Kara gave the children toys and stuffed animals to keep them happy. She said the best advertisement was to see a smiling child loving one of the store's products. Mind you, since Ariana had turned two at the end of July, the whole happy-child thing wasn't happening as often as it used to.

"You might want to go out in the evenings, though," Di said.

"Going out isn't on my list right now." She hadn't had time to make female friends here. As for dating, her history with men was a succession of screw-ups: from the musician she'd moved in with when she was fifteen; to the gorgeous African-American actor who'd hung around long enough to father Ariana but not to see her born; to the chef she'd fallen for last year before realizing he changed women as often as he changed his special of the week.

Aaron said she looked for love in all the wrong places. Maybe he was right. All she knew now was that this wasn't the time to be looking. And, though she had no affection for Destiny Island, she had to admit it was a good place to be if she wanted to avoid temptation. There weren't many eligible guys, and those she'd seen were way too wholesome and boring to appeal to her. "My spare time's for Ariana and for studying."

"Wise priorities," Aaron said.

She sent him an eye roll just as the kitchen door opened again. This time it was Kelsey, Eden's younger sister. She wore damp jogging clothes and with one hand flicked raindrops from her spiky, blond-streaked hair. "Eden, Aaron? Mom and Dad say you have big news."

A grinning Eden held up her left hand.

Kelsey squealed and threw her wet arms around her sister and Aaron. "I'm so happy for you! For all of us!"

The commotion woke Ariana, who let out a demanding screech.

Kelsey said, "Oh, sweetie, are you getting ignored?" She came over to scoop the child from Miranda's arms and made funny faces that worked magic in calming the incipient tantrum.

Eden repeated the proposal-on-the-dock story and then Di said, "Kelsey, Miranda wants to move out of Aaron's house and I've told her she and Ariana should take a cabin here."

"You totally should!" Kelsey said to Miranda, her eyes—the same blue as Di's—sparkling with excitement. "That would be so cool. More additions to our big, happy family." She gazed down at Ariana again. "You'd like that, wouldn't you? I'd see lots more of you. Mom and Dad would love it, too. They're just crazy about you, you little sugarplum."

Kelsey, at twenty-two, was seven years younger than her sister and almost five years younger than Miranda. She was spontaneous, generous, and optimistic, and she was also completely devoted to her mom. So much so that she'd taken a year off from university at McGill to move here with her parents to help out.

A big, happy family. It was the one thing Miranda and Aaron had always wanted. He was getting it, but she couldn't truly accept that it was being offered to her. Or that she deserved it. She glanced at her brother, who sat with his arm around Eden. His gaze met hers. A quarter of a century ago, the two of them had learned how to communicate without words. Now she knew he'd read her unspoken question.

Sure enough, he said solemnly, "Eden's right, that our place is yours, too. Never think you need to leave. But if you want to, I think you should accept Di and Seal's generous offer." His tone lightened. "Ariana would love having all these people to spoil her."

Miranda looked around the kitchen. A few minutes ago, everyone's attention had been on Aaron and Eden and now it was on her as they waited for her answer. Her brother knew exactly how to manipulate her. She'd do anything if she believed it was good for her child.

But could she really move to SkySong and be part of all this? The idea was overwhelming. She was so used to living alone with Ariana and had barely gotten adjusted to being in Aaron's house. Could she be a good guest here, pull her weight, ensure that Di and Seal didn't regret having made the offer?

Of course, she and Ariana would have a separate cabin. It wasn't like they'd all be living on top of one another. A lot of the time, she and her daughter would have more privacy than they did at Aaron's.

She gazed at her child, so contented in Kelsey's arms. Ariana was her anchor. Her heart.

Slowly, she said, "Di and Seal, if you're really sure, I guess that's what we'll do. But you have to let me at least pay something or cook meals or garden or—"

"Miranda, shut up," Seal said with a smile that deepened the curved lines bracketing his nose and mouth.

In the next moment, Di's arms came around her. Almost like a mother's.

Which was a dangerous way to think, because if there was one thing Miranda knew, it was that she couldn't rely on a mom.

More by Bestselling Author
Hannah Howell